Remedy

Remedy

Anne Marsella

Portobello
BOOKS

Published by Portobello Books Ltd 2007

Portobello Books Ltd
Eardley House
4 Uxbridge Street
Notting Hill Gate
London W8 7SY, UK

An excerpt from this novel was published first as a short story,
'Cooking with Djamila', in *Mediterraneans*.

A CIP catalogue record is available from the British Library

1 3 5 7 9 8 6 4 2

Hardback ISBN 978 1 84627 091 8
Export trade paperback ISBN 978 1 84627 100 7

www.portobellobooks.com

Text designed and typeset in Minion by Patty Rennie
Illustrations by Kazuko Nomoto

Printed in Great Britain by Cromwell Press

In memory of Carol Monpere

Feast of Saint Rosalia

As you presumably lived in a cave, dear Rosalia, and were possibly a twelfth-century nun – I'm afraid *The Concise Saints* allots you a meagre, wobbly blurb, pinned together by conjecture – it's unlikely you ever had your nerves quaked at six forty-five a.m. by mechanical jubilation, as mine were, here, this morning, whilst trying to get the most out of that last leg of beauty sleep. But Neighbour Jeromino was at it again, jackhammering a stolen-variety cobblestone from the Rue Saint-Dominique. And so I pulled my pink *peignoir* out from under the cat (to cover the Eve-wear) and knocked on his door.

'No noise before seven a.m. Neighbour Jeromino,' I reminded him sweetly, and added '*SVP*'.

Neighbour Jeromino smokes Marrakech weed and had been at the vapours all night.

'*Excusez-moi, Madame*,' he said all a-trembling. He always a-trembles when stoned. I said nothing about the jackhammer, nor about him calling me *Madame*, which I am not.

Mumly always says that Catholics can't get lonely because we have so many saints to chat with. No need to whine or pine alone, she says, when a community of divine ears are perked to hear you.

'Even in matters of love, Mumly, matters of... the love connection?' I once asked her, on the eve of turning sixteen, all a-tremble like Neighbour Jeromino, and blushing, too, at the thought of confiding my boudoir bumblings to the likes of you, Rosalia.

'Especially those, Princess,' she assured me. 'The saints have no shame, a result of the hideous trials they suffered in public. And they're all the better for it. I think they actually enjoy the juicy details, as long as you make them rhyme. And they'll oblige you in acquiring a love interest if you put in your request on time.'

Mumly says we should always use the occasion of morning coffee to toast a saint, seeing as the martyrs were ever on the go. And so I raised my *demitasse* to you, Rosalia, before downing a shot of black coffee, straight from the stovetop espresso-maker that Johannes von Krysler gave me. He is the Bavarian acrobat who stayed here for two days a fortnight ago, only to leave me (forever?) with a home phone number which was not his, but that of a family by the name of Smidtz. I have spoken to all the Smidtzes: the mother, the father and the two kids, Dieter and Monika – a very nice family, phone-friendly and eager to be of service.

Johannes, I should add, was the one who gave pedogasms – that is to say, orgasms of the feet.

I do appreciate the stovetop espresso-maker and use it every morning, including weekends, when, if I am a lucky girl, I have company.

I must admit, Rosalia, there are days when I wouldn't mind retreating to a Sicilian cave like yours, though only one equipped with lava lamps and a proper ladies' room. It would be such a nice place to read Balzac, I think. And maybe a bit of H. James. But the pull of duty, that competitor of gravity itself, got me to my desk at À La Mode Online at ten o'clock sharp. Twenty-two fashion photos awaited me, requiring my pen to pay tribute to the latest in calibrated couture: python trench coats, one-piece bloomer suits, strapless sheathes (Galliano); perforated dresses, narrow pin-tucked Bermudas, pump-kin pants (Givenchy); laminated chiffon skirts, tweed hosiery, dip-dyed duster-length peacoats (Chanel); and marmalade make-up (YSL).

I finished the work by noon exactly, just as the other girls were leaving for gym class, skipping lunch as they so often do. I politely declined the invitation to join them.

Instead, I headed for St Joseph's, down the street and to the left, where, as usual, I sat in the front pew next to Sister Dagobert and her guide dog, Yorik, for noon Mass. Sister Dagobert has been trying to get me to go on the Children's New Year Pilgrimage to Rome. She believes I am a child because I have an accent. I have tried to tell her otherwise but her belief will not be swayed.

'Remedy,' she tells me. 'The Lord has invited all the children of the world to Rome to celebrate New Year with His Majesty the Pope. I'm sure there will be room for you on Père Ricard's double-decker bus.'

Sister Dagobert is blind and completely dependent on the goodness of both the Lord and Yorik. Poor Yorik! Here is a dog far past his prime with senses less than keen, but most dedicated all the same. Yorik sleeps through Mass, at times emitting unpleasant gases. Sister Dagobert always has a kerchief, which she holds to her nose when poor Yorik cuts his cheese. Yorik's gas would be less of a concern if Père Ricard burned some frankincense from time to time in that silver censor of his, but really he has no sense of ceremony. He does nip at the bottle a bit (which could explain his lack of initiative and slurred homilies and lamb-o'-gods), but Sister Dagobert has unerring faith in Père Ricard. Even in his hastily delivered, three-point weekday homilies, which she listens to as only a blind nun can – that is to say, rocking back and forth in the pew. Sister Dagobert prays aloud and without discretion after holy Eucharist. Often I wish I didn't hear these disclosures. Really, only Jesus should.

Seeing as it's your feast day, Saint Rosalia, I decided to celebrate just a tad, if only in a culinary way, to make up for all the unleavened bread you used to nibble on. And so I stopped by the caterer on the Rue Montorgeuil for *tartiflette*, that creamy Savoy concoction of potatoes, crème fraîche, lardons, and *reblochon* cheese that's all the rage in Paris these days. But in no time at all, the girls, having foregone lunch for gym, arrived at my desk armed with those oversized French soupspoons. *Tartiflette* for one was consumed, quickly, by five, with much admiration of the French sort: *Oh là là!* But it is wonderful! It is delicious! *Oh là là!* By four o'clock I was starving and nearly went downstairs in search of a croissant concoction to make up for the potato concoction I'd missed, but Jean-Claudi arrived. I took a deep breath and stayed at my desk. Oh my heart! That man! Jean-Claudi was freshly showered, and perfumed by Kenzo; his chocolate-brown locks, slightly damp from the mists, curled coyly over his brow. Surely this was his wet look! I had never seen it before, and alas, it only made me desire this most inaccessible boy-loving Adonis all the more.

Jean-Claudi is a fashion photographer for both ladies' and men's apparel. He is a catwalk voyeur, a flesh connoisseur. He is the wizard spinning the couture cocktails that magazine subscribers all around the world are lapping up off the pages. Oh, I *have* to believe that this great lover of men also has room in his heart for a lady or two... Look how he comes into the office greeting each admirer, each adoring spoon, with that two-pronged kiss they call the *bise*. And he has a way of caressing your shoulder with his hand whilst doing so. Surely there is a fork in his road? I must believe there is. Boys-boys yes, to the east, but girls-girls as well, to the west. Jean-Claudi can have it all and I don't see that he would deprive himself an extra pleasure in favour of a singular affiliation.

Moreover, there is not an arrogant bone in his divine body! Today he lingered at my desk to tell me about a new hot spot called Le Swing Club run by a friend of his. It appears there is a giant swing in the middle of the club on which various astounding 'acts' are performed. *Pray tell, Jean-Claudi, what may such acts be?* He revealed nothing. When Jean-Claudi left me, I began to wonder if he spoke to me of Le Swing Club as a lead-up to taking me there in a man-to-woman date context. Later, though, I got word from Top Spoon asking me to call Le Swing Club's proprietor for an interview and possible write-up. Oh well. What can a girl expect? Jean-Claudi does get around and makes his desires clearly known to the right collocutor.

My earlier feast having been foiled, I picked up an entire roast chicken on my way back home from the office (in your honour, Rosalia) as well as a brioche with sugar on the top (for Jubilee) and a bottle of *Gigondas* as a party favour for all the saints. I was looking forward to this repast indeed, but just as I was about to sit down to table, the doorbell rang, interrupting my imminent dining pleasure. Who's there, pray-tell?

It was Neighbour Jeromino, asking for a roll of toilet paper!

In response to this needy request, I gave him a roll of extra soft, scented with a yellow (not red!) rose motif and got back to dinner, happily washing down the chicken with the *Gigondas*, a beverage recommended for *tête-à-tête* dining, but which also suits celibatarians like myself. Poured a drop into a thimble for Jubilee, though he nibbled on the wishbone instead. Which is fine for a cat, but I do wonder about those people who abstain from the fruit of the vine at din-din for the sake of the Lord. Why Jesus himself was both a celibatarian and fine wine drinker, preferring, I believe, the *Côtes du Jordain* varieties.

Ah! but is there anything better than retiring to a fresh-sheeted bed in the evening with a book? I'm sure there is, but at least five nights out of the week, I prefer to think not. It's best to keep content if you can, whenever and with whomever you can (not so, Rosalia?) I read Balzac's *The Girl with the Golden Eyes* before dozing off into a deep sleep, hosting a dream in which Jean-Claudi appeared sporting a *chartreuse redingote*. Was it a good dream or a bad dream? To be honest, I'm not exactly sure.

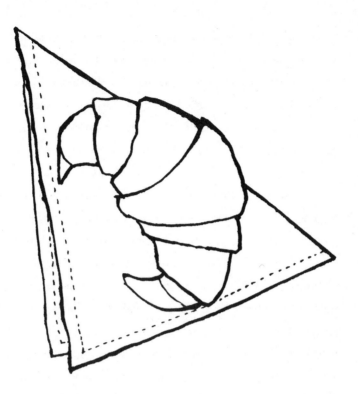

Feast of Saint Aigulf
(abbot of Lérins)

Oh, my poor, dear man. *The Concise Saints* claims your brother monks, sick and tired of your holy lording over them, arranged for marauding Moors to do you in. This was truly unkind of them, and yet your remarkable death by heathen hands, coupled with your reforms meant to harness the mutinous monks at Lérins (I'm not sure where this is, must look up on a map), earned you sainthood indeed. Please accept my belated congratulations.

The ululating of the Moors was surely unpleasant to your ears, especially as they swiped the dagger across your throat, but I can safely assume that you were never woken prematurely by M. Phet's downstairs lodger, as I was this morning, my ears nearly sticky with the sound of that syrupy torch singer from Taiwan. She's the girl you hear in all the Chinese eateries around town, the one with the sweet-and-sour voice, a millionaire herself with luxurious living quarters and guaranteed tranquillity.

And so I was obliged to put on my tracksuit and go downstairs. M. Phet's lodger, a man of childish proportions wearing a zoot suit, looked most astonished by this interruption to his easy listening. I sensed he would have liked to shut the door and banish my face from his morning, but was too polite (or too sugar-drunk) to do so. Bless his heart, nor was the head I presented such a nice one, as there had been no time to tend to coiffure. No matter, the essential had to be said before some curtain of incomprehension was pulled down between us.

As M. Phet's lodger understands little French or English, I aired my complaint in the most amiable and international of languages – that of the hands – to which M. Phet's lodger then responded with the head. I gathered from his singular nod that an arrangement convenient to both of us had been made, and so took my leave.

Unfortunately I was unable to communicate efficiently the ten p.m. to seven a.m. rule, that French law protecting the common flat-dweller from disruptive brouhaha. The torch singer's voice was taken down to a more intimate decibel, then raised again on high and left there.

I decided to leave early and have breakfast at the Café Beaubourg where Jean-Claudi can sometimes be found, never on a pouf but always in an armchair. I sat in an armchair myself in homage to that fine young gentleman, who was probably at that very moment wrapped around some young buck of a swing performer in post-coital sleep. And I asked myself, would I climb onto The Swing for Jean-Claudi? For the love of Jean-Claudi?

Had to admit, shamefully, to my deepest self, that I would not. The Swing, I was led to believe, is a Men Only contraption. And just as I would never dream of going into the Gents to relieve myself (although it is true that women in France have the gumption to do so in cases of long lines for the ladies' room), I would never, ever climb up onto The Swing. So be it. I am no Joan of the Bow. I will commit no travesty for the love of JC. How all these thoughts do sadden me a bit!

I left the Café Beaubourg in a melancholy mood made worse by the napkin invitation brought to me by a waiter just as I had reached the dregs of my coffee. The napkin read:

'The solitude of one is lonely at that. But the solitude of two delights you know who… Won't you come to my table, Mademoiselle?'

Oh dear, I thought to myself, not in the morning, not now! I really must get to the ladies' room. But I kept my cool and of the waiter I enquired, 'And who is the gentleman may I please ask?'

'Monsieur Lift,' he told me, indicating discreetly with a tip of the head where the M. Lift in question was seated.

It was not difficult to identify the gentleman who sent the napkin *communiqué*, for he was looking straight at me, bowing his head and tipping his beret when he caught my eye. I had a good look: manifestly, M. Lift was in his sixties, apparently bald beneath the beret, and shaped much like our beloved and belt-begirded nursery egg, Humpty Dumpty. He was seated not on a precipitous wall, but on a high-riding pouf and, like M. Dumpty, his feet, too, did not reach the ground. I cannot remember any distinct features of M. Lift's face, only his queer, come-hither expression rendered entirely ineffectual by a jowlish eagerness that seemed to consume his entire face. M. Lift was a desperate man and his position perilous; just one push and he was over. I took out my pen, brushed the croissant flakes off my napkin and wrote:

'Dear Monsieur, I thank you for your invitation. This solitude, however, must take herself off to work at this time. Alas! To each solitude its industry!'

I then gave this napkin note to the waiter, paid my bill and left the café, nodding but not looking in M. Lift's direction. It seemed to me that this was the way it was done. A woman declines, nods but does not look. Isn't it so? (But maybe you wouldn't know, dear Aigulf, such things being beneath your holy ken.)

This brief epistolary encounter set me up for morning pathos (a perplexing state you can perhaps relate to, Aigulf, being a pathological saint yourself). From ten o'clock to midday, I could not keep my mind from pursuing all the suffering solitudes in the world. I thought of the widows and the widowers (those freshly aggrieved), the divided divorcees, the bitter bachelors, the obsolete old maids, the freakish priests, bishops and their lonely lay-virgins (and of course all the abbots too!). All of them crept into my heart and therein found sympathetic soil until midday, at which point I washed them out of that mourning muscle with a torrent of tears in the ladies' room.

I do not cry like this often, but when lachrymation, much like the independent-minded virus, takes hold, it only stops when it has run its course. It cannot be medicated or tricked into dissolution. Several people knocked on the restroom door and several people waited. One person politely enquired. But what response can a vessel of sorrow be expected to give? Are not the tears heard through the door warning enough that a solitude is at work and should not be disturbed? But maybe these visitors were like me, and would themselves have drunk from the Cup of Sorrows. Who knows?

As it was, when I regained self-possession and left the relief lounge, they were no longer there: they had found deliverance elsewhere – inevitably in the adjacent men's room (we are in France, and this is always a possibility).

By then I was late for Mass. I tiptoed up the aisle of St Joe's to where Sister Dagobert was seated, by herself because of the Yorik problem. She had reserved me a seat next to her.

'It's me,' I whispered into her ear, and as always received her reassuring, petite hand in reply. It's Sister Dagobert's practice to grope for a person's hand, not to offer a common handshake but, rather, The Squeeze. The Squeeze, always affectionate, is executed with surprising force and often sets the nerves of your fingers aflame. But only for a minute or two. I must say that, although small in stature and known to frequent the meek, Sister Dagobert is no pushover. In the afternoons she works at the Hôtel-Dieu hospital in the Tropical Disease ward, dressing and undressing wounds, her blind hands guided by the hands of the Lord, yet unaided by Yorik whom she is required to park outside. She also teaches the picture-book catechism to bedridden converts. Like the Singing Nuns, she never asks for reward.

After Mass, Sister Dagobert had me sign up for the New Year Children's Parade to Rome. Of course, as I couldn't exactly enrol myself, I signed a list posted in the church's foyer under the pseudonym, Miss Dorothy Wayward. Within the month, a deposit cheque must be left to secure the reservation. I told Sister Dagobert that my (Dorothy's) parents would come by and leave the cheque with Père Ricard within the proper delay. She seemed happily reassured. In any case, she asked no questions.

Is it really possible that Sister Dagobert thinks I'm a child? So it seems. And yet she must believe me a precocious bloomer: a child with an independent current account and career; a child who chose to live abroad, a little one swimming thousands of miles from her birth continent to come ashore on the banks of the Seine at the foot of Notre-Dame. Sister Dagobert must think me a prodigy. And now she will have me trade in fins for feet and march on Rome. She will be the catalyst in my evolution from the piscine to the pedestrian, from Little Mermaid to Little Matchgirl.

I'm sure that many would say Sister Dagobert is only fooling herself, that by sublimating her blindness she has become a kind of phenomenological hazard. But to me this matters little. At times, an untruth is a better indicator of truth than some seemingly obvious fact. I may very well be a child after all. And this new continental life I lead could very well be taken as child's play. It all depends on how one looks at it. It's true that at times I feel I'm a smaller version of myself here. I've had to shrink to fit the proportions, you see. But could it be that I've shrunk too much? Sister Dagobert may be suggesting that I have. In which case I should, perhaps, pay attention and try not to put myself through the wash so often.

Sister Dagobert and I had a quick bite to eat at the café across the street. I ordered a *croque-madame* – a grilled ham and cheese number with an egg on top – and a spinach tart for Sister Dagobert, who does not eat ham.

Over lunch, she explained to me that she has had two conversion experiences in her forty-eight years of life. The first one occurred at the age of eighteen when she had a vision of herself on a date with Jesus. I believe they were going to a fireman's ball. At this point she quit her various Hebraic associations and joined league with the Jews for Jesus. The second conversion transpired during her twenty-fifth year, that year when unmarried Frenchwomen don hats on St Catherine's Day to attract potential husbands. But rather than parade her maidenhood with a hat, she cloaked herself in a habit, that most inexpensive and humble of wedding gowns, and was united by a mystic marriage to her former prom partner: Jesus himself. No comely vision visited her the second time around; she was swept away by the violent winds of whimsy. The conversion took her by force, leaving her in an ecstatic state for several days. She hardly knew what had come over her. When she finally did come around, she was no longer Mademoiselle Bibi Benguigui, but Sister Dagobert.

Sister Dagobert provided me with this particular history as she explained to me why she avoided ham. She could not help but maintain a certain prejudice against pork which she justified upholding by the fact that even her holy husband had never eaten it. She explained that she had once been sent for a year to a convent in Spain, that great land of a thousand and one hams, and had a terrible time of it. Some manner of ham on the plate at every meal. Since then, she has never quite had the same appetite, or so she says.

I happened to notice that she ate every last bite on her plate including the decorative condiments, the lemon shard and the parsley sprig. Fed Yorik pieces of my own ham and crust under the table whilst Sister Dagobert was preoccupied with an *après-repas* grace.

Back to the office, where I wrote the YSL article I was supposed to have written in the morning when pathos had struck. Pretended I was that *rive gauche* queen, Catherine Deneuve, and finished in no time.

Jean-Claudi arrived for a five-minute photo drop-off. I believe he was not insensitive to the Deneuvian transformation. Promised myself I would play Pretend more often, seeing just how useful this practice is for work and pleasure alike.

By the time I got home it was eight o'clock. Tired I was, but also somewhat distressed to find that Jubilee had exorcised all of his evil feline nibbles into my rug in the boudoir sometime in the late afternoon. I cleaned up the mess, then poured myself a glass of wine but skipped dinner.

At nine o'clock Mumly called from Florida. 'Princess,' she enquired, 'when are you coming home?'

I knew of course that she did not mean for a visit, but for good. I did not have the heart to tell her the truth, so told an untruth: 'When the money runs out, Mumly, when the money runs out.'

In fact I've been here a year now and the money has already run out, which is why the job at À La Mode Online has become indispensable. The money in question had never been all that much in any case. Most of it was spent on shoes.

I dislike upsetting Mumly, who is ailing with dropsy and unable to play golf at the moment. The last thing I want to do is trigger her Valium instinct. Pills became part of her diet last year when that Gérard fellow broke both her heart and into her bank account. For his love she had sold all of her mutual funds, despite the dissuasions of Mr Epstein, her banker.

Girard was Haitian but pretended to be Parisian. Mumly loved his accent. Whenever she told me about him, her voice changed, became much lower and I could tell she was talking in his voice.

'Last night, he took me to *zee Cha-Cha club* and we danced *all zee night*.'

I don't believe she even realized she was doing this. I would tell her to stop it and she would say, 'Stop what, Princess?'

In a way, I think he inhabited her. She was like an empty glasshouse, all fragile and transparent. I suspect this was partly due to those menopausal supplements she takes: anyone could see through her. Synthetic oestrogen derived from pregnant mare's urine aided Girard in his task. He saw clearly where everything was and had only to put his hands on it. Poor Mumly, she simply has not been the same since. I must say though, that when she was with Girard, she never once asked me when I was coming home.

Well, thank you, Saint Aigulf, for protecting my day from the treachery you once suffered. Lord knows what I would have done if marauding Moors had come after me with a blade today; a napkin *communiqué* certainly wouldn't have done the trick.

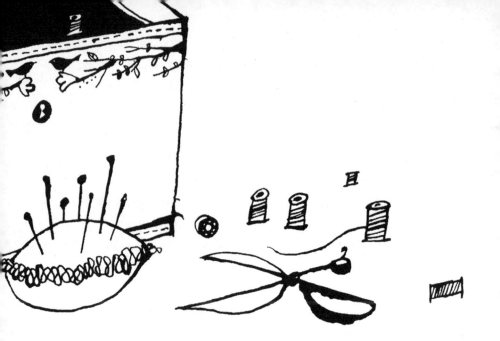

Feast of Saint Bertilla

Hello, Bertilla. I admit I'm puzzled by your report card. The *Concise* says you were strictly trained at Jouarre (must look on a map) and sent to establish an abbey at Chelles (isn't this where they now manufacture kitchen appliances?). Here, your rule 'gave the house such a reputation that Hereswitha (widow of King of East Angles) and Saint Bathildis (wife of Clovis II) both joined the community'.

Exactly what kind of a house were you running, Bertilla? The *Concise* remains vague, but to attract the noble figures of Hereswitha and Bathildis, you must have afforded certain comforts: perhaps you condoned bejewelling at Mass, like Saint Teresa of Avila, or the eating of lamb chops during Lent. In any case, your holy housekeeping earned you enough points to join the Communion of Saints as a lifetime member. No small achievement indeed.

Haute Couture Week is over at last. I skipped out at the Hôtel Costes party last night after watching Jean-Claudi French kiss the pierced belly button of an eighteen-year-old Gucci boy-model wearing a short bumblebee cropped top, low-riding track pants and size 46 snakeskin booties. Found the navel exploit awfully off-putting (wouldn't you have too, Bertilla?).

I finally had a quiet morning uninterrupted by the neighbours. The coffee made in the von Krysler contraption was really quite good. I sipped it while reading an article in *Belle* magazine concerning Adult Sex, and have subsequently been asking myself some very serious questions concerning amorous jaunts of the past five years.

I made a sort of mental checklist and examined each case up close (bear with me Bertilla, such things must be done for the sake of good housekeeping). What about Johannes von Krysler, for example? We had spent two rapturous days entirely together, never once leaving my boudoir. We ate only take-out couscous and pizza from Chez Shlomi's down the street. Von Krysler could not bear to see anyone but me, and so we would leave an envelope taped to the door for Mouktar, the behelmeted delivery lad, with payment and a request to ring the bell and leave the steaming semolina on the doorstep. Mouktar (oh, but what face hid behind that dusky vizor of his? How I'd love to know Bertilla!) executed this ritual perfectly and was awarded a tip in the form of a personal cheque drawn from an account at the Bundesbank.

Let me tell you, we were happy! We were in love! We played the dictionary game and invented new tricks. I once landed on the word 'Hashemite', and von Krysler did a double backflip, landing perfectly upright on the couch. Neither of us knew why he leaped as he did, but I felt as if I had won. Yes! I had won! Those were two unforgettable days and you cannot blame me for desiring a follow-up – a future invitation to Bavaria, say. Or even Romania.

Yes, I would have gone. And yet, having read this learned article written by a love-relations psychologist, I see now that Johannes von Krysler was right to leave me for good and that I never should have pursued him. I should never have called the Schmidtz family the twenty-odd times I did (how dear they were to me!). The truth of the matter is that clever von Krysler understood about Adult Sex and I, alas, did not.

And yet I take this experience as an invaluable lesson. In this day and age a woman cannot behave like the pubescent romanticist, that sitting duck stuffed with false notions of the love connection. No, she must take love as an assignment, fulfil the duties and dispense with it at term. Sister Dagobert is right: this isn't dress-up anymore. I must thank Sister Dagobert and Johannes von Krysler for the hints and guidance. Perhaps I should set up a practice schedule for the next few months, starting with an elementary exercise on how to de-helmet delivery lads. One must start at the home front, not so Bertilla? Adult Sex should not be so hard to master, I'm sure. And I really must write a thank-you letter to that psychologist at *Belle*. What is her name again? Doctor Dolittle?

I've decided to be 'counter couture' and wear a uniform to work. To make things easier in the morning, you see. Going directly from Eve-wear to work-wear, even after coffee, is no easy affair – especially in Paris, where women set the pedestrian chic standard rather high. These astute ladies know that what you put on in the morn determines how your day will transpire. Best not to be carelessly sloppy (although a studied recklessness is sometimes encouraged). And best to follow the vagaries of neck-, sleeve- and hemlines. At all times. I suppose if I were up for this risky business every morning, the uniform would not be necessary. As it is, to be capable of greater self-expression and freedom, I will put on that neutral something, a worker's uniform as such (not unlike your abbess's habit, Bertilla, only minus the wimple and with *décolleté*).

Let me say a bit more about my uniform. It is of my own making. This is not, however, to say that I stitched and sewed it, but rather that I picked and chose it, which is in itself a creative act, for it requires imagination to see possibility in the most disparate of articles. I found my items at the Guerisold, that discount clothesmonger on the Rue de Belleville. I waded through piles of abandoned garments: clothes that once lay against the skin of others, and enjoyed a seasonal ride through the world. I dug my hands deep into these barrels of cast-offs, rummaging for something crisp and clean, for something that was treated not as a mere fashion disposable, but as a garment for life.

I found three things of this sort: a pair of men's gabardine slacks (Brook Brothers, no less), blue and size 48; a long white child's gown used for Baptismal or Circumcismal celebrations; and a stainless nurse uniform, of a sturdy white wool blend (not rayon), long in length and sleeve. Of the three, I chose the nurse ensemble. Then I took to doctoring it a bit. I took the gown to the cleaners for a Bordeaux-red dye job (a flattering colour for blondes with freckled noses), then cut out the modestly high neckline and put in a scoop neck, which suits me better

19

and is, as we all know, better for the breasts as well. Or at least more propitious for showing them off, a consideration which is not negligible. I cut out the sleeves as well.

I've found that the best way to wear this uniform is with a hip-hugging belt. The belt I also purchased at the Guerisold. It came with an exceptional buckle from an earlier time, the size of a priest's Host (which Mumly called the Hostie) and of indeterminate alloy. At its inception, the metals had been melted and moulded to form the name of the legendary musical association, Led Zeppelin. As the belt itself was a bit tired, I removed the buckle and reattached it to a gold chain belt. The overall effect, I think, is handsome if not somewhat stylized, but seeing that the dress is no-frills, this should be permissible. This is my uniform, and I will begin wearing it as of the first of next month. I believe that will be December.

But today is a holiday. A war holiday, it seems. The war of 1914–18. Otherwise known as the First World War. In any case, people still make pilgrimages to Verdun to weep and to wonder. I read about it in the *International Herald Tribune*. Today we are to refrain from work and remember the tragedy that is a War Close to Home. The other kinds, we are not so obliged to remember. At least, not today.

I was once told in a history course that more people died after that war from influenza, than they did during the gassy slaughter itself. People become very tired after war and are susceptible to microbes. But this rarely makes the headlines, does it? We do not commemorate the end of influenza – only the end of the man-made devastation and a handful of heroic lives. And even then, only for a while.

They say that a history forgotten may well be a history repeated. For this reason I do try to remember my wicked little adventures, and those of others, too, sometimes. I have stopped going to confession, which also helps the memory. Before, I would cast forth my demons through the grating of the priest's booth. These evil ones would then be tried at the foot of the Lord, at which point I received absolution and a prayer assignment. All my trials told and forgotten. The trick, I had found, was never to confess to the same priest twice. In Paris this is quite manageable given the number of churches and the number of priests per church (usually three).

Still, attending confession does require a certain amount of foresight and planning, as one must also take their schedules into account. Priests simply cannot spend their entire day inside the confessional waiting for confessees, as they will tell you quite frankly (alas, Bertilla, it's not like the old days!). The confessional is, after all, a dreary little booth, musty and cushionless, designed for efficient mercy-giving. Therein all your personal sins are given the *coup de grâce*, in a swift and economical exchange. It's best to call ahead and either enquire for schedules or make an appointment. If the good woman answering the phone – and I rightly assume it *is* a woman, a kindly lay lady – tells you that only a certain Father Something sees confessees, and you have already seen this particular Père once, you must insist on her scheduling you an appointment with a different priest. Often she will be reluctant to do so, but you must insist that Father Something is a friend of the family and that you prefer confessing to a total stranger, hinting that what you have to confess is truly worthy of the priestly ear. You might say, 'I'd prefer this to be discreet.' The mere mention of the word *discreet* often works, at least in France, where discretion is valued over confession, and where even a whispered mouth-to-ear confidence must be discriminating.

But as I have said, I no longer confess. That is, I quit doing so as of six months ago. It occurred to me then that I was becoming very forgetful, and whereas previously these lapses in memory had guaranteed a rather happy insouciance, forgetfulness had now become an onerous habit. Rather than continue blithely and intrepidly ahead in my life, I found myself turning in circles, making my rounds from confessional to confessional on that curious circuit of Forgive and Forget. It was as if I were trapped on a giant Ferris wheel, rising up to the heights only to descend again, quite low, and never able to get off that revolving contraption.

As with all habits that lead to no ultimate good, this one was hard to break. Parting with it in the end required my making a rather fatal mistake. In a moment of distraction, I called upon the same priest in the same confessional twice. This happened on a Tuesday at noon. I was light-headed with lunchtime hunger but was determined to confess and forget before allowing myself the *pot-au-feu* or the eggs Benedict, whatever dish it was that I intended to dine on that day – I cannot remember. I would attend to my soul before attending to my stomach.

At first it was business as usual; while I might have recognized the priest's voice, in fact I did not – sensorially weakened as I was due to the hunger. When the priest addressed his commentary, it came at me like a north wind, blowing out the lazy fuzz in my head and the pangs from my belly.

'My daughter,' he said. 'This is not your first offence but the second time you have been driven to this sin. The road of temptations is long and the flesh is weak…'.

Oh dear! I did not hear the rest. Could not bear to listen on. No, I leaped from the confessional and ran from that church just minutes before absolution would be granted: I fled like an animal being hunted. Morality, after all, is a formidable hunter. Memory a more terrible one at that. And the priest, I realized with horror, remembered. My sins had not gone to the feet of the Lord for trial, but straight into the priest's souvenir shop. He had catalogued my demons, classified them in an instrumental database. They were all on file and he could look them up at will. At that moment all my illusions were discredited, as I saw that 'Forgive and Forget' was merely child's play, impossible in the adult world of responsibility, consistency and relentless addiction.

Since then, I have taken up the practice of memory, of holding myself to account by recording herein. Take the case of von Krysler. In the past I would have confessed the episode and begun another one shortly after with a von Krysler-type replacement. In the past, I would consider myself quite lucky if three weekends in a row offered three different variations on the von Krysler theme. Perhaps it may seem that, at that time, I was a more confirmed practitioner of Adult Sex. And yet how much further from the truth this could be. I may have confessed and forgotten the SIN, but I continued to wave the flag of hope.

Yes, hope!

It is, as dear Emily Dickinson says, the thing with feathers. How swiftly it flew, back then, after those one-stop hearts, those knights of convenience who would leave me on a Sunday morn! I loved every one of them, it is true. And from each of them, hope wanted more. Yes, plumy hope did!

Since I kicked the confession habit, however, the lamentable inefficiency of my amorous comportment and flighty hold on hope has become all too apparent. Adult Sex is just the storm that could abash the little bird. By looking the von Krysler episode straight in the eye, I have understood that the last kiss of the weekend must not have wings, but gravity. The whole affair should be brought down to earth and viewed sensibly, with an empiricist's eye and hand. Yes, with the senses and not with the heart.

Must write all this to that Dr Dolittle.

Feast of Saint Felix of Valois

I'm sorry to say, Felix, that the *Concise* claims you never existed save in the imagination of Trinitarian authors.

Undoubtedly they're being a bit hard on you. Nevertheless, you were presumably a hermit and founded a society for the redemption of savage captives. If you did exist beyond Trinitarian reveries (and I'm sure you did, Felix, because if you didn't they wouldn't have even listed you in the *Concise*) I think it was awfully kind of you to help those cannibals get a new start on things. After all, every day offers us a fresh beginning, isn't it so? Today I feel this could very possibly be true.

I awoke this morning with a kindly ancestral prayer on my lips, a prayer to my late and great aunt Glorietta. When Glorietta was among the living and I was but a child, she would sometimes take me out for ice cream at a very ladylike establishment called Plums. At Plums, the spoons were terribly long. Aunt Glorietta would arch a hand-painted eyebrow and say in that wispy voice of hers, after having taken a spoonful of the frozen cream (usually vanilla with a crème de menthe topping), 'This, my dear, is *not* hokey-pokey.' She would underline the word *not* with the ten-inch spoon and I would nod solemnly in agreement.

It was as if we shared a secret, albeit one I did not entirely grasp. The hokey-pokey secret. I trusted my response implicitly, although I could not explain it. Wasn't hokey-pokey that birthday-party dance performed on roller skates which I so hated? Perhaps, but clearly the one in question was not.

Not knowing what it meant in a semantic sense, I saw it as a piece in the puzzle of faith. Already, you see, I was being trained in Catholicism. There was a way in which one could *apprehend* while also seemingly failing to understand. I was learning to revere the mystery of the gap. (You of all saints, dear Felix, who exist most fully in the penumbra of Trinitarian imagination, should understand this.)

It was only much, much later that I was to find out that the hokey-pokey Glorietta once referred to was the cheap, street version of our select ices. Hokey-pokey is what Sister Dagobert and I treat ourselves to when we have an extra two euros in August. It's the summer pleasure of the poor.

But as I was saying, Felix, I prayed to Glorietta this morning upon waking. I asked her to please Godspeed the arrival of a significant prince – *not* a hokey-pokey one. I was unfortunately unable to give her any names. It does help to have a name (that is, to be as specific as possible) when requesting the intervention of an ancestor. Ask any Cambodian about this. I believe he or she will tell you the same although perhaps in different words.

In any case, I did supplicate with fervour, which should help Glorietta in her task as urgency creates a particular vibration that reaches the ear of the netherworld most effectively – if the ancestors can't hear your call, it will not be answered. The telephonic laws of the netherworld are not so different from our own. And who knows, perhaps one day we will call each other on Ouija-phones. I imagine such a thing will exist. Thomas Edison did try to design one himself a long time ago, intending to capture the sound of the soul leaving the body upon death, but could never quite establish the connection. I believe he called it the Valve.

Perhaps, though, I might have mentioned Roland in my prayer. I did not, because, in all honesty, it is my strong feeling that Roland would require a bit too much repair and maintenance. Princes, as all women know, come with a lifetime guarantee and are solid and sound from the outset.

I met Roland through my old college friend Joanna, who married his cousin last year. She used to be a translator of coffee-table books but now spends most of her time at the Ritz's La Prairie Institut de Beauté, or on the Rue du Faubourg St-Honoré with a shopping trolley which is pushed by her maid, Marie-Joseph. We met for tea last Saturday at her sixteenth arrondissement abode. She and her husband, Jean-Paul, live in a twenty-room penthouse decorated High Louis-style – which is to say that *all* the King Louis' are therein represented.

(Joanna, you see, has always been democratically minded, raised as she was in Philadelphia.) In any case the flat is a grand affair, though Joanna intimated they would be seeking something slightly more commodious shortly as, with their new live-in maid, the space had shrunk considerably. Still I must admit that by my three-room standard it seemed almost frightfully too large, the kind of home where even the master is unsure of the rooms and all too often mistakes the billiard room, say, for the maid's boudoir. The doors are always kept shut, you know. I got lost there myself, when I went to look for the bathroom and quite accidentally I found myself in Joanna's closet, a large walk-in the size of my bedroom. I must say that I've never seen such an overcrowded pantry: an unruly regiment of Rue du Faubourg St-Honoré clothes hung along all four walls, hundreds of shoes perched on a ledge above them and the floor space was taken up with baskets of more clothes – both dirty and clean – suitcases, and a hoard of accessories spilling out of hat boxes. The shopping trolley was there too, filled to the brim with Hermès packages she manifestly had not yet had the time to open. Poor dear Joanna, I thought. She really does need another closet!

As synchronicity had it, just as I found this sympathy in my heart for my friend, she, in turn, found the same for me in her own.

'Do you know, Remedy,' she said to me upon my return from the closet, 'that I have never been happier in my life.'

I shook my head to let her know that I did not. But Joanna was not looking at me just then. She gazed at her luxurious surroundings – the regal Louis', the Italian ceiling frescoes, the chandeliers and the crimson draperies – as if she were feasting on a sumptuous repast. And although such a meal would have given a diner of simple tastes some rough indigestion, she feasted with pleasure not complaint. Joanna smiled contentedly and turned to me again.

'And you know Remedy, I would love to see you be just as happy as I am. I really would. I have an idea. Listen.'

Sitting up, she shuffled her leather-frocked tush to the edge of the Louis (XIV? XVI?) armchair. Leaning towards me now, she spoke with the deliberate, theatrical air she always adopts when she wants to impress an idea upon you.

'Jean-Paul has a cousin. An unmarried cousin,' she insisted, 'who seems to be looking.'

I said nothing to this, but let those enigmatic words hang in silence over her stage.

'I was thinking,' she went on, 'of having you both over for dinner next week, but wanted to see what you thought of the plan first. I really think you would like him, Remedy. You know he's *very* Catholic. He goes to Mass every day like you. And you know the Ball of Marvels is coming up…'.

'What on earth are you talking about?'

My astonishment was sincere. I had never told anyone of my Mass habit and began to wonder if Joanna hadn't spied on me. True, we had taken a trip together once to Toledo and I had excused myself politely from her company once a day to attend service in that country of the once great *Reyes Católicos*, Isabella and Fernando. But I felt then that she had trespassed and laid bare a most intimate secret. I held my head high like a proud but wounded monarch.

'Oh come on, Remedy. I mean, I don't know if you go to Mass every day. It just seemed like you might. In any case, you really must meet this guy. He has just the profile we're looking for and said he'd be "enchanted to make the acquaintance of such a charming demoiselle". Get the picture? What do you say? Dinner next week?'

Eventually I agreed to meet the gentleman in question, for I could tell that Joanna was not going to give up easily. Having decorated her rooms to a suitable standard, she had decided to take me on as her season's make-over project and now envisions herself lining my existence with the finest fabric of men. Her goal – she sets these as others do their alarm clocks, for without them she cannot rise from bed – is to have me on the arm of a distinguished gentleman at the Ball of Marvels, that preliminary event, which, 'in three out of five cases,' she emphasized, '*leads to the real thing*'.

I could sense her discernment at work, the very same selectiveness she used whilst choosing Pierre Frey fabrics to cover her walls. She even did some mathematics in the process, adding up the particles in the patronyms. In the end, the winner of this careful selection was the aforementioned Roland. Roland de Bourdon, son of Madame la Marquise de Bourdon; his father, the Marquis, is already dead and buried. In fact, now that his papa is gone, Roland himself wears the title Monsieur le Marquis. Though only on paper, he explained.

The dinner party took place the following Friday and was a bit stiff, as French dinner parties in that particular vicinity inevitably are. Roland spoke little, but the little he uttered was profound.

'Mademoiselle,' he said when my country became the subject of conversation, 'we Europeans cannot help but see Americans as oversized children. And we find that you are often very naughty.'

'Merci,' I said to Roland, and began eating the rosy *magret de canard aux deux poivres* that had just been served to me by Marie-Joseph. Duck, I believe, must be eaten very hot.

I must say, however, that I found Roland's commentary enlightening in a fashion, as it offered yet another explanation for Sister Dagobert's conviction of my being a child, and perhaps also for my own personal perception of engaging in child's play and games like Pretend. Joanna, however, grew upset and spent herself on a tirade defending her motherland from the insults of the Franks.

It was all very tiresome, especially for Joanna, who was nearly weepy at the end and asked Marie-Joseph to bring her a Diet Coke at once. This of course only made matters worse. Even her dear husband couldn't bear the sight of that bottle on his table. It had to be poured into a highball glass and even then received looks of distaste. Joanna, now calm and fortified by the drink, lit up a Marlboro light and sipped at the coke with the detached grace of a Hollywood star. Just at that moment I was proud of my friend, for she was suddenly in possession of a quality that even the fiery French had to admire. In a word, she had become a mistress of nonchalance. Nothing more on the matter of the United States of America was mentioned by the two Frenchmen. Talk migrated to more pertinent topics, such as the European Union's threat to cheese. After coffee (not nearly as good as von Krysler's) Roland offered to drive me home.

How odd Frenchmen can be. They use their affections like a faucet, turning sentiment from hot to cold depending on their fickle whims. Roland, who could hardly be called charming at supper, became extraordinarily so in the car, and by the time we reached the Rue Cler, I had been invited out on a dinner date scheduled for the following week *and* received a slightly longish cheek kiss, which seemed to make its way down to the earlobe. Oh it was proper! But quite portentous as well.

Yes, things seemed promising with Roland during that dreamy week. But then D-day came: the Date-day. And Truth, so it seemed, had little time to waste.

It was over dinner at a restaurant called Maître Paul that Roland made a most revealing disclosure. Just as we were served our crême brûlée, Roland leaned toward me and said, 'I must tell you something Remedy. Something that is very important to me.'

'What is it, dear Roland?' (I was feeling very *intime* just then.)

'It is this,' he began, a critic's frown tightening his otherwise wine-relaxed face. 'There is something I find most detestable and it is women's underclothing. The only kind I can bear is the white, cotton sort. Yes, they must be very, very white and one hundred per cent cotton. Otherwise it's too difficult for me.'

'Indeed!' I said, giving him a wink. Perhaps he would have offered further explanation or continued his odd little joke further, but as it went, the proprietor, Master Paul himself, came by our table to enquire after the Marquise, Roland's mumly.

As they exchanged words in that particular French formality which bespoke a degree of intimacy Americans will never understand or know how to measure, I wondered a bit about my date's queer disclosure before putting it out of mind entirely, dismissing it as an unusual prelude to love. Yes, in the end I attributed it to a *mal de vivre* peculiar to the aristocratic race, one that might have been avoided with the arrival of plainer blood and wine. ·

I remembered that my own panties that evening were red and rayon. Very pretty and of a cut I believe is called Brazilian. I had put them on after showering with the same intention I might have had, had I adorned myself with an amulet. Most women do have the sense that panties replace the rabbit's foot. A good luck charm to be worn and used with care. I had no doubt that the red Brazilian would offer favourable auspice, a prosperous lead for the evening ahead. Yes, romance had been on my mind and these little red bloomers would be my conveyance to it.

And yet how wrong I was! Those panties did not win any amorous stab of cupid's arrow, but rather his frowning disregard and the lowering of the bow. The Marquis' words had not been prattle, but warning. There we were in my little boudoir, preparing for the flights of love ahead on the *canapé*. Roland's kisses roamed down my neck, a bit tight-lipped perhaps, but sure, and his fingers fumbled at the strings of my beaded halter top whilst I rid him of his frocks in record time, which, for a fashion functionary, comes quite naturally (sorry, dear Felix, but the truth must be told).

To countenance dear Roland, who was getting nowhere with the strings, I found it best to straddle him straight on and escort his fingers, perhaps afflicted with nobiliary rheumatism. The halter fell at last, causing my knight's brows to rise in delight, for there was nothing beneath that sheath but two shimmering champagne-glass breasts. He was surprised yes, but clearly pleased too, as I could tell from the pedigreed bulge in the briefs below, and now he unzipped my *plissé* skirt, or rather tried as best he could. In the end it was my own hand that brought the zipper down, that lifted the skirt up over my head and tossed it on the ground. My excitement at this *risqué* exploit would have heightened our adventure had not my lacy red panties caused Roland to gasp.

'Remedy, I… I… I simply cannot!'

'Oh Roland. What's wrong? Is it the rheumatism?'

'I told you earlier Remedy. They must be white. Otherwise, I cannot. And yours are red.'

'And rayon too.'

'They must be cotton. Or else...'

'Don't say it Roland. I don't think I can bear to hear it.'

Indeed my dismay was great. Love would not happen in its normal course. Ah! Had I taken his disclosure seriously, I would have made a polite rain check and prepared cotton undies for the following date. But then again, maybe not. Imagine this liaison were to endure. To even be considered a potential Madame de Bourdon candidate, I'd have to don the whities every day, day-in and day-out. Moreover, I do not even know where one purchases such underthings (though maybe Sister Dagobert might have an idea. Do I dare ask her?). But, in truth, Roland's simplicity of taste would entail endless complications, and I therefore did not suggest him as a possible prince in my supplicating prayer to Glorietta. No mention of the exigent, high-maintenance Marquis was made.

Oh, but I am worry-free today, having laid my burden in Glorietta's hands. She will do the job for me, I know it. Now I am off to work. Jean-Claudi is in Milan for two weeks on a fashion shoot, so I will pretend to be his lady-a-waiting. Off I go, there really is no time to lose! A good day to you Felix, and may the Trinitarians lift their glasses to you thrice. *A la vôtre!*

Feast of Saint Finnian of Clonard

They call you the 'teacher of the saints of Ireland'. Well, you must have had a great deal of work to do in your day, Finnian. My last name is O'Riley but I've never been to Ireland myself. I'd love to kiss the Blarney Stone though.

It was an important day for me, Finnian, because I wore my uniform to work for the first time and submitted myself to spoon inspection. Several paid their compliments: *C'est franchement original! C'est pas mal du tout!* Sister Dagobert noticed nothing although Yorik could not stop sniffing at me. I began to wonder if this smock once belonged to a veterinary nurse. I think I'll take the hem up a couple of notches.

Will Jean-Claudi ever come back? (Please don't answer, Finnian.) Asking this question with a longing sigh in my breast has become part of my daily Pretend practice. I wrote a fifty-word article on the bravery of Versace Man. I also wrote a ten-word blurb on the private pleasure of Medusa underwear *pour homme*. Thought of Roland, of course.

Neighbour Jeromino knocked on my door this morning to see if Jubilee wanted to come to his place to play with his tabby, Felix. 'Yes,' I said. 'He does, but I will not allow him permission because today is a workday. Maybe on Saturday afternoon.' Neighbour Jeromino does not work and forgets that others do. He is only thirty but lives off a pension plan already. When he is not drilling, sawing or hammering away on stolen goods, he's smoking away. In all honesty, I'd rather Jubilee stay away from such a hazardous environment! Gave Neighbour Jeromino a rain check and a handful of sugar cubes.

I stayed at work past the usual hour for an Yves Saint Laurent cocktail, which was really just a glass of champagne and a toast: *Here here, Yves!* Yves, of course, was not there at all. On my way out, I ran into Djamila, the wife of Hadj Mohammed, the Algerian janitor. Djamila accompanies her husband on his rounds, pointing out the office's dirty nooks and crannies. Sharp of eye and tongue, she never lifts a finger. It is Hadj Mohammed, a wiry little man with a saint's expression, who vacuums, cleans and empties all the waste baskets. He is called Hadj, which means pilgrim, because he made his holy pilgrimage to Mecca last year. I asked him once if he was any relation to the converted Algerian, Saint Augustine, but he thought not.

'And how is Mademoiselle?' Djamila greeted me, looking at me through her black horn-rimmed glasses.

Yes, there she was standing suddenly before me in her long velvety gown, a white rayon veil pulled sternly around her head. Often, these Muhammadan head curtains make women's heads appear smaller, but this is not so with Djamila, whose wide, serious face is strikingly framed by the kerchief. It endows her with more majesty than a three-tiered bun might. Yes, hair would cheapen her somehow, would render her authority less cautious and commanding.

I should say that many of the people at work are terrified of Djamila, especially the spoons. I was a bit surprised by this imperial lady at first but since the evening she asked me if I was a believer (to which I replied yes, I was), there has been an understanding between us. Djamila explained to me that she could not bear the sight of an unbeliever and that this particular office was polluted by these offenders.

'How do you know that for sure?' I questioned.

'Because,' she said raising her voice, 'I have asked them!'

'All of them?'

Djamila did not answer with a word but nodded her head slowly, closing her eyes like a woman ending a prayer for good health in pain. Then, raising an eyebrow over the black rim of her glasses, 'I have ways of knowing, Mademoiselle.'

Indeed, Djamila not only has ways of knowing but simply *knows*, and knows *all of the time*. Ask her any question and she will give you an answer which is less the fruit of personal reflection than of pro-verbial Koranic wisdom. I have taken advantage of this remarkable acquaintance to ask her a number of questions on a number of topics.

REMEDY   How long should a woman breastfeed her baby?'
(One of the spoons breastfed her newborn at work. Jean-Claudi left
editorial office looking a tad ill. I wanted to know more.)

DJAMILA   For two years. She must feed with the breast from the
child's arrival through to his second birthday. From this time on,
the child must never again see her breast for fear of temptation. It is
written in the Koran!

REMEDY   What is the best way to prepare steak tartare? (I was
having a dinner party that night.)

DJAMILA   The best way to prepare it is not to prepare it. It is
wrong to eat raw, heathen meats untouched by the cleansing fire. It
is written, I tell you, in the Koran!

REMEDY   Who does Allah love the most, the ladies or the
gentlemen?

DJAMILA   Allah loves those whose hearts are true and humble
equally. But he made gentlemen superior to ladies because of their
musclehood and because they are the ones who pay the woman's keep.
It is written in the Koran!

I thought then of Djamila's husband, Hadj Mohammed, that frail
pilgrim with the broom and dustpan, always bent or bending. How
hard he works to maintain his God-granted edge. And Djamila keeps
an eye on him at all times, making sure that he earns her keep. Yes,
Djamila does have all the answers. I must say that she is quite the
opposite of Sister Dagobert who, when she does answer a question,
provides several possible responses. You may choose one, as in multiple choice, or accept all as mutually inclusive. Yes, it is another game
altogether with Sister Dag.

38

This evening we spoke about different couscous recipes. Or rather, Djamila did. I listened and took notes. Learned the difference between red sauce and white sauce, mutton and lamb, halal and haram meats. Wrote all this down in my address book. 'No! Do not write this! Come to my home, I will show you.' I asked no questions but made an appointment with Djamila for Saturday morning.

'See you Saturday!'

'*Inshallah.*'

Oh dear, I thought. But *will* the Gods be willing? (No need to answer, Finnian, but if you don't mind, please note this appointment in The Lord's Agenda. I can't imagine he has time for so much willing or not willing.)

Feast of Saint Lucy (Virgin Martyr)

Do your eyes ever get tired, Lucy, from the supplications of so many sight-afflicted pilgrims? The *Concise* says your eyeballs are kept in a reliquary in Naples and have been known to cure the blind. I really must tell Sister Dagobert about this, for Lord knows she could use your help, Lucy. If you could just get her to the point where all she needed were bifocals, she would bandage better at the Hôtel-Dieu.

The *Concise* also says we can call you for SOS nightmare intervention. I wish I had known that last night. I was dreaming that a single-toothed sailor was in pursuit of me, when Jubilee pounced onto my bed, in hot demand for his morning sardines. Yes, he effectively put that awful sailor off my trail. I thanked Jubilee for ridding me of the stalker by giving him two sardines too many, which did make him sick a bit. I fixed coffee and lifted my cup to von Krysler himself: may he continue pedalling his unicycle on ropes both high and thin.

In the bubble bath I paid the kindest regards to my feet, once an *ami intime* of the von Krysler fellow himself. Here's what I love to do, Lucy: lounge in my *peignoir* whilst gazing out the window and waving a white Kleenex – as if to a distant knight on a moped. That's just what I did this morning before getting dressed. But before I knew, it was time for cooking class. Off to Djamila's!

I take the metro over, climb up to the sixth floor and ring the doorbell. I am ushered in and sprinkled with orange flower water as I am a guest, a guest student. There are some six women already there, all of them in satin or velveteen gowns, all of them in various stages of labour or repose on cushions and poufs. Have they come for cooking class too?

Djamila introduces me as the Nazarene, and I am pulled down onto a low couch by a young woman named Leila. Leila smiles at me and offers me a plate of dates.

'From Algeria!' she says. 'Not Tunisia! These are the good ones! Nazarenes eat dates too. Eat!'

I pluck a date from the plate obediently. Its skin is light golden in colour and its inner flesh honey sweet. There are no dates like this in Florida. Or in Paris for that matter, except for those who know how to find them. And only the Semites do.

'Have some of these,' says another girl who looks exactly like Djamila except for the glasses.

41

Daughter? I wonder. No, niece, I am told. Niece Sarrah offers cakes stuffed with fig mincemeat. I take one and wonder now where to put my date pit. Leila holds out a plump hand. *Here!* I hesitate for only a second. Clearly there is no shame in any of this. I feel small, cushioned against Leila's hams, but queenly too – everything comes to me on a plate. Yet another hand brings me a glass of mint tea.

'You're giving the Nazarene that glass?' someone questions. It seems to be Niece Sarrah. The glass bears the picture of a great and distant mosque. The mosque is gold.

'Please,' I say. 'It will be an honour.'

I try imagining a wine glass with the Cathedral of Chartres painted on it. It would be for tourists, I thought. A disappointment. Nothing like this one, which is for believers.

Suddenly the doorbell rings. Djamila says something to all the women in Arabic. It sounds to me like an order and is immediately obeyed. The women fumble in their purses and pull out scarves which they then attach to their heads so that no lock of hair is seen. On the armrest of the couch is a pillowcase that one of the women has been mending. Having no other recourse, I quickly pull this over my head like a surrogate veil. It will do, I see. The important thing is to mind Djamila. It is part of cooking class. The incipient stage.

'Oh the Nazarene!' Leila points at me, giggling and wagging her finger.

A chorus of mirth joins in. The veils are singing, but only for a moment. Djamila hushes them immediately from Pisgah, a foot-high stool upon which she stands to look through the door's peephole and behold the promised man.

In comes Mohammed, not the Prophet but perhaps a profiteer.

42

Mohammed is Djamila's son, a tall, fine-boned lad dressed in leather. He is here to ask for alms. Djamila pulls a fifty euro bill from her brassiere and wraps his hand around it.

'Go my son. God be willing, you will one day have a wife.'

Mohammed leaves and the veils come off, are stuffed back in purses. Leila pulls mine from off my head and swats me with it.

'Leila! Look how you treat the Nazarene!' It is Djamila, admonishing.

Leila laughs and takes my hands playfully. 'Shall I read your palm?'

But there is no time for clairvoyance. An immense plastic bowl with a mock wood veneer is set on the coffee table. Niece Sarrah pours a five kilo bag of semolina into it.

'Ablution!' cries out Djamila.

Leila nudges me and I take the cue, get up and go into the bathroom for hand washing. The soap is made of rose glycerine. Leila, who is washing too, tells me the rose scent perfumes the couscous. When I leave the bathroom, Niece Sarrah is holding a bottle of olive oil. Djamila raises the paring knife. The preliminaries are over. Couscous class has begun.

We wet the grain, we oil the grain, we steam the grain. We wet the grain, we oil the grain, we steam the grain. And so on. A concerto for six hands. Six hands play the grain. Djamila conducts with a free finger. It is only by a knowing touch that the passage from stone to willing wheat is made surely, without fail. The music is inconsequent to the process after all. Except that it is pleasurable. And can pleasure ever be called inconsequent? It is the music that sustains us. For several hours, the time that it takes the grain to swell. No-one seems to mind the time after all, not in this low-riding parlour which is on the sixth floor but close to the ground nevertheless. The minutes are not stern soldiers a-marching but dates on a plate, regaled at leisure. Ripe, not lazy.

I see I might stay here through to the evening and continue to ripen but obligation calls me away. On the Rue de Rivoli is a woman counting the soldiers this very minute. It is Joanna, awaiting me in a tea shop furnished with high-riding chairs, poufs on stilts raised up far from the soil. I thank the ladies and bid them goodbye. Djamila gives me the fruit of our labour in two Tupperware containers.

Come next week, and I will teach you to prepare mutton head.'

Inshallah!

Feast of Saints Theodore and Theophanes (brothers)

Not a wholly surprising fate for poets such as yourselves: twelve lines of verse tattooed on your foreheads during the iconoclastic persecutions for some saintly sin committed (the *Concise* does not specify which). Though the emperor of Constantinople, mindful of your reputations as poets, apologized for the literary shortcomings of the doggerel, a courtier interjected, 'Sire, such puny men are not worth better verse.' And so you spent the rest of your waking days bearing the marks of trivial impieties on your brow. Nowadays those tattoos would make you all the rage, my dear Theos, but in AD 841 they merely qualified you for sainthood.

Jean-Claudi just came back from Milan with a promotional Versace scarf in his pocket for each and every one of the spoons. Must say I am disappointed in Jean-Claudi's taste, particularly regarding his lady-a-waiting, for whom he chose a delicate orange-and-goose-poo colour. In all honesty I am slightly offended. Does he really think goose-poo becomes me? Why, it only brings out my freckles! Still, as it is only proper to thank the gift-giver, I did so. Jean-Claudi, it seems, came back two days early. Milano and its ephebes just could not hold his attention long enough. I suppose those Milanese swing-sets simply do not compare with their Parisian counterparts.

So I am no longer a lady-a-waiting. No indeed. I have turned that persevering girl out of my house, shucked her husk of homely longing. I stand here, alone and without illusion perhaps, but engaged in new purpose. Call me Claudia.

Claudia, you see, was my lunchtime purchase, although she is not an edible but, rather, a wearable. Claudia is an auburn ornament, a headdress commonly called 'a wig'. I found her at a store called Black Beauty Pride, a French boutique with an American name run by an African entrepreneur from Ghana. I spoke to the owner, a woman by the name of Gambi, I believe. I had been trying on an assortment of dark brunette wigs when Gambi came out from her back room to wait on me. In fact she did not wait on me long, but directed me to what she believed would suit me best: the redheads.

Gambi wears a wig herself but you can absolutely not tell it.

'See my wig,' she said, pointing at her hair.

'No,' I replied, admiring her long tresses, 'I don't.'

Not only was my response true, but it also seemed to me to be appropriately polite. What wig-wearer wants to be found out? But Gambi grew quickly annoyed by my lack of discernment and removed the hair as an entertainer would a top hat.

'No pins,' she said defiantly, before dropping the hair back on her head. It fell perfectly into place, impressing me greatly. Her locks, I saw, were of the highest quality. The value of a wig of course is measured by its degree of verisimilitude and holding power, and Gambi's are made especially for an international clientele. A clientele, she assured me, of standing.

'Look here,' she said, pointing to a corner of the boutique where four seemingly identical brown bobbed wigs were displayed. 'Those,' she said, 'are my kosher wigs.'

I had to admire the kosher few, not for their chic, but because they had been submitted to a number of tests and had passed. They were high achievers. Apparently she sells one of these every day. And on request will also ship to Tel Aviv.

It was due to Gambi's astute assessment of my coiffuratorial needs that I landed Claudia. Claudia is the one who looks best on me according to the word of Gambi. I tried on several others, longer and shorter, frizzier and straighter, but only Claudia satisfied the proprietor. Claudia is an American cut called Pamela, which is to say she is shoulder length, slightly wavy and layered. I have no intention of wearing Claudia daily, but only when I go shopping and perhaps to dance class.

Dance class, I must say, is going rather well. Last week my teacher, Samira, taught us the difference between the 'Hindu Head', the 'Chicken Head' and the 'Voodoo Head'. Of the three, I prefer the latter. Once I saw an African man perform the voodoo head in the Luxembourg gardens. I can't recall what the occasion was. Perhaps there was none. In any case I was terribly curious about it and must say I am proud to have mastered the move myself. Will show the spoons how to do so as well.

Samira is a wonderful teacher and most inspirational. She tells us stories about her life as a dancer in Egypt while we warm up our hips, bellies and 'grammars' – which is what Samira calls breasts, though I have no idea why. She also wears a wig. I must admit Samira has a tremendous influence over me; I shall thank her for Claudia after class, if possible. Often it's difficult to have a word with her in the dressing room though. She's such a nervous lady when she's not dancing and so distracted! And I think she gets the collywobbles too. Speaking to her then is like speaking to a government employee. I don't believe she hears anything. And yet this communicational flaw is understandable in light of Samira's recent history.

Samira you see, is an escapee. From whence did she escape? From Egypt it seems, five years ago. Actually it was not exactly Egypt she fled, but a man named Sir Reginald Hamly who resided at the Marriott Hotel in Cairo. Samira was a star dancer in the Marriott Cabaret, and at the time much in demand elsewhere as well. She had danced privately for Yasser Arafat several times (at least I think that's what she said) and also for the richest man in the world, who dropped seven Gomorrah rubies into her bra for the pleasure of watching her 'grammars' shimmy.

Whenever she was billed to perform at the Marriott, Sir Reginald Hamly would reserve a seat at the front centre table, to be her closest spectator. He always sat alone if you did not count the bottle of

Bombay gin, which inevitably accompanied him in the way of an appendage or protruding organ. He drank from it straight with the aid of a medicinal straw. Sir Reginald Hamly nursed, and while sucking upon the pharmaceutical teat he kept his gaze riveted upon the gracious Samira, eyes devouring her sleight of belly.

At first, Samira believed this most attentive Englishman was in love with her. She thought him yet another helpless admirer and expected the heap of floribunda roses to arrive upon her doorstep, the champagne to appear on her dressing table. In short she was awaiting the flattery of perks, the habitual progeny of amorous admiration. Yet, strangely, no such gifts came. For a time she thought him cheap, a trait which no Oriental can forgive. When she approached the edge of the stage and saw him sucking and gin-ing away, his gaze loveless and intoxicated, disgust rose in her grammar, and the desire to spit at him came strongly upon her. Indeed, once she did just that, but immediately regretted it terribly, for Sir Reginald Hamly lapped up this vehement oath.

Alas! Samira began to see that the queer Hamly had no intention of wooing her as a courtesan. No, he did not want her in bed in the least. Sir Reginald Hamly's heart wore a Britannic hat that kept it shaded from the light of an enquiring mind. His eccentricity could not be so easily divined. She came to understand that what he wanted was not to possess her as a man might a dancing girl, but to *be* her. He wanted to unzip her skin, remove the stuffing and step into this finest of female moulds. For him, she was simply ready-wear. He hungered to don the undulating Samira, the queen costume of the Marriott.

Perhaps it could have been suggested that he go to Morocco for an intimate surgery. But little good this would have done, for his desire was not operative. Nothing would fix or assuage it. It had no rule or runway.

Unable to reason with his queer desperation, Sir Reginald Hamly took to stalking Samira, sometimes hiding in her home disguised as a Nubian slave. She only saw him by way of his shadows and by the black stains on her furniture from the kohl he used to darken his skin. Several times she found a knife in her bed with a letter asking her to remove her skin with the implement and hang it in the closet when finished. The situation soon became unbearable and although a bodyguard was hired, Samira found no relief. Sir Reginald Hamly inhabited her imagination as much as her home. Indeed, he had succeeded in penetrating her through the fiercest of intercourse possible. His tool was terrorism. Terror had unlocked her, and now Hamly was lodged inside.

There was nothing left for Samira to do but make a continental escape. Disguised as a member of the French humanitarian society Doctors Without Borders, and carrying a medical valise filled with scenic cosmetics, she boarded a plane for Paris. Since her arrival, she has twice had the fright of believing Sir Reginald Hamly to be in the vicinity. Once she found a knife in her mailbox but with no accompanying letter. Had Hamly dropped by? She will never know for certain. So it is that Samira must always be on the lookout and prepared for the Englishman. The wig she wears, I should add, helps keep her incognito. Poor dear! I can see why she gets the collywobbles!

So, dear Theodore and Theophanes, that is the story of Samira as it was recounted during figure eight practice and warm-up. She nearly suffered a fate worse than yours, we must concede. Just think if Sir Hamly *had* succeeded in turning her into ready-wear: she might have been sent an application for sainthood too! Maybe it is best that I write her a thank-you letter. In the meantime I must remember to practise my pistol hips and maytag twist; one can never know when Samira might pop a quiz.

Feast of Saint Geneviève
(Patron Saint of Paris)

Paris is still waiting for another grande dame like you to come around, Geneviève. Only the Pucelle can compare but it's been a while since she saved Orléans, dressed in boys-wear I might add. How about Catherine Deneuve as a runner-up for grande dame-hood? She probably couldn't do much against Attila's hordes if they were to turn upon us again, but nowadays a woman can go quite far with couture all the same.

The holiday season was over in no time. I spent Christmas day with Sister Dagobert delivering gifts to the blind and bedridden; the Hôtel-Dieu was decorated with pink tinsel. 'Why pink?' I asked. 'Because,' explained Sister Dag, 'that's the colour of the baby Jesus.'

Odd. I wonder if it really was. Could the Christ child in fact have been a baby girl? Might there have been a swap with one of Herod's spared? And how would Sister Dagobert know what pink was in any case? Had she once been among the seeing? And never told me?

I gave Sister Dagobert a copy of *The Miracle Worker* in Braille. Hard to believe she's never read it. (Have you, Geneviève? If not, maybe you could find it in a Ouija edition.) Sister gave me a pair of hand-knitted booties size four. Believe that is the size for an eight-year-old. Might I wear them as mittens?

I called Mumly in Florida for the occasion.

'What do you want for Christmas, Princess?' she asks me on Christmas day clear across the Atlantic.

'Oh nothing really,' I say. 'Maybe a pair of shoes?'

Mother was celebrating at the clubhouse. Having Christmas brunch with her golf group, which included her banker, Mr Epstein, and his wife Rachel-May, and Father Flinn as well, from Our Lady of Perpetual Victory, mother's parish. I could hear someone sucking up a drink through a straw. Bloody Marys no doubt. My mind flashed for a moment on Sir Hamly. Suddenly I was worried about Mumly.

'Everything there okay, Mumly?'

'Oh yes, Princess. Wonderful! Do you know we're going to have a New Year's gala? There'll be that Cuban cha-cha band, you know, and a double blessing by Fr Flinn and a rabbi friend of the Epsteins's.'

I was happy to hear Mumly doing so well but had to ask about the dropsy all the same.

'Oh drop that! I'm doing great! Everything is just swell.' So it was.

And so it is. I did not march on Rome after all. Afraid of the lion's den, I stayed home with Jubilee. And declined several party invitations, including one from Joanna. 'Come and see the Works,' she suggested. Indeed! Her deck looks out upon the Eiffel Tower where the pyrotechnics took place. But in truth, I was not much in the mood for Joanna and her Ball of Marvels. And besides I was (and am!) white-pantiless yet and did not relish another encounter – intimate or otherwise – with the Marquis.

People are always tempted on New Year's Eve, are they not? Tempted to fly love like a kite? Freely, wildly and, in the end, disastrously? No, no, no. I am done with the great leaps of folly and faith. Love must rap at my door three times, give proof of identity and be submitted to the scrutiny of the concierge before there is entry. I believe I am finally understanding the notion of the temple as taught in the hearsay catechism. That is to say, of the body as temple of course. Perhaps it would have been easier had Sisters Mary Barbara and Virginia Marie simply told us about Adult Sex. Really, it would have been so much more useful, so much more up-to-date. I must mention this to Sister Dagobert as five sisters in her order are catechetical: Sister Doris, Sister Michelangela, Sister Sue, Sister Huguette, and Sister Rosemary. Yes, I will send them that article by Dr Dolittle.

But I must say that as things went, it was a good thing I refrained. For one thing, New Year's Day was all the better for restraint. No nauseous hangover to nurse, no regret to babysit. I began the year with industry. I:

1) Ironed my uniform
2) Shampooed Jubilee
3) Practised my camel walk and pelvic tuck, and
4) Took a walk down the Champs-Elysées.

Actually, on number four, I skipped rather than walked. I had no choice really seeing the disastrous state of the sidewalks. When I got back home, the phone was ringing. A call! From whom? Oh, just Monsieur le Marquis. Must say I was most surprised by this telephonic interruption coming by way of the sixteenth arrondissement. *Do you think,* he questioned gently, *that we could try again?* With my new door policy in effect, I told him I thought not. Only on the third call (I did not tell him this of course) might I consider another *sortie* (in the French sense, meaning date). Come to think of it (the whities!), perhaps even more calls will be necessary in this particular gentleman's case. But in all likelihood there will be no marks for the Marquis, be it three calls or four. No score for the bore. This being said, maybe I am not entirely without a regret concerning dear Roland, Knight of the White Panty, and yet I have learned enough from Dr Dolittle to believe, even if falsely, that I have done the right thing.

In order to recuperate from the lack of a need to recuperate, I have spent the last two days at the Cleopatra Club. The Cleopatra Club is an Arabian bathhouse on the Boulevard de Belleville. There, in the eucalyptus steam, I sat among Semitic and Berber ladies from Tunis, Algiers, Tangiers and Tel Aviv. It was not unlike being in Djamila's living room, only the robes were shucked for Eve-wear. The Cleopatra Club is a propitious place for womenfolk to get as clean as possible both inside and out. Exfoliation is done with a black-netted glove worn on the hand of a female wrestler. Actually, I am not sure she is truly a wrestler but, shaped not unlike a Japanese Sumo, so she appears to be. I believe her name is Samia, which is the feminine of Sam. Samia makes amends for biblical mishaps and grapples with evil, the hand-me-down fault of a trickster snake and its sidekick, Woman. She wrestles with modern-day ladies, the progeny of He-Snake and She-Eve, pinning us down on her board and taking that black glove to our bodies, putting all her weight and force into the scrub. Indeed, she removes our treacherous skin before we can think of shedding it ourselves, all of it, and leaves us with something rosier and quieter for covering. Then she sends us back into the steam where we will sweat with pleasure or with pain, depending on our nature and personal predicament.

It was as I was happily sweating that I met the Baptist. The Baptist was neither a Berber nor a Semite, but an islander from the Antilles. What's more, she wore a bathing suit. In other words she had shame and the prudency to cover herself. She too was the progeny of snake and woman, but had repented and put on a Speedo. The Baptist spoke English, which of course is the great language of the Baptists. *Do you know,* she asked me after she had enquired about my name as all good Baptists do, *that Jesus Christ is our Redeemer? Do you know him, Remedy?*

I must say that I was sweating copiously just then and breathing quite hard too. The fiery eucalyptus oil was snaking down my nose and lungs. Painful, yes. But pleasurable, too.

I shook my head, and I prayed this was the right answer. It was. The Baptist couldn't have hoped for a better response and took it as cue to perform the highest task of the missionary. Indeed, she had been sent to the Cleopatra Club to convert the Muslims and Jews, an ambitious and highly inappropriate undertaking with a lamentable success rate, but had come upon a mere Catholic, the easiest prey of all, especially in the case of a Catholic arriving from South America. I, of course, had arrived from Miami, which is not quite South America but almost. Still, she would not stand a chance with me. No, naked but armed with the Apostolic cuirass – that spiritual armour bestowed over the centuries by Holy Roman angels – I would stand my ground. (Thank you, dear Geneviève, for I'm certain you aided me at this very moment with your militant graces). *No*, I repeated. *I do not know him. But I do know the cross.* With this I lifted the two-inch long gold cross at my bosom. It is the only jewel I own, a family heirloom brought over to the New World from Spain on the breast of Lucia Irigaray de Valdez, my great-great-grandmother. Before reaching the family, it was believed to have belonged to the inquisitor Foulques de Saint-Georges, who operated out of Toulouse. At his death, the cross was stolen by the family of one of his victims – medieval cousins of mine thrice removed. And it has been handed down since that time, from bosom to bosom. Indeed, the cross has laid against many a breast, protecting its wearer from hasty conversions, probing inquisitors and pick-pockets.

I never wear the cross on the outside of my blouse but always keep it hidden within. Why? Because it is ornate and opulent in a way people no longer understand. It is covered with rubies and diamonds, you see, and all too many might take it for mere bijou, a comely commodity. But to me it is the cross, a holy remnant. No price will be put on it at Sotheby's, no tag at Salle Drouot, the Paris auction house.

I was told that Lucia Irigaray de Valdez wore it outside her corsage only in the face of heathens, for it blinded them with the light of the true faith. I thought of this, of course, as I raised the jewel, perhaps not unlike Foulques de Saint-Georges once did before the auto-da-fé, though I hope not. Yes, I raised it high so that it shone in the islander's eye. At first the gleam would not penetrate her sea-green irises, that kind so common to island girls, but then it did pierce them with a slight but immaculate ray. And her face, stretched like a cocky canvas certain of success, suddenly collapsed, losing all tension and hold. She looked, I have to say, like a wounded soldier of the Christian Armies. There are so many of them, you know. They are confident and crippled. They wear their souls in their fists.

Without a word, I left her then and laid myself flat on Samia's board and was delivered.

Feast of Saint Bernard or Barnard

The *Concise* has skimped a bit on your account, Barnard, and left me wondering what happened to your wife. Did you ditch her when you founded the Ambronay monastery, lock her away in a convenient convent? Or was it her untimely death that spurred you to such devout action? Suffice it to say that, according to their account, your marital life was more apéritif than dish-of-the-day – though how it piqued your appetite to become abbot, then archbishop, we can only surmise.

Speaking of marriage, dear Barnard, M. Phet's lodger was having

a domestic dispute with his overseas wife on the phone last night. It must have been around four a.m. Jubilee got quite upset by the High Cantonese and knocked over the vase of forget-me-nots. I heard the water dripping off the edge of the table and got up to relieve myself. Realizing that something must be done, I got out my broom and banged on the floor. Not sure this measure was sufficient, I then knelt down on elbows and knees. *Silence SVP!* I shouted through the floorboards. But M. Phet's lodger grew even more virulent, the High Cantonese higher still. There was nothing to do, but to return to bed with a candle and pray to St Wilgefortis, patroness of unfriendly marriages. Perhaps you've heard of her, Barnard? The Vatican supressed her veneration in 1969. But how little this matters. After only five minutes of supplication to St Uncumber (Wilgefortis's nickname), the dispute had ended, the phone had been hung up, and manifestly M. Phet's lodger had retired to his boudoir alone and unencumbered by strife.

I was happy about this resolution, but could not get back to sleep. There was little else to do but get up and make coffee in the Von Krysler stovetop. I had the coffee in bed whilst reading that Jean Rhys novel, *Good Morning, Midnight*, which of course made me think about ageing in a mouldy Montparnasse hotel room with only a balding fur coat and a half bottle of whisky to my name. I thought of the cruelty of gigolos too. That poor character, she really should have become a nun. At least then she would have had things to do during the day and a glass of wine every night at dinner. And the gigolos couldn't have got to her there. At least I don't think so. But Jean Rhys wrote that story so beautifully and probably didn't know much about the Dominicans back then. It's true that they keep awfully quiet.

Work was slow today as the top spoons have been sent to New York for the collections. The middle and bottom spoons are to hold down the fort, but many have scheduled numerous medical and dental appointments this week, which really do take up an entire morning or afternoon as we all know. So, really, there was hardly a soul at À La Mode Online today. Jean-Claudi of course went to New York with the top spoons too. I really do miss him so. And have been wearing the goose-poo scarf in memory of him, though it makes me look sallow. I have forgiven his lack of discernment and have found it in me to commend him on his graciousness in receiving an unattractive freebee. Someone else might have turned it down and offended the giver. But not Jean-Claudi. Instead he offended me, the giftee, which must certainly be the lesser offence. But as I have said, he is forgiven and now desired more than ever. Especially whilst away.

So there was no-one to talk to at work until the clock struck seven. At exactly this hour Djamila and Hadj Mohammed arrived with an assortment of brooms and buckets. The Pilgrim was immediately sent to work by the directive hand of his loving wife who stayed with me a moment for a chat.

'How are you Djamila?' Djamila smiled but did not reply. She reached out and touched the goose-poo scarf, admiring it with her fingers.

'How much was it?' she asked.

'Nothing,' I said. 'It was a gift.'

'You'll give it to me then, won't you?'

'Of course.'

I slid the silky Versace sampler off from around my neck and wrapped it over Djamila's shoulders. I did this without the slightest hesitation. After all, how could I refuse my cooking teacher such an obvious gift? I should have thought of it myself to save her the embarrassment of asking. Indeed, I should have seen that goose-poo was one of Djamila's preferred colours, that it gave a warm, dusky flush to her face and made her teeth appear whiter. Djamila of course had known, but I had not.

I admired the scarf on her and for a moment imagined myself disguised as some Muslim cousin of myself, riding a camel in Algeria, distributing Versace scarves to the womenfolk of Algiers. They would lead me through the kasbah into their homes where I would dance the Dance of the Seven Scarves, flying those diaphanous designer sheaths around the cushioned room. They would wave their scarves at me, then join in the dance, the Versace wrappers now tied about their shimmying hips. The party with its lady minstrels and sticky cakes would last for hours and no-one but the camel would know I was gone.

I enjoyed this particular round of Pretend so much that I was reluctant to mount the camel and take leave of the nineteenth century. In the end the move wasn't mine. Djamila brought me back with a sharp lash of admonishment.

'Ha! Where were you on Saturday?' she asked accusingly.

I shook my head and wondered confusedly. Yes, where was I? I honestly did not know.

'It was mutton head. Now you will never know how to cook it,' she chided me. 'And your husband one day (God-be-willing you will have one), will be disappointed by you. All husbands eat mutton head. It is the favourite dish of husbands. Don't you know this?'

I admitted that I did not.

'You must come this Saturday. Leila will be making pigeon pie. Husbands like this too. I will teach you about husbands!'

I agreed to attend, apologized profusely, and thanked Djamila for so graciously extending yet another invitation to her class in cooking and happy husbandry.

After several God-be-willings, I was able to make my way out of the building and onto the Rue Beaubourg, where, on an odd whim, I turned left rather than right as I normally would have and soon found myself in a padded armchair at the Café Beaubourg. Sometimes this can happen, a queer fancy will take hold of you and lead you to an unexpected chair. (Isn't it so, Barnard? Wasn't that how you ended up in the archbishop's seat in Vienne? After having made an unexpected pilgrimage there with Charlemagne to visit the thigh bone of St Bertha?)

The evening crowd at the Café Beaubourg bears little resemblance to the morning crowd, I'm afraid. No M. Lift after six. Only the beautiful people whose greatest pleasure it is to watch and be watched. A most particular comportment which originated, I would surmise, sometime in the Neolithic age, when hunting was quite the rage. Today this activity persists in Prince Paris, especially among the fellows here at the Café Beaubourg. These gentlemen voyeurs are quite attractive to watch and there is no worry about the risk of a napkin communiqué. At least in my own particular case. I ordered a beer and enjoyed this moment of relaxation, free now of that working plume that just an hour before had me scribbling on about unisex aprons, flirty mules and turquoise breastplates (de Givenchy).

Work at À La Mode Online gets quite tiresome. I must take a vacation sometime soon. Perhaps to Rome. In any case, I thought about Jean-Claudi and his Versace sampler. I thought about my love for him and my dislike of the sampler. I thought of the sampler around Djamila's shoulders. Suddenly, I realized that my long-standing

Pretend Production had undergone a shift, resulting in a newly shaped desire of triangular dimensions. Djamila, as the bearer of the scarf, stands at the tip of our reach. And yet she will never know this, nor will Jean-Claudi. Neither of them need to. Yes, desire, flimsy as it is, seems to borrow on the solid triangle, I discovered, whereas love, of a sturdier nature, requires the unwieldy spiral.

I thought of Mumly with that Girard fellow whom she dearly loved. Never had I seen her spin so defiantly out of control, losing her money and looks by the minute. And yet she was entirely in possession of her love. It sat within her like a vital organ, doing the work of a heart and a spleen. I must say that it is not so with me and Jean-Claudi. In all honesty, I do not love that boy. And yet I desire him mightily. It is a great relief to me that this desire can now breathe more easily, with Djamila, my protectoress, presiding over it. It is much more comfortable this way. Complicity, as any young schoolgirl knows, smoothes passion's uneasy edges.

I left the Café Beaubourg with my beer only half finished. A lovely couple – a kind of twin-set, wearing matching socks on their heads (they do make great hats) – took my table. I wished them well and headed home. Cooked up a liver steak for Jubilee and me. Neither one of us could eat it really, although we did try. We had cheese and crackers instead. A bit of green tea for Jubilee and then to bed. I read my favourite celibatarian sailor passage in *Moby Dick* four times which did have a marvellous impact on my slumber: I dreamed I was dancing a jig with a handsome harpooneer. *Rig it, dig it, stig it, quig it! Go Pip!* I could have danced all night!

(Farewell to you, Barnard, and to your lovely wife too.)

Feast of Saint Veronica

No matter what they say, compassionate Veronica, I have no doubt that you wiped the sweat and blood from the face of the Lord on his way to Calvary. Why, they still have that miraculous cloth of yours safeguarded at St Pete's! True, the Christ image you so beautifully captured on your linen is no longer discernible, but surely this is due to the wear and tear of time and not, as the *Concise* has it, to the fabulous nature of your legend. The *Concise* claims that the fraudulent towel was 'invented' first, and that the name Veronica – meaning 'true image' – was subsequently applied to its presumed owner, therefore reducing you, a great saint if there ever was one, to mere yardage!

How this upset me, Veronica! So much so that to lift my spirits I went straight to the Louvre, that *haut lieu* of true images, as soon as the clock struck noon.

An hour was all I had, which wasn't enough, certainly, but almost adequate for visiting the Michelangelo statue gallery, a haunt for lovers of loving men. I spent twenty minutes with *The Dying Slave*, and am convinced there was no knife, in fact, but the prodding of some instrument of pleasure typical of those times and now forgotten. I think you'll agree with me, Veronica, that no-one but a saint wears such a face when being mauled to death. And *The Dying Slave* depicts no saint I am sure: he is too beautiful, too perfect. Saints never come is such perfect wrappers. And if by fluke they do, they swiftly and irrevocably end beauty with quicklime acids, as did the South American saint Rosa of Lima, when her loveliness began to embarrass her.

There is no end to human suffering, really, which is why people come to the Louvre if even just for an hour. The Louvre is full of sufferings made beautiful by extraordinary tools and techniques. I really do wonder if Jean-Claudi comes to the Michelangelo gallery to admire these promiscuous gentlemen as I do. Such a pleasurable lunch-break activity. I really should suggest it to him. Maybe I will see if Djamila wants to come with me one day. Wouldn't she love it too?

The top spoons are back from collections. All returned with tanned skin and manicures. It seems their flight had a two-day layover in Miami. If I had known, I would have given them a letter to send to Mumly who simply loves to get letters from me. I really should write to Mumly more, although I do call which is quite nice too.

I left work at quarter past six, which to the spoons seemed awfully early, to go to St Joe's half-six service. Sister Dagobert wasn't there, nor was Père Ricard. I must say it was a bit lonely. Which is why I supplicated you, Veronica, to send me a new gentleman friend, one with *some* free time but not *too* much. Preferably one who dances the cha-cha, which I am dying to learn, and who can recite Emily's poems on command. You did hear my prayer, didn't you? The priest stayed awake through the entire Mass and sang a good deal of it in a language no-one understood. Could it possibly have been Polish? So it was rumoured in the pews. He refused our hands and made us take communion on the tongue. In any case he is nothing like Père Ricard who sometimes drops the hostie on your foot and usually takes a snooze in the burgundy velvet armchair afterwards. The half-six priest is certainly a visiting priest. And a stranger to our ways.

When I got home, there were two messages on the machine. One from Neighbour Jeromino's father, Bert Jeromino, who calls from time to time to see if his son is all right. The other from Joanna who wants me to help her chose a gown for the Ball of Marvels. That'll be in June at Versailles as it turns out. In the castle, so she says. She sounded overly excited on the machine, and expressed her Presbyterian determination to get me to the ball too.

'It'll be the make-or-break moment for both of us, Remedy. Socially, I mean. To be seen at the ball means you're IN, and for Americans that's no small achievement! Particularly for you, I mean... aren't you of Irish descent? Just think, Remedy, it might even be the occasion for Roland to pop the question. I'm assuming you'll be going with him? He's very with the times for a Marquis and has nothing against the morganatic...'

Dear, dear Joanna, always jumping the gun, always preempting like the folks back home. I suppose I'll have to call her back. Next week perhaps.

I then prepared an egg dinner for two and spent the rest of the evening painting with a set of watercolours (ages 6–12) I bought at the grocery store. I made a portrait of Jean-Claudi with only a towel wrapped around his waist. A bit runny but bearing a strong likeness nevertheless. I just might send it to him in the mail. Anonymously of course. (You won't say anything, will you Veronica?)

Feast of Saint John of Capistrano

I do have a hard time imagining any modern-day politician befrocked as a Franciscan, let alone a saint! But things were dramatically different in the Middle Ages, John, weren't they? And then you got an early start on things: you were married at eighteen, governor of Perugia at twenty-three, and a Franciscan at thirty. And if this were not enough, you lived to the ripe age of seventy and perhaps would have lasted longer if battling the Turks in Belgrade hadn't exhausted you so. Unfortunately, the *Concise*, in a shut-mouthed effort to live up to its name, leaves us with too many biographical blanks. As with your colleague, Saint Barnard, I am left with a nagging question: what did you do with wifey? As a potential wife myself, I'd like to know!

The doorbell rang this morning at eight o'clock. Who was it? The gas man come to do his annual safety check. I greeted him in *peignoir* and knee-highs (the only shoe-substitute around – slippers nowhere in sight). *Good day, Monsieur, the kitchen is to your right.*

Monsieur Gas de Gaz, ever at home in strange homes, proceeded straight to that hearth. He was efficient, I could tell, but not unkind. Jubilee ran between his legs, nearly tripping him. He did not bark. And I saw from behind that he was deficient in that lower muscle which Jean-Claudi flexed with glee. His pants seemed to be sliding danger-ously below the hips, but there was safety in his belt.

So there we were, the morning couple. He, the handyman. She, the home-maker. When he finished and packed his tools, I offered him a cup of coffee from the von Krysler stovetop. Handymen usually love coffee in the morning as it keeps them running, but Monsieur Gas de Gaz declined upon the doctor's orders. I gave him a quick glass of orange juice instead and wished him a good day. As he left the build-ing, I looked out my window above and waved to him below pretending to feel that heartfelt longing a woman feels for her man-gone-off-to-war, or her man-gone-off-to-deliver-pizzas (or, might I add, dear John, the saint-who-leaves-her-in-the-lurch). Whichever it might be, it was still a bit of home-making practice I suppose.

I got to the office by half past nine and wrote a thirty-word feature on freeze-dried Spatial Shampoo (de Givenchy) after giving it a try in the ladies' room sink. You just add water and shake. One of the spoons, who always has a hairdryer on hand, offered to style my hair. She did

70

a beautiful job with my bob, making the ends of my hair curl outward like a little shelf. I thanked her so kindly and wished her a pleasant gym session.

All the spoons are doing something called 'pump', which seems to be a kind of fitness technique from Australia. I'm not sure whence comes the name though. Could this have to do with the shoes worn whilst doing it? The spoons insist I try it too, but there is just not enough time in the day for a girl to do everything she wants. As it is, I hardly have a moment to work on my hip slides and paddle turns, which are certainly my priority. In truth, pump comes last, which is to say, not at all.

Sat next to Sister Dag at noon Mass. Yorik, whose peptic disorder grows worse by the minute, threw up in the aisle during consecration. Père Ricard did not notice but the others on our pew certainly did. One kindly woman offered us a generous supply of rose-print Kleenex for the clean-up. Afterwards I took Yorik outside for fresh air and relief. I missed communion but did light a candle for poor Yorik in the St Francis chapel. May that gentlest of saints kindly intercede today, and always, for all the furry beasts.

I asked Sister Dagobert if St Francis was a vegetarian. She said she didn't know but that like most saints, he probably only ate on occasion. The saintly diet, she explained, consists of stale bread and sour wine. Plus a pear and a piece of cheese when the saint feels too weak to pray. Seeing that they eat so few vegetables – which is to say, none at all – they cannot in all honesty qualify as vegetarians. Nor are they carnivores, exactly. The saints do have their mysteries. Jean-Claudi came in this afternoon to deliver his pics. He works directly with our artistic director, Willie (pronounced *Wheelie*) now, but still comes by to say hello to the spoons. I happened to have been pretending to be Joan of Arc when he walked in our office. It was the battle of Orléans at that moment, and I had just received an arrow through the left thigh (or was it the right?). The pain was agonizing but I held my ground. *Ça va, Remedy?* Jean-Claudi asked me with his deep, seductive voice, which would have been ripe with bedroom intimation had I perhaps been a John of Arc instead. Taking my courage in my hands, I bravely yanked that arrow from the flesh. *Fine! Ça va! Ça va!* I called out, not without a ring of triumph. Then headed directly for the ladies' room to dress the wound. What does Jean-Claudi think of me now? (Keep it to yourself, John.)

Appointment at a place called Chez Mathilde with Joanna after work. Joanna is over the moon about the Ball of Marvels and putting on the heat about Roland and me. If she doesn't stop insisting, I'll be obliged to tell her about the underwear problem.

Chez Mathilde, I should say, is a fine purveyor of haute couture rental wear. Both clients and clients' friends are treated with utmost care. While Joanna wrestled with the frocks in the dressing room, I sat comfortably in a candy-striped upholstered armchair helping myself daintily to the service of tea and *petit fours* set on the coffee table in front of me. How kind of them to attend to me, a mere sightseer.

Mathilde and her hired hand, Maxime, wrapped Joanna in party dresses, twirled her in front of the triptych mirror, commented, and unwrapped. In the end, a sea-green organza Dior number was chosen and reserved. I had to applaud. The performance was finished and our heroine was once again clothed in her work suit. Must say I admire Joanna for continuing to dress as a working woman when there is no apparent reason why she should. Since abandoning the coffee table translations, she has been free of that vestiary obligation. Yet, due perhaps to her Presbyterian sense of propriety (have you ever met a Presbyterian, John?), she maintains the impeccable, understated appearance of the translator-on-the-run. Such discipline! I do admire her so.

As we were leaving, Joanna explained to me that most guests of the Ball of Marvels rented from Mathilde, although personal friends of the grand designers were loaned dresses directly. Even closer friends were given gowns as gifts. She then expressed that she would like, one day, to become a *personal* friend. And, why not, even a *closer* friend! But for the moment, she had no choice but to be a Chez Mathilde patroness. Certainly there is some kind of membership system at work here, perhaps not unlike the one at Mumly's golf club.

Joanna impressed upon me that I really must take advantage of the handouts at À La Mode Online and get myself a fabulous dress for the ball – a Westwood number perhaps? But I explained to her that there were no freebees, unless you were a top spoon. I thought of the goose-poo Versace scarf of course, but didn't mention it. That's between Jean-Claudi, Djamila and me.

I declined on Joanna's last minute dinner invitation and headed home for a quiet evening with the watercolours. Decided I should enrol in a public course on drawing. There was one called 'How to Draw Your Pets and Loved Ones'. On Wednesday nights. I'll look into the matter.

Feast of Saint Frances of Rome

Not many saints, Frances, remained in wedlock throughout their lives, but you climbed the holy ranks whilst remaining a 'model housewife'. Maybe you should have a little chat with Barnard and John; I'm afraid they didn't manage matrimony quite as well as you for some reason. The *Concise* says your charity work surpassed what was humanly possible for a noble Roman housewife. But don't you think even the average Betty Crocker home-maker gives beyond what is humanly possible? When I think of all Mumly used to do, what with organizing the Junior League Charity Ball and dining with the bishop every week, *plus* mentoring fourteen Cuban girls at the golf course, I'm certain she deserves much more than that Catholic Mothers of America Achievement Award they gave her back in 1980. When will these wifely applicants for sainthood be given admittance? When, oh when will the Communion at last become an Equal Opportunity employer?

I'm no stranger to charity myself, Frances, thanks to Neighbour Jeromino. He knocked on my door this morning begging for bread and butter. Let me tell you, he was quite lucky I had any! I don't usually carry such items. Her Majesty's Weetabix are what I have for breakfast, or maybe a croissant when there's a gentleman around. I handed Jeromino his breakfast provisions and made coffee for myself. Noticed heavy tartar build-up on the von Krysler contraption.

After vacuuming the flat (I do my best, Frances), I headed off to dance class, which is just a block down from the Cleopatra Club. It's rumoured Samira sometimes goes there after class for relaxation and washing-up. Usually I don't go to dance class on Saturdays but sometimes I do. It all depends on my humour, which is to say my mood. My regular class is on Tuesdays, which makes the Saturday class an extra. Sometimes there are too many people at the Saturday class and we end up slapping and kicking each other, which is no fault of our own. Once there was a fight between two Algerian sisters, Mouna and Mimi, and the fire department had to be called.

Today, though, the class was medium size and we learned two songs, one called 'Fill the Cup O Beautiful and Give It to Me!' and another which begins, 'Oh my eye!' Both are love songs written for Samira by a celebrated Egyptian composer. He was ardently in love with her, she told us, but she would not have him because he was an aristocrat and his family looked down upon her as they would a petro-dollar courtesan. Her pride could not bear it. And so she kept that love at bay, reaping instead the fruits of his unclaimed desire. The songs, she explained, came to be associated with her in the hearts of many, and brought her even greater acclaim, for the Egyptians are a great sentimental people. She then taught us how to dance them as she once had at the Marriott, beginning with a *pas chassé*, flying the veil above the head, followed by a series of arabesques interspersed with camel turns. The veil is then thrown as if to the hapless lover, who has under-stood that the gossamer cloth is all that he will have of his heart's longing. She is sorry but relieved and dances now with wicked abandon. All emotion has come down from the heights and settles in her hips where a centrifugal force is at work, separating loss and pain from matter. The tremendous sensation of kinetic freedom over-whelms her. This abandon of the hip! The shimmy!

Half-way through class I had to take Claudia off. My head got so hot! I really don't know how Samira does it. Hers always stays on, even when she performs under blazing spotlights. Such admirable dedi-cation to her art and persona, I must say. There is so much to learn from her!

After class, I went to Djamila's for pigeon pie class. I have never eaten pigeon myself but Djamila swears by it. She recommends it espe-cially to parents of virgin girls refusing the hand of marriage, as it softens the female heart and wears down all wilfulness in the hour following its consumption. It is a Moroccan dish, she explained, and a special friend of hers from the imperial city of Fes would teach the class. I was looking forward to this lesson, but when I arrived at Djamila's I was too late.

'Pigeon pie?' she repeated after me, lowering her brow. 'That was last week! Where were you last week? Today we are making a circumcision gown for the joy of Leila's heart. He is seven and it is time. Come in. We will be needing you.'

And so I am invited in to that pouffy parlour, filled again with ladies in recline and repose. *She's about the right size*, I hear someone say. *Is that a thirty-four?* I ask. *Leila's boy is very big.* explains a cousin, Naima. *The circumcision should have been done last year, due to his size,* corrects Djamila, *but there is no telling Leila such things. Leila follows the prescriptions of the Koran. She follows the straight path and is not distracted by sizes and shapes!*

Suddenly I feel very small, and true, as if my shape does not matter in the least, as if it has been passed over by Allah himself as something indeterminate and of meagre age. I think of the book *Little Women* and begin to wonder just how little those March sisters really were. Does Allah really not care? Size, I begin to think, is everything. In the Bible there were giants and all the giants except Goliath were great men. Moses was fourteen feet tall, Noah one hundred and eleven. Why was this so? Were there giant women too? No, it seems there were not. Or if there were, they were folded at the knees and put away before the story was told. God, indeed, seems very concerned with size.

I stand still as the green velvet frock is pulled over my head and pins make their way around the hems. I am made to hold my arms out to the side. I am the Nazarene, a model for Muslims, turning my cheeks for each swipe of the hand. But my actions are meaningless here in the home of Djamila. I am more like a clown than a martyr and a fig is stuffed in my mouth. The ladies are cajoling me. They laugh and invite me to laugh with them at this enterprise, sewing the circumstantial garment for the boy-child whose skin will be cut from him in a fortnight. It is God who wants it and shall have it. Or so it is said. In my own heart, I say a prayer for the lad, for it seems unfair to separate the skins that nature knit together so pleasurably. Too pleasurably?

Finally all the pins are in place and the garment is carefully pulled over my head and given to cousin Naima who sews ready-made pieces of golden brocade onto it. The boy will be beautiful when he is brought down; the women see to it. Like a prince or a soldier.

'Will you be coming to the circumcision?' someone asks. 'It is a great party, not unlike a wedding. A hundred people will be coming. The boy will be very spoiled. Have you taught him, Leila, that he must not cry?'

Djamila who is all-knowing speaks. She claims that her son had not shed a tear with the tear. Not one! I go into the kitchen to help Leila prepare tea.

'No,' I hear someone say, 'it was you who cried, Djamila.'

'Did I? Now that I do not remember.'

All the ladies but Naima stop their industry for tea. I eye them carefully, sizing them up gently. They may not be tall, but they are large to be sure. Multiple motherhoods and the roomy robes they wear have widened their girth. Here, I see, are ladies who bring the sky down to the earth rather than reach out preposterously to the heavens. The heavens, in any case, would not heed their beckoning arms. They have been told this time and again. Instead they sift, shaking the celestial laws as they descend through their sieves, refining and forgetting. Here is work that giants cannot do. One must be close to the ground. And like the ground too.

I do not stay long after tea but take leave of the ladies. They insist I come to the circumcision of their dearest son, but I assure them I must be in Rome on that very day for a parade. And it is true that Sister Dagobert has had me sign up for the March of Pilgrims, which starts and finishes at the great basilica of St Peter. Will I actually go? It's very unlikely, but I do know that I would rather wear my togs down in Rome than sit on a pouf as a circumcisional spectator.

I went to the early movies from there. Saw a film called *Love Stream* about a housewife who is so crazy that she outsmarts her shrink. She loves and loves and loves. She reminds me of Jesus a bit, only without the rough edges which resulted from those primitive times.

Found a message on my machine when I got home. The Marquis had called sometime while I was posing for the dressmakers, requesting my presence at a horse derby, I believe. Could that be it? Phone call number two. I'll be keeping tabs. Charity will have to wait a bit. (But don't worry, Frances, Faith and Hope are still at work.)

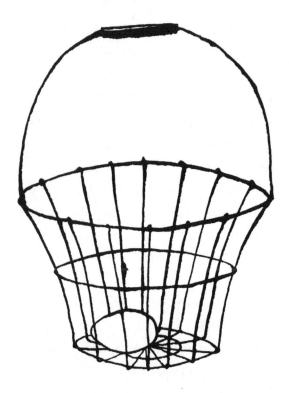

Feast of Saint Roderic

What I don't understand about you saints is why you are always getting beheaded by Muhammedans – or else beheading them! Wouldn't it have been more in the spirit of Christ to attend cooking school together; after all, culinary education promotes peace. Your tragedy, of course, was that your very own brother, a professed Muslim, betrayed you. Perhaps you could have dissipated his mean-spiritedness by inviting him to dine on a bowl of homemade paella with lots of jumbo shrimp and morsels of halal chicken and chorizo. In retrospect you might agree that it would have been at least worth a try.

What a morning! I had to rewrite that Dior cosmetics article – on how to make your mouth look like it's pouting when it's not – five times. I couldn't get it right. I still don't understand how that optical illusion works. Top Spoon said the article would do. They like things fast and sweet here. *Tout de suite!*

I met Sister Dagobert at St Joe's. Yorik seems to be doing better peptically, although he now has a fatty tumour on his left hind quarter. I lit another mendicant's candle at the feet of St Francis supplicating on behalf of all the fatty-tumoured beasts. May they be delivered of that budding burden divinely, without surgical intervention. Yorik, I hate to say, would never survive one. He is so frail and going blind himself, I'm afraid. Alas!

I had lunch with Sister Dag afterwards at the café across the street: *croque-madame* (me) and a hamburger patty with an egg on top (Sister Dagobert). Plus a little *quart de rouge*, which is always nice to sip after Mass. Sister Dagobert added a drop of water to her wine in memory of Mary of Magdalene's tears. Blushing wine, she explained, also quenches the thirst very well.

Having at last understood that accent is not a gauge of age, Sister Dagobert asked me to take upon myself the adult task of teaching catechism class on Monday evenings. Père Ricard is apparently hiring volunteers at the moment. I had to confide to Sister Dagobert that I didn't remember the catechism at all – except for the egg exercise. The egg exercise prepares young adults for future Roman Catholic parenting. The teacher gives all the students an egg (raw) to look after like a baby for a week. Coins are flipped to determine the sex of the baby egg. Students then build small egg cribs, sew egg suits in either blue or pink and make toys for the wee one's fun. It is a lesson in the fragility of life and unconditional love. For some, it is also a course in scrambled eggs.

I explained all this to Sister Dagobert who assured me not to worry, that she herself had forgotten much of what she had learned in Hebrew School as well. It's simply a matter of following the ready-made lesson plans in the *On Our Way* series. Sister Dagobert recommends that I work with the six-year-olds who require preparation for Holy Communion. I told her that I would have to think about this proposition, seeing that *teaching* communion is quite different to *receiving* communion and that I am only well versed in the latter.

Back to work just in time for a brief Jean-Claudi visit. He was showing the spoons a series of photos he had taken of Her Royal Highness Princess Lala of Morocco during her European tour. All of France is raving about Lala! Her djellabas are designed by YSL. Apparently she and Yves are *amis intimes*. She's the new Princess Diana, some will say, only so much more discreet! She is kept in palaces and only travels escorted by her brother, His Majesty the King himself. Jean-Claudi says he met an Italian director working on a new version of *The Princess and the Pea* based on Lala's life. The wardrobe budget is extravagant. Yves will be making a bundle on it. I wonder who the leading actress will end up being. Rumour has it that Madonna is high on the list, but I can't imagine her as a Moor (can you, Roderic?). Still, I think it would behove her to take on such a role; there is so much she would learn from pretending to be Lala. Lala has impeccable manners and moderate interest in humanitarian ventures. She is a true princess, a princess by birth, and has no seam at the waist or tuck under the chin. There is no flaw in her eating habits or sleeping practices. Her perfection is daunting.

I spent the rest of the afternoon working on Lala's posture both in seated and standing positions. I can manage it, only the long-term maintenance is difficult. Unfortunately, I developed a minor stomach ache, due perhaps to the royal carriage exercise, and was indisposed a bit. I ended up leaving work before Djamila and her pilgrim husband arrived for clean-up. Practised my hip snaps at home whilst holding myself erect in the royal carriage position. It was difficult but quite impressive, I must say. Could Lala, I wonder, do the same?

Feast of Saints Cyril (deacon) and Mark (bishop)

What an unfortunate duo you two make, though you, Cyril, were lucky enough to have been merely a deacon and therefore quickly martyred (*Concise* omits the means by which this was done, mentioning only that it was mercifully expedient). Sometimes it doesn't pay to climb the ranks, does it Mark? Julian the Apostate had great plans for you; that dip in the Roman sewers could have provoked your demise, but you hung on, surviving even the gnats which coated you after the Apostate poured a barrel of honey over your soiled person. But I suppose that gnats are better than bees and honey, better than tar. A saint must always look on the bright side, after all.

Spring is here at last, Paris' season of glory, and it is time, I believe, to change uniforms. Perhaps something lighter in colour would do. Something without a belt? I wonder if Joanna would oblige me with a hand-me-down. With a bit of imagination, you know, you can turn almost any outfit into a uniform. War wives and Catholic mothers have been doing it for years. Some call it making-do but I call it how-do-you-do, because you end up making acquaintance with a new creation. Call it a friend.

It is not without a sentiment of loss that I have put away the winter uniform, that form-that-unites. Yes, it united me with myself and the greater context of winter. Never, I believe, have I felt so shielded from quotidian, metropolitan aggressions. By covering in this way daily, an assembly occurs within, a coming-together of the selves. The result is a harmony, a bit queer to the uninitiated perhaps, but melodious and sweet all the same. Now I ask, what will spring bring? I think I will try the colour green.

I spent my lunch hour in the Tuileries gardens under the lee of a statue of Diana the Goddess, skimming through the *International Herald Tribune* and eating an egg-salad sandwich made and plastic wrapped at Marks & Spencer. This would have been a pleasant lunch-eon had it not been for Omar. Omar was the young man from Istanbul who took the seat next to me. A clever lad, he used my egg-salad sandwich as an entryway to the hall of conversation.

HE   Eating eggs? Looking for the husband?
SHE   I beg your pardon?

HE   Looking for the husband? Eating eggs?

SHE   I hardly understand.

HE   No need to understand, Miss Egg-eater. Omar is here! Doctor of psychology, instrumentalist, lover of life and sex. Omar! That is me.

SHE   *Mon Dieu!*

HE   Perhaps you would like a coffee? A Turkish coffee-delight? A Nescafé? Your wish, Miss, is my pleasure. I will take you there.

SHE   My wish is to be Swiss. To have fondue without you. Go away Sir Omar. *Allez-vous-en!*

HE   You are cruel. I have come all the way from Istanbul to know you. To share eggs and salt with you. And to take you back to my country where I have a sports car and a high-paying psychological position. Come away with me Miss. Come! Come!

SHE   No, you must go alone Omar. Do not think that because you know eggs, you know me. Besides, what would the Armenians say?

HE   The who?

SHE   Go away Omar and leave me in peace!

And so Omar rolled his *Turkish Times* between his hands and slapped it against his knee as he stood to take leave in defeat. His parting might have been bitter had the idea to leave me with a token of his hasty devotion not come and brightened his mood. He reached into his breast pocket and pulled out a calling card, looking now, somehow relieved.

'Here Miss, take this for when you will think of me.'

And so I accepted his complementary gift politely, for it is best when garden-variety encounters end cordially and with a card. As he

86

left, I nodded my head slowly as might have the tightly turbaned Simone de Beauvoir at Jean-Paul as he took leave of her at the Café Flore to pant and grunt over his eighteen-year-old student-mistress. She was gracious, Simone, a great lady. And an adamant Adult Sex advocate. I just wonder why she wrote so many books about those extraordinarily depressed ladies. They were all well-dressed practitioners of Adult Sex but so miserable all the same. I do wonder what Dr Dolittle would have to say about Simone.

I got back to work in time to see Top Spoon getting her hair extended by a foot. Two stylists from the European Institute of Hair and Aesthetics came especially to perform the feat. It's a promotional exercise, you see, and I was asked to write a hundred-word feature on it for the site. And so I watched for an hour or so, taking notes while the Institute's top beauty operators, Muriel and Jérémie, worked with surgical fingers, gluing the tried and true tresses of some financially desperate young woman to the short cropped locks of our well-paid Top Spoon.

It was quite fascinating to watch at first, but in the end grew tedious. And so I took a twenty-minute nap, arms folded on desk, head cushioned in the nest, before writing the article on the wonders of extension work and the Institute of Hair and Aesthetics. I had to write quickly before the yawns started. One of the spoons who studies yoga at the gym says that yawning is about the yin trying to meet the yang. It's much like a date, you see, or the preliminaries leading up to one. Thinking of it in this light does help. It evokes the possibility of an incipient romance, a reason to carry on, as it were. I wrote the article with a great plumish flourish, leaving out only the price of the extending. Why, after all, end the piece on a bad note?

Djamila and Hadj Mohammed arrived an hour early for clean-up because they had a train to Marseilles to catch at seven o'clock. We chatted briefly about their nephews who, it seems, are exceptional young men, outstanding in looks (beautiful as the moon, with eyes like husked sesame set aflame!) and achievements (clever as caliphs at calligraphy!). One lives in Paris and is a scholar of Medieval Arabian poetry (perhaps one day I shall meet him, dear Cyril and Mark?); the other is a Marseilles rap star who goes by the name Popeye Rachid. Djamila says Rachid has taken the straight path and raps Koranic verses in French. She hopes he will become a national star and in this way spread the true teachings by way of radio and discography. In the best of cases, she added, he will sing them in English so that the truth may go global.

'Is English difficult to learn?' she asked.

'Not to my knowledge,' I assured her.

Djamila was pleased to hear this and hurried off to guide her pilgrim husband through his rounds.

Before leaving the office, I gave Hadj Mohammed a copy of *The City of God* to read on the train. He thanked me so sweetly, which did make me wonder if he will really read it. (If he doesn't, maybe you would like it Cyril?) But no matter.

Back home I played my new Egyptian compilation CD which has Samira's song, 'Fill the Cup O Beautiful and Give It to Me!', over and over again whilst practising my grammar rolls. Last week I did a demonstration of this movement at the office. The spoon who studies yoga explained that it stimulates the fourth chakra which is the heart chakra. And so, as I grammar-rolled this way and that, I began to sense that I was being guided by the vagaries of heart more than head, of feeling rather than thought, of love rather than logic. When I was done, I called Mumly.

'Is that you Princess?' I had to admit it was. 'Did you get my package yet?'

She was referring, it seems, to a Christmas gift she had sent last month, which is to say February.

'No, I'm afraid it hasn't come yet.'

'Oh damn them then!'

Them of course, refers to the French postal service, which is actually quite good, strikes notwithstanding. Last year the same thing happened: the package never came. I believe Mumly doesn't write the address correctly but I'm afraid to tell her. It might hurt her feelings. The dropsy afflicts her hands and makes her cursive careless. She is already vexed enough as it is!

'Say, Princess, when are you going to Rome?'

'Sometime soon I hope, Mum.'

If Mumly doesn't ask me when I'm coming home, she asks me when I'm going to Rome. Just like Sister Dagobert, she believes a trip to St Pete's would behove me (though watch out for those sewers, right Mark?). But what should I really expect from that Papal Village? Fruit of the Womb (not ready)? A double conversion experience (have heard they're great)? A visitational vision of the Padre Pio (good Lord!)? It seems there are myriad possibilities and then one must always take into account the butterfly effect which may change the course of events so abruptly. The best way to prepare for the fluttering wings is to leave your expectations at the foot of an angel. Perhaps this is the point of going to St Pete's, where there are, of course, very many angels flying about. But then again, you must not expect to find angels there because it is precisely the lack of all anticipation, which makes grace possible and the flight of the divine messengers visible.

'Yesterday was Daddy-gone's anniversary, Princess. Did you remember?'

Indeed I did. Fifty-five candles at Notre-Dame for my *papa disparu*. I have a photo father you see. All I have ever seen of him is tucked away in Mumly's love album, now kept in her safety deposit box. Images of Daddy-gone in pilot-wear, on the beach in Bermudas, at grandma Josephine's table with an arm around a laughing Mumly, pie on his plate. Such photosensitive bliss.

A simple life we had until that plane went down in Vietnam while I was the tiniest of living creatures, swimming still undiscovered in the watery womb, a little love-fish with hardly a care in the world. But how things changed with that crash; what should have loved me as flesh-father, was merely mute paper in the hand, to hold (only for a few minutes) and to cherish, perhaps, but also easily misplaced and, as with most pictures, misunderstood.

In time, I was succoured by my games of Pretend, and Mumly had Richard II, her second husband. But we still have not forgotten Daddy-gone, king of our hearts. And every year on his birthday, we light candles as if he were yet with us although parted, and could blow them out with an oboe from the heavens. Dear, dear Daddy-gone, I never really knew him.

'Do you think he likes the candles, Mumly?'

'It's hard to say, Princess, but he always did like fireworks.'

I wished Mumly lots of love before hanging up, and curled into bed with Jubilee at my feet and a book about a Prince and a dwarf simply called *The Dwarf*. A wonderful, Nobel Prize-winning saga though somewhat disquieting at bedtime (and definitely not appropriate for saints). Fell asleep all the same.

Feast of Saint Gregory Makar

Though few have heard of you today, Saint Gregory Makar, you were haunted by celebrity in your lifetime. Your fear of growing conceited caused you to flee eleventh century Armenia where your bishophood was overwhelmed by the adoration of fans and Gregory Makar wannabes. As a hermit you then lived near Orléans, austere and still famous. Stardom, it seems, was your destiny. Odd it is that you found what you did not seek. And what you sought you did not find. Have you brought this conundrum up to the Board of Saints?

I have to say this riddle does puzzle me too. Last night, when

Jubilee and I sought nothing more than a quiet evening with H. James, we received an unexpected and, I must say, most auspicious visit. It began like this:

KNOCK. KNOCK.

'Who's there?'

''Owdy!'

'Owdy who?' I pressed the gentleman further before opening, for a girl must be careful.

'Junior,' came the reply. 'Jeromino's brother.'

'Owdy Junior, Jeromino's brother,' I repeated, establishing the name and its kinship. 'Do come in.'

I opened the door, for clearly there was nothing to fear in an Owdy Junior if he truly were Jeromino's flesh and blood.

''Owdy Pardna!,' the gentleman in question greeted me once again, now that the door no longer stood betwixt us.

Before me stood a cowboy of sorts, clearly Jeromino's junior by three years or so, dressed in Wrangler jeans and a turquoise Panhandle Slim Ropin' Cowboy shirt, yoked in black with embroidered caballero cuffs. His feet were decked out in Durango harness cowboy boots (two-tone blue and black), polished and slick-heeled (no spurs). His face, though resembling his brother's in its shovelsharp features, had none of Jeromino's fume-induced fogginess, his shaggy dewiness. No, nothing slack about Junior. Everything taut and tight. Even his short clipped hair stood at attention. He tipped his Stetson, tugged at the lasso resting on his shoulder.

'Howdy,' I replied, getting my bearings at last, exchanging what I had thought a name for a greeting. 'What can I do for you?'

'Excuse me Miss, but my brother says you could oblige me with a libation.' My my, so Neighbour Jeromino thinks I run not only a country store but a saloon too! With an extended credit line!

'A libation? Well, I suppose I could do that. Tell me, what'll you have?'

'That'll be a Bud, Miss.'

I didn't miss a beat, just like Mumly when she entertains the bishop and the banker. Never let a guest get thirsty, she always said. Never second-guess what your guest will guzzle. With a gracious arm extended toward my boudoir, I invited my gentleman caller in. Junior took off his hat before stepping through the threshold. And held it against his chest.

It should be said that I had never before had the pleasure of entertaining a cowboy – a French one at that! All the more piquant! (Believe me Gregory, it would never have even occurred to me to seek an Owdy Junior!) Being out of Bud (can such a thing be found in these parts?) I suggested another ranchero remedy recommended by Richard II whenever Mumly's glum quotient fell perilously low and even shoe shopping wouldn't perk her up.

Whisky on the rocks it was.

Junior tipped his hat to the highballs; we toasted and made acquaintance.

So it seems that Junior has been in cowboy practice for the past five years; he has lassoed down Fama and Mercury, Coysevox's rearing horses in the Tuileries gardens and many of the other statues there, both modern and old, with the exception of the Roy Lichtensteins. He hopes to obtain a scholarship to attend Rodeo College in the Camargue, for the garden gendarmes are always blowing the whistle on him and how can he possibly improve with such constraints?

I expressed my admiration, for imagine trying to become a cowboy in the first arrondissement! We really were getting on marvellously, I must say and I couldn't help but notice how his jeans fit him beautifully both in the front (just tight enough to tell...) and the back (a treasure of a tush). He was like the Dying Slave in Wranglers! Oh bless him!

When I went to fetch our fourth round of libations, tottering a bit I must admit, he surprised me by lassoing me from behind ('Oh my!') reeling me in towards him (getting the girl by the girdle?), and gently, gently singing a country song that went something like, *'Do you love as good as you look? Well, I 'ope you do, because 'ey, baby I got you.'* Indeed!

He certainly did have me in his tether, that lasso looped around my hips. I saw no other possible course of action but to camel-walk my way to him. To be honest, in my deepest heart I would have preferred camelboy to cowboy, but as my ancestor Glorietta had manifestly sent me this bovine version for Ouija reasons we cannot hope to fathom, I was certainly willing to make do. Junior's nasal-toned tenor, his affected country twang which vowelled out in pouty French ways, must have been hard earned indeed and I was all the more appreciative of course.

'Say,' I asked. 'Have you ever ridden a bucking bronco?'

I was curious to know just how far his Tuileries training had taken him.

''*eeeee 'aw!*' he yodelled. 'This is just what I am going to show you, good lookin'...'.

And so that lasso for one became a girdle for two. In each other's arms we tumbled about the boudoir, lassoed for love, turning garden-variety rodeo into amatory art. His loving was nearly nip and tuck with Von Krysler's, less seasoned in its expressions of nimbleness perhaps, though he had tremendous strength and staying power. I held on the best I could during our half-diamond hitch, held on to those soon-to-be-saddle-clinging buns, while our pleasures gained momentum. In short, it was a most satisfying night-o-love with nothing to mar it but the morn.

I woke up at ten feeling a bit under, I must say, unaccustomed to so many whisky libations. A song Richard II used to play to tease Mumly came to mind, '*I got in at two with a ten and woke up at ten with a two.*' Oh dear, thought I. I really must freshen up before Junior arises. And attend to coiffure too! Don't want to be taken for a two! And so I quietly went to soak in the bath, cucumbers over eyes, as my cowboy slept on.

There really is nothing like the unexpected adventure, which Dr Dolittle simply does not stress strongly enough. It's only the whisky I regret, but then again I must thank it for loosening the lasso, not so? And now that I know what I want (more of my bronco!), Saint Greg, are you telling me I shall not receive? May you be forever wrong. Celebrities so often are. Oh dear Junior, do come again!!

p.s. Forgot to mention that Junior refused coffee made in the von Krysler. Might he suspect something, Gregory?

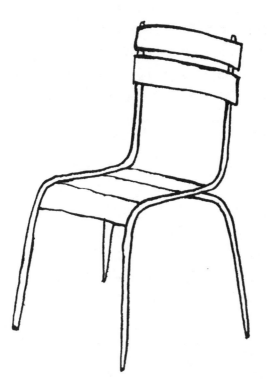

Feast of Saint Catherine of Sweden

What dumbfounds me, Catherine, is how you managed to live most of your life with your mumly (also a saint) and survive! I just can't imagine living with Mumly that long. Oh, I adore her, I do! But she would be the worst roommate *ever*; her dropsy days make her so feisty and prone to collywobbles. If you're not a saint it just doesn't work!

I had a dream that I was invited to a VIP wedding in London and arrived without my underwear (did you ever have dreams like this, Catherine? So embarrassing!). Actually my panties were in my purse but I couldn't seem to find a discreet corner to slip them on surreptitiously. Men invited me to dance and so I danced (it's rude to refuse) fearing all the while the flight of my skirt and an indecent exposure. Then the bridesmaids gathered around me as I was queuing for champagne jeering the childhood mantra, '*I see London, I see France, but where are that girl's underpants?*'

Mortified I was but where could I go? What could I do? Luckily, M. Phet called and woke me up.

'The leak, the leak! You must stop that leak!'

It suddenly occurred to me that I might have wet the bed.

'Beg your pardon?'

'The leak that is ruining the property value of my flat! You must stop it at once!'

'How do I do that?'

'By calling the Fire Department, by calling the plumber!'

'I'm sorry, M. Phet, but can you call me back in an hour?'

I hadn't, of course, had my coffee yet, and couldn't think through the problem properly. M. Phet responded by hanging up the phone. Thirty minutes later, however, he was at my door a-buzzing. I was still in *peignoir* but fortunately with hair done, sparing him, then, what he might have perceived as a coiffuratorial aggression. To assuage M. Phet's homeowner inquietude, I gave him a full tour of the flat, praising its fine points but also pointing out its prevailing weaknesses. M. Phet does, I suspect, do some real estate. He took an active interest in my tour, verifying with great care that no leak had been sprung in the water ways, then offered to take me on a tour of his own. And so I followed him downstairs, Jubilee running ahead of us (he loves visiting the neighbours) to that flat where that small, zoot-suited lodger resides.

He was dressed and eating some kind of pork-chop soup when we arrived, and so I offered my excuses for interrupting his morning repast by bowing and holding my hand to my heart. M. Phet, however, unaware that he was disrupting a quiet matinée, began his tour promptly with the kitchen where, indeed, the ceiling was a bloated mess, dropping patties of waterlogged plaster and paint. And the floor was entirely stained with this pasty splatter as if some indecent and oversized bird had pooped it from above. Oh dear, I thought, dropsy! And for a moment a nauseous terror seized me at the grammar level. *Haut-le-coeur!* say the French. *Up-goes-the-heart!* But then the heart descended, almost instantly, fearing the unnatural height, and I felt quite all right again. The leak, M. Phet and I ascertained, came not from my home or his but from that space between our homes. This was a convenient conclusion for both concerned.

'Good day, M. Phet.'

'Good day, Miss Remedy.'

And so we left each other amiably with best wishes for the day ahead.

Yes, the day ahead, now the day-gone-by. But it was a fine day all the same. I wrote a brief article on Calvin Klein's latest funnel-neck felt shell jackets and fake sleeved trenchcoat dresses. Surprised myself by making a catchy pun which earned me a congratulatory smile from Top Spoon. Usually I'm not so clever at punning although in French it's much easier. The French, as everyone knows, are a very punny people. They're a bit embarrassed by it, but they just can't help themselves.

Sometime around ten I overheard a conversation between Jean-Claudi and Willie (*Wheelie*) at the coffee machine regarding Le Swing

Club. My my my! Almost wish I hadn't heard. It's hard to believe such things happen in semi-public places. So daring and love-defying! And how clear it became to me that I simply cannot compete with those swing performances. If that is truly what Jean-Claudi requires for love, than I am lost. Lost! Perhaps I will have a chat with Djamila about this. Is she not the guardian of our desire, looking down upon us with one hand on her heart the other on the Koran? She will have the answer.

I had lunch in the Luxembourg gardens having stopped beforehand at Dalloyau to purchase a cucumber tea sandwich and a chocolate macaroon. Once inside the garden gates, I followed the orb of statues depicting Europe's queens, princesses and noble damsels. (Wonder if Junior has tried roping these ladies. Oh my!) Yes, I followed these great dames gracing the palace grounds until I found the right pea-green chair, under the lee of a lovely princess, sold by way of marriage to the de Médicis tribe, immortalized here happily or unhappily on this primrose path, and sat watching the tots push their toy boats on the pond with rented sticks. I espied the daffodil rising to the north and the high-school girls swinging their blooming vines over their shoulders, laughing with their beauty. A man sitting nearby was being driven mad by them. Such girls! The garden is full of them!

Men come here to weep and desire. Women come to read books. If ever the need to feel safe takes hold of me, here is my home and leafy hearth. True, the risk of a garden-variety encounter is great, but at times this too can be welcome after all. It all depends on who and when. On when and who. Omar, for example, was the wrong *who* coming at the wrong *when*. His score was zero out of two – which is to say, the losing score. When he learns to perfect his *who*ness and *when*ness, he will be a winner, I am certain.

The same undoubtedly holds true for myself, only I am getting a helping hand from my ancestor Glorietta. Hokey-pokey Omar could use a hand too, but he needs to learn to ask for one. It's the simplest of things really, yet so few people nowadays think to call up an ancestor with that most obvious of requests, 'O Ancient One, Help! Help!'

In any case, my noon repast went uninterrupted which was not so bad a thing at all. I dined lightly and pleasantly, my back straight against the back of my garden armchair, the crown of my head attached to the heavens by an invisible, auric thread. I adopted, in a word, *posture*: Her Highness Lala's *regal posture*. And I was picky too, as all princesses must be if they are to be taken seriously. With my trusty pair of tweezers, I delicately pulled a piece of bacon (Moors don't eat this as you well know, Catherine) from the tea sandwich, cursed it for the fatty gristle it was, then dispensed with it over my shoulder. For the beasts!

Luncheon finished, I then took a stroll down the chestnut tree-lined lanes, past the pissing ponies pulling chariots of applauding children, then out of the park gates. Made a quick pit stop at Guerlain to be perfumed then headed on down to St-Germain-des-Près. I considered making a left and stopping at the Café Flore for an after-lunch coffee with the literati, but turned right instead and walked through the portal of St Germain's church. Why? I would be hard-pressed to know. More whimsy of the feet, I suppose. But once inside I did not regret the pedal instincts, for I managed to step auspiciously into a polyphonic assembly, a queer chorus of lay voices, singing at once but not together some Latin phrase.

An affable layman, dressed in his business best, handed me a paper on which were written the words *'Pange Lingua Gloriosi Corporis*

Mysterium Sanguinisque Pretiosi!' Which I believe translates as, 'Sing Oh My Tongue the Glory of that Pretty but Quite Mysterious Body!' Or something to the effect.

Taking the cue, I joined in, raising my voice to a contrasting note, then wavered it above and below in the manner of a Corsican crooner. How extraordinary, I thought, without knowing the way, my voice hath found it. Yes it did! That lyrical path to some divine gate. Perhaps one of the seven Djamila has often spoken about, opened by the Houris and housing fruit trees for the faithful souls and martyrs. It's hard to tell, but I do know that something soulful in me rose up through the voices to the gothic vaults, where, manifestly, it knocked as if upon a door – for when a priest came and put an end to this lay-communion, I found myself with my hand extended for a shake and the words, 'How do you do?' on my lips.

Who was I about to meet? Upon whose door had I knocked? That, I'm afraid, I cannot remember. The abrupt ending of our song brought an equally abrupt clip to my wings, the sights I must have seen on high and the personages I was to meet there. But manifestly it was time for the lunchtime Mass, and as Bishop Chauvin had recently issued a monitory regarding tardy starts, many priests are now trying quite hard to begin service on time. Bless them! Their lives are preposter-ously lonely and entirely without any sugar-on-the-top. If only out of pity, one will obey.

I got back to the office at two in time for tea. The spoons now serve tea in the afternoon following pump. Excessive tea drinking is supposed to keep the metabolism a-moving speedily, so that a few extra pounds can be shed even while a-seated at the computer. Unfortunately, I had one cup too many and was shaking so terribly

102

that I had to go downstairs to avoid swooning, which is a highly inappropriate thing to do at work. I bought a piece of cheese and a box of treacle cakes. Oh cheese, cheese, that remarkable fruit of the cow. It did save me. I was feeling much, much better and even accepted another cup-o-tea. Treacle cakes were donated to the Spoon Foundation.

On my way home, I stopped by a bookstore and came across a book on a subject called pornocracy, which is the ruling of the government by lady porno stars. In this most unique form of government, conflict is resolved in much the same manner as it is within the bonobo monkey tribes. And, alas, pornocracy, like its mimicking monkey friends, is on the verge of extinction too. The last one occurred in tenth century Rome (way before your time too, Catherine).

I did not buy this most interesting book but instead a pocket-sized copy of Baudelaire's prose poems, which I read on the way home pretending to be the poet's lifelong mistress, Jeanne Duval, reclining on a cheap Montmartre *canapé*, sipping absinthe.

I had a bit of a run-in at the Gare de l'Est with one of those Foreign Legionnaires in tortoise-wear. Finding me a tad suspicious perhaps (ladies on absinthe do appear somewhat altered) he asked to inspect my purse. Always obliging when there is a gun about, I agreed.

'It's a small purse,' I explained to him. 'I only carry the minimum.'

Which indeed is true. Yet apparently convinced that I might be the carrier of some minimal-sized but potent explosive, he peered into the private life of my handbag, more with his nose than his eyes, before grunting and signalling with his hip-slung weapon that I was to move along. I really do not like the machine guns these legionnairing gentlemen tote in the train stations. In a pornocracy they would simply not be allowed!

When I got home, I found a message on the machine from Sister Dagobert, insisting that I come teach catechism Thursday night. Père Ricard is apparently quite desperate for young recruits, having lost three of his prized teachers to the Dominicans of the Incarnated Verb. Tomorrow I will see Sister Dagobert and have an in-depth talk with her on the matter. First Communion was so long ago!

For dinner I ordered a kosher pizza from Chez Shlomi's downstairs (they're very good, Catherine. Have you ever tried one?). Mouktar delivered it fifteen minutes later wearing, as his job requires, a scooter helmet. Surprised perhaps to see me alone and not with Johannes von Krysler, he removed the helmet before handing me my order and said ever so eloquently, 'Here you are, Mademoiselle.'

So it was that I saw Mouktar's face for the first time. And my! What a handsome face! If the moon herself asked him to illuminate the night, he'd rise up and become its halo! Such marvels are within his power I am sure. A man with golden eyes is worth four with hazel, it is said. Mouktar's eyes are pure gold, shaped like summer almonds. There is a rosiness to his cheek and his dark locks curl in thick rings about his fine head. And he is perfumed, not by the cheesy concoction he delivers, but by the dew of musk and amber.

My perusal of his infinite charms was beginning its descent below the neck when I heard his call for payment. Waking as if by the toot of a klaxon from a reverie, I quickly found my way to the wallet and pulled out the required sum. *Thank you! Thank you!* I cried out down the hall after him. Then, from the stairwell below he turned around and beamed me up a smile so ripe with beauty and intimation I nearly swooned! *Au revoir! Au revoir!* (But do come back!) How lithesome was his step! Much like a rabbit's. But of course delivery lads must be spritely. A pizza delivered cold is a pizza sent back. To Shlomi's!

I then had to calm my emotions before eating, so said grace facing what I believed to be the East. Praised the Lord for all good things such as dinner delivered by the gorgeous, and hopefully celibatarian Mouktar. Scraped the anchovies off the pizza onto a saucer for Jubilee. The rest of the evening I spent with an illustrated copy of *The Arabian Nights* in which I found a lovely drawing of a prince in a peach tree. It looked so very much like Mouktar. Ah! Mouktar the Moor!*

*Dreamt I was Desdemona dressed in YSL Egyptian style beaded jet-fringed skirt and black lace tulle bikini top. *Love me! Love me!* I was heard saying. But to who? (Have you any idea, Catherine? How I would like to know!)

Feast of Saint Guntramnus

Though we apparently cannot 'admire your private life' (the *Concise*), we must nevertheless find 'merit in your zealous promotional work for the Church' (*ibid*). I hate to think of what you were doing in private back then, Guntramnus. But pray tell, did it have anything to do with a swing?

Not to worry, Guntramnus; numerous are those who lead a dubious *vie privée*. Just this morning I read a book review on a recent biography of the legendary Marchesa Casati that got me quite fired up. True, I had never heard of the Marchesa before, yet this did not preclude me from responding immediately to the morsel of risky exposé I had just read by pretending I was that Belle Epoque heroine herself, descending fantastically into debt while draping myself in live-snake jewellery and calling on painted servants to fetch my diamond-studded whips. Jubilee became my pet cheetah. I wrapped my rhinestone necklace twice around his neck and he played the part splendidly. It was a decadent morning, I must say. I didn't get through my bowl of Weetabix and was very, very late for work.

After Mass I had a lunch date with Sister Dagobert during which we discussed catechism class at length. I am quite anxious frankly; First Communion A1 begins in two days. (Oh Guntramnus, help me be an enthusiastic promoter!) Sister Dagobert is now wearing a pluviometer on the holy rope that girdles her waist. It was given to her by a patient at the Hôtel-Dieu, a *retiree* by the name of Lecoq who once manufactured weather gauges of all sorts in some seaside town of Brittany. As Sister is unable to read it herself, I deciphered its messages for her. West winds, it seemed to say, and increasing showers through Monday. It rains so often here you know. Sister Dagobert says that this will help her forecast precipitation if her arthritis fails her. Usually her bones know though. I left Sister Dagobert with the instructor's copy of *Change Your Heart* from the *On Our Way* series, under my arm.

Back at the office with the catechism book tucked away beneath my seat, I could not resist the call of the Marchesa, far more potent in the afternoon than the morn due to the general laxity of the hour. In no time at all, my haphazard desk became a lavish boudoir strewn with love-lies-bleeding and the feathers of the peacock princes. The fax machine became my gold leaf dictaphone and into it I recited poesy. With a ruby quill pen, I devised the intrigue for my next amourette.

Perhaps a handsome, bean-eating pauper this time? Ah I will seduce him with titbits of skewered meat! How happy I was! Chirping like a strident blue jay and cracking my whip at the feet of my boudoir attendant, Angelo Crispo.

But then a missive came, brought to me on an Etruscan platter by one of my many Adamite servitors. It was from my banker, Mr Epstein. 'Minus twenty-five million' it read. It is over, my dear Marchesa! You are lost! Lost! Realizing that there was nowhere to go but down, I fell to the floor where I wept with bitter regret. Mercy! Mercy! I pleaded. But who was to hear me? Perhaps someone after all for there were footsteps approaching. Frightened though as I was, I could only think: They are coming to get me! Already! Ah! The *coup de grâce*, for I am doomed!

In marched the spoons, freshly showered after pump practice with shopping bags in their hands.

'Look at Remedy! What's wrong? *Oh là là!*'

'It's nothing, girls,' I said lifting myself up off the floor quickly. 'Just a little spill.'

Indeed! Mine was as hefty as any oil spill, but no sense in telling the spoons about it. Let them think it was just a wee bowl of milk.

'Tea?' I suggested.

All agreed, for the dietetic and diuretic beneficence of tea is a true spoon pleaser. I spent the rest of the afternoon working at the fax machine, alas no longer a dictaphone. No Jean-Claudi visit and no Djamila after five. No Junior anywhere either, for that matter. And cell phones simply don't work out on the range! Where have all the flowers gone? I couldn't get that song out of my head!

At home, as I prepared to prepare the catechism class, I realized that I would have to teach the children about Lent first since they certainly didn't know what it was. The Lentil Season has just begun after all. And so I drew up a lesson plan called 'The Forty Days Till Easter' from the instructor's manual, along with a worksheet for the children who are not quite readers yet. The worksheet, which I will read to them aloud, asks them to cross out the things they are not to eat during Lent. From *Belle* magazine's kitchen corner, I cut out true-to-life pictures of 1) a roast beef; 2) a chocolate marquise with a raspberry coulis; 3) cod prepared *à la portugaise* and; 4) a bottle of Coca-Cola. These I glued to the worksheet, which I will photocopy tomorrow at work. I hope this is not too difficult an assignment for the little ones (but if it is, will you give them a hand, Guntramnus?).

Feast of Saint Gladys

As far as I can tell from reading the *Concise*, Gladys, you were granted sainthood for mothering St Cadoc. Of course the Board of Saints also took into account your valiant conversion of your heathen husband Gundleus, who, it should be said, stole you from your first hubby (a certain Brychan of Brecknock) during a raid in Wales. Rather than pine for Brychan, you applied a healthy Adult Sex attitude and bedded with the chieftain Gundleus, reaping the fruit of this no-nonsense union by way of your saintly son. Really, Gladys, I think you should tell Dr Dolittle the whole story. It's absolutely inspirational! And don't feel bad that the Board of Saints missed the point; it's just not their field. (By the way, any advice to give me on the cowboy and lonesome me?)

Djamila and Hadj Mohammed just got back from their trip to Marseille. Earlier than expected and in none too good shape. Hadj seems to have developed a goitre condition due to the air there, and Djamila is in grief over a family feud which resulted in their precocious return.

'Djamila!' I said when I saw her distress. 'What has happened? You don't look so well.'

'No, I am not so well, daughter' (she taps at her heart). 'But God-be-willing I will stay alive a bit longer. Allah is merciful to those who follow his ways. I may not be so well, but it is my sister, Aicha, who is worse off. Still, she will not see it. Ever since she was a little girl, she has loved jewels and her bank account more than Allah. And now that golddigger has ruined her sixth son, Rachid, who once sung the Koran so beautifully. She pushed him to sign a contract with the United States of America and they will be going there to live and sing abominations. Do you know the United States will not pay him to sing the Koranic verses but only songs about drug smokers, sodomy and other sicknesses prohibited to Muslims? What is wrong with that country of infidels?

'Certainly it is that there aren't enough Muslim faithfuls there. I told my sister that she and her son were driving down the road to damnation, but all she saw were those American dollars raining from above. And so I called the Imam and asked him to reason with her, but when she saw that holy man at her door and opened her mouth wide to protest, a djinni flew in and took possession of her throat. She began screaming in English, a language she had never spoken or heard before, and threw all of our luggage out the door. And so we left, praying for their souls, which have already been sold. But I am pained that I will never greet my sister at one of the seven gates when it is time to return our souls. She will go south while I will take the right way, which is north. Ah, my heart!'

Never before had I seen Djamila so distraught. Certainly she had reason to be upset and yet I tried with a twist of optimism to help her see brighter possibilities than familial damnation (perhaps this was also how you handled your husband, Gladys?). I remembered the Baptist, that Cleopatra Club converter, and thought of redemption, our last saving grace. Perhaps, I suggested to Djamila, once in America they would have a change of heart. Perhaps they would arrive there as an Adam and Eve among all the other Edenites and redeem themselves with their own freshness. How could Popeye Rachid sing about sodomy when he's never been tried? About hashish when he's never puffed the pipe? No, I told Djamila. In America, where all manners of abomination have been attempted and accomplished, no-one would ever believe him. But if he sings about them and repents wholeheartedly afterward, chances are he will be loved and forgiven, perhaps even *believed* in the end. He might become a star of sorts. And only a star, I assured her, could sing the Koran. Djamila seemed to be thinking this over when I excused myself to leave. I didn't want to be late for A1.

Went directly to St Joe's annex where classes are held and was greeted by Sister Dagobert and Yorik who had made a special trip over to help me find my class. How very dear of them, for my anxiety was on the rise, and a peek into my book bag revealed I had forgotten my copy of *Change Your Heart*, which had all my notes in it. Sister

Dagobert kindly reassured me that for the first lesson, I wouldn't have any need of the book or the notes, and led me to what appeared to be a small library where the seven-year-olds were awaiting me in kindergarten chairs arranged in even rows.

Twelve lovely children, bewildered certainly by the blind nun, her tumescent dog and recent recruit, remained quietly seated. Where are we?, they could very well have been wondering. Why is it that *maman* insists on sending me here? I am only seven. Oh, I'd rather be with *maman*! *Maman*!

I could feel that cry for the maternal embrace rise in their wee breasts. But rather than panic, I called upon the Holy Mother of all requesting her reassuring presence to nip the nascent bud of *mal de maman*.

'Hello children, I am Remedy, your teacher. Please arrange your chairs in a circle here, as Jesus would have liked it.'

And so I had them all rise and showed them how to make a circle out of mere chairs.

'Please be seated.' The children sit. 'Do you know, children, the story of Jesus' forty days in the desert?'

Two children shake their heads, no. Others are about to cry.

'Children, Jesus went to the desert without food and water and was tempted by the devil from morning till night with roast lamb and potato dinners, pitchers of iced lemonade and cream pies. But he would not have any of it. He was there to be alone with God and only God would sustain him. Today we remember these forty difficult days during the season of Lent.'

Having finished this brief preamble, I distributed the worksheet along with felt pens and coloured pencils.

113

'Now children, during Lent we remember Jesus in the desert by trying to be a little bit like him. While of course we can't stop eating altogether, we do do our best to pare down and eat simply. Please, children, I would like you to cross out the items on your worksheet, which we should not eat during Lent. Take a moment to think about it.'

I then gave the children fifteen minutes to work as I began to prepare the next activity, which required scissors, paper, glue and *Belle* magazine. The children worked quietly and hesitantly, often looking over at their neighbour's worksheet: several times I had to remind them to do their own work. I believe they did the best they could, yes, their application was honest, but it was perhaps not an easy assignment. Only one of the twelve crossed out all but the cod *à la portugaise*, a dark-haired girl named Maria-Helena who happened to be Portuguese herself.

'Children, Maria-Helena is right. We are only to eat fish, which is a humble thing to eat. Traditionally it is the poor who eat fish because they are so easy to catch. Today, this is not so true. Fish is now quite expensive but we continue to eat it during Lent because it is also a symbol of Christ.'

Realizing that I was about to touch upon Eucharistic doctrine, I did not continue for fear of confusing them. I wanted them to understand Lent first, so that the Last Supper, when its time came, would be fully appreciated for the highlight it indeed is. I then asked the children to come up to the table where I had set the magazines and arts and crafts accessories.

'Now, I would like you to imagine that you are pilgrims on a forty day journey. Yes, it is a long and tiresome one but at the end of it is an Easter basket filled with chocolate fish representing the resurrected saviour. As a symbol of this journey, 'I would like you to look through these magazines to find a picture of your journey path. It could be a great highway, a little path, footprints in the sand or even a picture of a brand new car. Once you have found this picture, cut it out and glue it to a piece of construction paper. Afterwards you can take them to your family for home display.'

The little ones then freely skimmed through *Belle*'s glossy garden, their humour now lightening. Perhaps they found the magazine's familiarity heartening: it was one that *maman* kept in the bathroom, or the babysitter brought in her comely basket along with her home-work. It is not a magazine intended for them, but they know it through and through – even the French boys, who, although under ten, already kindle a burning love of Woman in their hearts, a love beginning with *maman* but turning so quickly towards *that girl there*! Such prodigies! Like a deck of indiscriminate cards, *Belle* offers up Queens of Hearts to whomever the taker, be he tender of age or hard of ear. How little it matters. And the girls, through their reading and sightseeing of this wondrous world of beauties, fruit all the more precociously, folding and unfolding their limbs, just as they do their latest clothing pur-chases. What they ask for they receive. And it is always love. Yes, Love!

And isn't this the whole reason for A1. Is it not love that motivates it? Love, yes, and nothing more! My heart beat in time with the little ones as they searched the pages for a symbol of their inner journey.

'Love!' I burst out, unable to keep my revelation to myself. 'Look for love!'

And the children did so, without giving me the slightest quizzical look, for that had been their ambition from the start and they knew just where to find it.

One had cut out a picture of a young model with a poodle licking her toes. That was love. Another found a pair of twin lovelies, a blonde and a brunette, in the throes of rapturous embrace. That too was love. Still another came upon the picture of a post-coital couple loosely sheathed in sheets (Dr Dolittle's column). That we do indeed hope is love, too. However, we cannot be sure. I did not contradict the children as discussion on Adult Sex, which is indeed an adult pre-rogative, would have been entirely inappropriate (I'm sure you'll agree here, Gladys). And so I shook my head. 'Yes,' I said softly. 'Love too.'

The children then began pasting their images onto construction paper, making with great pride the journey posters which would sustain them through those moments of Lent when it is so hard to be an abstainer. A bell was then rung in the corridor, signalling the end of our course.

'Goodbye children. We shall meet again like this next week, God-be-willing.'

And so the little ones, with faith that God and Mother would oblige, ran out into the hall to find their awaiting *mamans*. I was a tad sad to see them go so soon, but, like any good teacher, tidied up my classroom and scribbled a few notes about the class and each student's participation. Really, it was nearly enjoyable for all concerned.

I got home in time for dinner – leftover coq au vin heated up bain-marie style – which I shared with Jubilee who of late has refused to eat all cat kibbles. I can't say that I blame him really. It's perfectly normal to prefer rooster. Whilst dining, it came to me that I had forgotten to tell the children that poultry is quite all right if fish is not a possibil-ity. The real cheat is red meat.

Joanna called twice during dinner (I never answer when I'm eating) about the Ball of Marvels. She says it is urgent. Must get back to her ASAP. Must remember to get back to her ASAP. Yes, must remember (would you have a post-it, oh Gladys?).

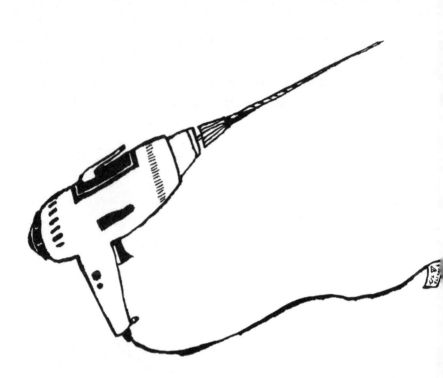

Feast of Saint Hugh of Bonnevaux (abbot)

Well Hugh, the *Concise* gives you just a single, twenty-five-word sentence bio. Maybe this is because you are one of many Saint Hughs, including the legendary Saint Hugh of Lincoln (sixty sentences) and your uncle, Saint Hugh of Grenoble (four sentences). It's best to ignore the hagiographic parsimony and join in this party of saintly namesakes, remembering that in French the 'H' of your name is strictly not pronounced. Here you are called Ewegh.

Lo and behold! Here's what I found this morning: a bathroom sink sitting on the sidewalk right outside my door waiting just for me! A most extraordinary basin really, green and shell-shaped, somehow Mediterranean. I wondered who had abandoned it so cruelly? Some brave and unnatural sea fruit? A gigantic mollusc from the sub-kingdom of soft bodies, now grown hard, still alive and wandering our streets without water or home but claiming humanhood?

Never mind. There it was at my feet, clearly a castaway. And now it belonged to me. I picked it up and began a treacherous and encumbered ascent to my flat. As I was on my way up, Neighbour Jeromino was on his way down. Down the stairwell. Sober it seemed. Yes, off the weed.

'May I?' he asked, looking wild haired but knightly. Sometimes he is awfully polite.

'Yes, please help me,' I said.

And he did, relieving me of the weight for two flights. I nearly ventured to ask him about Junior before we parted, and if he had a home phone number because there's no reaching him on the cell, but refrained. (Was Jeromino *au courant*? Like you, I really do prefer discretion, Hugh).

At my door I took the shell back and set it lovingly into my tub for a bath. I washed it with Mr Clean, scrubbing its belly and back. Then, drying it off with a negligée-gone-rag, I set it in the corner by the window, its privileged place.

Really, most serendipitous this find. Just last night I came upon a suggestion in the *Change Your Heart* instructor's manual to recreate a small holy water fount in the home. Yes, a fount, a daily reminder of my baptismal day which is, of course, impossible to remember. How wee I was when the watery rite of passage took place. Now, however,

119

with the help of this sink, I should be able to remember precisely that which I cannot remember. What amazing fortune really. Seek and you shall find, isn't that right? But the truth of the matter is that I wasn't even looking. The sink was simply there, awaiting a new home and owner. Yes, it was the sink who was looking. Not I.

I took a bottle of Evian spring water to Mass today and asked Père Ricard to bless it afterwards. That he did, which was kind of him because, as Sister Dagobert explained, he only has time for one thing after noon Mass – lunch. Père Ricard dines everyday at Madame Maréchal's. She sits in the front pew and wears a Bodega diamond. It's reassuring to know that the Père is fed at least one meal a day, but perhaps Madame Maréchal should consider subtracting the apéritif, the Bordeaux and the *eau de vie* from her midday menu. Sister Dagobert said she would suggest this in the name of Père's health.

Skipped lunch myself and made a quick trip home to fill the fount with the freshly blessed Evian water. It's better not to wait too long, you see. Holy water, unlike certain mineral waters, does not age well in plastic. Pilgrims headed for Lourdes should know about this: it's best to bring an empty wine bottle with a fitted cork. Once home, I plugged the sink's – now fount's – drain with a stopper and poured the healing waters into its loving basin. Jubilee came over as a spectator. Soon he was blessed, his forehead anointed.

'Go, my cat, and spread your peace in this world.'

Jubilee lifted his rear amorously and rubbed his head against the fount's porcelain edge. It was a moment of bliss and I blessed myself too. Yet still, I could not remember my own baptism so long ago when Father Flinn dipped me in Our Lady of Perpetual Victory's fount. No recollections appeared. The repository that holds this secret would not open its doors to my knocking. Perhaps though in time it would.

I got back to À La Mode Online in time for tea. Jean-Claudi joined us too for a quick one. I had to ask him if he had any more news on Lala whom I think about quite a lot. Jean-Claudi explained that she is back in her palace and that we wouldn't hear much more about her until her next European tour. Apparently she naps quite a lot which is her beauty secret. And travelling does tire her so.

Jean-Claudi is growing a chin-tuft. A very manicured one, which I believe is called a goatee. I was inclined to compliment him on it, but he explained that he would be shaving it off that very day as Horace didn't care for it. Who now, is Horace? I didn't dare ask but knew in my heart that this gentleman must be his latest pendulum conquest. Perhaps even a full-time conquest, the seriously swinging kind, a live-in lover, as it were. Does Jean-Claudi care to have my opinion? No he does not. I must face the truth and inhibit my desire, which inspires not even the slightest curiosity in its glorious object. Djamila can come down from her mount for the pyramid is soon to topple. It was built, I will now admit, with mere straw. In Paris it is difficult to find better building materials. Thatched desire is as good as it gets. And although this may be thought flimsy, Parisians do prefer the lightness of it. Moreover, straw burns splendidly. Perhaps all I need to do now is light a match.

Top Spoon had me write an article on a famous thaumaturge named Hiri Kadini for the site's new health section: Wonder-Workers of the Fashion World. Hiri Kadini is currently all the rage as he has discovered a new chakra which he calls the 'curious ambulance'. The curious ambulance is a moveable energy centre that cures on-site. Kadini explains that, through meditative exercises which draw on the curative powers of this ambulatory chakra, one can heal a saddened prostate or a withered ovary. Headaches go away and colds disappear in a sneeze. He is most often found backstage at the London and Paris Collections where he works as an in-house healer, training the models to manoeuvre their curious ambulances so as to stay in tip-top shape. The girls absolutely swear by him.

One of the spoons here actually had a session with him behind the curtain at last year's Fall Collections. At forty-five she believed that motherhood and its joys had passed her by. Yet within the week following her session, she conceived. Triplets they were, who now born, go by the names of Hiri, Kiri and Biri. This spoon suggested I use her story in the write-up as a case history, although she forbade me to use her name. I did as she suggested, protecting her privacy with the pseudonym, a certain Madam Spoonful.

I left work as early as I possibly could and picked up two fish, a lemon and a lettuce head on the Rue Cler for din-din. When I walked in the door, there was Jubilee drinking from the holy fount as if it were a common feline watering hole! I stamped my foot with righteous anger, which sent him under the sofa. But how useless! Jubilee would try, try again. He had found his source and wellspring and would even fake thirst just to drink there. Manifestly, I would have to hang the fount on the wall.

While contemplating how the fount might mount, I cooked dinner. It came to me then that the best course of action would be to ask Neighbour Jeromino, who seems to be so handy with hammers and what not, for help. I rang his bell but could smell the Marrakech vapours from outside his door. Perhaps not such a good moment to enquire, I thought and was about to go back inside when Neighbour Jeromino answered the door all a-tremble.

'Oh it's you,' he said, losing his balance at his doorstep.

Physically, the lad was all undone. No nerve or muscle tone hooked him up. Rather something had left him limp.

'Yes, it is I,' I replied. 'I'm sorry to bother you but I'm having some trouble with my sink. Could I possibly call on you for help?'

Neighbour Jeromino, still all a-tremble, nodded his wobbly head. Just as I began to fear that his head would topple off that flimsy coil, he shut the door. Very well, I said to myself. No matter. I will look elsewhere for help. But two hours later there was a knock on my door announcing the arrival of Neighbour Jeromino himself. Yes, there he was with toolbox in hand, now looking slightly more the master of his motor skills and clearly better cemented.

'Here, here!' I cried out leading him to the fount. 'And thank you so much for coming!' I added politely.

Neighbour Jeromino took one look at the sink and understood everything; he saw it for the fount that it was and the holy fixture it would become. Such fine-tuned perception and foresight! I suppose those Moroccan wholesalers really do provide the finest. Neighbour Jeromino then unearthed his drill from the pile of implements in his toolbox and proceeded to do what was necessary to mount the fount. The operation was terribly noisy and rather off-putting to M. Phet's lodger who twice came upstairs and knocked on my door with a pipe. Neighbour Jeromino and I preferred not to hear his pounding, as interruptions of this sort would only prolong our work. Neighbour Jeromino worked deftly with drill and screw and the operation was quite a success. In record time the holy baptismal fountain clung to my white wall.

'Please, dear Neighbour Jeromino, how can I thank you?' I asked him sweetly.

'Baptize me,' he said most seriously. And I saw that he meant it.

I nearly protested as I am not of course an invested priest. I'm not even an acolyte. And yet I could not refuse him this service seeing how kindly he had helped me and so late in the evening (you don't mind dear Hugh, do you?).

'Very well,' I agreed.

I then had a good look at Neighbour Jeromino's head and decided against dunking him. He suffered from the oil-dandruff duo hair type and dunking him would dirty the water unnecessarily. Seeing that getting this holy water home is no easy task requiring as it did the blessing of Père Ricard (or an abbot like you, Hugh) which is not so easy to procure, I decided to adopt the cup and towel method.

'Please kneel,' I asked Neighbour Jeromino. And he did so, right below the fountain. 'And hold this towel. You will be needing it.'

He held the towel in front of him, draped over his hands like some noble linen, one which might have depicted a unicorn, say. Perhaps a rose as well. 'Now you may bow your head,' I guided him.

Neighbour Jeromino bowed like a knight before his lady, his pride dressed in the more humble cloak of humility. Such chivalry, I thought. How was I to know the French were still capable of it? Certainly Junior was not! (Still no word from my lasso-lover! What should I do, Hugh?) I dipped my cup into the fount filling it to the brim. Then I paused, wondering how a priest might go about this. In this moment of prayerful silence, I requested the sacred words required to fulfil the task at hand. When they came at last, it was in the form of a latiny prayer long ago taught to me, a prayer to the Queen of our hearts, Our Lady. How appropriate I thought, for this young knight before me. And so I began.

Mater Dei memento mei… Slowly, I poured a thin rivulet of the holy beverage onto his head until the prayer and water were spent. Then I made the sign of the cross in the air using the papal technique saying, 'Rise my Neighbour and go in peace.'

Neighbour Jeromino did rise and without a word, picked up his toolbox to go home.

'Please, wait just one moment, I have something for you,' I said, making my way to my purse. From it I pulled out my sampler of astronaut shampoo, a present from Givenchy from which I have greatly benefited.

'Here,' I said holding it out to Neighbour Jeromino. 'It's really quite wonderful. You just add water and shake.'

Neighbour Jeromino, still under the sacramental influence, silently accepted my offering with a nod and proceeded out the door.

'I think you'll like it,' I added. 'Good night Neighbour Jeromino. Good night! Good night!'

I practised my inner and outer eights before retiring to write herein. A lovely evening really. I do hope Neighbour Jeromino feels like a new man in the morn.

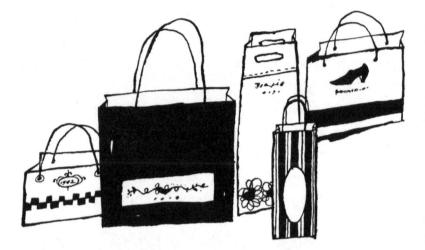

Feast of Saint Irene

Another sad story! Your sisters Agape and Chionia were burned alive for refusing to eat sacrificial meat and toting the scriptures in their book bags while you were sent to do service in a penny brothel! I'm afraid that in such dire circumstances, even Dr Dolittle would be of no help. After only a week in the infamous institution, ravaged by priapic pagans, you pleaded to be put to death. Poor Irene! Technically speaking, you are not even considered a Virgin Martyr like your sisters. You really should petition the Board of Saints; I've heard they're finally coming round on such issues. Who knows, they might even offer workers' comp now.

I have finally found my spring uni, Irene! A discount item this time from the Bon Marché department store. I went there yesterday after work wearing Claudia, my shopping companion. Actually I had a coupon; Top Spoon passed it along to me last week. Top Spoon receives many of these coupons and freebies as well. Usually though, the trickle-down theory doesn't work so well at À La Mode Online due to various stoppers. Why a bit of the wealth leaked through on this occasion, I'm not sure. I suppose it is only human nature to pull the plug from time to time. In any case, I did appreciate this coupon which allowed me to purchase any item on the third floor (ladies' apparel) for half price. I would really have liked to get shoes as well, but they were on the second floor, making it impossible for me to benefit from a coupon reduction. I did consider taking a pair of shoes from the second floor up to the third floor, leaving them for ten minutes in the day-wear section, then coming back to them to claim I had indeed found the item on the third floor, justifying thus a purchase at discount. But I was not in the mood for this kind of hokey-pokey. Not really up for it, I must say.

But how I do love shoes! Mumly and I used to have the nicest shoes when she was married to Richard II. Splendid shoes often with a bow or patent toe. Even several years following the divorce and annulment we still had wonderful shoes. Richard II was very kind to us but also terribly old. I'm afraid that when he died all his money went to the state of Texas. Fortunately he had bought Mumly a lifetime membership to the country club before passing away. Golf is what saves her and when dropsy keeps her from the club she really does get all undone.

I believe that Mumly loved Richard II dearly, but he was simply too antiquated to be a proper husband which was why she obtained a rapid annulment. She was still in her childbearing years and the Bishop Mahoney, founder of Catholic Mothers of America, believed she should be freed of a fruitless marriage for a further go at a more fruit-o-the-womb one. I believe he acted as her attorney before the Pope. So Mumly left Richard II but never did marry or conceive again. I was her only babe and wore magnificent shoes until it was time to go to Vassar College, Mumly's alma mater.

Since that time, I have struggled to maintain the shoe standard all on my own. The uniform, you see, helps, permitting as it does most of my wardrobe allotment to be put toward shoes. By now I must have shoes of every colour, including canary yellow and parochial violet.

Unfortunately, as I have mentioned, there were no shoes on the third floor. What I did find, though, were twin uniforms: matching cigarette-girl dresses with wallpaper patterns in navy (uniform #1) and mauve (uniform #2). I was immensely pleased to have found such appropriate attire for uni-wear. And as the weather is beginning to warm, I am better off with two rather than one because of the perspiration problem. Indeed, I nearly purchased a third, but decided against it, as the colour of this last matching dress was baby food green, a colour which would have become the olivey Djamila but, alas, not the freckled me. And so I left the Bon Marché with my good deal, making my way to see St Catherine Labouré at the Miraculous Medal chapel next door.

St Catherine now lies procumbent in a glass casket on the altar of the Miraculous Medal chapel. I try to stop by and see her whenever I shop at the Bon Marché (and if you were around these parts, I'd visit you too, Irene). It's the Neighbourly thing to do; moreover, she can be most helpful with petitions. All you have to do is write your request down on a petition paper and drop it into another glass box, which sits at the foot of her glass casket. I don't know how she gets to these supplications, seeing that she is hermetically locked into her box, but like all saints she works in mysterious ways I am sure.

I was making my way down the long entryway to the chapel with all the other international pilgrims when I spotted Sister Dagobert and Yorik talking to Sister Samuel, the Sister of Charity who runs the gift shop. Usually at this time of day Sister Dagobert is at the Hôtel-Dieu reading scripture to patients in the Tropical Disease lounge; indeed, I was a bit surprised to see her so far from home at such a late hour.

'Sister Dagobert. Is that you?' I asked, as if not trusting my own eyes, which in truth are very good ones.

'Remedy!' she cried out, grabbing my hand and squeezing it hard as is her habit. 'Lead me, my daughter, to Saint Catherine!'

And so I escorted Sister Dag and Yorik into the chapel and up the aisle to the front row where we both knelt before the casket. Each of us silently said our prayers. Then Sister Dagobert whispered in my ear, 'She's not looking so well today, is she?'

I have found that Sister Dagobert often knows how people look without her eyes as witness. To tell the truth, I believe she sees quite a bit with her groin where, according to a recent medical discovery, retinal cells abound. I had a very close look at Saint Catherine myself then and saw that she was not looking so fresh indeed.

'A bit pale,' I said to Sister Dag.

'Pasty,' she added.

'Yes, waxy,' I admitted.

129

And we stopped our evaluation there. Neither of us is, after all, a certified aesthetician. What do we know? Saint Catherine requires, I believe, the help of a beauty professional. Perhaps with a bit of string pulling, I could arrange for a beautician from the European Institute of Hair and Aesthetics to drop by the chapel. Careful application of make-up by a certified aesthetician could certainly render her complexion less cadaverous. I am a bit concerned that soon people will mistake St Catherine's incorrupt body for a Madame Tussaud wax dumb-dumb.

As Yorik was growing whiney due to his disruptive entrails and the fatty tumour upon which he cannot sit too long, we took leave of the Miraculous Medal, whispering farewell in our hearts to the many pilgrims in the pews. Once outside I checked Sister Dagobert's pluviometer. Showers tomorrow morning, it said, followed by afternoon clearing. I realized then that I should have purchased a rain bonnet to go with the twin-set unis. How forgetful I am with details! This being said, accessories are on the first floor, which is a full-price floor. I suppose I will just have to ask Top Spoon if she would possibly spare a first floor coupon. I do wonder which is truer: *ask and ye shall receive* or *waste not want not*? If I do not ask for the coupon, is it because I do not need it, or because I am a-feared to ask for it? And if I use the coupon for all its first-floor worth, will I not want my purchases in the end? Does *not*-wasting result in the loss of desire? Perhaps one day I will have an answer to these most formidable questions. In the meantime I will continue to ask in hope of receiving, and not wasting in the hope of not wanting, whatever this may mean.

I bid goodbye to Sister Dagobert who was a dinner guest that evening at the Sisters of Charity's dining room. From the smell in the walkway, we surmised they would be serving cod *à la portugaise* (no sacrificial meats here, Irene!). I made my way home on foot, stopping off at my favourite Rue Cler caterer to collect a dinner of patchouli salad (I call it this because it's the most perfumed salad ever, with coriander, ginger, lemongrass and a drizzle of potable eau de cologne). Picked out the shrimps for Jubilee. After dining, I practised the left vertical shimmy, which is really the most difficult of the shimmy variations. Hung up the twin-set. Retired. Good night Irene, Good night Irene.

Feast of Saint Hunna

It seems there are as many ways to earn sainthood as there are saintly souls. You, Hunna, were hoisted up to heaven for doing the laundry of the poor, a service which earned you the nickname 'Holy Washerwoman'. What an unusual take on charity; most holy helpers heal the sick and feed the downtrodden, whilst converting and redeeming souls. But who takes into account those overloaded dirty clothes hampers that never get carted to the cleaners? The poor of the seventh century just couldn't afford dry-cleaning, let alone soap!

It's tankini time: this summer's beach look, especially recommended for ladies with a tummy bulge. I wrote an article all about them this morning (only wash a tankini in Woolite, Hunna), an exercise which prompted me to ask the becouponed spoon for a first floor Bon Marché discount ticket. Shoes, accessories and tankinis are all first floor favourites. Coupon Spoon promised to see what she could do.

Joanna called me at work all in a state. I begged her to pardon me for not returning her calls, but explained I had been awfully busy with summer collections and the bathing suit advisory. Fashion cannot wait, I tell her, which is exactly what the spoons tell me every day. Joanna, I believe, has forgotten just how treacherous the work imperative can be. I often forget myself, and so am hardly the person to remind her of it.

Of course, what Joanna has been dying to talk to me about is the Ball of Marvels. Joanna confided in me that she would very much like to have a baby, but that she cannot do so until after the Ball. The idea of it has become so dear to her, you see; she has put all peripheral activities on hold until then. It seems that the Ball of Marvels is in fact a cotillion, presenting young lady debutantes from Europe and Japan. The girls will all parade in a rehearsed performance, which will rely heavily on sound and lighting engineers. Joanna has changed her mind about the dress she put on hold at Chez Mathilde and is currently working on developing a *rapport intime* with a young but highly esteemed designer by the name of Eléanore de la Motte de la Motte-Piquet. If Eléanore takes the bait, Joanna just might be presented with a Motte de la Motte-Piquet ball gown. If not, she will return to Mathilde's.

Joanna was also *most* persistent about the Marquis. So much so that I had to break the news about the panty problem.

'What does it matter, Remedy?' she insisted. 'If that's what he likes, then just wear them. I mean, what's underwear after all?'

Indeed! Joanna, I should say, is a most practical Philadelphia girl, a descendant, she claims, of the Winthrop line; she simply cannot understand how a woman with less sense and lineage might invest panties with the powers of an amulet. But I am a descendant of Killarney and Cordoba, a hybrid, crossbreeding the panty lines. I am, alas, little more than a freckled Moor. And the purity of white-wear may well be beyond my attainment.

'Look, Remedy, just go to the Bon Marché and buy yourself some nice cotton panties and bras. White ones, right? They have the best selection in Paris. And I'm sure Roland wouldn't mind some lace, if it's cotton lace.'

'Maybe,' I said, beginning to see her point.

'You know, Remedy, relationships are about compromise. It's easy to forget this when you've been single for so long. But listen, I'm sure you can find panties that both of you will like. It can't be that hard.'

As usual, I admired Joanna for her optimism and level-headedness. She is always so sensible, so sure-footed in the world. When she goes Rue du Faubourg St-Honoré shopping, she takes a shopping trolley with her. Her life skips to the beat of a readily recognized rhyme, a perfectly wrought reason. And her house is not cluttered by Poesy and its sidekick Pretend. There are no Johanneses and Juniors in her closet. Dear, dear Joanna. She thinks me a fool, yet still sees to it that I have the best. And the Marquis, she believes, is top-of-the-line. How, she wonders, could I even consider turning him down? And because of a panty problem?

'Yes,' I acquiesced, 'if he calls, I will talk to him.'

'Well, I should hope so! Has he been calling you, Remedy?'

'No, just leaving messages.'

'Well, I hope you've called back. He's trying to invite you to the ball, I'm sure of it.'

'Listen Joanna, don't give it another thought. It'll all work out, *Inshallah*.'

'What's that?'

'Got to go, Joanna, the boss just walked in.'

In fact, it wasn't Top Spoon at all, but Jean-Claudi, that former boss of my heart, still bossing it around just a bit, I must say. Jean-Claudi is so extraordinarily beautiful that it's a wonder he's behind the objective rather than in front of it. He is himself, a photographer's delight, and could easily earn his object's keep. Yet perhaps it is his own beauty he is trying to attain by photographing the beautiful, just as the sick man will spend his life curing those with illness. In the end, if fortunate, the sick man manages to cure himself. Perhaps Jean-Claudi, will one day set down his camera and pose before it, discovering at last his inimitable handsomehood. And perhaps then he will move on to other activities, such as stardom.

I finished the article on swimsuit styles describing further camouflage techniques for the wide-waisted and cellulite-*derrière*d. I couldn't help but wonder why women put themselves through it every summer. I thought of Iranian women bathing in chadors and having fun. Nothing exposed, nothing lost, and perhaps nothing gained as well. Who, I wonder, is the freer? I then pretended I was tankinied on the Azure Coast. Yes, at Cannes, strolling down the Croisette after a morning at the pebbled beach. I walked around feeling rather naked and pale seeing it's so early in the season. Yet no-one noticed a thing.

I wondered if the tankini was truly the right model for me. I wondered if I should submit myself to the 'flaw test'. Instead, I left the office and its swimwear ponderings, and, on my way out the door, crossed paths with Djamila and Hadj Mohammed in the foyer.

'Djamila!' I cried out. Then, remembering my manners, '*Kayf halek?*' employing the North African greeting perhaps once used by Saint Augustine himself.

'*La-bes, barak Allah fik,*' replied Djamila. 'And God-be-willing, this weight will be lifted from my heart.'

'Your sister?' I asked, enquiring after the weight in question.

'No, my son, my own son, my heart!'

'What's happened, Djamila?'

'He has brought home a girl to marry.'

'Yes?'

'And she is an atheist! I will not have her as a daughter, I tell you. It is an impossible marriage, forbidden by the Koran.'

'Did they announced their engagement?'

'No, but they might as well have. He brought her home to me and then took her into his room for the night.' Djamila's voice trembled with the gravity of the situation.

'And he's never done that before?'

'Never!' replied Djamila. Then, after some reflection, 'Once or twice perhaps.'

'Yes. And they came and went didn't they? For the moment, Djamila, you mustn't worry,' I reassured her. 'Love nowadays is fly-by-night. A young man brings a girl home to his mother just as he might bring her a rose. It is his way of showing you he's a man of success. Think little more of it. Next week, he might bring you a young Muslim

136

lady. But think nothing of it. The week following, it may be a Jewess. Again, set no store by it. When it is time for him to marry, you will choose the wife. A good mother always does.'

Djamila nodded her head slowly, her expression now more hopeful. Must say I was surprised by all I said. Was I channelling for Dr Dolittle?

'Thank you, daughter. God-be-willing you are right. May the atheist be out of his bed as quickly as she fell into it. Come by this weekend for sewing class. Leila is making a wedding dress for her cousin in Constantine. You must learn to sew to become a good wife one day. And may that day be sooner than later, *Inshallah*. We will find you a husband, child, a believer who will appreciate your talents in the kitchen and beyond.'

I thanked Djamila for the invitation and agreed to stop by. How timely! I'd been needing to take the hem up on the mauve uni and could use a lesson in alterations. After several promises and *Inshallahs* regarding Saturday, and my future husband whose face only Allah can know, we parted.

I went directly home without buying dinner and practised Samira's choreography which we're to perfect by next Fall when we perform before a live audience of standing.

Before retiring, I separated my whites from my darks (in honour of you, Hunna!). Off to the cleaners tomorrow.

Feast of Saint Rumold
(or Rombaut – aka Saint Rambo)

Well, the *Concise* is certainly imprecise when it comes to your bio. Were you Irish or English? Was your name Rumold or Rombaut? Since we really do not know, I suggest we call you Rambo. This will make it so much easier for modern believers to remember you. And isn't it your saintly duty to be remembered? Why, if no-one supplicates you to help out, you'll grow lazy and slothful and cease to be a saint!

Oh but there is nothing like a Sunday morn after a Saturday night at the rodeo, Saint Rambo. I don't expect you to understand of course, but could you please, on blind faith alone, start preparing my next Wild West Show? Say for next weekend? And put some muscle in it please!

Junior surprised me with a late-night visit, got me up from bed whilst I lay reading Melville in Esperanza, a pink, peek-a-boo negligée with a black lace trim. I don't usually read in peek-a-boo negligées, but thought I would for the sake of adding something girlish to Herman's boys-only tale. But how pleased I was to be so prettily attired whence Junior came a-knocking. In truth though, he did not knock. Perhaps to make up for his absence whilst out on the range, he now returned with a song, '*If I said you had a beautiful body, would you 'old it against me?*'

His twangy, aitch-less song serenaded me whilst I tended the saloon. I quickly took stock. No Bud, I saw. No whisky either. Apple brandy down to near dregs. Just a bottle of Philippe de Rothschild Mouton Cadet 2002. Do cowboys drink this? Oh, I will hold it against you! I crooned back as I popped the cork. Come-hither! Let us Drink from the Cup, Oh Beautiful!

But really this talk of the Cup was something a girl should only say to a camelboy. In the West they do not bother with cups but drink from the bottle directly. Junior began his second number, '*I changed her oil, she changed my life*,' which reminded me I needed to moisturize, which I did, very quickly, in the ladies' room using an À La Mode Online freebee lotion (Dior).

'Howdy Owdy!' With the door open I now revealed what would soon be held against him.

''Eeee 'aw!' yodelled Junior, visibly pleased with Esperanza's peek-

139

a-boo effect. I held a finger to my lips, for it occurred to me that we mustn't waken Jeromino from his vapours. He was such an impressionable lad and I do believe, an abstainer himself.

'Care for a drink, cowboy?' But before I could even reach the Mouton Cadet, Junior swept me up in his arms and landed me on the couch, nearly on top of Jubilee!

'Let us ride the breeze, baby'

'Oh let's do!' I eagerly agreed. But then I noticed that something was missing, a prop that made love all the more prodigious. 'Where's the lasso, love?'

'In the chestnut tree. Impossible to undo it.'

'You mean it's caught in a tree in the Tuileries?'

'It bit the dust.'

'Never mind. We'll do fine without it.'

I was careful to hide my disappointment, to console my cowboy who mourned the loss of his loop.

'But let's do have a drink. How does Mouton Cadet hit you?' I raised my voice to a cheerful hostess high.

Junior accepted his glass and even made a proverbial French toast: *A la tienne!* Health to you too, cowboy. And lotsa good ridin' to boot!

'Do you have any snacks?' enquired Junior.

'You mean nibbles?' I queried to clarify his enquiry. 'Something to accompany the wine?'

I refrained from telling Junior that cowboys don't ask for nibbles to go with their wine. It would only have added insult to the injury that was losing his lasso. No, but I would have to get him back in the saddle ASAP.

'Cowboy up!' I shouted.

And the next thing I knew, the four little black bows that unite my wrapper were loosened and Junior's tongue, warmed from wine and song, was licking me pleasurably. Making my grammars tingle and swoon. There was no more talk of nibbles now. Oh, the Call to Ride has been heard! And now we were on our way, 'orray!

As Dr Dolittle has explained in her column, Adult Sex practitioners often broaden their acquaintance after, not before sex. How right she is, for it was in the morn that my knowledge of Junior would branch out beyond the biblical. I learned, for example, that he has a day job selling hot dogs at La Vallée des Peaux Rouges, a Western theme park replete with simulated cowboy and Indian battles and a real Wild West Show. Cowboys, he explained to me, always eat a hot dog before performing in a rodeo. Nitrates are luck enhancers it seems.

The exciting news is that Junior just auditioned for the Wild West Show! He'll know two weeks from now whether he makes the cut. I'll certainly keep my fingers crossed! With the extra money earned, he'll be able to go to Rodeo College. (You can help him, can't you Rambo? Sometimes a little saintly nudge makes all the difference in the world.)

We really did have a lovely morning-after. Once again, he declined on coffee. But not because he had sniffed out anything von Kryslerlike. The truth is he drinks hot cocoa (please don't tell anyone, Rambo). Cowboys do have their surprises. And their little secrets too.

Feast of Saint Anselm

The English have you to thank, Anselm, for encouraging the devotion of 'rustic' (*Concise*) English saints despite the efforts of William the Conqueror's crew to replace them with Norman holies. Why, they almost struck St Dunstan out of the calendar! But you very carefully put him back on, and others as well, to heal the emotional schism caused by that French marauder. But perhaps you took things a bit far when you tried to officially condemn sodomy in the English church. It just didn't go over. Cross-cultural sensitivity is a requisite when living abroad, Anselm. Why look at how careful

I am with the spoons; always pluming away and never a vexatious word!

I had a dreadful headache this morning brought on by that after-dinner liqueur I had at Chez Wong last night. It was served in a Chinese thimble with a picture of a naked man at the bottom of it. Quite a cute one at that, resembling Junior not a little (please no judgement, Anselm. He's too adorable for condemnation!). All the spoons were offered a thimble but I'm the only one who got a little naked man. The rest of them had little naked women. A nice evening all the same, made even more agreeable by a gift envelope containing three first floor Bon Marché coupons.

The coffee made in the von Krysler contraption was much too bitter; the tartar control treatment can no longer wait. It would have to go to Djamila who is a plaque-removal specialist. In the end my breakfast consisted of two fizzy aspirins which did help a bit, although certainly not enough. I thought about making contact with my 'curious ambulance' for a more rapid recovery but didn't know where to find it. Locating this circulating chakra can only be learned in a private session with the master Hiri Kadini himself. Rumour has it, however, that he will soon be finishing a book on the subject, making public the discovery and use of this most complex and potent healing force. Soon, the curious ambulance will become as much of a household term as fizzy aspirin. For the moment, though, it remains shrouded in mystery, available only to a happy few behind the Collections curtain: the designers, their models and the top spoons who write about them.

And so without recourse to the curious ambulance, the headache lingered on throughout the day. Uncomfortable yes, and yet this discomfort, apart from incommoding me, had the beneficent effect of inspiring compassion in my breast. Compassion for the suffering, for those consumed and weakened by illness and whose hearts have been sold to despair (oh Anselm, hear my prayer!). I thought of Sister Dagobert working day in and day out at the Tropical Disease ward and lounge. How, I wondered, do her heart-bands stretch so far and not snap? The finer the elastic the better, it seems. My own remains as thick as the bands that bind broccoli; it will not go the full round. I am merely an apprentice of compassion, which, I am told, can even appear cruel at times. Jesus' fury in the temple, Sister Dagobert explained to me, is a fine example of compassionate behaviour. For compassion means understanding with the heart, which was how Jesus apprehended the temple problem, not so? I began to wonder if the daily use of the curious ambulance precluded or enhanced compassion. Might it be a promoter of perfection? And is not perfection the tightest and securest of bands? Custom made and self-contained?

As the day progressed, I felt the elastic loosen, my heart widen. I read an article in the *International Herald Tribune* about the horrors committed against women in Afghanistan. Tears burned in my eyes, my fists clenched my desk. Called an Afghan travel agent but was told I could not purchase a ticket without the consent of husband, father or brother. Went instead to the coffee machine and wept into an espresso goblet. Useless! I thought. No good! Yes, with the elastic so far stretched, I was a useless spoon. Not even the ladies' room could succor me, for it was not comfort I was seeking, but some exercise to accommodate the expanding heart.

Saw no other option but to leave the office and, like so many searching souls, get on the metro. With no particular destination in mind, I simply rode, measuring each stop instinctively to see whether or not it beckoned me with some variation of hope. In the end, I got off at Victor Hugo, that second-to-last stop named after the great patriarch of French letters and compassion. Yes, a great lover of the poor, the miserable and the poetically oppressed. Were he alive today, he would get me on that flight by claiming to be my father. Yes, my Father! My Victor! Men can help women in their great womanly tasks but do not know it. How amazing this is to discover! All we need to do is tell them! Tell the men! Never before in history has it been so clear and simple. Victor! Victor! Come to the phone and get me on that plane! But alas, I do not have a Ouija-phone, and while Victor can hear me, the airline cannot hear him. Imagine! Victor Hugo not being heard! I am sure he cannot bear it (if you can help us here Anselm, please do!).

I walked around the eponymous circle with small groups of professionally dressed people until I came upon a young woman in a waxprint dress seated on the sidewalk at the foot of the Société Générale. She was painting her toenails. I immediately identified the golden plaited wig she was wearing as coming from Gambi's. Yes, it was a Gambi original to be sure. I wished for a moment that I had Claudia on as proof that we shared this point in common, for of all the people milling about Victor Hugo circle, this young lady was the only soul with whom I felt encouraged to speak. Why? Perhaps because she was seated whilst the others were standing. Or perhaps because her home, with its blanket foundation, appeared so wide open. The invitation was indiscriminate, addressed to Victor's entire circle. Still, no-one paid her a visit. I fumbled in my bag for a housewarming gift and found a roll of mints.

'Care for peppermints?' I asked at the threshold. My hostess took the roll and, with a flippant gesture of her hand, indicated that I take a seat on her blanket.

'Toenails!' she announced, rattling her bottle of polish. I believed she was offering to paint mine, although it was difficult to say. Here was a lady of few words, a hostess of great seriousness. I was very concerned not to vex her. Tentatively, I began to take off my shoes, searching her expression for a sign to inform me if my action was appropriate or not. Whilst there was no hint of encouragement, nor, more importantly, was there any sign of disapproval; and I deduced, therefore, that I should remove the knee-highs as well. My inclination proved correct. The kneeling hostess promptly, if not a bit roughly, took my right foot and set it on her firm, massive thigh. Looking down at her hams, she inspected my toes, which because of my attention to excellent shoes, were in naturally fine shape.

'I see nothing,' mumbled my saturnine hostess, seemingly displeased.

Suddenly it occurred to me that she might be a toe-reader. Yes, toe-reading, a branch of clairvoyance I once read about in *Belle*, largely practised in Haiti and uncannily accurate. I was terribly surprised by this and began to worry dearly as to why she saw nothing! Had my shoes perhaps been too good? I was growing increasingly upset awaiting an explanation, and nearly took it upon myself to question her directly at the risk of being impolite. Yet my hostess, more inclined to speak with gesture than words, dipped her wand into her pot of polish and began painting my toenails. Carefully and with artistry in a sparkling lavender. Not toe-reading, I saw. Just cosmetic pedicure, less costly than the medical kind. No removal of corns, nothing to be skinned off and removed. How I had everything wrong! She was not a hostess at all but a sidewalk pedicurist. And when she finished I was charged five euros. Not a bad price it is true. Perhaps even a price for a friend, and yet I had suspected nothing.

'Excuse me,' I said, having paid for my paint, but remaining on the blanket still until it dried. 'But do you go to Gambi's?'

The pedicurist looked askance at me. Was it my question that disturbed her or was it simply the fact that I had asked a question that did? How difficult she was to discern!

'I've never seen you before,' she replied. Clearly, she would not talk to me about Gambi, our mutual purveyor of changeable hair.

'No, I don't believe we've met before,' I agreed. 'I'm sure that we haven't. But your hair is very familiar to me.'

Taking courage, I ventured on, 'What do you call it?'

'Cindy,' she replied after a moment, looking at me for the first time and smiling, perhaps despite herself. 'Cindy of Hollywood.'

I heard the square, almost loving intonation of pride in her voice.

'How lovely,' I said, hoping that her smile would bloom more fully. That uninhibitedly she would share her haughty beauty with me. She the rose, I the rosarian. And vice versa.

The exchange could be so happy. Yes, I desired more than the mere commerce she offered which in itself is never enough. But the smile died quickly on its vine, and the transparent fence around it resumed its guard. I had mistaken so much, even the open house invitation that was, of course, only rudimentary marketing.

'Goodbye Cindy,' I said having dressed my feet. 'Wear-well!'

Receiving neither a nod of recognition nor a wave of the hand, I left at my own bidding – my feet perhaps enhanced but my heart gently oppressed. As I made my way back around the circle to the metro, I felt somehow at a loss: *tristesse* filled my breast. I wondered if Victor Hugo used to feel this way after having made a chancy, mercantile encounter on the street. Oh, I was certain he had made them in his day, but could his heart be nearly bullied like this? Just before arriving at the metro, I slipped into a phone booth, inserted my card as instructed and wept. Fortunately, thanks to a trusty tree, I was kept hidden from the indiscreet view of passersby. I could cry all I needed and did so whilst listening to the weather line, Allô Météo.

How I wished that Sister Dagobert were near. Yet there are moments when we are meant to find consolation on our own, just as Jesus did in the desert. Indeed. And so I got back on the metro and headed home, where I discovered – with a sense of marvel, it is true – that my headache had disappeared, returning undoubtedly to that treacherous kernel from whence it comes, ever unannounced and unwanted. What gratitude I felt then! Gratitude towards my sidewalk chiropodist and her Cindy. Gratitude towards Victor! To that man who will help me when he can. He helped! (And to you Anselm too, for as they say, 'a saint a day keeps the doctor away'.) I went to my fount and blessed myself with great reverence and thanksgiving.

'Thank you O Holy and Dear ones, for the headache departed.'
And with that retired for the evening.

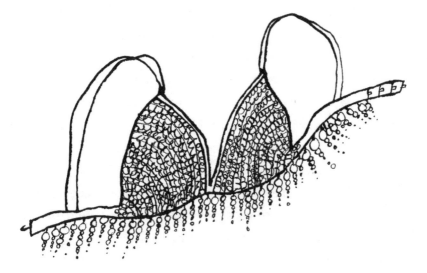

Feast of Saint Zita

From servitude to sainthood: a remarkable path, Zita. I certainly hope the miserly family you served for forty-eight years appreciated that all their dirty work was done by a saint. I can't imagine! The *Concise* says you condemned the work-shy and applauded the industrious, setting a miraculous example now lauded by butlers and maids alike, in England, France and Texas too. Mumly used to keep your holy card on the door of the refrigerator so that we'd always have enough domestic sustenance. It came down though, when she married Richard II.

Sleep, that Saturday morning's prerogative, was undisturbed today by my hazardous neighbours. Even Jubilee did not begin his kibble call until nine o'clock, respecting thus the ten p.m. to seven a.m. law that holds in the French Republic. I did have a fine sleep and lingered this morning draped in my *peignoir*. Read, and sipped Nescafé (von Krysler stovetop still in repair: could you help, dear Zita, Godspeed its return?).

There were no guests unfortunately, though it would have been a rather lovely moment for one, a gentleman guest, freshly showered and with a bakery bag of warm crescent rolls to offer. I've often wondered why there are not any industrious crescent roll boys in Paris. Door-to-door croissant hawkers on the seven a.m. to ten a.m. route. Of course a crescent boy is not the guest I have in mind. I am thinking more in terms of a Moorish gentleman (named Mouktar say?) who, having purchased the crescents rolls from a crescent boy on the stoop, climbs my four flights of stairs to share them with me in the breakfast boudoir.

After sufficient lounging, I packed my dance bag and headed to dance rehearsal. Samira has chosen six students to perform in her autumn season's ballet: it seems I have made the cut. We have started rehearsing on Saturdays at noon, which is not always so convenient, but it's best not to complain. Samira won't have any of that. Samira says that she will never get used to the French, who are the biggest complainers of all. Perhaps this is how I made the cut, not because of any superior talent, but because I do not complain, especially whilst in class. All of Samira's other chosen ones are of Arabian descent. None of them banter or chaff. And then there's me, the freckled half-Moor, a diligent student of the eight, both with and without shimmy. We are a happy ballet, flying our veils under the eagle eye of Samira.

Today was a dress rehearsal: Samira brought a suitcase full of imported Egyptian costumes and assigned one to each ballerina. Much to my delight, I was given a revived cabaret classic of emerald green with a pearl-fringed sequined bra and belt set. The skirt is a three-toned verdant-hued chiffon *plissé*. I could not help but express my pleasure and gave Samira the *bise*. Samira smiled warmly and kissed all the girls.

'Now,' she said becoming very serious. 'I must ask all of you for a deposit.'

She required, I should mention, more than just a penny per pearl. Samira is no fool. And we, the obedient ballerinas, addressed our cheque books to give our professor guarantee. Ballet of course is business too.

Now that we have all learned the choreography for 'Fill the Cup O Beautiful and Give It to Me!', we are currently working on perfecting our expression and gestural attitudes. Last week Samira handed out a worksheet on the seven gazes and we were told to memorize and practise them in the privacy of our boudoirs. Each gaze, you see, expresses an emotional twin-set. All of the seven will be used in 'Fill the Cup', especially the *come hither/touch-me-not* and *leave me/never-let-me-go* combos. If we are up to par, there is even a chance that we will perform for the King of Morocco and her Royal Highness Princess Lala! Samira is extraordinarily well connected in the Moorish world and seems to have several shoo-ins. Oh! How I would love to dance for Lala! And the King too! But will we ever be good enough? Samira seems to have great faith in us. Yes, faith in what we will yield and, alas, doubt in what we will return.

Our dress rehearsal was more in fact a dressing-room practice. We spent most of our time trying on the costumes, all of which were at least a size or two too large, seeing that they were made in Egypt where women tend to be two sizes wider. According to Samira, Egyptian women have no notion of dieting and would spurn such a thing if they knew about it. Only their aristocracy go on diets – and do so even more fervently than their European counterparts, with the same passion once devoted to pharaonic mutilations (which were also a prerogative of the courtly class in days gone by). So it seems that the upper crust distinguishes itself from the lowlier crumb by the practice of unnatural *bizarreries*.

The Marquis of course came to mind. He is, indeed, as much a victim of the crust as I am of the crumb. Or perhaps I should not say victim, but performer. When I reminisce upon our dinner date, I see him as a most extraordinary actor, performing with perfection his crusty role. How curt, how irritable he became upon finding the crumbly underpinnings! And how the crumb herself understood nothing, for to her such crumb-wear was so wholly natural! Yet in the aftermath of this rejection, she turned the prodigal crust from her door, for he was still under the illusion that crumb will cater to crust and had returned for the catering. Ah, the strange private life of crust/crumb politics!

I was a bit relieved to find that the costumes, as their large sizes proved, were surely Egyptian crumb-wear. One must be true to one's performance after all.

From rehearsal I went straight to Djamila's for the sewing circle (more industry, Zita. You can't say I'm work-shy). Brought with me the mauve uni and the emerald costume for adjustments. I was greeted with rose water, sprinkled as usual by the mistress of the house herself.

'Welcome daughter. Come in and set your sewing down.'

I enter carefully, stepping around the spread of pale pink satin voluptuously carpeting the floor. This, I see, is the wedding dress to be. But for the moment it is more like a thick, expensive cream found in a pot, one that can be eaten as well as spread into the skin. The bride will be covered and soaked in it. *Does the Nazarene know how to sew?* I make my way around the spilt cream and set my bag down at the foot of the couch. *She has brought her own sewing.* Leila, who is calculating her yardage, smiles at me.

'My cousin is a big girl. To cover her is costly.' Djamila speaks while pouring mint tea into mosque-covered glasses. There is, I see, some twenty metres of silk-satin. 'A woman her size can have many children. It is Allah who wants it so. He has given her that shape and the appetite to satisfy it.'

Niece Sarrah brings out a plate of datemeal cakes.

'It would not harm her to eat one chicken less,' remarks Leila. 'Sometimes she will have two at supper. Her father is rich but will her husband be able to feed her?' Djamila offers the tea on a platter. 'She is marrying the son of a restaurateur is she not? And the owner of the finest cake shop in Constantine. She will have enough to eat. And her children too, God-be-willing.'

In the meantime we eat cakes in her honour. In honour of the Constantine Cousin: a quick toast with the tea.

'To her health!' I say. 'What is the cousin's name by the way?'

'Fatima! Fatima the Fiancée!'

This name sends my mind through its Marian files. I am reminded of Our Lady of Fatima who appeared to the Portuguese children Lucia, Francisco and Jacinta in 1918 and nearly had them miss their First

Holy Communion Class. She warned them of Stalin, the perils of Communism to come and told them to say the rosary every day. My immaculate heart will triumph in the end. I find myself whispering the words of Our Lady of Fatima on the eve of her last Portuguese appearance.

'What is the Nazarene saying? What's that?'

Just some famous last words, perhaps best not repeated in mixed company. No, there is no point in bringing up Our Lady of Fatima's geopolitical predictions and prayer prescriptions. All that is Christian history now. May we remember and proceed.

The future of the Muslim Sisterhood here is our cousin Fatima. Fatima the Fiancee! The Constantine Cousin. Soon to be a great mother herself. Due to make appearances in the hearts and minds of her children throughout their lives, enduring past her own, God-be-willing.

'Can I be of help?' I ask setting my tea down on the coffee table.

But no-one answers me.

'What's in your bag, Nazarene?'

It is Leila who wants to know. She sees a green light arise from it.

'A star of sorts. Look! It's for dancing.'

I pull out the shimmering, reptilian thing. Glamorous dance-wear made from siren's skin.

'Ah! The Nazarene! Does she know how to dance? She will dance for us!' Niece Sarrah claps her hands. 'Djamila! Some music!'

Leila reels in her silk-satin. All its pinkness goes into a basket.

'Yes, something from Egypt, Djamila! Something to dance to.'

I wonder for a moment if Djamila will oblige, if she considers the proposition Koranically-correct, but see that I am wrong to. She flips a switch and the Arabian airs of Radio Orient bring Egypt into the low-riding salon. Coin-fringed scarves pulled from purses and drawers are fastened around hips.

'Here Nazarene. This one makes music.' Djamila herself ties a musical wrapper around my hips and pushes me gently into the circle of seamstresses.

'No! The costume. Nazarene, put on the costume!'

I shake my head. No, too large. Egyptian size. I spread my arms out wide to give them an idea of the girth. But never mind.

'Put it on Nazarene. Put it on! We will pin you.'

Djamila speaks this time and as guest, I cannot disobey her. I pull on the *plissé* skirt, its top and belt and stand cruciform while the Muslim Sisterhood pins me down. Fastens me to belt and bra.

'Beautiful! Now dance Nazarene! Let us see you dance!'

Leila claps to the rollicking music. A Lebanese song now called 'Oh Heart, My Heart!'. A favourite dance tune of Beirut's celebrated male belly dancer, Mousbah Baalbaki.

'Anybody can shake his body and get money,' Mousbah Baalbaki once said. 'But to me dancing is an Art.'

Yes, if Baalbaki were not an *artiste* he would have been arrested by now. And even so, he continues to cut it close with the moral authorities and always dances with a bodyguard near to hip. Art, in the end, is a fragile exploit, so easily arrested, I daresay.

'Dance, Nazarene!'

I am being called back to the salon, away from sniper-shattered Beirut and its Saturday night fevers. 'Dance!'

I reply with hip flicked seamstress-ward.

'*Yallah!*'

The ululating begins, a three-throated chorus encouraging further and more furious shimmy. The contagious kind. The sort that draws up the sodden earth through the feet and legs to spin-dry it in the hips. Ah! We can clean the soil with our hips. We can! The dancing ladies, the daughters of the Eight. I am no longer a soloist but because of costume only, a minor *étoile* of sorts. I stick out like the thumb of the hand. All the women dance with an abandon I have not yet learned. But I am learning. Those things acquired at home, not in class. Such as cooking. And this, I see, is a kind of cuisine. The cooking that is done in a very large pot, conducting heat through the very centre of things. All the mysterious rudiments become alimentary in the cauldron, are consubstantiated by the fire of our hearts. For heat rises, does it not? From hip to heart?

Ah! And Djamila's smile! Shut the curtains for it will set the moon aflame. There is no prescription for such a smile, no laws for it. It blooms when the cards are wildly shuffled, in moments of delightful disorder. And here the disorder lasts. Not through one song, but two, three, four until the music is interrupted by an advertising voice which sends the women to the poufs and *canapé*, out of breath and pleased. Five chickens for fifteen euros, a side of beef for forty-five, a whole ready-to-roast mutton for one hundred euros, a dozen eggs for two ninety-nine… The Boucherie a-Salam's bargain list continued on, offering one hundred per cent halal *viandes* to the hallowed hungry. But we are not hungry – the cooks never are – although we are all wearing halos of heat.

'Turn that off! Silence!'

It is Leila who obeys Djamila this time. Not me. I am happy to hear from the Boucherie a-Salam. The message helps me practise my Arabian accent. In ten minutes, it is time for prayer.

156

'Where are the carpets? You are always hiding them Sarrah.'

Djamila lays the cards down flat and square. Her halo has descended and now lies around her neck, giving her voice a gold-timbred authority.

'But can't we pray with the radio? It's convenient with the radio muezzin.'

Sarrah is pulling the carpets from behind the couch.

'We are not that kind of people.'

Djamila raises her eyebrow like a whip.

'Please! I am all pinned into the mermaid skin. Please, can someone undo me?'

Leila comes and begins unpinning.

'We almost forgot the Nazarene! We almost forgot our guest!'

She laughs to make me feel better. I do feel fine, but it is time to go. When the Muslims pray, the Christians stray.

I repacked my bag but Djamila stopped me.

'Leave that here. We will take care of it. Leila is very good at it. Take this.'

Djamila hands me the von Krysler stovetop, detartared and spotlessly clean.

'Thank you so much Djamila! How can I thank you enough? Thank you a thousand times!'

Hugging the von Krysler gift to my chest, I kissed my friends goodbye: 'Enjoy your weekend! God-be-willing, next week we will sew again. God-be-willing. Goodbye!'

Feast of Saint Mafalda

First of all they tried to marry you at age eleven (my God, were your grammars even developed then?) and to your crusty cousin, King Henry I of Castile. But in the end, the marriage was rapidly annulled because of consanguinity and you were sent to the nunnery, where you subsequently attained sainthood. Too much crust and the cake caves in. Yet somehow it's good to know the crusts contribute to sainthood too, though I certainly hope, Mafalda, that you don't look down your nose at crumbly colleagues like our dear Zita.

All's quiet at À La Mode Online. The top spoons have flown down to Cannes, hopefully in time to meet the Victoria's Secret Concorde, which should be full of top mods and their bevy of underwear. A grand VS fashion show and benefit dinner are to be held on the Film Festival grounds, adding under-glamour to upper-glamour. All the cinematic stars and their directors are cordially invited to purchase a pricey entry ticket. The most fabulous amongst them will be tabled close to the catwalk whilst the lower bidders must rent opera glasses. Proceeds are believed to go to a cause although, as of yet, nobody can gather which.

The Riviera rendezvous for both top spoons and top mods is the Hôtel Carlton, which is where Mumly and Richard II used to stay in their travelling days. I have a Polaroid picture of Mumly in the Hôtel Carlton lobby looking smashingly lovely and tanned in an Oscar de la Renta chiffon mini. Richard II should have been in the photo too, but all that you can see of him is his third leg, which is to say his cane. I believe it was taken by some Mumly-admirer in the environs. Yes, I do suspect it. She was so beautiful, so young and vacationing on the Riviera! In a way, those were grand days for her which perhaps would have been grander indeed had the permissive notion of Adult Sex, which can adopt adulterous forms in such Riviera vacationing cases, been more widespread and promoted at the time. For the Riviera, without the love that a cane renders difficult, may as well be a sleepy Florida key. The sensual natures of love and glamour unite on this azure coast for those willing to wed it. But Mumly was caught by the crook of a walking stick. True, she loved Richard II dearly, but more continentally surely than coastally. What a far distance to travel for naught, I say. But Mumly never complained, except perhaps to the Bishop Mahoney.

I would have liked to go to Cannes myself. Especially now that I have a tankini, my latest purchase made possible thanks to a hand-me-down spoon coupon. Why am I not tankinied on the Croisette with all the other spoons, accepting invitations to champagne cocktails? Because I am not a nomadic spoon, but a sedentary one. I am the trusty ditty spoon, rewriting the hazy glamour calls, the slipshod modem-sent communiqués from the coasts and capitals. And I enjoy it, I do. But wouldn't I enjoy it in Cannes too? Perhaps I would, but in the grand scheme of things how little this matters (thank you Mafalda for helping me renounce). Going to Cannes would be a minor conquest, a bit like winning a party favour from the prize *piñata*. A treat, yes. Hokey-pokey for the jet-set, a member of which I am not. Glamorous perhaps but riddled too with required rituals – too many for the taste of some. I have even heard that certain celebrities go there only grudgingly and out of a sense of starbound duty. This is unfortunate, for one should go to Cannes with a great desire for crusty encounters and profit well by it.

But there was a great deal to do in the office whilst the spoons were gone! First of all there was desk cleaning to attend to, then reading hour (*International Herald Tribune*), followed by some catechism class preparation and a brief write-up on YSL safari suits. Then out to St Joe's. Ten minutes late for the *midi* service. Tiptoed up to Sister Dagobert who was pewed in the first row with Yorik lying procumbently at her Hush Puppies.

'Hello Sister,' I whispered in her ear. And got The Squeeze.

Père Ricard, I must say, was not looking so well. He must have started earlier with the nips than usual and taken above the daily dose. His homily on the Fruits of the Spirit and the Fruits of Sin was terribly muddled – a veritable fruit cocktail I'm afraid. Where does the divine begin and the profane end? How does one distinguish between a good fruit and a bad fruit? Père Ricard no longer seemed to know and we, his parishioners, even less. Sister Dagobert, who often manages to put these homilies through a goldminer's sieve, extracting only the rare, more valuable nuggets, shook her head after this sermon. Nothing would come through that strainer: all silt and sand. Ah! Poor Père! Poor parishioners! Fortunately the pulpit stint was short and the Mass soon gained the altar. The rest was recipe.

I had a look at Sister Dagobert's pluviometer during the kiss of peace. Rain, it said. Rain and more rain. Honestly, that's all it ever does here. Why did the Romans civilize Paris anyway? For bathing purposes?

Sister Dag and I went out to lunch, not at the corner café but on the Rue des Rosiers for a falafel special. Usually Sister Dagobert avoids the Rue des Rosiers because of her previous Hebraic associations and their disapproval of her marital choice.

'But Jesus was a Jew,' I remarked.

'Yes,' said Sister Dagobert, shaking her head. 'That is the problem.'

Indeed, to the minds of many, mystic marriages make little sense and are esteemed fruitless, barren ventures of the blind. In Sister Dagobert's case, the reproach lay in her choosing the wrong tribe member, for she opted for the lamb-o-god over a flesh-n-blood man-o-god. And while she knew that pardon would not come from her blood family on earth, she had the notion that the heavens promised an all-faith reconciliation, a oneness which does not yet exist here but for which the National Committee of Catholic Bishops exhorts us to pray.

161

I suppose it was the general spiritual muddle cast upon our minds by Père Ricard's sermon that weakened Sister Dagobert's resolve. Like her father's name, her love of Hebraic cuisine precedes and pursues her and yet how often she refuses to indulge it! Still, it is true that if fortune cushions us, confusion can lead us unexpectedly to the portal of a pleasure renounced. So it happened after Mass with Sister Dagobert. And never once did I question her, but pretended this was the most normal of courses. Still, for her sake, we got take-out falafel rather than a sit-down one.

Accompanying Sister Dagobert back to the Hôtel-Dieu after our luncheon, taken under the lee of my umbrella, I found she was in great spirits. Several times she reminded me, 'We are what we eat, Remedy!' True indeed. A wise alimentary maxim, more pertinent today surely than the time it was first pronounced.

Parked Yorik and bid Sister Dagobert goodbye in the Tropical Disease foyer. Then I hopped on the metro to get back to work ASAP, arriving in time for the postprandial tea, although no such beverage was being served due to the number of spoon absentees. I put the kettle on myself and prepared a pot of green for potential tea-timers. Yoga spoon was there as well, although deeply entranced in the raven position. Amazing how long she could support the weight of her bum on two hands! And on top of her desk! She is no small spoon! Commended her with mental applause which, according to her master, the Swami Vishnu-Parnapada, is superior to handclapping. *Bravo! Bravo!* Yoga spoon descended from the raven high and reemerged as a wingless biped, radiant and ready for tea. Indeed, tea-time is indispensable for all the spoons even perhaps for our Cannes counterparts who, the moment we indulged in our leafy brew, were sipping a smoother kind on the Croisette. Probably a version of slimmers tea, highly advised for the tankinied.

My entire afternoon was spent working on a diagram linking designers to their perfume progeny. A kind of perfume tree as it were, covering the last three generations. I do hope to benefit from this exercise myself. A gift set of eau-de-toilette, *parfum* and matching soap would be most appreciated. Especially coming from the Coco house.

On my way out, I bumped into Djamila and was given a large shopping bag with the mauve uni and the dance costume.

'Thank you Djamila! You're a love!'

'You will thank Leila. She is the seamstress,' she corrected me.

'Has she finished the wedding gown?'

'The gown will take thirty days to finish.'

'Not forty?' I asked, enquiring in truth, to see if this pronounced time frame were at all related to Lent.

'No,' replied Djamila, shaking her head. 'Only thirty.'

Indeed, thirty rather than the Lentil forty. It is written in the Koran! But it was not Djamila in the flesh who said this but my own private Djamila, the one who speaks to me in times of dire ambiguity – when my ears hear double and all equipoise fails me. Then, it is this Djamila's voice, endowed with pyramidical powers, which descends upon me like a conical canopy, protecting me from all overhead congestion. So it was in the case of Jean-Claudi upon whose person I had projected many ambiguities in the hope that one of them might lend me a key to unlock a minor chamber of his heart. I believed at first that Djamila would preside over this passion. And she did, although from the elevated vista of her throne she saw what I could not and took then the appropriate course of action, which was to end all lopsided longing.

It was this Djamila's voice which informed me that Horace had become a household name. Jean-Claudi's path presented no fork leading to the girl-folk after all. It never had. The ambiguity was my own, arising no doubt from excessive Pretend-ing whilst ignoring the clearest of clues and all kindly, but unmitigated intimation. I am grateful to both Djamilas and have come to rely on them dearly. Yes, quite a bit though not excessively so. We do not, after all, share the same good book.

I thanked Djamila again and transmitted my further thanks to Seamstress Leila before heading out of the office and making my way to St Joe's annex for catechism A1. Oh my dear little students. So timid and true. As usual they were awaiting me in neat, scholastic rows and needed to be directed towards a more Christian configuration.

'Please, children, let us gather in a circle like the twelve apostles. Jesus prefers it this way.'

Of course, I have no way of knowing if Christ actually minds the rows or not. The noblest practice of religion requires a bright imagination and successful catechism, fancy for inspiration. This too, the children would have to learn. Hopefully, my example would teach them.

'You must get out of your seats to do this, children. Please, make the circle quickly.'

Timorous and needing encouragement, these minor apostles at last began to move their chairs around and into a circle.

'Very good. Now, children, do you remember how last week we spoke about the Lord providing for the starving Hebrew people in Egypt by turning the morning frost into a crusty treat? They could only eat this in the morning because it was perishable. And so lived for a while on the breakfast alone. Now, could each of you tell us what you had for breakfast this morning?'

This was an exercise suggested in the *Change Your Heart* manual and it seemed to me like not such a bad one. The children, being French and, therefore, naturally gastronomically-minded, began without further prompting their descriptions of croissants and chocolate buns, buttered brioche with jam and day-old baguette, toasted and dripping with melted half-salted butter.

'Children, by listening to one another, I believe you can see that breakfast is a celebration of bread. It is the bread that nourishes our bodies. But children, there is another kind of bread. A more mysterious one, even stranger than the bread that spreads like frost on the morning earth. This bread is the Bread of Life. And soon you will be celebrating it, which is to say ingesting it. Next week we will talk more about the Lamb-o-God and maybe have a demonstration too. But today I would like to tell you about a miracle. The Miracle of El Paso.' Again the manual highly recommends that instructors recount the testimony of a modern-day miracle, similar to the one Jesus enacted in the parable of the loaves and fishes. It is believed that experiencing a miracle, either directly or by procuration, stimulates the autonomic nervous system. Sister Mary Paul MD, author of the catechism manual, claims that the stronger the hypothalamus gland, the more the child is likely to develop a spiritual aptitude and imagination. And so I prepared for my students an account of one of my favourite miracles, told to me long ago by Richard II.

'Children, it was in El Paso, Texas, that this extraordinary happening happened. Texas, Children, is the size of France but it is not at

165

all like France. It is a state in the United States of America. Do you know it?'

The small faces looked at me blankly. I'm afraid none had heard of the Lone Star except for Xavier, a child who claimed to have an Uncle Pierre there.

'Well, Children, in El Paso, Texas, some years ago, lived a priest named Father Thomas. Father Thomas wanted to celebrate Christmas as Christ would have wanted him to, which is to say, not with family and friends but with the outcast and poor. And so Father Thomas crossed the Rio Grande, which is a great river, to invite the poor and miserable of Juarez to his Christmas dinner. When he got to Juarez he found that the down-and-out were angry and fighting dangerously with one another. "Please," said Father Thomas. "Stop your strife! I have come to invite you to a Christmas party. Cross the river tomorrow night and come. We will celebrate Mass at midnight and feast at my house after." But only some twenty people said they would come and so Father Thomas crossed the Rio Grande again to prepare a meal for the twenty. When Christmas Eve came, however, and Father Thomas opened the doors of his home, there were not twenty guests but two hundred! "Lord Oh Lord," he prayed. "May all these men eat else I am a victim of their violence!" Father Thomas was serving ham for Christmas and had bought one that could feed fifty but no more. And so he began carving that ham. He began at one in the morning and did not stop until six. The ham that should only have nourished the twenty, fed in the end the two hundred. So busy was Father Thomas with his carving that he did not notice the meat was evergrowing. And it continued to multiply until every man had eaten and could eat no more.'

As I ended the Miracle of El Paso story, I saw that the children's eyes were alight with the mystery, their breathing now slow and steady. The effect of this miraculous ham on their hypothalamus glands was immensely positive. Sister Mary Paul MD's hypothesis proved correct. The students had begun to 'change their hearts', their automatic pilots (Sister Mary Paul refers to the autonomic nervous system as such) now endowed with the loftier wings required for such a trans-formation.

I certainly had not expected to have such a successful class and was pleased beyond measure. I suggested then that we have our own humble feast with the orange juice and cakes Maria-Helena's mumly had brought.

'The best parties, children,' I said as Maria-Helena went around the circle with her cookie tin, 'are those hosted by the Lord. We are always sure to get enough convivials.'

Micheline, whom Maria-Helena had asked to pour the orange juice, missed one of the paper goblets entirely and poured half the bottle out on the floor.

'Not to worry, children,' I said cheerfully as any catechist would. 'There will still be enough for all, we will just take smaller portions. Thank you Micheline, for because of that spill, we are going to deepen our experience of making a little go a long way.'

I did insist upon this brighter aspect of our situation, for I was afraid the children were being led dangerously close to the materialis-tic expectation that miracles should occur and reoccur at the most minor of needs. Especially the multiplication sort. What if they began demanding a miracle of the juice say? And lose their budding faith because of its failure to transpire? Was it time to tell them about free will and the sparing interventions of the Divine? Was this the moment to confuse their minds with the subtlety of paradox by explaining how the Lord works in mysterious ways? Do I tell them about the Virgin Mary's ear? No, I decided, A1 must for the moment remain rudimentary and focused on First Communion. But how terrible it is to be an instructor seeing the connection between all things and having no means of rendering such awesomeness simply to the seven-year-olds (perhaps you have a tip for me, Mafalda?)!

'Please, children,' I began, 'let us have a moment of prayerful silence before we leave.'

Silence, I thought at first, was our only recourse to this awareness of infinite connection. But then another possible path came to mind, one that seemed somehow happier, perhaps more straightforward.

'No, children. On second thoughts, I'd rather you stand up now. I'm going to teach you an exercise, which will prepare you for many things in life, including First Communion. Once you have understood the movement, please continue practising it until it becomes your own. Then you can do this whenever you like, at home or in the playground. This movement is called Oh Infinity!'

I then began to trace a figure eight with my hips, the simplest of eights in the Oriental Dance repertoire. The basic Egyptian eight as it were. The students copied me as they could, some acquiring the movement more quickly than others of course, but all managing to push their pelvis around the eight track in some manner. Yes, even the boys had their way, perhaps not unlike the Lebanese cabaret king, Mousbah Baalbaki, who womanizes his hips to experience the joys of eternity. Yes, all of us, man, woman and beast should know this bliss. Even if it calls for travesty. There is no shame in it. None at all, although the experience may be perceived incipiently as odd. Such was the case with the pupils.

At first there were giggles and the general silliness of children at a new game, but then they grew quiet whilst continuing the figure. And the eight grew, its sliding circles reverberating and fattening out into the classroom. With it a silence so profound, thickened like a muscle, arresting all sound, which might have escaped our inspired hearts. There was a tyranny to it, but a generous one, forcing us to broaden our berths. Yes, we now had more room to come about in our proper places. More room to swing at anchor. For infinity is a matter of being still and throughout at once. A binding paradox which liberates. Is the eight, after all, not a knot? A knot upon which the ship depends for its safety whilst navigating the infinite sea. Our chests may well be our grammarians, but our hips, I saw, are our boats. And the eight, their most natural tacking figure, unites our earth and its heavens, our seas and their constellations. So much gained and understood whilst staying moored and anchored! How can this be? I thought of dear Emily (c.1865):

> *I never saw a Moor –*
> *I never saw the Sea –*
> *Yet know I how the Heather looks*
> *And what a Billow be.*

Indeed she did, much as the children and myself in the classroom felt, without any palpable guide or stimulus, the tidal pull, the rushing wave. There we were, twisting mariners of the earth, Christians as it were. Fishers of men, it is said. But Roman Catholic ones here, of

Latiny dispositions, my own slightly tempered by Anglo-Saxonity. From our sciatic schooner, we throw our lines, over and again, starting right then to the left, a weaving reel without hitch or pause. There was no need, I saw, to explain the earth or the sky to these apostles, for they easily possessed both.

Then, from up and down the annexed port outside our door a siren sounded, calling in all ships. It was Sister Dagobert who bore the bell. Diligently she rang, calling our sails down.

'Children,' I said, gently encouraging them to release the eight and return to a daily hip stance, hopefully now more fully aware of infinite love and altered for the best. 'Go in Peace, children. They will know you are Christians by your love, won't they? And, Xavier, will you bring the snack next week? Please don't forget the cups. Goodbye!'

The pupils skipped out of the classroom and into the arms of their respective *mamans*, that most loving of harbours. Ships they would continue to be. Fishers of men.

Left St Joe's annex after tidying the classroom and having discussed my lesson plans with Sister Dagobert. Sister Dagobert is so full of love, you know. And so supportive of the work I do!

Got home in time for a phone call from Joanna. On and on about the Ball of Marvels.

'Never have I wanted something so bad for myself and for you. Do you realize that I've found you a Marquis, Remedy. A Marquis! The guy has got his own castle! My God, can you believe it? All you have to do is say yes, and you'll have it made! You'll even get your own chapel! With a priest too – you know how they always seem to have one of those around. Just think of it! Tell me, have you found a dress?'

Glass of sherry and cheese crackers for din-din. Chinese freeze-dried shrimps for Jubilee. A lovely evening. To bed, to bed. But will she ever wed? (No distant cousin or other, Mafalda. You'll make sure of that won't you?)

Feast of Saint Solangia

Poor dear. All we know is that you took a vow of chastity and died in defence of it. But maybe you could teach me some of that resolve you're so famous for; Lord knows today would certainly have been a propitious day for it.

Oh Dr Dolittle, where are you??? Six months since Johannes von Krysler's last disappearance. And now a telephonic return! From the Charles de Gaulle airport. At eight in the morning! In time for coffee? *Remedy darling, I am coming. Wait for me. I will come to you.* Ah those words! So casually spoken and yet so seriously received.

All practice of forbearance for naught, Dr. Dolittle! All attempt at a sturdier independence, at rooting in a firmer emotional soil failed. Failed, Dr Dolittle! And so I waited, against my better judgement which advised me to tell him I was busy but perhaps another time thank you. Playing it cool, you see, would have served me well. A kind of non-action as it were, actively not acting. Leaving the gentleman with the hunger and the need to appease it. Myself propped on an ermine-upholstered pedestal, not waiting but reigning. It certainly could have happened this way, and yet life's tests are delivered spontaneously. Study all you will, they steal upon you in your greatest hour of unpreparedness. Whilst you stumble to find your pen, the exam will have reached its finish. These tests are never written.

And so, having lamentably failed that propitious occasion to prove my expertise in Adult Sex training, I sheepishly waited for the Bavarian. From eight to eleven thirty I remained in my flat, listening for the blithe upstep of my acrobat in the stairwell. Listening for that loving rap on the door, rhythmed like a bugler's reveille. True, Johannes von Krysler had been in the army a bit. True he announced himself like the morning's captain. But wasn't that all part of his endearing mien in the end?

I waited. At eleven thirty there was a spoon-call enquiring after my whereabouts. I was in the middle of changing the sheets for the third time, having opted for the purple *Congratulations* set I bought at Tati, Paris' discount department store. I call these *Congratulation* sheets because the word *Félicitations* is embroidered on them, most likely meaning they are nuptially inclined and made expressly for rural Moroccan families who exhibit them with RVM (ruptured virginal membrane) stains. I thought von Krysler might like them for a change.

Acrobats usually sleep in hammocks, you see. With a duvet maybe, but never a sheet.

'I'll be right there,' I told the spoon on the other end of the line. 'Just a minor health problem this morning. Nothing to worry about.'

True, not a lie. After all, abandonment provokes a number of common complaints, generally of the digestive sort. It is indeed a health hazard. Took two spoonfuls of dietary charcoal, brushed the soot off my teeth and left my post to go to À La Mode Online. Taped a note to my door in case von Krysler ever did come, leaving my work number and email address. *Could not wait!* I explained very simply.

Got to work in time to see the spoons head off to pump practice at the gym.

'*Ça va, Remedy, Ça va?*'

'All is well,' I reassured the spoons. 'Have a good pump!'

Went immediately to work on fashion communiqués:

1. Sailor-striped evening gown with ivory-and-navy lacquered ostrich feathers (JP Gaultier)
2. Camouflage tulle knickers with open-back gabardine raincoat (YSL)
3. *Clochard* chic jumpsuits in canvas, rope and leather lace (J Galliano)

Worked very hard, passing on lunch, passing on tea-time. I have been told the mourning businessman will bury his sorrows beneath the nerve of frenetic labour. Thought I would try this technique myself. Did it work? Quite well indeed, but only in the short term.

At half six, that labouring nerve sprang like a wild coil, leaving the wound open and unguarded. That was in Mass. In the last pew. I came undone whilst the evening priest, the presumed Polish one, invoked the saintly community of four: Saint Mark, Saint Mathew, Saint Luke and Saint John. Pray for us! we all cried out. But I cried the loudest. My cry was the boldest. Still, it was not to the foursome that I spoke, but to the Virgin Mary herself, the Mother-o-God. Where are you? Where are you? Oh Mumly of God!

But no sooner said, then a soothing warmth flooded my chest, dissipating the confusions and tension therein. It was the flush of love that came upon me, the love of the Virgin Mary. She had not abandoned me at all, only Johannes von Krysler had! And so I understood that the gods were not treating me with disfavour in the least. How easy it is to confuse human folly with divine action. And how difficult to bear the charge of free-will.

Must discuss this fundamental truth in A1. Yes, even the children should begin grappling with this notion. The earlier the better I would think. I've been much too easy on them, haven't I? One is never entirely immunized against such confusions; the dividing line between the divine and the human is difficult to discern. That frontier is a foggy one, rendered perhaps less opaque through the cultivation of prayerful practices. Why, look at Djamila who prays five times a day and has no doubts about the borders. She would never mistake, say, a mortal foible such as absenteeism for a sacred messenger. And she is right: there is no mystery to the manmade flaw. Although its blatancy can be painful to bear.

Divesting my morning abandonment, then, of all godlike responsibility, I left St Joe's feeling remarkably relieved. Clarity, after all, is a wonderful reliever, at least incipiently. It has always been my belief that it is better to be affronted by ignorant Man than by knowing Angel, for the *savant* insult hits harder, with wings and exactly where it hurts.

Johannes von Krysler was merely a Bavarian. Prone, undoubtedly to acrobatic accidents. His no-show was a minor offence.

I made my way home, newly reassured, stopping by my Rue Cler caterer to pick up a ready-made dinner: two slices of pork roast, potatoes *allouette* (really just a gratin, but so light and deliciously frothy that I call it a lark), apple tart and a bottle of '93 Médoc. Peace of mind encourages my appetite. It always has. Took this repast up to my flat where I set my table for one, lighting a candle as further mood enhancer. I was feeling quite all right. There are many who complain about dining alone, yet this has never bothered me. It is quite possible that I enjoy eating more than I enjoy most table company.

Misanthropic as this may sound, I believe it is true of gourmets, many of whom are otherwise – that is to say away from the table – affable people. The lover of delicate fare often finds the need to dine free of distracting conversation. The French who have raised *gourmandise* to the level of an art, know that gourmets should be paired at the table or remain dining alone. Of course, the great *gourmande* Julia Childs spoke superbly and at great length on the subject. How often we saw her on television at a table for one! Suffice it to say that I sat down quite contentedly to my dinner and that the roast was a savoury one indeed.

I was midway through this supper when interrupted by that rudest of horns, the telephonic *brrring*. I very nearly did not pick up, but then, perhaps pushed to do so by some telepathic persuasion, did.

'Remedy, darling,' said the voice on the line, 'meet me at the Café Beaubourg in an hour. I'll be waiting for you.'

'I'm sorry Johannes, but I'm not available this evening. Maybe another time.'

My tone was cool but not cold. Firm but not fixed. True, I had not anticipated his call, yet I was ready for Johannes von Krysler this time. The Communion of Saints (headed by you, Solangia) had loaned me an evening anchor. Moored, I was not going anywhere, and from my docking could effectively shoot from the hip. All midnight seafarers would have to swim out. And even then, there was no promise of being permitted on board. This was made very clear on the phone so that the acrobat understood all risk was his to take. No more precarious waiting for me. No more flighty hope that the tides would change.

Went back to my dinner finishing the last bites of potatoes *allou-ette*. Poured myself another glass of the Médoc. The velvety drink slipped into me, warming and softening my hardest notions. I was proud of myself, yes, for I had acted wisely and in the name of self-preservation, and yet the sweet memory of my weekend with von Krysler came rushing at me like a diluvial catastrophe.

Dr Dolittle! Dr Dolittle! What now?

Within minutes of finishing that second glass, I was all awash. Unmoored by emotion. So many months of being alone with only the bite of a panty-perturbed Marquis and an Owdy Junior on my line. And myself, a fisher of men! How is this so? Oh, the gods had abandoned me! All my Mass ruminations had brought only temporary convictions. Hope again, had me believing they were bedrock. Flighty hope! And now I had pushed him away on the faith of a feather.

I poured yet another glass of wine.

Liquor does unleash the emotions, but a very good wine reasonably consumed can also sharpen the voice of logic. Descartes, that rationalist extraordinaire, was a lover of the ruby juice himself. Managing to calm the emotive toil, I then began to reason that, as the von Krysler pattern was to appear and disappear, there was every chance that after that evening's telephonic appearance, there would have followed a Café Beaubourg no-show. True, I had not consciously refused to see him for fear of being stood up, yet this logic must unknowingly have guided my dismissal.

Recognizing that the situation offered no guarantee of a love encounter and that I had done well not to take the bait, I began to regain confidence in my decision. To have been made a von Krysler fool again whilst sitting on a Café Beaubourg pouf would have humiliated me, perhaps beyond recovery. In that café, human emotions are showcased *à la carte*, listed on the menu. Cooked to the amusement of all the *beau monde* – and then, finally, consumed. How the Café Beaubourg loves to see a lonely man such as Monsieur Lift made lonelier or a toasted girl made toastier! Going there could very well have had a miserable me on many a plate. And so, as I went to do the washing up, I congratulated myself on my mature refusal of an offer that might have reduced me to petty fodder.

Happiness was again within my grasp. To celebrate this positive advance, I stepped into my shimmering green dance costume, fastened the stays and slipped into an undulating camel walk. Radio Orient was playing Oum Koulsoum's 'A Thousand and One Nights', a song that requires several dance veils to illustrate this Egyptian diva's extraordinary range of musico-emotional states. I only had one, but did my best flying it as rapidly as I could so as to create the illusion of volume and multiple flyers.

Ah! Truly there is nothing like belly dancing, nothing so kinetically surprising as this hipdom of gyration. For once the shimmy starts, it does not want to stop but climbs the body with the freedom of heat, bringing the face to its fullest and headiest bloom. All cares are shuffled out and sifted down. The entanglements of love unravelled, their yarn loosely strewn around the feet. I kick them away with a pointed and outstretched toe, led by the momentum of the Tunisian hip, one of the basic moves in the repertoire. The veil is now behind me like diaphanous dragonfly wings. I gracefully raise and lower my arms sending a message of parting, then bring the veil in front of me to take it in one hand. Here now is the most decisive moment, for the drapery is to be dropped, denoting both adieu and if-you-dare. Ever so slowly, undulating in the camel manner, I turn nonchalantly, letting the veil suggestively fall to the floor when at the turn's halfway point. I was about to finish this move and continue on with a maytag shimmy when the doorbell rang.

Who's there? Junior? But no, Junior doesn't ring the bell. Neighbour Jeromino then? With Neighbour Jeromino, one never knows. He is likely to call at any time of day or night with sundry requests. (Because of the pension plan, you see, his biological time-clock is off.)

'Coming!' I called through the door, picking up the veil and wrapping it around me to cover my bare midriff. Then, 'Who's there?' before opening, just to be sure it wasn't some stranger trying to get in and rob me to death.

'It is me, Remedy, darling,' said a voice from the stairwell. 'Open up!'

Ah! there is only one man who addresses me by that avuncular and outdated endearment. *Darling!* Young lovers no longer say it. Only grandfathers, uncles and Bavarians do.

Indeed! It wasn't the pensioner a-knocking at all but Johannes von

Krysler, some twelve hours late for our rendezvous. Not a no-show at all but a *late* show. The late-night show featuring the trapeze artist himself.

'Johannes!' Within seconds I had unlocked and opened the door. 'Remedy darling! Darling Remedy!'

Presence means everything. The phone is merely theory. The body, I believe, speaks the truest and often the loudest truths. Swept up in the von Krysler arms, those muscular wonders which can sustain the weight of four flying ballerinas whilst hanging from the trapeze by his knees, yes, held and cradled there, forgiveness came. It is not an exercise after all, but a phenomenon that occurs of its own volition. At least this most basic brand of pardon, the kind a woman might bestow upon a late but beautiful man.

Ah, indulgence!

All trespasses forgiven. Johannes von Krysler was scot-free, but then again so was I. How free I was for the rope-walk of love, the funambulist tumble. A soirée with von Krysler is a better tonic than any session with Hiri Kadini. No curious ambulance can compete with his kisses. He is my amatory acrobat, my late-night victor, my medicine man extraordinaire! No wonder I had called the Smidtzes again and again! How can a girl possibly get enough?

At least that's how it seems after he's come and gone. Yes, it's hard to think otherwise. Surely Dr Dolittle has never known the likes of von Krysler. She is distant and so wise, but has she ever had it this good? Has she ever had the tips of her toes a-humming with pleasure? If so, then she is truly all the more remarkable, her forbearance worthy of great admiration. Still, it is my suspicion that she is at least a part-time abstainer. In any case, how would she have time for acrobats with that busy advisory business? Acrobats, after all, are not hit and run. True, they may never stay in one place long, but while they are with you, they require your utmost attention. Von Krysler's gravity-defying stamina sets a commendable pace. One must keep up, of course. But it's a pleasure to be up to par. To be a love peer, as it were. A love contemporary, happily swinging wherever the breeze of a rotating fan might take us. (Johannes insists on having the fan on at all times!)

Yes, it is tremendous fun. Yet like all amusements, this one too has its favours and its *finis*. This time I was presented with a glow-in-the-dark star, which I attached to the ceiling over my bed. I must admit it's wonderful for making bedtime wishes. I thanked von Krysler profusely for the party favour, and in my joy made a double cartwheel pointing my toes in the air for extra leg extension.

'*Hashemite!*' I cried.

Johannes took the cue and did a double backwards flip landing upon Jubilee's sardines. Washed his feet, not with my hair like the Magdalene, but with a squirt gun and dust cloth. Gratitude does encourage love, I must say

Finis came on the morn of the second night. Von Krysler stole away at an hour so early it is not even appropriate to drink coffee then.

'Goodbye, Remedy darling. I am off to Rome!'

Ah! *Roma*! Von Krysler will visit it before I do.

'Say hello to the Angels,' I whispered to him.

But my acrobat did not hear me; he had already taken flight and was certainly halfway to the Gare de l'Est, where he would catch that train across the border. *Bon Voyage* I wished him, through my intermediary agency, the star. Stars, as you might know, do godspeed messages.

Needless to say, I could not fall back to sleep. For who can sleep when her lover leaves the nest, perhaps forever? I tossed and turned for what must have been several hours, then left the boudoir to fix some coffee. The stovetop worked beautifully and a feeling of gratitude came over me as I sipped the coffee (thank you, Saint Solangia, for foiled forbearance.). Yes, odd at a time like this, but it was gratitude. True thanksgiving! And without a regret. Thank you, Johannes! Thank you, my darling! It mattered so little that he was not there to hear it. I was happy to say it, again and again!

Fell back to sleep around ten but woke up at noon to the sound of Shlomi yelling out his pizza orders and the revving engine of a scooter. I looked out the window and glimpsed Mouktar just moments before he slipped on his helmet. A divine vision to be sure, filling me with the light of revelation. So stunning and sudden it left me dizzy. I grabbed the fount to steady myself. Made the sign of the cross as any Christian maiden would thus caught in the perilous grip of desire. *Inshallah!* I called from my tower window as he sped off on the horizon with the steaming kosher pizzas. If only... Oh, hope! God-be-willing we will!

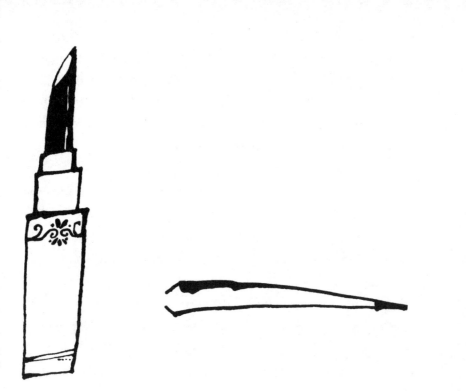

Feast of Saint Dunstan

Let us, Dunstan, salute our dear Anselm, for thanks to his high EIQ (Emotional Intelligence Quotient), you survived the Norman Invasion and remain to this day, a favourite Saxon sainty. The *Concise* mentions that you absolutely loved to paint and draw and cites a marvellous portrait you did of yourself adoring Christ. Well, I'd just love to see your images some day! Especially the self-portrait, because apparently you were simply gorgeous, a kind of blond Jean-Claudi in monk-wear. If you were living today, Dunstan, I'm afraid you wouldn't be a saint, let alone a monk.

Do you know Brigitte Bardot? (If so, Dunstan, please forgive her.) I recently read an article on her animal rights campaign, her love of the furry beasts and disregard for the Southern Hemisphere's human populations, which prompted me to sit down this morning with a blue pen and a sheet of Salvation Army stationery:

Dear Brigitte, (I wrote)

People are animals too. Why is this simple fact so easily forgotten? Brigitte, like so many in the preservation business, is drawing rather unnecessary lines, giving privilege to one fragile few over another. We all need protection after all, even the sweet earth we stand upon. Suggested she do some reading on Saint Francis in any case as I think this was precisely his point. As the great holies have often said: Love thy Neighbour as thyself. Does it really matter if your neighbour is a German businessman or a cow? Just love them! That is all that's required. I hope that Brigitte can get the hang of it and quit saying belligerent things about Southern Hemispherians in the press.

I've been busy writing letters these days as you can see, and just sent the von Krysler journal entry to Dr Dolittle herself so as to share my personal triumph with her and possibly the larger *Belle* readership. As we know so well in America, stories of personal triumph are highly inspirational. Recently, I read about a woman who survived an alligator attack. Being from Florida myself, I know something about those choppers. Personally, I would never take the risk of getting near them or foolishly row a boat in the swamplands, but this woman was not from crocodile country and had no idea that when a hungry alligator gets a whiff of you, he will capsize your canoe to get at you. And so, while rowing along, she was tipped and caught by those treacherous jaws. Of course, the inspirational part is that she survived the numerous rolls and managed to pull herself up on a slippery shore where against all odds she was found by a roving ranger. Apparently she has borrowed on this harrowing experience to formulate a new philosophy – which, incidentally, Brigitte Bardot should read, because it is all about the food chain – and insists that we are inextricably part of it. This, of course, means that many animals want to eat us and manage to do so. It merely takes the whim of a hungry crocodile to put us in our place. Are we indeed the masters and mistresses of the animal kingdom? I'll be interested to hear how Brigitte responds to this when she writes me back.

Life has been breezy since von Krysler came and left. This is not to say that it's any easier, of course. Or that I no longer yearn for a jaunt with Junior. Or have stopped cursing his cell phone, out there on the range. Only that my heart feels lighter, as if the weight of a small stone has been lifted from it. I wonder how many people go through life suffering from heart stones? Judging from the closed, clogged expression of a good number of Parisians, I would say quite a few.

And yet how simple is the cure, the sure-cure! A weekend of love does wonders. If only I had a Ouija-phone I would call up Saint Paul, that fervent proponent of abstinence, and have a word with him on the matter. Why all those letters to the Corinthians telling them to either knock if off completely or at worst get married? He certainly set us back a number of years and that was a long time ago. It's hard to believe that we are still weighted down by his stubborn heart stones and I suppose we ought to be saying, 'Oh, poor Saint Paul! So many stones upon one heart.' But at this point it's simply too late. The best thing to do is have those epistles removed from the New Testament entirely. Of course the Church Fathers have been cutting and pasting that book for years. Manifestly, an updated and freshly re-pasted version is overdue (am I not right, Dunstan?).

It certainly seems like more could be done for the public's health and well-being, especially in Paris, which is supposed to be the city of love. Perhaps that sobriquet was once well earned, but today it is only kept alive by and for tourists, who love and then leave. The truth is that there are far more would-be lovers than lovers in practice, hence the need for a Dr Dolittle and the increasing number of 'encounter' clubs and gymnasiums. At the moment, though, I feel relieved of all heart-stone weight and anxiety, and certainly am much better for it.

Jean-Claudi came into the office today with his beau, Horace. Considering them both as dear, old friends, I made them tea, serving it Moroccan style, which is to say, deferentially and with lots of mint. In my breast, there was not the merest trace of a hard feeling. No spark of jealousy or pang of disappointment. On the contrary, I was delighted to see such healthy human beings creating even better health through the practices of love. As the two gentlemen drank the beverage, their cheeks grew rosy and their humour more solicitous. Mint tea will have this effect.

'Please,' I might have insisted, 'Have another cup!' And yet there was no need: the men were serving themselves from the pot, laughing and caressing cheeks. Willie (*Wheelie*) then came in from the design studio and was served too. A beautiful man in his own right and an *ami intime* of both Jean-Claudi and Horace. A delightful threesome they made, coyly sipping the beverage and exchanging bits of tittle-tattle.

Seeing that their menage no longer needed its hostess, I excused myself from the tea-room which, in all honesty, is really my desk, and directed myself to the ladies' room. Fortunately the facilities were not occupied seeing that the spoons were largely out to lunch or at the gym. I took advantage of this liberty to pluck a few hairs from my eyebrows – a thoughtful habit, making you focus on your brow, that epidermal gauge of emotio-intellectual activity. Apparently there are women nowadays who prefer to freeze their brow with sausage poisoning and lose the gauge. Of course this makes me wonder if they also don't freeze their brains a bit in doing so. What I like to do is read my brow as I would Sister Dagobert's pluviometer. A slight tension rising in the north with several mood swings to the east, it said, but calm in the central valley. Not such a bad reading really. Those northern tensions dissipate quickly and the eastern swings can even be warded off if one prepares for them. How fortunate that my gauge is in tip-top shape, helping me to live and love better, and not frozen over.

Sprayed myself with a promotional bottle of Miss Dior sitting by the sink, and spared one last thought for the beautiful Jean-Claudi, former man-o-my-heart. Sighed. Perhaps with relief but perhaps not. Adorable and devoted, Horace was his perfect match. Jean-Claudi was getting all the love he could ever need plus more. Both on and off the swing. Certainly, this couple was one of the rare masterpieces of that often mistaken schemer, the Matchmaker.

Sent off another request to Glorietta for a *new* man-o-my-heart. A stay-in-town man, preferably one who can dance. Of course I could hardly ask her for another acrobat or lasso looper. Not only would she not approve, but why would I choose a part-time lover when I could have a full-time, stay-home love-boy? An Arthur Murray man would do fine, a young gentleman with rudimentary merengue training at Mr Murray's studio.

Returning to the tearoom, I found it empty now of the three *mousquetaires*. Where had they gone? I cleared the dishes off and resumed work at my desk, editing an article on the Viva Glam III conference in New York. Top Spoon, Queen Bee, and her mid-spoon sidekick went and brought back Viva Glam lipsticks for all the stay-home spoons. The lipstick is a cat nose pink shade called Twig. I immediately gave mine to Djamila. Twig is simply not for pixy blondes. Djamila pretends not to wear make-up for Koranic reasons, but I know for a fact that she loves it and will wear it when she's with the girls. Moreover she outlines her eyes with kohl regularly, claiming to do so for purely hygienic reasons. Muslim women have a bag of beauty tricks each with a medicinal flipside. Of course this is quite useful when the moral authorities buckle down on the womenfolk which inevitably happens when the menfolk are uneasy and out of work. The ladies who are always labouring are hit the hardest indeed. Suddenly it is dangerous business being a woman, let alone a coquette!

At half six, I went to attend Polish Mass and miraculously came across a copy of the *National Catholic Reporter*, an RC publication which reports on the Good News – and the Bad News a bit, too. It must have been abandoned by some broad-minded RC American tourist. A miraculous find yes, especially in an Old World RC establishment like St Joe's. And I found it just in time. The NCR is sponsoring a Jesus 2006 Art competition. Artists both amateur and established are requested to send in bold, new images which best represent Jesus in the year of our Lord 2006. Winning entries will be made into a keepsake album.

I went home then and got to work right away on my watercolours. My first picture was of a shirtless, beardless Jesus in a low-slung flannel pants (Galliano) walking with a little lamb. Then a second depicted a womanly saviour Maria-Jesus in a white silk fish-print evening gown with diamanté straps (Lacroix), an inflated globe on a string attached to her finger. My last attempt limned a man-loving Jesus-Maria dressed in a lilac georgette suit (Versace) holding the scrotum-shaped sacred heart in his hands.

How difficult to imagine Jesus, Maria-Jesus or Jesus-Maria in anything other than couture. I suppose this is because of my profession. But even so, why shouldn't Jesus 2006 enjoy the raiment of our great sartorial minds? Moreover, it only seems right that he/she should be dressed in something at least as nice as the Pope's Versace cassocks. I'll write a short letter to the NCR along with my submission to explain all this.

When I finally set down my brush it was midnight. Art does require such terrific dedication and endurance (as you well know Dunstan)! Tea and caviar toasts for din-din. Three-minute egg for Jubilee. Hung drawings on clothes-line to dry. Retired.

Feast of Saint Laurence
of Canterbury

If Saint Peter hadn't cracked his whip on you in a dream, you probably would have led a well-fed ecclesiastical life in France and not returned to England to accomplish the formidable task of converting the depraved King Ethelbald. It's a relief to know somehow that even sainties need to be flogged from time to time if only in their dreams. I've never been whipped myself, thank God, but lassoed yes. Indeed!

At last, dear Laurence, my Saturday Night Cowboy has made a

rodeo comeback after weeks out on the range roping Giacomettis and Ernsts.

It'll drive a cowboy crazy. It'll drive the man insane. And a broken home and some broken bones is all he'll have to show. For all the years that he spent chasin' this dream they call Rodeo.

Hearing his heartbreaking ditty through the door, I went to the kitchen and rummaged through the cupboard. Not a bottle to be found. Dry, dry, dry, like a Mormon bye-the-bye. We would just have to drink holy water. Cowboys don't complain. My coin-covered Egyptian belt jingled as I went to answer the door; I had been practising my paddle hips and was in full rehearsal attire: hareem pants and short cropped Indian top, crowned by Claudia. I could tell from the slight fall of Junior's face as I swung open the door that I did not fit the familiar fantasy. Cowboys caroused with brothel wenches in tight corsets that made their grammars pop out, not sequined seraglio sweeties. Still, the sight of so much midriff did please him, I could tell. Cowboys don't complain in any case. Only Frenchmen do.

''Owdy, baby. Look what I bring you.' Junior thrust a six-pack of Budweiser beer at me, proud as can be.

'Oh! But where did you loop that? It can't be true!' I was most impressed by the find though I don't drink Bud because it gives me pimples.

'It is a cowboy's secret. And this is the truth!'

Well said, I thought. A cowboy never lies but knows how to keep a secret. Lord knows but those broncos do talk. Junior then took a can from the pack, pulled the aluminum tongue. The metallic snap heralded our (h)appy (h)our.

'Can I have a glass?' he enquired. Should I tell him, I wondered, that real cowboys don't drink from the Cup? Deliberated over this for ten seconds then decided to drop it. He will learn the true ways at Rodeo College; who am I after all to teach him the mores and manners of the West. I'm from Florida after all and know nothing of cows, though I do know a bit about crocodiles and their accessories. I fetched us both a glass and poured our libation; pretended then to sip the beverage whilst surreptitiously pouring it into a pot of African Violets.

'Oh my!' I exclaimed of a sudden, for now the full impact of Junior's cowboy couture hit me: he was wearing a most extraordinary leather leg-wear, studded down the sides with silver dollars and which formed a frame around the family jewels meant to venerate the highlight that they are.

'Chaps! Oh my!'

I was confronted, just then, with a vision of Jean-Claudi wearing the likes, and this most seductive mental picture coupled with this junior-in-the-flesh before me, piqued my desire in the most extraordinary manner. *It'll drive a cowgirl crazy. It'll drive the woman insane. Chaps on a lad make a girl go right mad!*

'Come on, baby. I gonna make you see the daylight.'

'Oh, but I'd rather see the moonlight!'

My plea for the softer illumination of night's satellite was not heard, or at least not heeded. Junior was already fixin' for ridin' in the bright light of day. I flipped back on the main switch and bent down to mine the jewels, kissing them to bless the journey ahead. On the pleasure trail to the diamond D ranch!

I must say that Junior's hard work at rodeo practice has certainly paid off and not only in the boudoir *paraît-il.* I learned over coffee and cocoa in the morn, that he passed his audition for the Wild West Show and will be performing in a number called 'Good night Lovin'' (how *à propos*!) in which he is to play a buckaroo who saves the life of an Indian Maiden whose braid gets caught on an evil sheriff's saddle horn. Moreover, he has been offered a fully paid scholarship to Rodeo College.

'Oh don't tell me you're leaving soon!'

'Never (h)old on to a cowboy, Remedy. When a buckaroo's got to go, he's got to go.'

Very well. So it's a bit like having to go to the ladies' it seems. Dr Dolittle would say as much, of course. Adult Sex eschews hanging on to the ropes of Saturday Night Cowboys. *Unloose the noose then. Untie the tether. You're on your own boy, just never say never.*

I wished Junior all the best as he took to the wind. But do come back, dear man! And if you fall off a bronco, remember Remedy Ranch out on the romance range! We'll fix you up in no time (you'll give me a hand, won't you Laurence?).

Feast of Saint Godric

Pirate, hermit, trusted friend of bird and beast, fortune-teller, popular songwriter: if ever there were a Saint of all Trades, it was you, Godric. Apparently the Top Four Holy Songs you wrote are still being played to this day, though you have to go to Durham to hear them. I'm not sure I'll be able to make it there, Godric, what with all my spoon responsibilities. Why I hardly manage to get to Mass as it is!

Today, for example, I was ten minutes late to midday mass, having had to stop by the grocery store first for a bottle of water. The baptismal fount is nearly dry, you see, and needs a holy refill. Blessed water evaporates so quickly! Plus, I did manage to bless Junior three times over the course of our *amourette*, using more water than I had anticipated. Oh, but it was worth it! I'm pleased to say that Junior liked it! Very much!

Was a bit concerned about bothering Père Ricard again, but as he is my parish priest, and therefore responsible for blessing my bottles, I did not hesitate to ask. Fortunately, Père Ricard was of a reasonably sober disposition and operated the blessing matter of factly, without commentary. *Merci, mon Père!* I do wonder why in French we must address a priest as 'My father', which seems so appropriative. It's on equal footing with Daddy! Only slightly more formal of course.

Took Sister Dagobert out to lunch and asked her about this. Sister Dagobert explained that it was not appropriative but filial. That the Catholic church is modelled after a family consisting of fathers, sisters, brothers, sons and daughters, and the Communion of Saints as ancestors. Indeed, I saw her point. So it seems to be. But where, I had to ask her, were the mothers? Sister Dagobert was at a loss for a moment but then found her answer in her own back yard.

'Why there is a Mother Superior in most convents,' she offered.

True enough, those mothers do exist, although their numbers continue to dwindle drastically. Mothers there may be but fathers far outnumber them in this family affair. And, as in China, where gynocide has set the country on a third, crooked leg, this imbalanced Mother/Father ratio may well lead to family dysfunction. Sister Dagobert did see my point and suggested that we pray for restored balance in both China and Rome.

Ran the bottle home, poured it into the fount and returned to the office. Hardly had time to pay the spoons a post-gym hello: the phone was ringing too urgently.

'Remedy!' Joanna was shouting into the phone. 'You won't believe this.'

'Believe what?'

'That I'm going to be hosting a luncheon for Eléanore de la Motte de la Motte-Piquet. Two weeks from Thursday. You have to come!'

I looked quickly at my calendar to make sure there was a clearing. And yes, the coast was clear. I could make my way to the luncheon safely.

'Just tell me what time.'

'Twelve thirty would be good. And, oh… I was maybe thinking that you could do a feature on her for the site? You know, just a little spotlight or something. That wouldn't be too hard, would it?'

'Oh, Joanna, I'll do whatever I can!'

'You're a doll, Remedy.'

'Am I?'

'Oh! And do you think you could get that photographer friend of yours to come. What's his name? Jean-Claude?'

'Jean-Claudi,' I corrected her. 'Best to send him and his friend Horace an invitation directly. I'll say something to them when I see them.'

'Can you believe it, Remedy? Eléanore – we're on very familiar terms now – was absolutely lovely when I suggested the luncheon in her honour. She's so down-to-earth – for a designer that is. You just can't believe it! And her couture is to die for! I mean to die for! Who knows, maybe I will just have a Motte de la Motte-Piquet gown for the Ball of Marvels!'

Joanna was almost giddy with happiness. I wished her all the best and promised to pray on her behalf to Saint Evrard, patron saint of seamstresses. May she, for all her troubles, be fashionably awarded.

Fortunately, Joanna was so engaged in her luncheon ministrations that she did not ask me about the Marquis, who I certainly have been avoiding. True, I have returned several Marquis phone calls, but most carefully, making sure to speak to answering machine rather than to nobleman himself. And always presenting polite excuses. Yes, I am always terribly polite, exhibiting the innate gentility of the crumb-class.

I spent the rest of the afternoon writing a communiqué on bustle dresses with leg-o-mutton sleeves (Lacroix). Couldn't get the song, 'Fill the Cup O Beautiful and Give It to Me!' out of my head, which in fact behoved me, as I was able to practise the dance in the ladies' room for quite a while. But then there were too many knocks on the door and I could tell the girls were tired of using the Gents, even though they are used to the detour. And so I did leave the WC and its mirror, which is an excellent aid for practising dramatic expression although I am not used to observing myself minus Claudia. Nothing is quite the same without her.

Samira is insisting we perfect our facial interpretation of the song's passionate tale. At one point in the dance, we are to appear as if fighting off tears. This is not so simple, for once you evoke that saddest of emotions, the tears do want to flow. And how! We have all cried at one time or another, which Samira declares highly inappropriate. I'm sure she is right, but how difficult to learn lachrymal restraint! Several of the girls in the ballet have been discussing the possibility of going on tour in Egypt. I quite like the idea myself but had to remind them of the Sir Reginald Hamly problem. It seemed entirely improbable to me that Samira would risk the trip.

'What about Morocco?' I suggested.

And the girls agreed, especially if we could dance for His Majesty the King and Princess Lala. Or if not, at the very least, the Minister of Finance.

Before leaving the office, I visited Djamila and her Hadj. Hadj Mohammed's goitre has almost entirely gone away thanks to the repeated and efficacious prayers of the celebrated marabout, Hadj El Kadhir. Djamila explained that El Kadhir was not only the most sought after Algerian healer in Paris but also a second cousin on the maternal side. Apparently there is a year-long waiting list to see him, but Djamila, being kin, gets into his office the very day.

'When are you going to Algeria?' I asked Djamila, remembering the Constantine cousin. It seemed to me that her wedding was some-time soon.

'The wedding is next week but much of the cooking is done. I'm flying to Algiers tomorrow with four suitcases of cakes and a trunk filled with the bridal attire. God-be-willing we will all arrive alive.'

'Yes, God-be-willing. Please give my kindest regards to the Constantine cousin.'

'Yes, I will. It will interest her to know that a Nazarene assisted her seamstress.'

Djamila then took my hand and spoke to me with concern.

'Please, Daughter, while I'm gone, would you keep an eye on my husband? I'm afraid he is lost without me. Just do like I do. Point your finger.'

'I'm sure he will be fine,' I reassured Djamila as we both watched the pilgrim pushing the vacuum cleaner behind and underneath the desks. Indeed, he knows the job by heart. There is no need for a pointer.

'Yes, God-be-willing he shall be.'

Wishing Djamila *bon voyage* again, I left the office and made my way to St Joe's. A1 class was to start in fifteen minutes and, alas, I was not entirely prepared. Snuck into the annex through a side door and quickly organized the classroom, apostolic style, so as not to waste precious class time. True, the students understand Jesus' preference for the circle, yet they will only rearrange their seating at my request. Such respectful wee ones. All very dedicated to *maman* and, by long but sure extension, to me as well.

Once the circle was set, I slipped a long Moroccan muumuu over my head in preparation for our mock-communion celebration. Djamila's Leila had given me this djellaba to wear to her son's circumcision, which I did not in the end attend, and while I was at first bewildered by the roomy gown, I now understood its purpose. It was essential to be robed for today's A1 lesson, for without such attire, how would I have made a convincing priest?

Now, a Eucharistic celebration rehearsal was not suggested in the *Change Your Heart* manual, and yet it seemed to me indispensable. The best way to learn anything is to try your hand and heart at it. I wanted the children to receive a preliminary communion before being dressed in white and sent to the altar for the veritable First Communion. True, I am not officially vested with the priestly powers to consubstantiate the bread and wine, but by exercising the imagination – an essential practice of the faithful – perhaps something would come of it. Certainly it was worth a try.

199

I emptied my bag of the necessary class accoutrements – the bread basket, the ginger snaps, the chalice (a wine glass) and the grape juice – onto the table behind me. Here was our altar, manifestly makeshift, yes, but perhaps its nakedness would force us to keep our undivided attention on the essentials, which is to say the bread and wine (here cake and juice) being turned into flesh and blood. Soon the children appeared in the doorway, looking timidly in. They are so dear and do need constant encouragement.

'Please, come in children and take a seat. Let's get ready for class.'

And so they entered our humble chapel, smiling shyly, the girls whispering to their neighbours as little girls are wont to do, the boys comparing those miniature Renaults they keep in their pockets.

'Do you realize that in two weeks you will be walking up the aisle of St Joseph's to celebrate your second sacrament, which is First Communion? Children, are you excited?'

I found myself growing enthusiastic just thinking of the big day and felt my charisma, which according to *Change Your Heart* is a gift granted by the Holy Ghost, spread around the circle. Maria-Helena clapped her hands. Little Xavier put his pinkies in his mouth and whistled. And Marthe, a quiet child whose voice I had not yet heard, asked to be excused to go to the ladies' room.

'Yes, children, it's a wonderful day. And to make it an even better one, we will use our class time today as a First Communion rehearsal. It is important to prepare for this major event in your lives. We have spoken a great deal about Jesus' multiplication miracle and how afterwards he taught in the synagogue that his body was the good food and his blood the good drink. Many people refused to believe him including many of his disciples. Only the truer ones did and they proclaimed "Yours are the words of Eternal Life". These same apostles partook in the Last Supper, which we continue to celebrate at Mass.

'Now, it is important to remember that Jesus is present in the Eucharist, but *invisibly* so. The bread and wine become the real, true, authentic body and blood of Christ, only you cannot expect to see this with your eyes. How is this so? Because the Holy Ghost, who is himself invisible, descends upon the bread and wine to work the body-blood miracle. The bread still tastes like bread and the wine like wine, and we are grateful for this. The invisibility of the miracle is a blessing. For what would it be like, children, to actually eat raw, human flesh and drink the blood of a man? Would this not be an abject and inhuman transgression? Indeed. Therefore, the miracle must be kept so secret as to be invisible. Do not expect to taste and see. What you will be ingesting is everlasting life.'

Having finished this explanation coming almost directly from the *Change Your Heart* teacher's manual, I asked the children to stand up and make a line. Suddenly I was feeling a tremendous fatigue, due, surely, to the difficulty of rendering the complexity of consubstantiation to rudimentary form. After our myriad discussions of multiplication miracles for which visibility is a central feature, I was concerned the children might find the notion of invisibility less appealing. But one must begin somewhere with the lessons of faith, and while we can protect our young ones from the difficulties of belief in their early years, by communion time, the truth must be told. Or at least some of it, to be sure.

My students, however, were not put off in any manner to learn that apprehending the intangible would be the crux of their budding faith. No, they were soldiers, I saw, lined-up and circumscribed. They were ready for rehearsal.

I carefully explained the rules for Eucharistic reception, both the tongue and the cupped hand methods. Then, at the altar, I poured the juice and lifted the chalice and plate of thin ginger rounds I had made the night before, and began the invocation of the Holy Spirit for the consecration. The words flowed freely, from the heart, for what church-going Catholic does not carry these Eucharistic speeches inscribed in the breast? How obvious it was to be a priest and how naturally it came to me! The Lamb-o-God rolled off my tongue. Have mercy on us, Dear Lamb, grant us peace!

With a nod of my head, I gave the signal to move forward. The twelve apprentice apostles slowly, with hearts and minds on the gift of Everlasting Life, advanced to receive rehearsal communion. And how splendidly they did so! There was not one drop or spill, not one missing 'amen'. When they regained their seats, they diligently prayed with bowed heads and folded hands, just as it had been taught to them. I was immensely proud of my apprentice apostles. And of myself as well, for I must say my execution of the priestly duty was nearly flawless. Yes, even Père Ricard would not have performed with such precision. Manifestly, I was a natural rehearsal priest, and my wee but worthy parish took me as their torch-bearing guide, lighting the obscure path of faith.

There I stood, humble princess of my parish, above a deaconess but below a bishopess. The moment was so perfect it nearly became unbearable: yes, I could continue our catechistic Mass with the bene- diction and rite of sending off, indeed, I was prone to do so; yet it dawned on me that for the sake of the children's concentration, it was best to begin anew rather than plough on to *finis*.

And so the second round was begun, this time with cupped hands, whilst the children's attention and Eucharistic devotion remained rapt. Once again, the children performed splendidly, leaving me with no doubt as to the success of their First Communion celebration due to take place in two weeks' time. They were solidly prepared and duty inclined: the sacramental day would be a delight.

When we finished our rehearsal, I removed the roomy robe and helped this week's snack-porter, Marthe, distribute her treat.

'Children, I think you noticed that communion was rather sweet today with cake and juice taking the place of the usual bread and wine. But you should know that when you go to the altar for your First Communion, the hostie will be a thin wafer, more like paper than bread. Sometimes it sticks to the roof of your mouth. If so, let it remain there until it melts. Otherwise you risk choking which would be such a shame. As for the wine, it will have a slightly sour taste although the priest will water it down in memory of Mary Magdalene. I suggest you ask your parents to serve you a small glass of watery wine several times before your communion. This is an excellent way to prepare your taste buds.'

True, it is. At an equally wee age, Mumly used to serve me this preparation every Sunday evening when the Bishop Mahoney arrived as our honourable dinner guest. It made me feel quite grand really, to drink this cordial with the Bishop and Mumly. And so I did not cringe at my first bitter sip of the beverage, but let it warm me sweetly. Bishop Mahoney would sometimes tilt the Burgundy my way saying, 'A topper for you Miss?' but I would graciously refuse, for it is important to show forbearance as a child, especially before such a governor.

Unfortunately it would not have been appropriate of me to offer the watery wine to the catechismal learners. They would have to request this preparation at home, and hopefully most of them would.

'Now, children, peace is not the absence of war but the presence of happiness' (Sister Mary Paul MD, *Change Your Heart*). 'So now, go in peace. They will know you are Christians by your love, children. Yes, by your love! Go and spread peace!'

The bell was rung and my amorous army took leave leaping with joy in their hearts. How lucky their mothers were, reaping the love we had sown in A1.

I headed home, stopping by the corner market for food. All caterers closed by that hour, all pre-prepared dishes now unpurchasable. Catechists should have spouses. And priests too, for that matter, including rehearsal priests. Spouses to greet them with hot roast and potatoes *allouette* when they're done. Had no choice but to make myself scrambled eggs with lardons. Not so bad really with a bottle of Sidi Brahim, that Algerian wine sold after nine p.m. Began preparing this repast for two when I was called away. Who's there? But it was the phone a-ringing requesting a pick-up. I picked up.

'Hello?'

'Remedy? This is Roland speaking.' Indeed it was. The Marquis himself. And now no polite subterfuge available to me. No choice but to speak in direct telephonic discourse to the gentleman.

'Roland! How have you been?'

'Very well, Remedy, very well. I am fortunate to finally reach you. You are a very busy young lady I see.'

Roland speaks very formally I should say, addressing me always as *vous*.

'Oh yes, *en effet*. I work quite a bit in the day and teach in the evenings as well. In fact I just got in.'

'Yes? So you see how very lucky I am!'

'Oh, yes.'

'Tell me Remedy, would you be free a week from Friday? I have two tickets to the opera. Poulenc's *Les Carmélites* is playing. Do you know it?'

I could tell by his superior sounding Marquis de Bourdon tone that he did not suspect I did. Perhaps he perceived this date as a crusty lesson for a Florida crumb.

'Yes, I know it very well in fact, and I would love to go.'

By appealing to my sense of pride, the Marquis succeeded in procuring my assent. And whilst pride may be seen as a sin, it is some-times quite helpful for upholding crumb propriety. And so I made an exception to the no-date policy I had established according to Adult Sex principles – if only for the sake of democracy.

As for *Les Carmélites*, I did know it well. In his Golden Years, which is to say the years he was with us, Richard II had become a prodigious opera aficionado. Our days were rhythmed by the operatic seasons and our happy house grew and quivered with the vicissitudes of those ecstatic voices. He would fly us up to New York for every production at the Met and fly us down when it was over. I had piles of opera colouring books and operatic paper dolls, which I glued to Popsicle sticks, dressed and undressed. The Marquis, I'm afraid, had nothing to teach me. I knew them all.

After several minutes of uneventful chit-chat using the formal *vous* pronoun, the Marquis and I wished each other a good week and hung up. It was all very crusty and polite indeed, which considering how near we got to love on that first, red-pantied date, is perhaps slightly odd. But so it is with crusties. I went back to the kitchen to finish cooking dinner. The eggs were not in good shape but the lardons fared better. Filled Jubilee's dish, then mine. Blessed us both. Retired with Herman (Melville) whilst humming a tune I had never heard before, a kind of Latiny 'Amazing Grace.' Believe I was channelling again (one of your Top Four Holy Songs, Godric?).

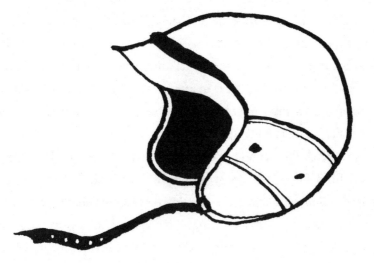

Feast of Saint Rita

Oh 'Saint of the Impossible', can't you turn me into a four-star Adult Sex practitioner? I just need a little push from an Advocate of Desperate Causes like yourself to make the big league. Already, I've come along quite a-ways through personal effort, but if you could just tap me with your 'magical rose that achieves the impossible' (*Concise*), I'd be much obliged.

Here's the twofold news today: Dr Dolittle just sent me a letter informing me she could not publish my von Krysler letter in her column. Why? She was loathe to tell. For someone so frank in her column, she is surprisingly uncandid in her epistolary correspondence. I would simply like to know why! Why, Dr Dolittle? Was not my experience with the acrobat exemplary of correct Adult Sex behavior? Would my story not inspire other *Belle* readers on to Adult Sex success? Now I'll have to write her back, demanding an explanation, adding a paragraph or two on my Rodeo Nights with Junior, which, though not exemplary, are not so far off the mark. Moreover, I still have not heard from Brigitte (I'm afraid she needs a bit of help, Rita). The mail from Saint-Tropez is a bit slow these days because of all those private helicopters taking up the runways.

Now here's the second piece of news (saving the best for last): I got a card from Junior who's now stationed near Béziers at the Rodeo College. *I Still Miss You, Baby, But My Aim's Gettin' Better*, it said, a point he illustrated with a drawing which in a pornocracy would have been considered High Art indeed! Oh I was simply charmed! But sad, too (though I certainly won't tell Dolittle); his semester runs straight through July. No holidays for cowboys. No leave or reprieve from the Ro-de-o! Alas!

At noon, I made a trip back to Gambi's with Claudia in my purse. She seems to be losing hair these days, and seeing how infrequently I wear her (which is to say, to dance class, dance rehearsal and whilst shopping), there shouldn't be so much fall-out. Fearing a flaw, I saw no other choice but to render her to her maker. Perhaps for repair, maybe an exchange. At the very least, for reassurance. Little did I know going in that Gambi would offer none of these. No, instead, that remarkable proprietor huffed and puffed. Accused me of accusing her merchandise! Dared I detect a defect? No, I dared not, for fear this woman would pull out my *own* hair. I merely posed a question and

Gambi pulled the seams before my eyes as proof. Handmade in the Philippines. Hand stitched by happy hands, she insisted.

I tried hard to hide my dismay. Dismay over the hard-working hands, dismay over the loss of the lock. But I knew I could hold back my complaint no more.

'Gambi, I want a refund!'

I could see from how her legs tensed-up like tree trunks that Gambi was not about to hand over the tender. She made no move toward her register. Instead, admitting at last that my distress could not be expediently angered away, she went into her back room and began to reinforce the stitch with her own needle and thread, adding several strands of replacement locks. She worked quickly but patiently. It seemed to calm her, as working with the hands often does. Gambi had not bothered to close the door and several other customers came around to watch her too. She was fascinating to observe; it was not unlike watching a queen at a typewriter. The sight was unexpected, the personage both lessened and aggrandized. I thought for a moment of the Lord who belittled himself to come down to the size of Man. Some loved him all the more for it. Others less.

Being one of those who honour the humble downsizing of the self, for it in fact creates a larger self, I admired Gambi immensely and could not refrain from exclaiming in awe, 'Jesus! Look at her go!' As if in response to my outburst, a woman who had been standing beside me spat on the ground. Had I spoken wrongly? I turned to take a reading of my neighbour's brow, to check her gauge as it were, and saw, to my great surprise, that this lady was Cindy of Hollywood, my side-walk pedicurist. I almost cried out, but refrained. Was put in check by the cool glance she sent me down her nose. *Dare you?* she seemed to be warning. I replied by turning my gaze away. Still, I could not help it. I pushed my sandalled foot out in the balletic third position. Perhaps, I thought, she would recognize the labour of her hands. Indeed, my toenails were still painted with her lavender polish. A stubborn polish it was. With terrific hold and staying power. Surely she would see it and recognize a client. Someone who sat with her at the Victor Hugo circle and offered her feet. But my pedicurist did not look down on her work. Instead she advanced, laying all her stepping weight upon that foot of mine until I could no longer refrain from crying out again.

'My foot! My God! My foot!' Here were words a trained chiropodist knows by heart, a kind of *bismillah*, a call to action as it were. But this woman had not gone to foot college, had received only the training of her observation. An autodidact of the foot decor profession, she had no medical or ethical sympathies to date. '*Excusez-moi*' was the only compensation she offered for the wrong. A quick, terse formality, uttered with disdain. But I accepted it, my foot now in my own hand, being loved and rubbed there.

Gambi then came out, with Claudia duly repaired. Handing her to me, she was about to say something when the pedicurist flew at her with a sickly Cindy of Hollywood. Their conversation was in Swahili; I could not follow it, but other women in the store joined in, shouting and flying their arms at each other. I tucked Claudia into a shopping bag and limped out of the boutique. No sense in staying around for the scene.

Back at the office, the spoons greeted me with concern. *Remedy! What's wrong with your foot? Oh là là!* and so forth. Yoga spoon made a tea-bag compress for the swelling. I was much obliged. *Tell us what happened! Oh là là!* So I told them about Claudia and my trip to Gambi's for the repair and about my neighbour's trespassing upon my foot. The spoons were entirely sympathetic but mostly quite impressed that I was the owner and bearer of a genuine wig. How odd! I explained to them that they're the easiest things in the world to get your hands on and that Gambi's prices are very reasonable. Wigs are wonderful to wear when you go shopping for example, I told them. No-one recognizes you! Of course all the spoons wanted to try on Claudia, a request to which I gladly consented. How wonderful to share your blessings with others! What a pleasure to hear the spoons cry out in delight at their Claudia debut! How I do love Show and Tell! At the office or anywhere.

I spent the rest of the afternoon with my foot propped on the desk. The tea compresses were quite effective. Wrote article on toe cleavage, this summer's latest trend. Toe cleavage and tankinis are all the rage. It's best if you can manage both, which means wearing a tankini whilst remaining togged in Wonder Sandals, a toe cleavage enhancer. Women may not enjoy keeping their shoes on at the beach, but now it's recommended to do so and I suppose that many will oblige.

I stayed at work until Hadj Mohammed showed up. For the sake of dear Djamila away in Constantine, I offered the pilgrim a cup of coffee which he gladly accepted. We spoke a bit about St Augustine, but mostly about Averroës, a Medieval Arabian philosophical doctor who taught his students the entire medical repertory through poetic recitations. Hadj Mohammed began reciting the celebrated doctor's litany on obstetrics for me. It was absolutely lovely, so sing-songy. I must say I was impressed by his ability to recite at whim – not unlike myself in the role of rehearsal priest. Perhaps this is what Catholics and Muslims

211

have most in common: the ability to commit to memory and chant. I bid the Hadj good evening and happy cleaning. Though I did not point the finger.

Getting home was quite an adventure. As I stepped forward from the sidewalk to cross the Rue Cler, a helmeted man on a scooter nearly ran me over! Fearing for my life I jumped to the right, and he, for the same reason it should seem, steered away the best he could and skidded to a stop. Then we both turned around, myself ready to fire invective, and caught sight of each other. The man removed the white protective bubble from his head, dropped his scooter and ran to me, 'Miss, are you fine? Did I hurt you in any way?'

My chest heaved, then descended. All the accusing words I was about to cry out recoiled and were as if vacuumed up from some aspirating force within me. A wave of woozy pleasure rippled through my belly, for it was Mouktar! Handsome Mouktar! And his brow was furrowed with concern.

'Miss, are you fine?' Then recognizing me, he added, 'How have you been? It is a great pleasure to see you again, though I regret these circumstances. Tell me, are you fine?'

I was hit, literally bowled over, not by the scooter, but by the beauty of the man who had sat astride it and was now at my side caressing me with his voice. 'Please' I said, trying to gather my emotions. 'Please...' And rather than misinterpret my intention, Mouktar repeated the very same word as if to confirm me. 'Please' he said with warm tenderness. 'Please' he said again as his mouth came alive with a smile that could set the thousand and one candles of a vizier's palace alight with incandescent flame. And now looking into his golden eyes, I was just about to say, once again, what had become our hypnotic, amorous word, when Shlomi himself emerged from his restaurant, waving his arms at Mouktar:

'Get it to them while it's hot! No-one wants a cold pizza. Get cracking!'

Called to attention, Mouktar responded by putting on his helmet. But I could see he was loathe to leave me. He looked at me imploringly, yes, as if there was more he desired to tell me before he turned away to get back on his scooter. 'Please,' I said at last, though somewhat differently due to Shlomi's interruption. 'Go in peace.' And so Mouktar sped away, though not so peacefully I should add.

I arrived home, my nerves and emotions greatly excited by this fortuitous encounter, to a ringing phone. Oh not again! I said to myself, both worrying that it was and hoping that it was not Roland. But it wasn't the Marquis complicating an already delicate dating situation with a rain check or game plan alteration. No, it was Mumly, calling from Florida.

'Princess? Is that you?' She always does an identity check when I leave off the 'h' in hello.

'Yes, it is.'

'Oh good! How is everything in Paris? How's the weather?'

'It's raining Mumly, but I'm wearing my sandals anyway.' I had to let Mumly know that although the weather was terrible I had not given up.

'That's a good girl. Listen, did I tell you I was going to Pebble Beach?'

'No, why there?'

'On a golf tour, Princess. I made the cut this year! I'll be playing in the Ladies' Open.'

'Oh! Congratulations Mumly! That's wonderful news!'

'Oh it is Princess! It's absolutely fabulous, isn't it? I'm already starting to pack.'

'Don't forget your rain gear, Mumly. And your woollies.' Mumly has been living in Florida for so long that she's likely to forget cool weather essentials.

Pebble Beach is a bit like Miami except that it's foggy and almost nobody speaks Spanish there. Pebble Beach is where all the overheated wealthy people go. The people who have made their money in the sun. Miami is just the opposite really. Wouldn't it be wonderful if Mumly could meet another Richard II type, only slightly younger and on the overheated side? It would do her a world of good, I think. I am really very excited to think that both Mumly and I have made the competitive cut in our respective activities.

'Did I tell you Mumly, that I may be going on tour to Morocco with Samira's dance troupe?'

'To Morocco? Now why would you go there, Princess? Isn't that like Tijuana?'

'Not at all, Mumly. It's a royal kingdom with a King and a Princess Lala. Haven't you ever heard of them?'

'No, Princess, I'm afraid we don't hear much about those people here.'

'Well, it is a-ways away. Listen, Mumly, have a wonderful tour and do remember the woollies.'

'I will Princess. Give my love to the Pope when you see him.'

'Will do, Mumly.'

I hung up the phone happy to know that Mumly is doing so splendidly. No mention of the dropsy. Indeed, to have made it to the Ladies'

Championship, all ills must have subsided. All swelling must be down. I went to the fount and made a special blessing for Mumly at the Pebble Beach Championships.

Retiring to the *canapé* with Jubilee, Herman and a glass of Sidi Brahim, I offered a toast to Mouktar and trembled a bit. To the beautiful Moor! I had some crackers and cheese too but then fell asleep on Herman and my cheese platter, waking up at four a.m. in time to put myself into bed. Slept on with dear dreams of fairy godmother Glorietta granting all desires (thank you for lending her your magic rose, Rita). Wish-fulfilment mechanism working beautifully.

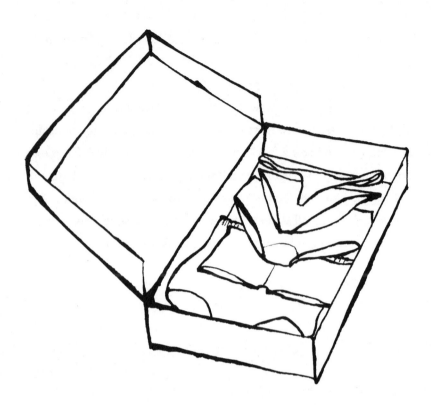

Feast of Saint William of Rochester

I wonder why that foundling boy you adopted murdered you near
Rochester one fine day. Was it that he didn't want to go to
Jerusalem with you, yet you forced him into it, pulling him by his
orphaned ear? Perhaps you've noticed how Sister Dagobert uses gentle
persuasion to commit me to pilgrimhood; true, I've not yet begun the
march, but when I do, I certainly won't assassinate her. We reap what
we sow, not so, William?

Neighbour Jeromino appeared at my door this morning at eight,
not solo but with Felix wrapped in *Rouge*, the Communist canard.

'Please,' he supplicated lifting his bundle for me to peer into, 'the last rites, Felix is finished.'

Looking into the newspaper, I saw a contented but vaporized Felix, fat and in favourable health, reeking, like my neighbour, of the Marrakech weed. Clearly, this was a hallucinatory concern, the whim of a wandering, herb-steeped mind. And yet how could I refuse my neighbour? My only neighbour on the stoop? And Junior's brother at that! Indeed. In any case, Neighbour Jeromino's request was simple and, when all is said and done, within my power to fulfil.

'Come in,' I said welcomingly but solemnly. 'Please have a seat.'

But Neighbour Jeromino did not sit down. No, the poor pensioned soul stood all a-tremble in my living room, awaiting the sacrament. I knew I would have to work quickly.

In the bedroom, I threw on the muumuu. Would this do? Suddenly I wished I had a stand-up collar, that choker that makes the priest. As a facsimile, I fastened a white silk scarf around my neck and went so attired into the kitchen to prepare the unction: a tablespoon of olive oil on a saucer (rapidly blessed, using same gestures and words as water-blessing Père Ricard), plus a lemon wedge and a tablecloth. Covering the table with cloth and, with all preparations in place, I commenced.

'Please,' I bid Neighbour Jeromino, 'bring me the beast.'

Neighbour Jeromino obediently stepped forward with the tabby comfortably dazed and dozing in sheaves of labour union news. I laid my hands over the creature who, for all I knew, could very well be severely indisposed and simply not show it. With cats it is hard to tell, especially cats who are excessively exposed to hazardous fumes. The thought that dear Felix may indeed be ill, moved me to quick action. The priest's passion, I saw, is not unlike the empathetic persuasions of a paramedic fireman or emergency room intern (or a saint who bosses a foundling?). All are called to save. Be it vital flesh or soggy spirit. Every rescue is a passion play. Every rescue worker, a passion flower. And so I began my ascent as a climbing instrument of passion, upright, branching, in bloom. Drawing upon the precedents set by the veterinary Saint Francis himself (a good man, William, never once wounded by his adopted beasts), I anointed the feline's head and paws with the holy oil. Immediately, Felix began a-purring. His response to the sacred unction was instantaneous. How sensitive the wee ones are to the intangible, to the elusive manners of the divine. And how our saint of Assisi tried to spread the word! Neighbour Jeromino bowed his head and joined in the Our Father which unfortunately he interspersed with the Act of Contrition. Of course it's wrong to medley prayers but more and more hasty Roman Catholics are opting for such two-for-one miscellany. Perhaps one day the Vatican will greenlight this practice, but for the moment mixed company is not tolerated. Poor Felix. Would he know of his Master's mix-up? No, he would not for I covered by singing the Our Father in High Latin. To Felix everything sounded fine. The sacrament was now administered with only the benediction remaining.

'Go in Peace,' I advised Neighbour Jeromino and Felix. 'Be good and love.' I then washed my hands with lemon wedge and dried them with tablecloth.

Felix shucked the communist newspaper and ran to the door with Jubilee at his tail. Shockheaded Neighbour Jeromino bowed and handed me a thanksgiving envelope filled with home-rolled cigars.

'Oh! I don't smoke, Neighbour Jeromino. Please take this back.' But my Neighbour would not allow the return.

'Perhaps you don't smoke today,' he said with his usual solemnity, 'but tomorrow you will.'

My, my! Neighbour Jeromino is full of surprises, I must say. If these little hashies endow a soul with prophetic powers, perhaps tomorrow I will puff!

'Goodbye, Neighbour Jeromino. Please pray to Saint Francis.'

I shut the door and made a quick cup of coffee as well as a verbena infusion to calm Jubilee, which I had to induce medicinally with a dropper. Jubilee gets much too excited around Felix. There is certainly chemistry there but obviously the wrong kind. I must ask Glorietta to send Jubilee the appropriate friend, one who will complement him coolly. I threw off the muumuu and put on my mauve uni. A raincoat over that and off to work.

À La Mode Online is now launching promotional campaigns with lots of prizes to win. One of these, I just learned, is a Motte de la Motte-Piquet evening gown with a pavé diamond chronograph over each breast. I called Joanna immediately to let her know. 'You have to give it a try!' I encouraged her. 'It's a lottery but there are also three questions to answer. You might win, Joanna!'

Indeed there were three questions to which Joanna could easily have provided three correct answers, seeing how *intime* she has become with Motte de la Motte-Piquet. And yet because her Motte-Piquet courtship was in full swing and sure to reap a gown, Joanna would be no vulgar player. It was the means of achieving the prize which counted, she explained. The work that one put into it. Indeed, Joanna has devoted a great deal of her personal time and energy to the Motte de la Motte-Piquet cause. In the end, she will bear that gown away and know that effort, not chance availed her. So it seems that in Presbyterianism labour is favoured over fortune. For why else would Joanna think this way? Answered the three questions myself under the name of Dorothy Wayward and sent in my electronic coupon.

The spoons have been arriving to work increasingly late due to morning appointments it seems. Today five of them showed up together at eleven all dressed in python: python coats, boots, pants, skirts, and even panties (Top Spoon). I must say I felt a bit out of place in my mauve uni. The whole reason for the uni after all is to free me of fashion imperatives. Yet today python-wear has become the official spoon uniform, infringing thus upon my liberties. This is our uniform, the spoons seemed to be saying, wear it or weep! Oh, I did cry just a bit – if only for those poor snakes. Thankfully though, theirs is only a come-and-go uni – tomorrow all python pieces will be taken to the cleaners and forgotten for a time. Few spoons have uni staying power like I do.

But the big surprise today was the powder room. That chamber which I knew so well, formerly designed for polite dot.com lady lounging, now resembled a Turkish hammam. Only without the steam and the lady wrestlers. A kind of Cleopatra Club, as it were, but in facsimile form. This transformation appealed to an Oriental sense of beauty and refinement: emerald Marrakech zelliges blanketed the walls and floor, coloured glass lanterns lit the room like a dim jewel and thick, silk draperies collected with tasselled brocade ropes curtained the stalls. The sweet murmurs of a fountain seemed to whisper to the ears of ladies-only. Rose petals floated in its pool. Where am I? I wondered. In Lala's boudoir?

Just as I had posed the question, a toilet flushed and from behind a green silk curtain appeared yoga spoon. She went to wash her hands in the sink, a sea-green ceramic basin depicting exotic birds and pomegranates. To dry them she conveniently found a canary-yellow and Byzantine-blue gazelle motif linen set on the mosaic countertop for this purpose.

'What has happened?' I asked my colleague as she made to leave. 'Where are we?'

'Didn't you hear about this, Remedy? We're doing that feature we talked about, you know, "What designers do to bathrooms?"'

'Oh!' I said pretending to remember, whilst remembering nothing at all.

'Yves Saint Laurent sent someone here over the weekend to do all this. Next week it'll be Gaultier's turn. The camera crew already came through and took all the shots they needed. Don't worry about messing things up.'

Indeed! Mess things up? At times, I clearly do not understand the spoon mentality. Manifestly, I could not use this royal chamber for restroom purposes. Read a book by the whispering water-spring yes, but discreetly pee behind the draperies I would not. Went to the Gents instead where, luckily, all stalls were free.

Most of the morning was spent browsing on the Internet looking at unofficial Pucci sites, the most distinguished of which was Lulu-Maria Ortega de Zaperfield's site, *Pucci4thepoor.com*. I had never heard of the Ortega de Zaperfield but apparently she owns the *very* distinguished, very *carated* Zaperfield diamond, which she wears with a security device on her ring finger. If she were to lose the ring she would lose her finger with it. She prefers it this way as she could not bear to look upon that digit without the diamond crown.

'Take them both or leave me in peace!' Such were the words she once uttered to a thief in Brindisi.

A brave woman, she nearly lost her entire hand. Fortunately the villain had no saw. Ortega de Zaperfield explains all this on her personal welcome page. *Pucci4thepoor.com* is an auction site where Pucci owners donate their Pucci perennials which are then sold to potential Pucci buyers. Proceeds go to the P.P. Foundation whose mission it is to dress the orphans of London, Paris and Milano. Downloaded info for Top Spoon who wants to throw an Online Pucci party.

With a sense of spring-inspired joy, I skipped out of the office at ten past twelve sharp. Not for Mass but for a picnic lunch in the Tuileries gardens. I picked up comestibles at sidewalk bakery: club sandwich, pistachio macaroon, lunch-sized bottle of Evian (profane, not blessed). Ah! But there was bit of sun betwixt the clouds today. And a girl must know how to appreciate the rare commodity, how to soak the sun in and save it for the rainy days. Of which there are so many! Alas, so many in pluvial Paris! There I sat within that surround of sculpted Tuileries nudes, gazing at the Obelisk of Luxor, my lunch on my lap.

Ah Luxor! Love in Luxor! It is a song as much as a tempting thought. Samira played it once, only once, and yet its melancholic, Oriental strains came back to me as if it lodged in some deep coil of my ear a-waiting to play. Imagine, I thought as I unwrapped my club sandwich, a Luxorian boudoir with a Luxorian prince, trained in the arts of love. As skilled as Johannes von Krysler but with princely talents too. Mouktar immediately came to mind. Now *there's* a peach of a prince! Fruit trees would be his trapeze, and our love would swing amongst the branches. Ah! Luxor! Perhaps one day I will go there for a royal amourette. But before Luxor, alas, there is Rome, my outstanding obligation to Rome. I will go when I am ready. Ready with a pilgrim prince by my side. Ready to hold loving hands and gaze upon the angels.

Turning my gaze from the obelisk, I observed the garden locals around me. Tourists mostly, but also a good number of celibatarians like myself, sitting alone with sandwiches. I then heard a voice beside me, speaking words I well knew.

'Soul of Christ, sanctify me,' spoke my neighbour.

'Body of Christ, save me!' I responded. My neighbour turned to look at me and I, him. It was a brother I saw, a hooded Capuchin.

'Blood of Christ, inebriate me!' he continued

'Water from the side of Christ, wash me!' I followed.

'Passion of Christ, strengthen me!'

'O good Jesus, hear me!'

We remained silent then for a moment and did not continue the *Anima Christi*. Why? Perhaps we both felt we had said enough. Acquaintance was made and the Lord had heard. For a moment all was still between us until the bearded brother pulled out two foam rabbits from his hidden habit pocket.

'Watch,' he said. And so I did. He then closed the rabbits in his fist and made a wide figure eight with his arm several times. When he finished this gesture, he opened his fist again and on it now sat five rabbits! The same two he began with plus three wee ones, obviously the progeny of the first two. I simply could not believe it. A multiplication miracle before my very eyes!

'Brother, please,' I implored, 'could you do this for the children in my catechism A1 class? They have heard all about the parable of the loaves and fishes and the El Paso story. As RC learners, this would mean a great deal to them.'

'Call me Brother Gabin.'

'Pleased to meet you, Brother Gabin.'

'I'm not sure, Sister, that this would be a good thing.'

'Oh, I believe it would be. Certainly it would. What they need is a concrete demonstration of the multiplication principle. Honestly, yours is the best I've seen yet.'

'The Lord's work does keep a humble servant busy, Sister.'

'And is the humble servant not rewarded for his troubles?'

Manifestly, Brother Gabin needed an incentive, which, after all is entirely understandable. I let him know that he could expect recompense and to prove that I was trustworthy, I offered him half of my club sandwich.

'No thank you,' he said, eyeing the pistachio macaroon.

'Please,' I said, with filial comprehension. 'Take the cake.'

I left the garden in very good spirits due to this fortuitous encounter with the multiplication man, soon to visit A1 with his procreative demonstration. Oh the minors will love it I know! Stopped by the Café Beaubourg for a quick espresso. The bartender was terribly busy but gave me a chocolate wedge all the same. Seeing I had donated dessert to Brother Gabin, I was most grateful for that wedge. The coffee and wedge were consumed in record time. True, in an ideal world one would not make stop-and-go visits to the Café Beaubourg where there is so much to see. Yet I tried my best to see most of it in the short run: the table of bleach-haired foundlings in skintight tees (best to stay away, William), the cinematic *tête-à-tête* on the settee, the

Three Graces puffing on Gitanes cigarettes, rotting their pearls, the twin brothers sipping apricot juice, holding hands beneath the table. Yes, I saw what I could see and blew them all a kiss. Paying with kindly gratuity, I left promptly to get to work on time. Most of the afternoon was spent in a spoon meeting discussing the Online Pucci party. Top Spoon has already taken several ideas from the Ortega de Zaperfield site. Though I expressed my concern about this conspicuous plagiarism, I was outvoted. Certainly because of my accent, that Florida marker. Sister Dagobert has finally come to understand that I am not a child, but rather an alien, registered with French immigration. Legal for the moment but one never knows. She has taken me under her wing as a near peer, no longer as an *orpheline*. The spoons, however, have trouble with the alien feature at times. They are dear, yes, but so impatient with any new twist on their tongue. So protective of their language. I did do my best but was vetoed all the same.

Fortunately I was able to leave early for the half six Mass where I prayed for the forgiveness of all spoon trespasses. The priest ended today's homily with the Miracle of Warsaw. A remarkable story indeed about the artless virgin Weronika who was seduced by the lascivious voice of Lucifer.

'Go my beauty, and fetch the knife,' he whispered with blatant bedroom intimation. 'Cut out your heart, my love, and offer it to me.'

Weronika, an impressionable virgin, obeyed the devil's orders, believing herself in love. Not long after the sacrifice, Weronika's brother came into the room and found her close to dead, her heart lying unhooked upon her sleeve.

'Oh Holy Mother!' he supplicated. 'Restore to Weronika what is lawfully hers in the name of our Lord, Your Son!'

The brother did not cry or wail: he had belief. He was also a photographer and began taking pictures of his distressed sibling intuiting that such snapshots would be needed as proof in the coming days. Then, before his very eyes, he saw the heart crawl like a crab back into her chest, and the skin close over the wound. Weronika was resuscitated and her ears were henceforth made Lucifer-proof. Rumour of the miracle immediately spread throughout Warsaw and when the film was developed and proof made apparent, the Bishop ordered a special conversion feast to be held. It was a great success with sausages and drinks a-plenty. Enthusiasts flew Weronika banners portraying her both with and without the wound. Three Musulmans and one Jew converted. Confessees far outnumbered the exhausted, belaboured priests.

My, my! Truly an amazing miracle, recounted with a formidable accent which was not discredited or vetoed by the more charitable believers. Mass ended at half seven making all Mass-goers late for dindin. I arrived at the Rue Cler caterers just in time to get the last half of roast chicken and a serving of potatoes *allouette*. A brioche for Jubilee who does love that sugar on the top.

Upon my arrival home, I found a package awaiting me with the concierge. Who was it from? Joanna! My dear friend! I opened it up immediately upon entering the flat with the help of Jubilee for whom everyday is a birthday. Inside was a La Perla box containing five pairs of size thirty-six white cotton panties in five different cuts from the tiny thong to the waist-high granny panty! Oh, Joanna! Dear Joanna! She does think of everything! And how she looks after me! Ever since our studentine days at Vassar when she would find me a date to every Black and White Ball. And always with a Harvard collegian. Someone she used to go to school with in Exeter, a dear-old-friend, now out of uniform and since become a gentleman of sorts. How little things have changed: today she still wants the best for me, yes, the best, which in our current context, she believes to be a marquis. It is difficult and ultimately useless to disagree with Joanna who is so certain of her perceptions. She will never need glasses, my friend, not even at a ripe old age. She sees the field all too clearly, knows every ploy played by man, understands the subtle sways of timing. In short she is a winner, and surely one fortunate enough to be the recipient of this victor's care and amical attentions has no reason to balk. Impossible now to shirk the duties Joanna has so kindly assigned me. The panties must be worn, I saw. To the opera and in the company of Cavalier Roland.

Suddenly the usual volant play of my sentiments was ballasted down with the weighty matter of inevitability. I had accepted the Marquis' invitation, if only out of crumb pride. And because of crumb pride there was no turning back. I sifted the soft, French cotton *dessous* between my fingers. Each had a prim, white satin bow. Would this be too much? Took the panties to the fount and blessed them, for they were a portentous gift and would determine whether the operatic evening would end on a high or low note. In cases of win or lose, it is always best to bless.

I put them in the drawer and sat down to dinner, though I could not eat. I turned on Radio Notre-Dame for the rosary, led, I believe, by Sister Véronique de Varenne – sisters of noble blood get to keep the participle. And whilst listening to the Marian hymn, I got out my watercolours and made several drip paintings depicting a Luxorian Prince in the shower (no foundling that one, William). Retired shortly thereafter.

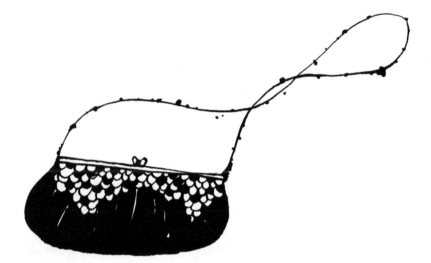

Feasts of Saints Donation and Rogation (twin-set martyrs)

Good third century Christians you were indeed, Donation and Rogation, enjoying your sacraments and lamb-o-gods till the day Maximian noticed your fervent faith and had you put on the rack and beheaded. Max was a bit oversensitive on the piety issue, yet this imperial weakness fuelled that fury which created two new saints. So let us give it up for Max! Without him you might never have made it to the communion, with him, you learned that holy heads that roll straight to heaven do go.

Encouraged this morning by a soft stream of sunlight through my curtains, I left my raincoat and umbrella behind, skipping to the metro in strappy sandals. Free and breezy. *Tonight! Tonight!* I sang. *The Marquis and I. Oh yes! To the Opera we go. Oh no!*

At À la Mode Online Jean-Claudi and Horace were photographing the Gaultier bathroom, a bejewelled Indian-odyssey affair, with ostrich feathers for hand towels. Jean-Claudi took a picture of a half-dressed Horace in one of the sailor-striped stalls feigning a very private pleasure. So risqué! Will they be putting that on the site? Or will it go to Mr JP Gaultier himself?

'Tea, my friends?' I offered. And the two loving lovers agreed to the pause. I was delighted to have their company. The spoons have all fled to London for collections and a curtained *tête-à-tête* with Hiri Kandini. Their scribbled communiqués will be arriving any day. Addressed to me, the stay-home girl – Remedy the fax machine queen. Jean-Claudi was supposed to go as well, but declined because Horace's mother is ill in hospital and they both felt they could not leave Paris. Oh how rare a thing such true devotion, this extension of the love connection! Imagine Johannes von Krysler saying, 'I will not leave you until Mumly calls. I'm concerned about the dropsy. Let the circus go on without me!' He would not say it, I tell you. It would be beyond his devotional capabilities. Adult Sex after all precludes enthusiastic addictions and extended loyalties, as Dr Dolittle has explained numerous times in her column.

I met Sister Dagobert at noon Mass. Yorik slept at her feet, his fatty tumour growing in girth by the minute, even as we prayed for it to shrink. So it seems that fatty tumours possess the gift of free will too. Prayed instead that the tumour would find itself overweight and, of its own volition, begin a slimming regime. Otherwise a girdle will soon be required, for the thing is becoming pendulous. I explained this to Sister Dagobert as kindly as I could. Sister Dagobert is susceptible when it comes to Yorik, which is entirely understandable, as the bond between the blind and their guide dogs possesses the strongest of bindings. Not only is he her walking guide in life, but also her brother and babe. An operation is out of the question for what would Sister Dagobert do while the beast lay in bed? No, we would have to rely on prayers and girdles alone.

Over lunch at the corner café, I told her about my date of the eve. Usually I do not share my private life with Sister Dag. Never, for example, would I have told her about the von Krysler expedition or even the misled Jean-Claudi crush. Yet there is nothing private about dating a marquis and therefore it is appropriate to confide most details (panties notwithstanding) to a holy sister. Today's noblemen are a queer breed, no longer paid by taxpayers, but reluctantly recognized by them as a branch of history. Indeed, they are the flesh and blood of historical monuments. Monuments made flesh. Without them we would have to admit loss. With them, we can do little. My date with the Marquis could not therefore be kept confidential. Like all other commemorative goods, his title now belonged to the people. What he did with it would also be their concern.

'Have no fear,' Sister Dagobert said. 'These are modern times. The Marquis will not harm you.'

Indeed, deprived of any former *droit de cuissage*, that lordly law entitling the nobleman to the pick of female flesh in his fiefdom, Roland had no allowance for abuse. He would have to win a woman over like any man of the people, only without the benefit of doing so privately. I had not, in any case, expressed any fear to Sister Dagobert, only a small dose of apprehension. Sometimes her frontal readings, that is to say her manner of interpreting my forehead, run slightly askew.

Whilst waiting for communiqués to arrive at the office, I visited the Catholic Forum's new website and clicked on the Apostolic jukebox to play some of the old post-Vatican II hits such as: 'If I had a Hammer' and 'Hey, Sinner Man'. You simply don't hear these songs in France or anything like them for that matter. From there I stumbled upon the Miracle of Warsaw's official website. An astonishing find to be sure! But there she was – Weronika, former virgin since become beauty queen – professionally presented in a comely photo gallery. So, we are presented with Weronika having just been named Miss Warsaw and bearing the victor's red satin bandoleer across a bikinied chest; Weronika in a Lacroix gown kissing the Pope's ring; Weronika consoling unwed mothers forced to give progeny up for adoption at the Verbum Dei Convent; Weronika with black lace mantilla head cover (Pierre Balmain, I believe) saying the rosary with her mumly; Power-suited Weronika on the phone in her office, organizing fund raiser for converted courtesans.

I must say this was a tremendous surprise and surely an indication of changing times. Formerly, recipients of extraordinary grace such as Miracles or Virgin Mary Visitations were left to suffering fates. One only need look at the life of St Bernadette, discoverer of that now great multi-national, the grotto at Lourdes, to see the truth of this. Subsequent to the apparitions and ecstasy, she was tortured by a jealous nun until the end of her days. 'I cannot promise you happiness in this world, but in the next,' the Virgin had warned her. Indeed! Yes, in the past, the price of the miracle was excessively high. Few people were accorded these graces, and understandably, few people wanted them. Today, however, it seems that hap rather than hopelessness will win out. Grace recipients are now accorded here-and-now joys, permitted first world successes. Could this mean a spiritual policy change has been effected? One does wonder.

Downloaded Weronika info for Sister Dagobert.

Though I tried to leave work early for my date preparation, I was detained a bit by Djamila and Hadj Mohammed. Djamila had just returned from Constantine. A double cheek kiss was exchanged betwixt us all.

'And the wedding?' I asked after our sweet greeting.

'Ah! There were too many gifts! And in a time of difficulty! How many of her cousins will go without mutton now so that she can have her four chickens a day! Already it is bad to spoil a woman, but to spoil a fat woman is worse!'

'I'm sorry to hear that Djamila.'

'Don't be sorry, daughter. Allah will attend to the wrongs and excesses.'

'God-be-willing.'

'Say, where are you going in such a rush?'

'I've got to get ready for a date.'

'With who? A good man? A believer?'

'He's a marquis. And a believer, or so I've heard.'

'Ah!' said Djamila frowning in disapproval at the public hearsay. 'We will find you a surer one, daughter. Have no worries.'

Djamila too, misreads the frontal gauge at times. Clouded worries did not wrinkle my brow. A correct reading would have been: high pressure system with no sign of precipitation – clear and sunny skies. Perfect weather for the evening ahead I dare say.

'Come by tomorrow. We will be making stuffing for a fish. Do not forget your apron.'

'*Inshallah*. I will try to remember. *Bonne Soirée!*'

Got home and immediately withdrew into the bath, soaking in a geranium-scented foaming product as long as I possibly could. Then plucked my brows: frontal gauge forecasting steady, light winds and sun. A slight but subtle fluctuation on the former report. Not to worry.

I dried off and went into the boudoir. Taking the five panties from their lavender-scented drawer, I laid them in a graduating row on the bed according to size of cut. Startling white they were, aggressive in their purity. I took a deep breath then and began the inevitable stratification: one pair, then another one over it, and so on, until I stood with five under-layers forming one very heavy-duty white panty. A bulky wrapper, nappy-like and hugging. And yet sturdy, solid, not unlike a Plaster of Paris Panty. Imagine being draped in muslin and plaster for the passing pleasure of a Marquis. Has he handled the hammer? With a chisel, could he crack the coop? Set the hens free? But no, he specified that the fabric be of vegetal origin, fibrous and downy. Not the mineral gypsum. Nothing from the Montmartre quarries, far too north of the Seine for his ilk. Bleached cotton he would have, five layers of it. Indeed, the more, the merrier.

Or certainly one would hope.

Of course, no-one knows for sure. Yet it seemed to be the right thing to do. The Marquis could use the suspense the peeling off would provide. The Russian doll effect to stave off ennui, make the pleasure protract not subside. Judging from our former encounter, brief though it was, the Marquis was no supple swinger; what he required was acrobatic training of the A1 sort, with limbering games to stimulate the initial connection, and tricks up the sleeve to coax open the libidinal pen. Surely there have been books written on the subject of Marquis seduction.

In truth, it was not seduction that I sought to master, nor even the Marquis. No, it was my role as facilitator I was preparing. Joanna had clearly understood my role early on. Her package was a reminder to me of the need to facilitate the conjugation. Nothing could be taken for granted with the Marquis. Expectations should be kept to the strict physiological minimum. Just as Christ was a great proponent of teaching and transformation, so would I attempt to follow the example set and show the Marquis the way.

Such were my thoughts as I put on a long, Lycra and lace ruby red dress and observed myself in the mirror. The fit was snug as intended although now revealing extra hip. This was the layered look and there was little I could do as a facilitator to modify it apart from de-layering which was clearly not an option. Manifestly I had a new shape, perhaps a more womanly one, if indeed the addition of bulk enhances womanhood, as is the case, say, in Egypt. Certainly in Cairo, this girth enhancement would have its hasty admirers. In Luxor it would subjugate several princely players. But in Paris? To be honest I was not so sure and for this reason layered anew, slipping over it now a black redingote, a covering which did the trick. The Marquis would divine nothing and be all the more exhilarated at the unveiling.

It was then time for *toilette*: I made myself up with À La Mode Online promotionals, re-curled fallen locks, filled evening bag with soirée essentials. And left the flat. Not skipping now, but because of pelvic encumberment, walking slowly with languorous pause between steps, not unlike Princess Lala as she approaches the orange tree in which her personal-trainer awaits her for love. Every princess has a crumb love, not so? But I was in opposite shoes, walking awkwardly although at regal pace toward my Marquis. With as much dignity as could be mustered in the circumstances. This was not a car date initially, although Roland does have a car – an English one by the looks of it, for the steering wheel is wrongly stationed for the continent. He had offered to take me but I declined. It is better to end a date in a car than to start one there as any girl knows. I had told him I would meet him on the steps of the Opera house. Not Garnier but Bastille, the Opera house of the People.

A timely arrival upon the steps for me, which, considering my handicap, deserved applause or at least a corsage as reward, preferably a pink orchid. But this was not the Black and White Ball, merely an opera run, and Roland, when he motored up ten minutes late, offered neither recompense nor excuse. *Tout de suite!* Indeed, not right away, but I suppose soon enough. Perhaps he was slowed down a bit by the steering wheel, and yet I waited patiently, properly covered by redingote. Yes, not only properly but pleasingly too. When, parked and returned, Roland eyed me with undisguised pleasure, I knew I had dressed for success. Now on foot, both of us, we climbed arm-in-arm to our destination. Around us were other goers pushing their way up the bleachers. We pushed too, conversing breezily like the others all the while. Ours was a kind of small talk, appropriately mundane and begun upon a phantom note.

HE *Plaît-il?*

ME I beg your pardon?

HE *Comment?*

ME What's that?

HE I didn't understand what you said.

ME I didn't say anything.

HE *Très bien.*

Yes, everything was fine, despite the aural misses. Perhaps while pushing, Roland had difficulty hearing. So it appeared. We pushed some more but remained quiet. There would be time to talk after. The important thing now was to get through the crowd and into the People's Opera where we would sit in the manner of spectators with programmes upon our laps. It is never really so difficult, but only looks so from the outside.

'May I?' I saw that he meant the redingote, that he offered to rid me of it and assign it a cloakroom.

'I'll keep it, but thank you.'

'As you wish.'

How pleasant to have one's wishes respected and not contradicted. The redingote would stay on and my hip harness would remain hidden. Roland went to dispose of his overcoat and returned just as the lights were turned down. The opera had begun.

Before us unravelled one of the most remarkable stories of the French Revolution, the history of the Carmelite sisters of Compiègne recounted by internationally-renowned prima donnas. With trepidation, we watched the singing sisters, victims of those bloodthirsty times, being rounded up on the public square and there beheaded by the anti-clerical revolutionaries, one after the other, while they sweetly sang the *Memorare* and walked fearlessly to their deaths (thank God the guillotine spared them the third century axing you went through, Rogation and Donation).

I fly unto you O Virgin of Virgins! O Mother of the Word Incarnate! There was no need for guards or bindings, the nuns offered themselves (*to you I come!*) quietly and courageously to the guillotine. *Despise not my petitions, but in your mercy hear and answer me!* At the sight of this, the wild, pushing crowd grew silent, grew frightened and when the last head rolled, became certain of their mistake. *Before you I stand sinful! O Gracious Queen I sit sorrowful!* Two days later, the French Revolution had ended. Amen!

Standing ovation, three curtain calls and a question in all of our minds: did the Carmelites put an end to the Revolution? Or did the Revolution put an end to them? It is impossible to know for sure. Most of us would have to rely on speculation. Roland, as we left the opera house, looked around himself nervously, drummed the sides of his legs. Was he speculating on the nuns or on the what was to come next? I could only speculate myself, and came to the likely conclusion that post-opera concerns provoked his agitation. I put my hand into the redingote pocket and felt the layers, still bumbled and intact. He would be fine.

'Could you give me a lift?' If I proposed, he would dispose. At least it often worked that way.

'*Bien sûr.* It was my intention.' And when we arrived at my flat: 'Care to come in for a drink?'

'*Volontiers.*'

Yes, I did expect the volunteer spirit. A spontaneous acceptance to the unknowns of my offer. Joanna undoubtedly had worked him over too. Knowing this gave me confidence, encouraged me on as facilitator. As long as I offered he would accept, but only because he knew that I knew the game. We were both in the know as it were, complicitous while pretending otherwise.

'Champagne?'

'*Avec plaisir.*'

It seemed to me that the Clicquot widow would facilitate the tasks ahead. Certainly she has come betwixt countless men and women with the intention to unite them for a night, warming cold limbs, heating hearts.

'*Aux Carmélites!*' said Roland, lifting his glass for the toast.

'*A la Révolution!*' I added, as Roland took his first sip. Perhaps he downed too quickly, for he choked and spewed. I quickly found a dish towel and began patting him dry.

'*Ce n'est rien.*'

Yes, it's nothing. An easy spill. I dropped the towel to the floor and pushed it around with my toes to mop up below. Then I went to the CD player and pushed play. The strains of 'Fill the Cup O Beautiful' emerged from the speakers. Was he, I wondered with alarm, a royalist? For if he were, this could go no further. Even Joanna, loyal to Philadelphian principles, would have to renounce. But the Marquis said nothing to confirm this worry, made no attempt to dispute my toast. He was a lone marquis after all, with no personal investment in the kingdom. I camel-walked toward him. Slowly, rolling my grammars in a delicious undulation. My cameleer perked and pulled in the reins.

'*Oh là là…*'

Indeed, what was to happen happened very quickly. And the layers, I should say, were not taken as preliminary play but as a challenge, a calling to account. What goes there? the Marquis might have called out. For I could tell he saw himself as summoned there, called to by some sentry from below seeking help. Yes, he seemed to sense his duty, one that could be acquitted only by removal. And so the layers went, not in one pull, but duly, like dishes that succeed one another at table. A table where only one is seated and served the five-course fare. Where was the jesting, the good-humoured ease, the amorous toying? Such dallying in the five-tiered procession is discouraged by the noblehood.

And so I understood that Roland was a gourmet, yes, but a joyless one in the arts of love. What he needed was not a facilitator but, like Marie Antoinette, a dance instructor teaching the play of tempo and step, a candid lesson in entrechat, that laughter of the feet. For the Marquis could rise to the call, which indeed was reassuring to know, but unfortunately without the charm a dose of playfulness provides. Love happened as a matter of course and from there, was submitted to rules of astounding stiffness. I did what I could, graciously initiating him to rudimentary limbering. Yet even the simplest calisthenic move, suitable for producing a most productive pleasure, became a complicated caper, immediately rejected once the difficulty was perceived. Still, with teeth gritted we persevered.

In a word, our eve was consummate.

Yes, it was somehow complete, although more of a cordial success, than a *succès fou*, it must be said.

Whilst lying prone after our sport, a kind of longing for Johannes crept into the unfulfilled places. But there was no sense in lamenting the Marquis and pining for the flying acrobat or the yodelling cowboy.

239

There is nothing worse for Adult Sex than this pitting of one partner against the other which only leads to unreasonable discontent. Yet I could not help thinking in comparative terms. I wondered at the crusty prefix, *von*. Could von Krysler possibly be of the marquis ilk? But this von in the Krysler patronym is merely a circus additive. Von Krysler, like Junior, is as much of a crumb as myself and yet both are kings of the boudoir by right of talent.

I watched Roland slip down into slumber. How tired he was, and perhaps hungry, too. With my hands above his crown, I said the Prayer for Renew. He would sleep a princely sleep, gently caressed by white, layered dreams. Perhaps he would hear the piping of the Carmelites or the litany of the Rogation days (a tribute to you Rogation and Donation). *Bonne nuit, mon ami!* Good night, dear Roland, and may you remember your lessons in the morn.

I helped Jubilee say his prayers, then puffed on one of Neighbour Jeromino's cigars, an excellent après-sporting treat. Turned off light and hummed.

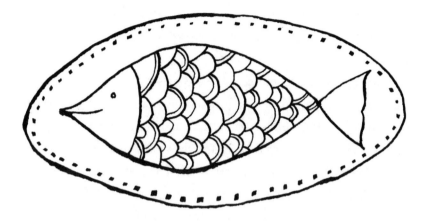

Feast of Saint Joan of Arc

Oh Joan, you are such an inspiration to me, pushing Pretend beyond your pastoral solitude to the flesh-n-blood battlefield. (Ah! To think that it all started at the fairy tree and finished on a lump of burning logs!) May your guidance show me how to forge beyond the frontier of my little game and become a true player in the action-packed field of love and life. Amen.

I slept in till ten, waking to the pitter-patter of rain and finding myself all alone. Manifestly Roland had slipped out at some near dawn hour. Perhaps he had early morning Marquis duty. He nevertheless left me a note written with amorous flourish. *Tu charmes comme le soir, Nymphe ténébreuse et chaude! Tes hanches sont amoureuses* etc. I believe that translates as '*You charm like the night, You hot, gothic nymph! And your hips are in love…*'. Baudelaire, I believe, but so sweet to repeat. Awfully kind of him, I must say. Much more thoughtful than von Krysler who left me the stovetop only accidentally. And yet do niceties ever compensate for lack of expertise? In all honesty I must admit they do not.

Finding the coffee canister and Her Majesty's Weetabix box empty, I decided to call Le Nôtre for a breakfast delivery as Top Spoon often does when her cupboard is bare. *Allô?* Good morning Sir. Two crescent rolls and coffee with cream. *SVP.* The delivery arrived on linens and tea tray, just twenty minutes later whilst I was still in *peignoir. Oh merci!* I tipped my gallant deliverer, a darling lad, entirely leather clad and eager to be of morning service. For the gratuity I was offered glass of freshly squeezed OJ. *Oh you mustn't!* But I accepted of course and toasted my gift-giver. *A la vôtre!* Yes, here's to you and yours, my charming morning man. Where the Marquis has failed me, you have made amends. Of course this goes to show how curiously we come by gifts, the most auspicious of which motor to us on wheels unknown. Waved to my lad from out the window as I watched him mount his moped. *Adieu!* Oh, if only he were Mouktar!

I then sat down to a repast of delicate, buttery croissants and coffee whilst flipping through the pages of *Belle.* There was an article entitled 'Tweedy Birds' all about the comeback of herringbone tweed and plumage, and another on 'What Men Really Want' which, it seems, is nothing in particular.

Went then to the Cleopatra Club for a steam, which is simply the best way to celebrate the love connection *après coup*. It's said that the Farah Diba had her own private hamman equipped with a Water Weenie to prolong the fun and games. I can understand her desire to splash and frolic in the baths. Unfortunately one cannot do this at the Cleopatra Club without attracting the attention of Samia, which is highly inadvisable; her redressing techniques employ a harsher wrestle than her massages. At the Cleopatra Club you sit and steam. Sometimes you visit your neighbour who you hope is not a missionary trying to put you in the right position, that is to say, properly orient you toward the Lord. Fortunately today there were none of these.

I spoke briefly to a woman about her neighbourhood hamman in Tunis where she would get all the perks for the equivalent of only two dollars. Ten times less than what you pay here! And so much cleaner. And there's none of her! My neighbour pointed at Samia who was kneading hard into a brown, fleshy back. The lady from Tunis shook her head condemningly at the Cleopatra Club. Having never been to Tunis and, therefore, with no point of comparison, I could enjoy these facilities without regret. How lucky I was in a way, and yet I understood my neighbour well. I could not help returning to my own preoccupation, which was the von Krysler/Marquis comparison. How easily we are spoiled, I thought. Best not to be discriminating. Best to love the one you're with. Advised my neighbour to engage in a round of Pretend. Imagine, I said, that you have been invited by a vizier who wants to see you at your most beautiful which will be three hours after you bathe. Go now and perfume yourself. Remove that hair above your lip with honey wax. Have your ladies prepare your dresses. My neighbour drifted away from me dreamily, gave an order to Samia and continued on to the beauty salon.

Dressed and left the vapours at twelve. A quick glass of mint tea at Chez Bichi, then over to Djamila's for cooking class.

I climb up the six floors all a-puffing. Ring the doorbell. *It's the Nazarene.* I ring again.

'O Infidel! I do not at all adore what you adore. You do not at all adore what I adore. I do not adore what you adore. You do not adore what I adore. You have your religion and I have mine.'

(It's best that sura 109 is clearly stated before entry.)

'It's the Nazarene.'

A second time. Leila speaks on the other side, the warm, cushioned side of the door. The portal opens and I turn my cheeks left and right. The kisses are hasty but true. Not Parisian kisses for show only, but signs of peace to the infidel. A glass of mint tea is set before me. Pinenuts float at the top.

'Look! From the port of Casablanca. Just this morning.'

A two-foot fish is pulled from a suitcase and plopped on a long flat pan. A gilt-head, I see, although not golden. Pure silver this one. How? I wondered. Who?

'On the windowsill!'

Djamila will have nothing foul her home and points her finger window-wise. The briny fish, ripe from the journey and its valise, has brought in too much of its port.

'It's a fresh catch! Just this morning!' Leila covers it with ice and sets in on the wide sill. Pitter patter of rain.

'Mouktar brought it. You know Mouktar?'

I shook my head. Who? I ask, is he?

'Djamila's nephew. The son of her sister, Saadia. Just returned from vacation. He's a beautiful boy. Would you like to marry him?' Leila slaps my shoulder with her plump hand. Runs her fingers through my hair and pulls at a lock. Then moves in close.

'The Nazarene has made herself beautiful today.'

Djamila sets bushels of parsley, coriander, garlic, a bag of pinenuts, lemons and olive oil on the low-riding table.

'She is very clean. The sign of a good woman. Do not corrupt her.'

Leila throws her hands out at Djamila.

'Not me! I'm a good friend of the Nazarene sister! Would I ever harm her?'

Djamila sets down the heavy chopping block. Sarrah runs for the knives.

'That fish must be in the oven within the hour. Else, may Allah who is Great forgive us, it will perish.'

As it is best for women not to beg for mercy which is granted more favourably and easily unto their brothers than they by the great Allah himself, we chopped furiously, hammering down on our nuts and leaves. To avoid any need of forgiveness which we would most certainly not be accorded, we speedily stuffed our fish with the fresh-smelling mix.

'Why this parsimony?' I tried to ask. 'Allah and his daughters...'

But Djamila was too busy to explain. Yet even if she were not, she still would not. Explain the why of the matter. Her Koran is a *what* book, not a *why* book.

'Look! Is he not beautiful?'

Leila stands and holds the platter high, too high for us, who are yet propped on cushions, to see really. But we knew we had dressed it splendidly, added golden buttons to its silver coat.

Sarrah turns up the radio and lets forth a piercing ululation. Leila burps and touches her heart. Praise be to Allah! The fish is in the oven before the hour is spent. More tea now, and lemon cakes. But no-one takes a seat, not yet. The music is gaining on us. Leila lifts her arms over her head, flicks her hip.

'*Haiwa!*'

The Arabian call to joy has us all lifting our arms. Scarves are distributed and tied around hips.

'Watch the Nazarene dance Egyptian style!'

I begin with a *déboulé*, then ease into a maytag shimmy. Djamila claps for the infidel. She has hers, I have mine, but we both have this!

'*Haiwa!*'

Leila cups her left ear coyly and undulates. She invites me to do the same while Sarrah shimmies her shoulders. I undulate and shoulder shimmy so as to dance with both. Djamila joins us with pistol hips. I add to my dance the pistol hip move. Clearly I am now on my way to transcendence. I feel myself slip into that rapturous space. My soul is as if rising. Passing through and on its way out. But where is the door and will it open when the time comes? Will my soul have the key? A siren then. Once, twice it blows. The music comes down and the scarves are taken up several notches, brought up and over the head. Djamila looks through the peep hole in the door. I am just awakening, coaxing my soul back down the ladder. No time for head curtaining.

'Mouktar!' Djamila undoes the bolts and opens for her nephew. 'You are here in time for lunch! We have cooked the fish!'

She ushers him in. But he cannot stay for lunch. He has only come to get the suitcase. The suitcase that had the fish in it. Now he is out from behind Djamila's girth and I can see him. I make him out clearly. Indeed it's Mouktar! Yes it is! My gorgeous Mouktar, the one who nearly ran me down! So he is Djamila's nephew as well! Djamila kisses him twice on each cheek, pulls his chocolate brown locks. He is beautiful. As beautiful as the rising moon with fine eyes meeting brows and limber limbs. None of the cousins are insensitive to his charms, although he is family and should not be noticed in this way. Djamila raises her finger to end all nonsense.

'Leila, fetch the fish. Sarrah, set the table. And the Nazarene?'

She is introduced to Mouktar. 'How do you do?'

But he smiles with recognition and obvious pleasure.

'How are you, Miss?'

'Oh it's Remedy… please. Do call me Remedy.'

'It is a great pleasure to see you, Remedy.' I begin to feel slightly faint.

He is well and marvellously tanned. The pleasure of gazing upon him is nearly extreme. O eyes of love! Lover true! Fill the Cup O Beautiful, and give it to me! Leila places the cooked fish upon the table, Sarrah sets the plates.

'You must eat with us Nephew. Our fish is ready. You cannot leave us with your belly empty.'

The nephew protests, then concedes. Is seated next to me on a pouf. The fish, now more delightful than the day it lived, certainly more fragrant, is served on our plates. Mouktar pours me a glass of Fanta soda. I pretend to take a sip but leave the orangish fizz untouched. I do not adore what you adore. Unfortunate, for I do wish to toast with him on the friendliest of terms. But a Catholic must drink wine with her fish, a Pouilly or a Sancerre, a glass only at the noon hour in commemoration of the Virgin Mary's *accouchement*. For she gave birth to a fish. Ichtus was his name. Since that time, red wine is drunk for the sacrifice of the lamb, white for the persecution of the fish.

Our catch, flown in from Africa on a chartered plane, is a delicacy beyond compare. A herb-stuffed fondant, buttery and exquisite. Mouktar serves me seconds. He is a man who serves rather than waits to be served. A new kind of man, I saw. An Algerian-Frenchman who vacations in Morocco where the risk of losing his head is nil. We eat quickly without conversing which is the Muslim manner of dining. Fanta soda does not loosen the tongue or encourage unhurried table-talk. It is nothing like commemorative wine. Within minutes we have finished the fish.

'I must leave you, Aunt, and thank you for your graciousness.'

Mouktar is standing, positioning himself for the door. We stand too, to bid him goodbye. He gives us two kisses on each cheek, which means he lives in a suburb. For the double *bise* is the suburban manner. In Paris we are thriftier, and kisses more costly. There is so much to learn about Moutkar but I am learning it.

'Do come by sometime. When you're off duty?'

Oh dear! Have I, I wondered, been presumptuous?

'Take her some couscous, Nephew. She needs to eat! The Nazarene ladies are too thin. How do they expect to continue? Perhaps they will not.'

It is hard to know who, at this point, will bear it away and who will perish. For the moment we do what we can. Say our prayers. Wear our girdles.

I stay through the cleaning up, dipping my tingling hands in the water to cool my excitement. I'm nearly feverish, for Mouktar's presence will not rinse off. That mere flutter of his long black lashes as he bid me goodbye has caused a climatic upset and now the amatory

248

collywobbles are setting in as the temperature mounts. Can I tell the Muslim daughters? Can the Muslim daughters tell?

'Thank you, dear Djamila. God-be-willing we will do it again.' (With Mouktar, yes, with my man of magic fire!)

Djamila promises a lamb dish with prunes and saffron. A dish revered by husbands, one of which I will soon have.

'If Allah wants it so. So Allah will have it.' Indeed.

I left cooking class in a rush, late for my appointment with Joanna, and taxied down to the Louvre, running across the *parvis* to the Café Marly where all the top mods go to use the toilet. The Café Marly is something like the Café Beaubourg only more for mixed groups of ladies and gentlemen, with a certain preference for ladies-only tables if the truth be told. Joanna was waiting for me inside seated at a corner table with an uninhibited view of the ladies' room. One of the favourite Café Marly pastimes is to watch who goes in and who comes out. It is also important to observe how they enter and if there are any noteworthy changes upon exit.

'Remedy!' Joanna was waving at me madly. I hurried over and slid onto the velvety couch next to her.

'How did it go?' She lit a cigarette. I could tell she was worried.

'As well as it could, I suppose. Fine I think. But maybe he isn't my type.'

'Remedy, you don't have a type! That's just the problem.'

'Well, how do I get one?'

'Listen, Remedy, you had better shape up. I just got word that Roland is crazy about you. Did you know that he has only dated two women in the last ten years? I mean he's tough. He's choosy. And you've got a great chance.'

Joanna was certainly irritated with me and for good reason I am sure. She had planned our match so carefully, so delicately and indeed, for my very own good (like you, dear Joan, Joanna has unflagging faith in the French crusthood). But my mind was on Mouktar. Came back to his handsome face in waves. I was filled with a creaturely kind of excitement.

'Joanna, I'm in love.'

'You are? Remedy, that's great!'

'I'm in love with Mouktar.'

'With who?'

'Mouktar! My Man o' the Moon!'

'Oh stop it, Remedy! I mean it. Get serious. Listen, I can only do so much. The rest is up to you. Now if you keep up this nonsense, you're going to ruin your chances. Right now the odds are in your favour. Don't blow it!'

Joanna certainly has her point and speaks it clearly. So it seems that the Marquis is enchanted by Remedy who in turn is enchanted by Mouktar. I would have to give this some thought.

'By the way, thank you for the panties. They're lovely.'

'I hope they were OK and everything.'

'Oh lovely, really.' Joanna took a long drag on her Marlboro Light.

'I'm glad to hear it.'

'Joanna, look!'

Just at that moment two models wearing toffee and mint chiffon date dresses respectively, snakeskin mules and matching totes with Pat Nixon style day coats over their shoulders made their way to the ladies' room. A third, in a lime green-paillette chiffon shell with matching acid-coloured ostrich bag and faux peacock mules, followed behind, pulling a small suitcase.

'Oh them,' said Joanna with easy recognition. 'I saw them down the street earlier at Chanel. They're on their way to London this evening. The seven o'clock train. See the one with the suitcase? She's from Saint Louis although she now lives in New York. She has a loft in the meat packing district – it used to be a pantyhose factory. The other two are Danish, but you wouldn't think so because they're so darkish. But let me tell you there's nothing *naturel* about that! The dark look is in and the blondes are doing anything to get it. I talked to them a bit while I was being fitted.'

It occurred to me that Joanna would make an excellent top spoon, that the métier of fashion journalist of which I was a minor, stay-home apprentice, came naturally to her. Her stint in the coffee-table book business had clearly been an *erreur de jeunessse*. Perhaps one day, for one never knows the course of destiny, I would at last be able to avail my ever-obliging friend by showing her the quickest route to spoon-dom. For the moment, however, Joanna sees no reason to write about couture when she can wear it so easily.

'Will they be in there long?' I asked.

'Undoubtedly,' Joanna replied knowingly. 'Probably half an hour.'

'What are they going to do?'

'What all models do, change their clothes.'

Of course. Models are inevitably caught on the run-and-change cycle. A clean, well-lit toilet serves the purpose when the dressing cabins are tied up or nowhere to be found. Moreover, the Café Marly's proprietor is delighted to oblige these young mannequins whose frequent frequentation has earned this ladies' room international standing. It seems to make no difference that the girls neither eat nor drink here. It is enough to be beautiful, international and use the toilet.

251

'Here they come.' Joanna doesn't miss a beat.

Our three ladies exited the WC now frocked in matching tweed bubble dresses with snap slits, their hair which upon entry had been bobbed, now coifed into comely beehives.

'Those are Chanel. They were picking them up when I was in the shop. It's a new look. A bit finicky for the Coco house, but the croc purse gives it a supremely finished look. It's the proper lady rage but with a cool quotient. Look, they're heading straight for the photographers.'

Indeed, several photographers had arrived armed for a fashion shoot. Joanna smiled enticingly at one of them and got her picture taken. I looked at my watch, saw it was time to go.

'I've got to get to my dance rehearsal, Joanna. I'll see you later.'

'Yes,' said Joanna, concentrating on the foxy trot of her six-foot sisters. 'Oh, and don't forget Thursday. The luncheon.' She blew me a kiss.

'See you there.'

I made my way past the contorting photographers and their contortees, past the ogling spectators and out the door to the metro at Palais Royal. I arrived at the dance studio just as the others were changing – in a dressing room expressly erected for such purposes which indeed seemed to lessen its glam quotient not a little. Be right there! I told the girls and went into the WC to change into a russet leotard and Turkish hareem pants swaddled hip-wise with a black sequined cummerbund. I must say that playing fashion Houdini in such poorly adapted quarters is no small feat, which only made me admire the dear mods even more for their perseverance. But I came out of that closet looking rather stunning if I do say so myself, now a mid-length redhead thanks to Claudia. Unfortunately, there were no photographers to meet me on the dance floor, just Samira with her FYI announcements.

The FYI is that we will be dancing at the most prestigious El Salem Theatre with the entire Egyptian consulate in attendance. The consul himself wrote a personal epistle to Samira insisting on his delight at the prospect of our performance. He invited all of us to a private, eleven p.m. soirée at his consular home. With a select few of his dignitary friends and would we have the kindness of performing in preview? Samira refused for reasons obvious to all but me. Manifestly I will never know the hearts and minds of Egyptians. It does seem, however, that there is a *droit de cuissage* practice in Egypt, which lamentably allows consuls to claim rights over the thighs of dancers. Samira is so wise; I trust her implicitly. If it hadn't been for the depraved Sir Reginald Hamly, she would certainly now be the greatest living ballerina in Egypt. Queen of the desert! Star of Caliphed Cairo, balancing hips like sailing ships, dimpled and dancing and white as milk. Wavering breasts with crimson crests, like golden birds that shake their nests.

Samira taught us the words of the most recent addition to our repertory, 'Eyes of Magic Fire', and as usual we had to study the song's emotional content for expression purposes. To help us, Samira showed a video of the Red Sea, to which, upon a second viewing, we interpreted freely in dance. The idea was to become wood and water. Tree and Sea. So that our hips would sail as ships and our grammars rise like the birds so prized. It was a gruelling rehearsal requiring tremendous concentration. There was no music you see, only the voice of an Israeli commentator. Nobody understood him. Alas, we had to rely on the images alone. Still, nobody complained, for Samira's sake, but all did their best to come about and waver. Next week we will learn the choreography, which should fill in so many of the missing blanks.

I left rehearsal at nine p.m. rather exhausted really. A long day with quite a lot of steam in the morning. Moreover I was famished and finding there was nothing in the fridge but an expired yogurt, nothing on the shelf but a can of sardines (for Jubilee only), I had no choice but to call Chez Shlomi's. A Princess Pizza for one *SVP*, with anchovies on the side. A Princess Pizza has lots of nice things on it like pickled crudités and pepperoni. It's what I usually order when all alone.

Twenty minutes later the doorbell rang. Mouktar? I wondered. Mouktar indeed, but a Mouktar on the run making the rounds for Shlomi. A Mouktar marvellously moulded so it seemed from moon-light, but with little time for talk. Folded my cheque, and putting it in his heart pocket, he said:

'Next week. Day off. Will call.'

I closed the door slowly, listing to his spritely feet, limber and lean on the stairs. A promising sound, I thought. Though best at the moment not to make promises. At least not to myself. Men are like a tree of golden oranges. Some are for juice and some are for salads. Try not to mistake the one for the other, else your drink be oversweet, your dinner rather bitter. Expectation is that hammock in which errors are made. Do not rest too heavily in it. Indeed, one never truly knows what to expect or what to promise and so should expect and promise nothing.

Ran to the window and waved good-by to the back of his white helmet, leaving me like a waning moon. *Mouktar au revoir! Mouktar à plus tard!*

Feast of Saint Kevin

That the cow who licked your clothes whilst you prayed produced fifty per cent more milk than its sisterly bovines is one of the most charming of those legends to which the *Concise* alludes but fails to deliver. I first heard about your devout cow straight from the mouth of Bishop Mahoney at an impromptu meeting of the Catholic Mothers of America club held in Mumly's living room. Was his aim to incite the RC branch of *La Leche League* to increase lactation through prayer? That could very well be, though with the Bishop one never knows; like the Lord his parables aim straight yet stray in the light of interpretation. In any case, when I'm low on milk for my Weetabix, I'll give you a ring, dear Kevin. Maybe you could send Moutkar dressed as a milkman to succour me; yes, Mouktar dressed in white with a bottle-o-milk tucked under his arm for his Lady. Thank you in advance, Saint Kevin, for milk miracle to come.

I ran into M. Phet on the stairway this morning and talked shop for a few minutes: pipes, leaks, repairmen, insurance companies and relatives in Singapore. He invited me to view the damage in his flat once again but I declined. Top of the day, M. Phet and best wishes to your lodger. I do dislike disturbing my neighbours at breakfast or being disturbed then myself for that matter. Unless of course, it's the milkman, Mouktar (*n'est-ce pas, Kevin?*). Otherwise there's nothing worse than that early morning doorbell whilst I'm still in Eve-wear and enjoying it.

At work I found all the spoons back in place and looking radiant, I must say. The London blush I suppose, that high tint of rose that flushes the cheeks both above and below. One of the spoons was guiding her curious ambulance towards her ovaries, which were aching from the high-speed train ride. Hiri said that ovaries don't like speed, nothing too fast you know, she explained whilst ecstatically massaging the air above her abdomen. My, my! What a lot of kneading! Nearly wished her ovies a speedy recovery, then remembering the speed problem, wished them a slower one. Got to work on communiqués and editorial exercises. Wrote an article on the retrograde stewardess look, now the latest rage in London where women have been spotted in nightclubs sporting airline tea and coffee trays. Stewardess brooches revisited with cabochon emerald studded wings (Chaumet) and Saudi Arabian Air's veiled pillbox hat done over in black *crêpe de soie* (YSL) top off any ensemble with transcendent charm. Sent article to Top Spoon.

At the coffee machine I chatted a bit with the workmen who were painting the ladies' room black and removing the toilet seats. Looks like a difficult one, I said. Who's the author, pray tell? An up-and-coming French designer, apparently, although they couldn't remember the name. It seems he wants our toilet to mourn the passing of the twentieth century in black. Oh dear, couldn't they have done this in the Gents this time? The look would be decidedly lunar, they explained, with gloomy galaxy motifs. Any stars on the ceiling? Apparently not, nothing too glow-in-the-darkish. Just enough satellite illumination to make it to and from the stalls. I wished the workmen a happy day and headed back to my desk, where I pretended from eleven till noon that I was Barbarella, booted to the knee and with a bubble gun. Those were grand days for Jane Fonda, days of free love and dining. Yes, before the fitness years set in and dinner amounted to five walnuts and a bowl of berries. Wondered a bit about Jane in the here-and-now. Is she eating more for menopause? Mumly says it's important to do so. I squirted one of the workmen ogling the spoons with bubble gun. Got him in the eye.

Off to Mass. I thought of picking up a bottle of Evian for Père Ricard to bless as my fount is running perilously low. Then decided against it seeing that I can bless the bottle myself! No sense in taking up Père Ricard's precious lunch hour. Even lay beginners can change plain water into holy fount material. It's the easiest sacerdotal man-oeuvre in the RC repertoire. Odd that the Church doesn't spread the word.

A quick hamburger lunch with Sister Dagobert afterwards. Yorik's tumour, I should say, seems to have stabilized. Perhaps this is a sign that shrinkage is due to transpire. Said a special prayer to St Rupert, patron saint of slimmers (have you met him, Kevin?). Sister Dagobert revealed that she will be going on pilgrimage to the Holy Land before the end of the year. She showed me the Quality Christian Travel brochure, which she had just been sent in the mail. It promised a fully escorted custom pilgrimage with daily Mass on-site and a deluxe, private motorcoach with two toilets (ladies *and* gents) and a soda bar. I imagined Sister Dagobert at the Sea of Galilee, carrying the cross along the Via Dolorosa. I saw her in Nazareth and the Old City of Jerusalem bravely feeling her way through history.

'And Yorik?' I asked.

'Free of charge. It's a Jubilee year special. For every five pilgrims, one dog travels for free.'

'That's wonderful news!'

'Yes, it is.'

'So who are you travelling with?'

'Sisters Marie-Joseph and Marie-Martin. They are twin sisters. Born and reared in the convent. This will be their first time out.'

'They've never left the convent?'

'One's a cook, the other a laundress. But now the Lord has called them to make the Holy Land pilgrimage and they will have to leave their posts. Of course there will be many people on the tour whom we don't know: priests, deacons, religious and lay leaders. Child, you are certainly welcome to come.'

'Thank you Sister Dagobert, but now is not the right time. Later, perhaps when I am ready.'

I did not want to tell Sister the entire truth, which was that I still had not yet fulfilled my primary RC travel obligation to Rome. Seeing that she had tried on several occasions to get me there by bus, it was better to say nothing. How could I even dream of traipsing off by charter plane to the Holy Land when a mere night train could get me to the Holy City. First things first.

'I don't think you'll need your pluviometer,' I said, thinking it would be nice for her to leave the weighty device behind. 'They say it's always sunny in the Holy Land.'

'I believe you're right. I'll just take that Perrier fan you gave me.'

The Perrier fan was a promotional Café Beaubourg gift, which I received for ordering a Perrier with lemon wedge. It is green, held in the hand, and uses two AA batteries.

'Good idea. Don't forget to take extra batteries. They could cost twice as much in Jerusalem. I've heard the prices in the Holy Land are not always accommodating.'

I left Sister Dagobert and got back to work, busying myself with feng shui dossier from two till closing. Feng shui for love and prosperity. If it works for the Chinese, why shouldn't it work for us? But there are many rules to remember, moreover, you must be proficient with a compass. For this reason, former girl guides have a good shot at feng shui fortune.

Here's how it works: stand in the middle of your flat with the navigational tool and divide your home into eight sectors corresponding to the eight directions. Each direction corresponds to a particular aspect of life (love, money…) which in turn corresponds to a particular colour – either a yin colour (grey, blue, black) or a yang colour (red, yellow, white) which in turn corresponds to a particular element (wood, water, fire, wind, earth) which in turn corresponds to *yet another* particular direction and another aspect of life as well as an internal organ. Sounds complicated, but Master Woo insists that once you catch on to the logic of the spiral, the gestures follow *de même.* Master Woo, I should say, is the feng shui man of the moment. He's the Chinese Hiri Kadini only for the home. He suggests that single women eat yang-coloured food to attract men. This means lots of egg whites for example (Angelfood cake) or spaghetti with tomato sauce. Steak tartar is also excellent, as red stimulates the heart. No blueberries however, or Muscat grapes, which you should only eat if you want to join the celibatarian ranks. Master Woo insists upon the importance of flowers in the home, although never next to the bed, which creates a yin/yang imbalance detrimental to the love connection. Contrary to one of our most ingrained western practices, Master Woo states emphatically that the gift of red roses creates bad blood between the giver and giftee due to the thorns. Also, absolutely no mirrors above the bed! Never talk on a cell phone when facing south-west. And plant bamboo to the east!

A long cup of tea before leaving work was required to clear my head a bit. Master Woo's imperatives come at you hard and fast, which is perhaps effective but nevertheless a bit overwhelming. Manifestly there are many rules and regulations which one must simply learn. But is there a definitive book of feng shui prescriptions? I only enquire because such books serve as excellent reference sources. Djamila for example has the Koran, which puts down all the rules quite clearly and comprehensively. It helps her dearly, day in and day out. Must ask Top Spoon who recently had her flat feng shuied by the Master Woo himself. Certainly she would know. Apparently she was advised to hang a crystal chandelier above her earth sphere and throw rice and salt at the moon. Has she done so? I don't believe so. Still, she swears by Master Woo as do so many in the couture spheres such as Jean-Claudi and Horace who have an appointment with him next week. They just bought a flat together and want to do everything right, activate the love sector properly and avoid the shar chi (the breaths that kill)! Truly they are a paragon of perfect couplehood. I adore them, I do!

Putting my papers in order, I went to the special cabinet where promotional products are kept under lock and key. Anyone, even office passers-by, can help themselves to the products on the right side of the cabinet but not on the left, which remains under the authority of Top Spoon. I rummaged through the goods on the right side then, looking for some form of retribution. Something to serve as an offering to Brother Gabin, due to appear tonight at AI. I went through several shelves pushing aside the polishes, creams, compacts and elixirs. Only for the fairer sex. Not for the brother gender. I dug deeper still, pulling up vermicular belts and scarves till at last my hand alighted upon something square and packaged, already a presentable. I pulled my hand out of the cabinet to see what I had caught.

The package I held was in fact a box of Medusa underwear, *pour homme*. Yes, a Versace treat that had once sat patiently upon my desk while I wrote it a ten-word blurb. A delightful titbit I believed to have been claimed by Jean-Claudi months ago. Or by Willie (*Wheelie*). Perhaps even by one of the spoons, as a gift to a special gentleman. Who exactly I did not know, but I was certain such a treasure could not last more than a week in the closet. Yet it had endured months, surely because some hasty cupboard mishap had pushed it far down into women's accessories, where normally, no men's briefs will go.

Here, I reasoned, is what must be the perfect gift, for there was nothing else in sight and time was running short. And yet even so, I had the suspicion that monks enjoy a private pleasure as much as any man. Surely they do! And who knows what they wear under those robes? Most likely something soft, not scouring. Or perhaps only Adam-wear. I wrapped the package in a red velvet tissue pilfered from a box of Vivian Westwood garter belts and tied a lingering Hermès bow around the whole. *Voilà!* Fit for a monk no less!

With this scarlet package under my arm, I headed back out to St Joe's for my very last A1 class. Yes, the last class of the year, the last chance at proper First Communion preparation. If the children didn't have it down by tonight, how would they make it through Sunday? Told myself to remain as hopeful as possible for the sake of their autonomic nervous systems. According to Sister Mary Paul MD, children register the hope and faith quotient of their elders with remarkable accuracy. There could be no fudging on my part. Prayed to the zealous Saint Paul for confidence that convinced. Then prepared the classroom. Desks in a circle with a small table in the centre for Brother Gabin and snack-time.

As I was happily arranging, it occurred to me that I didn't have a lesson plan. Indeed, I had merely planned the visit of Brother Gabin, who I was relying upon to carry all pedagogical weight by performing the multiplication miracle and remaining thereafter for a question and answer session. According to my hasty calculation, snack-time would then take up some twenty minutes if we allowed it to, which we would. But what if Brother Gabin didn't come? What if all he had to offer us was a no-show? I went to the door to see if he was somewhere in the hall. But he wasn't, only the children were. In they arrived, cautious for having left behind *maman*, but confident too I could tell. Something of import had transpired in A1 after all, something which had led us all trustfully to the same table. We would boldly feast on the mystery of fish and lamb, sing songs with our mouths full and show others, by our example, how to do the same.

'Children, please be seated.'

I hesitated as to whether I should mention Brother Gabin's impending appearance, but then decided to say nothing so as to protect them from the potential disappointment of a no-show, which, at this early stage, could upset their budding confidence in the faith of their Fathers. Instead, I chose to work directly upon the hypothalamus glands, which can always use a boost at the beginning of class.

'Children, prayer is an international language although people pray in hundreds of different languages. God understands them all because he understands the hearts of women and men. God is called hundreds of different names throughout the world, but God is always God. Do you agree?'

The children nodded their heads in agreement. Little Xavier raised his hand.

'What about that god called Allah?'

'A very good question, Xavier. Allah is the Arabic word for God. When God hears the word Allah, God knows that the heart is a Muslim one. In rarer cases, it might also be a Christian one but from the Middle East. Allah is just another one of God's names.'

'Does God love the Christians better?' Xavier persisted.

Oh dear, thought I. But remembered I was in Europe where the crusades were still fresh in mind, where villages and towns throughout France proudly put up 'Richard the Lionheart was here' billboards. Yes,

263

on his way to Jerusalem, the crusading Cœur de Lion made a good number of pit stops, for travel was then a slow, shoddy affair. This history and the bad blood it stirred has not been forgotten on the Continent but passed down by way of fearful notions. Patiently but firmly, I would do what I could to help little Xavier drop his weighty baggage filled with ancestral sundries, now of little use.

'No, God does not. God loves all men and women equally. All women and men!'

I thought of Joanna, which gave me a charge. I spoke charismatically and with an authority that inspired trust. I felt as if the Lord God were speaking through me. As if my lungs were the pipes of a holy organ.

'All women and men are equal in the eyes of the Lord!'

Indeed, the force of my words made Xavier sit up straight in his seat, bright eyed and visibly relieved of his onus. How I wished that Djamila could have been here to recite the Al-Fatiha and offer us a short course in Islam for beginners! But that would have to wait for Catechism B2. At least now the children were freed of age-old antagonisms and with lion hearts could now pray and live as true brothers and sisters, loving, like God, with equipoise. I made no mention of course of the prodigal son parable, for to hint that the Lord may well have a slight preference for the sinner, if only because of the pleasure that redemption brings, could well have upset my A1 apostles at a critical time. This class must go well, I reminded myself, take not the tricky risk.

'Maria-Helena, could you say the Our Father, Hail Mary and Act of Contrition in Portuguese? Children, listen carefully to the words of the Lord in Maria-Helena's mother tongue.'

While Maria-Helena dutifully recited the words she had learned at her grandmother's house in Lisbon, I went to the door and had a look. Still no Brother Gabin. Would he not come after all? Was he afraid the miracle might fail him before the wee ones? Were his rabbits shy of crowds?

'Thank you Maria-Helena. That was lovely. I believe the other children appreciated your prayers very much. Rodrigo, could you say the Hail Mary in Spanish three times? The Spanish language is very pleasing to the Virgin's ear because there is such a devotion to her in Latin America. This is not to say that she has a preference for Spanish, but only that she enjoys it quite a lot.'

Again I went to the door to check the corridor. Still no multiplication man. The scarlet present sat on the table. Perhaps I would have to offer it to Roland. *Santa María, Madre de Díos.* The Latiny cadence was like a lullaby, nearly too sweet, too soporific. Rodridgo, I saw, was lulling the minors to sleep. Xavier who had just straightened his back to embrace the democratic principles of divine love, slumped again, his head drooping over his shoulder. Maria-Helena had closed her eyes. Her chin nodded gently against her chest. The fine line between prayer and sleep was not being respected. The fibre required for obtaining intercession was weakening with this lax surrender to slumber. Clearly this would not do. It was time to get all of the children out of their seats for a round of Oh Infinity! I clapped my hands to clear out all sluggishness in our common energy field.

'Thank you, Rodrigo. Children, please stand for our next exercise.'

The children rose to their feet yawning, their expressions dreamy and vague. And yet as usual, they were willing to continue on, soldiers that they were. Dear, dear soon-to-be communicants.

'Children, next Sunday, you will be receiving your First Communion which is the gift of everlasting life. To understand the notion of eternity, which is a very difficult one to fathom if we only use our minds, we are going to do a callisthenics exercise we have already practised called O Infinity! It is another means of understanding. Do you remember it?'

Maria-Helena and Micheline clapped their hands with delight. Xavier corrected his posture and the others looked at me expectantly. They did remember, how good of them! As a refresher, I demonstrated the oriental eight for a minute or two, explaining the concept of the figure and its energetic typology. Just as the children began to join me, swinging their hips left and right, around and over, there was a knock on the door. I stopped my eight-making to turn around and see who it was.

Standing in our doorway was the hooded Capuchin, fingering the string of fat wooden beads that hung from his waist rope. He smiled shyly at us from underneath the hood. Bless you, Brother! How wrong I was to doubt; his arrival was only a matter of time. Yes, time, a notion, which concerned acrobats and religious men so little it must be said.

'Children, this is Brother Gabin who is our guest of honour today. He has come to share a particular gift with us on this last day of class before the sacrament. Please, let us greet Brother Gabin with applause.'

The children and I eagerly clapped as Brother Gabin came and took centre stage. Without further ado, for he is a man of few words, trained in all matters of silence, Brother Gabin proceeded with his exercise in rabbit multiplication.

The children saw one rabbit become two and two become five and five become ten. They shrieked with delight and clapped their wee hands. The rabbiting occurred miraculously before their very eyes and what joy it was to be a witness! Witness to a miracle. Or so it was thought though in truth it was mere magic trick. Still, how little this matters in the end, for in the early stages of catechetics, development of the imagination takes precedence even above and beyond the precepts of doctrine. So insists Sister Mary-Paul, MD, who knows something about the subject. It was important that the children understand the import of the Eucharistic sacrament not just intellectually, but by experience, which is to say with the heart (as you showed us well with your cow, dear Kevin).

'Children, put your hands on your hearts and feel all the joy there. Feel it rushing up into your palms like the warmth of sunshine. Remember this feeling! Never forget it, for this is the joy of the Eucharistic celebration. May you jubilate throughout your lives, particularly as you make your way up the aisle for the hostie!'

In great spirits then, we ended our class with snack-time. Brother Gabin stayed until the end, snacking and performing other ploys with his rope, delighting the children in a number of ways.

'Children, Sunday will be a very special day. I will be thinking of you every minute and wishing you the best. Go in peace now and with love in your hearts! Perhaps we will meet up again for Catechism B2 next year.'

I blew all the wee ones a kiss and watched them part in search of *maman* who by way of cooking and sewing was also deep in sacramental preparation. So much work to be done for the A1 graduates. I had done mine.

'Thank you so much, Brother Gabin. This is for you.' I handed him the ruby red gift and, feeling the tears of completion well in my eyes, took leave.

'Please, open it at home. In the privacy of your boudoir would be the best, I think. Thank you again!'

Went directly to the ladies' room where I wept into a paper towel direct from the dispenser. My sorrow was sweet but the hand towel rough. I wiped my eyes instead with a sleeve of the mauve uni. Eyes now dried, I left St Joe's powder room. From the corridor, I spied a curious Brother Gabin in the foyer opening the piquant package. I slipped out the side door.

Perhaps it's odd to feel weepy after such jubilation, and yet any episode of life that comes to an end must be mourned, if not a great deal, then at least a little. Good riddance, you might say when the commensal leaves your table at last, but mourn all the same. For if you do not, the commensal may well mourn you and return in ways you did not expect. Mourn the changing of the seasons, the hours, the changing of the guards. But jubilate, jubilate, jubilate too! Who said that sadness is all misery, for it can be tinged with a sweetness, a *douceur* so subtle that it strains you with the pleasure of half-hues. A piercing comfort it affords in passing Calvary. Emily knew the sweetness of suffering too. She took the circumference of grief betwixt her fingers and gave it many names.

> *I measure every Grief I meet*
> *With narrow, probing, Eyes –*
> *I wonder if It weighs like Mine –*
> *Or has an Easier size.*

A comparative study of sorrow. This too, I knew. A way of looking into faces, reading eyes and brows, studying the slope of cheek and then the unmentionable things, the queer apprehension that a person is dying when no other forecast augurs alike – and yet you weep, for in the end it is found you are right, or that your lover has become a cheat which you know from how he pronounces your name in the morning before, not after coffee.

But what is sweet in the end is not the pedestrian suffering but the very mystery of grief. For ultimately we are left as puzzled as we are dispossessed, and curiosity provides most, though not all, with an odd kind of comfort. Perhaps it killed the cat, yet the human heart will die without it. The mystery, when one relinquishes oneself to it and poses all the unanswerable questions, issues a balm so soft as to be thought untrustworthy. But trust it for the sweetness. Yes, that immeasurable sweetness.

Such thoughts gently absorbed me as I made my way home by way of metro and foot. I walked down the Rue Cler, past the merchants throwing buckets of soapy water out their doors, passing mops up and down their aisles. Cleaning up what the day's customers had brought in. As it was too late to pick up a ready-made dinner, I went to the Moroccan grocer and purchased a package of rigatoni, fresh cream and half-salted butter. A can of Ron-Ron for Jubilee. A bottle of Sidi Brahim for me and any late night guest on a drop-by date – one never knows, 'tis best to be hopeful.

The concierge waved to me as I walked in.

'For you, Mademoiselle.'

In her arms a bouquet of red roses. Long stems with thorns intact. Attached to it on a small florist's card were the words:

269

'In less than a month, dear Remedy, at the Ball of Marvels? With love from the Marquis de Bourdon.'

So he pops the questions with flowers. Not a bad way to do it at all although Master Woo would strongly disapprove. According to the feng shui master, the yang intensity of the red rose in particular, along with the menacing presence of the thorns, invited shar chi which, as I've understood, are small poisonous darts that weaken the immune system of the rose receiver. Eventually contention sets in between giver and receiver due to the exhaustion and overall bad humour of the latter. Perhaps it is so.

If Master Woo speaks the truth, I would have to take vitamins E, C and B-minus, for extra resistance. There was no chance however, that I would abandon the roses which are not only my favourite flower but Our Lady of Guadeloupe's too. How I miss her now that I am no longer in the Americas! She is Celibatarian like me, ever alone and never with bambino. A velveteen portrait of her hangs in Notre-Dame which I do visit when I can. Last Fall I set an ear of corn at her feet and a Montezuma rose too.

Sitting like a carbuncled crown on my table, the bouquet added a truly exuberant yangish touch to my otherwise yinish decor, which after all, is what a girl celibatarian needs to attract her male homo-logue. Looked once again at Roland's note. Next month, he suggested. The Ball of Marvels. And until then? Manifestly, what he proposed was a longish reprieve, a suspension in our dating game till the cotillion itself. Perhaps this was a crusty custom dating back to the times of chivalry. Wasn't Abelard separated from Héloise for a time? Tristan from Iseult? And now Remedy from Roland. According to the theory of reverse, a theory largely practised by the noble classes,

270

our separation would lead us to reunite all the more touchingly.

Perhaps. I should say, however, that Dr Dolittle is a right strong advocate of the Pleasure Now theory which precludes reversal games, ploys to prolong pining, and other practices which do not guarantee immediate libidinal gratification. Dr Dolittle is a doctor of today. Roland is a knight of yonder years. And what am I? Oh I'm just a Remedy girl, with a taste for a bit of this and that, yes, a smite of every-thing but anchovies. Indeed, I could abide by the rules of separation and get a taste for them too. What's the rush after all? True, Roland does need practice but we could also make-do couldn't we? Perhaps the ball would remind him of more playful years when he would run under his mistress' skirts and shout *Me Voilà!* And what if he were to do this at the ball? Oh it would be wonderful, wouldn't it? To see the Marquis so at ease and on all fours! Looking for the crumbs. Very playful, slightly naughty. I do hope there will be a treat or two!

Once home, I made a very white plate of pasta (yang-charged) which I accompanied with a glass of hearty Sidi. *See you then* I wrote on the back of a calling card, which I then put in an envelope addressed to the sixteenth arrondissment. *Le Marquis de Bourdon, Paris 16ème.* Thought that should do. Blessed myself before getting into bed. Read more *Moby Dick*.

'Pull – won't ye? What d'ye say? I say, pull like a god-dam!'

'Yes, yes, Mr. Stubb. I will try!'

Accidentally dropped my oar. (Thank you Saint Kevin for leading me out of that nautical pasture! I nearly got the whip!) Slumber.

Feast of Saint Sancho
(martyr... and virgin?)

We know precious little about you, Sancho, except that you would not abandon the True Faith, even as the Moors held the hatchet above you in Cordoba. You did not renegue and, therefore, you were impaled upon the ground, impressing onlookers by your love of the Lord. That was back in AD 851, before Spanish holies were granted private bodyguards, as they were when Isabella and Fernando headed the helm. It certainly helps to have a king and queen behind you; even an aristocrat can come in handy. But unfortunately, Sancho, no royal tutelage softened your fate. So it seems that not all saints are created equal, though sanctity, 'as necessary to the saint as high speed is to an aeroplane' (*Concise*), levels the discrepancies quite nicely in the end.

I had a dream last night about Daniel Boone, one of Richard II's ancestors (he was the founder of Kentucky, Sancho, a godfearing man who believed in predestiny rather than royal tutelage). In my dream he was the size of Tom Thumb and dressed exclusively – but scantily – in raccoon tails. A premonitory dream apparently, for at work several of the spoons were wearing touches of raccoon. Around the collar, belting the waist, as pom-poms on booties, hanging from the sleeve, as muffs etc. It's the Pocahontas look, or so they are saying, but rather than wear buckskin, it's advised to wrap up in velveteen and *crêpe de soie*. Queen Guinevere meets Indian maiden really. Tattered hems, uncouth fur, heathen helmets, quilted underskirts, and king-o-turtle stockings look smashing on modern-day hunter-gatherers. So explained Top Spoon as she took off one of her raccoon skin shoes and removed a cornflake from its sole. I would never have suspected that she ate breakfast cereal in the morning. So she *is* like the rest of us after all, only propped up at the top.

Spent most of morning looking at raccoon websites for more information.

At noon, I went to find Jean-Claudi to see if I could get a ride to Joanna's luncheon. As usual he and Horace were with Willie (*Wheelie*), discussing aesthetics in the dark room. I had to remind them that it was time go. Joanna, I'm afraid, would certainly not forgive tardiness. Today could be a grand day for her, if the Motte de la Motte-Piquet takes the bait. With each passing day, that potential gift gown grew more and more dear to her, increased significantly in its value. Of course, she could *buy* the gown, if her seduction plans are foiled, but surely this would be a bitter defeat. Joanna is extraordinarily principled, and hard-working, too. Women of her ilk expect success. It's a Presbyterian prerogative, with widespread implications amongst New Englanders. In Florida, where there are so many underheated vacationers, we worry perhaps a bit less about success. A balmy evening with cocktails at the country club does make up for the non-performance, for any running short.

Crawling into the back of Jean-Claudi's sports car (which in fact is really a two-seater), I held on wherever I could and squatted upon naught. Never have I been so glad to see the Hausmannian buildings of the sixteenth arrondissment. Jean-Claudi parked his little rig upon the sidewalk, as many civic-minded Parisians do. We then entered, as a fashionable threesome, direct from À La Mode Online. Joanna was all nerves, running around from Louis this to Louis that, plucking at the bouquets and table settings. She looked splendid, though, in a black velvet mini fringed with raccoon tail. Her long blonde hair was parted down the middle and braided on both sides – more like Pippi Longstocking than Pocahontas, but entirely stunning! We were the first of the guests to arrive, which was exactly how Joanna wanted it.

'How can I help Joanna?'

'Just start taking notes, Remedy. Don't miss a beat.'

And so I got out my notepad immediately and began scribbling. Little poems at first, things that Djamila has said:

Allah writes for eternity. But even He cannot rewrite again. Alas! Alas!

But also comments on the decor:

Red Dandy roses with mixed pine and fern foliage, excellent yang concentrate.

And on the arriving guests:

Madame de Tournevile, in Barbarian fleece coat with matching mother-of-pearl bag and mules; Mademoiselle Félicia Samson Ortiz y Dupont in rouge slip dress with matching panties and bra; pet dog Wilbur dressed in leather motorcycle doggie coat with silver-studded collar; high dosages of yangst throughout.

Indeed, with these high doses of yang-side chi, Joanna was sure to pull it off. The only possible foible would be overheating, a short-circuit due to an excessive yang charge. The yin-yang line is a fine one to walk indeed. What she needed were several guests dressed in blue. And indeed they came, the bluebells and morning glories emanating the necessary doses of salutary yin. I breathed more freely then. Yes, with relief that Joanna still safely gripped the tightrope with her toes. That her equipoise had indeed won out.

At last Motte de la Motte-Piquet arrived, dressed in a candy-green mid-length velveteen suit, with mink bustle and matching mink collar. Vegetal yang. Desire to meet a man. Weak in the kidneys but willing to try. Joanna rushed over to greet her, lavishing her with compliments and taking her by the arm. Motte de la Motte-Piquet was reserved but perhaps not unfriendly, although it is difficult to tell with Parisians who close their faces. Talking to them is a bit like talking through the confessional grill. The exchange is slightly tense, verily uncomfortable, but fortunately guided by a common code of intercourse. Ultimately you do not know to whom you are speaking. Yet one is led to appreciate the mystery of this and, over various encounters, to glean the hints caught through momentary apertures. Who is my collocutor? But then, on the third or fourth occasion, the sleuth in you deduces slyly and jots down the find in a register. Manifestly, Motte de la

Motte-Piquet was of the sort that required this careful probing through the grill.

I continued taking notes. Jean-Claudi was snapping away with the digital. Joanna's luncheon *would* go online! Horace charmed the ladies by complimenting them on their handbags. A silver bell was rung. To the table! Foie Gras on its bed of gingerbread, onion confiture and braised Sutani citrons. Joanna had outdone herself. *Oh là là! Que c'est exquis! Tout à fait! Oui, Oui! C'est un repas tout à fait heureux.* Yes it was a happy meal, made even happier by the visible approval of Motte de la Motte-Piquet herself, who smiled so slightly, and ever so tightly, that it might have been taken for a grimace. And yet I guessed that it wasn't affectation really, but as much of a veritable expression of pleasure as she could muster. I clapped my hands for the thrill of Joanna's triumph. More, I wanted to shout, more for Joanna!

And more she would have.

Lamb leg on its coulis of confited tomatoes, tapenade of Tuscany olives and potatoes *allouette à la méridionale.*

Madame de Tourneville delicately tapped the edge of her empty wineglass with a ruby-studded ring finger. A subtle sign, but she was served immediately before she continued talking, as if to nobody in particular and yet to every one of us guests:

'The castle belonged to my great, great grandfather, the only son of a great Brugian family. How he came to France I am not sure. But he bought the castle and used it as a beach house for he loved to swim in the Mediterranean. He invited fifty Jesuits every Fall for a swimming party that would last an entire month. The priests would dance and trample the autumn grapes, then swim and sun all afternoon.

'My family has continued this tradition ever since and our wines have always been superb, only now it is no longer possible I'm afraid. The priests are very costly guests. Everything must be provided, even their swimming trunks! Moreover they are now loath to trample the grapes for fear of discolouring their feet. Last year I had to hire a foot-washer, a young Romanian boy who was certainly too talented to stay on – I believe you see what I mean. The Jesuits have now demanded night excursions to Monte Carlo. Last year we were obliged to buy a double-decker bus! I don't know why it is that when you own a castle, you are expected to host the clerics.

'Next year I will invite no-one. How I do need a rest! And a good deal of oral surgery I hate to say. You know, I am an artist, Monsieur. And so very sensitive in the nerves. I am writing a musical comedy about the life of Marie Antoinette.'

Horace smiled charmingly at Madame de Tournevile while eyeing the tiny, pear-shaped mother-of-pearl handbag on her lap. Jean-Claudi squeezed the Horatian knee under the table.

Madame de Tournevile tapped her wineglass again and did not have to wait long. Assorted cheeses on their bed of radiccio, slices of nut bread. Joanna spoke enthusiastically about one of Motte de la Motte-Piquet's avant-garde performances, the evening gown with pavé diamond chronographs over each breast, generously donated to À La Mode Online's sweepstakes:

'It's fabulously futuristic and yet so *Gone with the Wind* too. It's like Scarlett boards the Star Ship Enterprise! Is it postmodern or post-romantic? I don't know but it's simply fabulous!'

Motte de la Motte-Piquet's expression remained fixed in the same trim smile. Her posture, too, was impermeable; rain could not bring her down. She held herself closely fastened with little slack of flesh on which to pull in case of emergencies. And she ate very little, which was understandable for a woman of diminutive size who fastens herself tightly at the waist for fear of growing there. Certainly she was a hard nut to crack, and yet Joanna was handy with a hammer. With soft but persuasive knocks, she was coaxing the nut from the shell. Motte de la Motte-Piquet was pleased by Joanna's praise, which rang true because she meant it dearly. If one looked closely enough at the guest of honour, one saw the slightest loosening of the joints, a very subtle shifting as if something wanted to emerge. Perhaps this was Joanna's dress itself, getting ready to hatch.

Chocolate marquise cake with a raspberry coulis and almond-crusted rounds. Jean-Claudi took a photo of Madame de Tournevile's silver spoon dipping into the marquise.

'Get the ring!'

It was Horace, whispering from behind his cupped hand. Madame de Tournevile poised her carbuncled finger for a perfect shot.

'You two must come to the Château. Artists are always welcome to our swimming parties. I do believe that artists are our modern-day clerics, purveyors of a more sensual theology, don't you?'

(Apparently, dear Sancho, the noblehood has had it with holies.)

Jean-Claudi took another shot of Madame nibbling the almond-crusted round.

'And I assume you have your own bathing trunks, or do you go in like Adam?'

Horace gave Madame a knowing wink. Turkish coffee, with its five sugars. Three-tiered petit fours and truffle assortment. Motte de la Motte-Piquet downed her *demitasse* in one gulp, which seemed to do her a great deal of good, seemed to make her hum now. She picked a small lemon tart from the petit four platter and pursed her lips in anticipation. A lovely, tart little pick, decidedly right for her palate. She popped it into her mouth, then lit up a cigarette.

Joanna on the other hand, was looking droopy all of a sudden. Even her stiffly sculpted braids hung now without their previous hold. Oh dear, thought I, not now! Not yet! The party isn't over! I excused myself from the table to go to the ladies' room, then came back and went over to Joanna as if to ask her where I might find a particular feminine something. Joanna took the cue and went back with me to the ladies'. Concerned as I was, I spoke to my friend earnestly.

'What's wrong, Joanna? You're not looking well.'

'I'm not? Oh God! I'm afraid it's not working, Remedy.'

'Oh, but you're wrong, Joanna. I've been watching her like a hawk. She's delighted! Did you see how she drank her coffee? Everything is perfect, Joanna! You've done a faultless job.'

'But she's hardly said a word.'

'She's an artist. Why does she need to speak?'

'She hardly ate a thing.'

'She's a smoker. Why does she need to eat?'

'Remedy, I'm just not sure. I've worked so hard, you know. I want this to go well.'

'It *is* going well. Like I said, I've been watching her closely. She loves it! Every minute of it. Just keep up the excellent work, Joanna. And lots of compliments, you know. Now is not the time to slump!'

Visibly my words had a positive effect on Joanna, for she re-applied lipstick, re-sculpted her braids and applied a liquid scarlet stain to her cheeks for a rosy flush.

'Exotic dancers swear by this stuff for nipple-staining.'

'Well, it looks great on your cheeks too.'

Indeed, Joanna was radiant again, compact and perfectly groomed.

'You just have to be careful not to overdo it. When it's done right the look is refined but sexy.'

Indeed. Here was just the touch of ruby yang she needed to finish the luncheon in triumph.

'There's less than an hour left, Joanna. You're going to do great.'

I followed Joanna out then, walking behind her and admiring her carriage which at that moment, was not so unlike Princess Lala's, a regal posture that inspired ladylike confidence.

Around the table guests were conversing in hushed tones. Madame de Tournevile was peering intensely into Horace's *demitasse*, her brow strained by some mental exercise. She had tied her linen napkin around her head like a turban. It was the coffee grounds she was reading, I saw, like a Turkish cup reader.

'What I see here are wedding bells and then a trip to the islands, a honeymoon trip, no doubt in a private beachside bungalow.'

The ladies listening in broke out in peels of *Oh là là*. Horace and Jean-Claudi smiled at each other so knowingly, so lovingly.

'For those of you who doubt. Know that I was taught this art by the great Turkan Kamel the year I resided in Istanbul with my first husband, the Comte de Constance. This master taught me to read the cup with perfection, count my future wives on an abacus and read the songs of migrant birds for news from abroad.'

Someone from her audience asked if she had actually had wives, and didn't she rather mean husbands?

'I've had quite a few. At least seven so far. Yes, wives. Women who have cooked and cleaned for me because of a sentiment of love.

Women to whom I've recounted my dearest secrets. Wives of a fashion. I have loved them all.'

Indeed! Madame de Tournevile was beginning to sound just like a Frenchman. What would she say next, that woman was a mystery?

'Madame de la Motte de la Motte-Piquet, would you allow me?'

But the couturier's cup was bare, there was nothing to read. In her haste to drink, she had slurped up the grounds as well.

'Excuse us, but we must be getting back to work, most unfortunately. Thank you Joanna dear, for such a sumptuous lunch. You are simply marvellous!'

It was Jean-Claudi introducing our departure. Several more shots with the digital and out we went, blowing kisses on our way. It was a French workday after all, and while a four hour lunch may pass before the boss's eyes without receiving a blink, a five hour lunch is no longer tolerated as it once was, due to the global economy which does hasten all mealtimes, lunch in particular.

Unfortunately Jean-Claudi got a parking ticket, which made him rather sore. Thank goodness Horace was there to minimize the blow and massage Jean-Claudi's solar plexus. Horace handed the ticket to me, and told me to get rid of it, which I did by dropping it into the public garbage bin. Off we sped to À La Mode Online, myself holding on to the back of Horace's headrest for dear life. Jean-Claudi is quite a car pilot indeed!

Once there, I raved to all the dear spoons about the luncheon. As the stay-home spoon, I knew it was important to highlight my one outing to the best of my abilities. Went through the entire menu which the spoons accompanied with a second round of *oh là là*s. Then was put to work on a calculator to estimate the shelf life of handkerchief tops. Multiplied the strength quotient of the fabric fibre times the daily wear-and-tear quotient, divided by the time on the shelf recorded in seconds. Hid my answer in the drawer. Have always found mathematics quite embarrassing. Managed to get Yoga Spoon to do the job instead.

Began to get the collywobbles, probably because of such rich midday dining. Asked the spoons if they had any anti-collywobble tea, which they gladly did. Fixed myself a cup and retired to my desk for a brief rest before it was time to go to Mass. It had been a long day after all and not without its tensions from all that note-taking! Said a quick hello to Djamila and her Hadj before leaving. Djamila was wearing the Viva Glam Twig lipstick. She looked smashing and I tried telling her so in Berber, a language I've slowly been learning thanks to dance and cooking class.

I found my seat in St Joe's next to an elderly lady who would not stop talking. I supposed she was talking to God but still! It was very hard to concentrate and yet I did my best to pray for Joanna's happiness, which at this point was obviously contingent upon securing the gown. To simplify matters, I prayed for the garment, too (thank you for putting in an extra word, Sancho). Said a blessing for the Polish priest's accent at the end, and left St Joe's feeling quite all right. Yes, cured of the collywobbles and rather chipper.

Which meant I could comfortably spend the evening dancing with Jubilee who is a rather fine dancer, I must say. I practised the entire repertory including the latest, 'Eyes of Magic Fire', and worked on intensifying my gaze by looking intently into Jubilee's wide, golden eyes. I was bitten on the nose yet did make improvements. Retired to bed with a cup of tea (chamomile for Jubilee) and more *Moby*

Dick, (Chapter LXXXI). '*Don't be afraid, my butter-boxes*,' cried out Stubbs to the hell-bound harpooners, whilst looking straight into the whale's eye.

'*Pray tell, dear Stubbs*,' I would have queried on the Ouija-phone if one existed, '*what exactly is a butter-box?*'

Slumber.

Feast of Saint Pelagia of Antioch

The *Concise* doesn't know whether to call you a martyr or not, as you took your life in your own hands and threw it off the roof of your house – but only because the Christian-hating Romans were coming after you. They chased you from room to room and up the staircase, till at last you had no choice but to leap your way to sainthood. To think that at the age of only fifteen you found that quick route into the communion's ranks, avoiding perhaps years of self-inflicted deprivation and cruel Coliseum tortures! A quick glance at the pain-riddled lives of your colleagues will support my conclusion:

you got off easy, Pelagia. And even better, because of this you have become our Patron Saint of Expedient Exits.

I wonder what it was that woke me up so early. Perhaps the yangst in Roland's roses? I pinched my spleen point, which Master Woo recommends for calming an excessive yang reaction in the morn. Then I thought about Roland for a moment. Perhaps I should send him Mumly's Jack La Lanne exercise book. I did a few jumping jacks myself, and a cartwheel too. Jubilee got terribly excited by the callisthenics and ran out the door, which I had opened for a knocking Neighbour Jeromino.

'Carrots please. Felix has the flu, please.'

I went to the kitchen and looked in the crisper, where two floppy carrots, very limber and perfect for boiling down, limply lay. I was glad they would be put to good use. I myself only eat crisp carrots.. And Jubilee will only take them when shredded. Feeling generous, I gave Jubilee permission to play with Felix whilst I got ready for the day. Von Krysler coffee, Her Majesty's Weetabix and vitamins A, E and B-minus. Put on mauve uni, grabbed raincoat and was out the door quick as a flash (thank you, dear Pelagia, for boosting my exit efficiency).

As is so often the case, I got to work before the spoons had arrived (so on second thoughts, Pelagia, perhaps you should lighten my dose just a little bit). On my desk was a fax, addressed to me, from Top Spoon herself – who is presently at a spa in Corsica – listing her daily itinerary: would I write it up as a feature for the site? And so I did as requested, enjoying the pre-spoon hour, which offered the perfect conditions for my journalistic flight of fancy. I imagined myself on the Island of Beauty, taking a dietetic breakfast on a terrace overlooking the Mediterranean, later working with a personal trainer in the exotic garden, before spending my afternoon on a waterbed wrapped in red algae and massaged by a hundred hydrojets. In the early evening, a facial with the essential oils of Moroccan roses and macerated bamboo. Dietetic candlelight dinner with personal trainer overlooking terrace, exotic garden and sea.

I finished the article just as the spoons began arriving in various waking states. The À La Mode Online crowd is certainly not a morning one. A round of tea, coffee and cigarettes is the key for starting the work engines. I helped prepare the beverages but was called away by a telephone call.

'Remedy, I think it went well.'

'Oh I'm sure it did, Joanna! Tell me what happened after we left.'

'Well, before leaving Eléanore invited me to her *atelier*. I'm meeting her tomorrow. I think that's a good sign, don't you?'

'Absolutely!'

'I have to say that I am very, very pleased. Oh, and about the Ball of Marvels, Remedy. You know that all the guests are formally introduced with a mention of their "claim to fame" as it were. Yours, I was thinking, would have to be Richard II, the Texas Tycoon.'

'But he was only my stepfather and then Mumly got the thing annulled. Now he is my dead ex-stepfather. I don't think that counts.'

'But he was with you during your formative years, Remedy. The years when you needed him most which does count for a lot.'

Indeed, the formative years. Joanna was right. Those years when my very *being* was forged, my personality percolated and put through the strainer for refinement. Richard II kept me beautifully shod for the journey and guided me along to the strains of Verdi. When a problem arose, he taught me to percuss it, tap it gently with a finger for diagnosis. It was a musical suggestion that has served me well. He trained my ears to listen for the answer. I cannot say that Richard II was ever a father to me. No, he was more like a paternal conductor, somewhat distant, speaking to us with his batons, which he wildly waved whenever the music came on. His presence provided Mumly and me with the happiness that comes from fine shoes and food for the ears.

'I see your point, Joanna. Go ahead and use his name. It's the only name I have. If I remember right, he did adopt me for a time.'

'And what are you going to do about a dress? The ball is in three weeks. At Chez Mathilde they need *at least* that much time to do the fitting.'

'Don't worry about that, Joanna. I'll get it taken care of.'

'Well, just don't wait until the last minute or you'll be out of luck.'

'Don't worry.'

I was sure right then that Joanna's frontal gauge was reading thunder showers in the north. She really does take too much on. Imagine worrying about what I'll be wearing! Even I'm not worried! Poor Joanna, she's so overworked these days. She just doesn't know when to stop!

I hung up and wrote a scoop on one of the latest lines of bubble baths with aphrodisiac properties, simply called Aphrodite, developed by an Australian sexologist. Has Dr Dolittle come up with her own line as well? With her experience in the field, she could even take product efficiency further by adding Adult Sex properties. This way a girl could soak with her bloke and have a nice time, but in the end, pull the plug and leave nothing behind! Now that the cosmetics industry possesses the *savoir-faire* required to provoke precise emotional states in their product users, there is a whole new realm of possibilities to explore. A joint venture with Master Woo, bringing together the best of Feng Shui *and* Adult Sex, would surely provide the ultimate bubble product. Perfect yin-yang balance plus modern day-efficiency. A winning combination! Shall I suggest it to her in my next epistle?

Left for St Joe's at midday sharp and was only five minutes late for Mass which, by divine time standards, is hardly late at all. Sat next to Sister Dagobert and Yorik, whose fatty tumour was at last tucked into a girdlesque wrapper. Apparently, one of Sister Dagobert's patients had designed the bandage himself, and strapped poor Yorik up in it every morning. He was an animist, she explained to me later, who worshipped the carved branch of a chestnut tree taken straight from the Luxembourg gardens. I could not help thinking of Melville's queer Queequeg, at the Spouter-Inn, saying his prayers to his Congo idol. I have never met an animist myself, but I said a prayer for them nevertheless: it is said that many of them are head-peddlers – or they were back in the nineteenth century – and it is important to pray for past events which have influenced the present so clearly and dearly.

Finishing the Mass, Père Ricard made mention of a parish pilgrimage to the Holy Land, the very same that Sister Dagobert had spoken about. He encouraged those interested parties to sign up in the foyer. It looks like Sister Dagobert has chosen the most popular of the pilgrimage buses; she is so *very* with it and has an eye out for what's best.

We had a quick, hamless lunch afterwards. I couldn't wait to ask Sister Dagobert how the children's First Communion went. I didn't go myself, of course. Never on a Sunday, I told Sister Dagobert who seemed to understand. *As long as you go on Saturday.* Indeed I often do catch the Saturday night Mass, though not always.

'How were the children? Did they do well?'

'Beautifully!'

'No drops or spills?'

'None whatsoever. Even Père Ricard didn't miss.'

'I'm so happy to hear it. That they were true apostles.'

'They were, Child. And as dear as angels.'

Ah! My darling students, my apostolic learners. May they continue their sacramental itinerary without delay! May they understand that, (as Sister Mary-Paul MD says), while totalitarianism is quite bad in politics, it is so very good in relation to the Lord! And may they find comfort in the hard work required of them as Christian Soldiers. Yes, in their love of the Lord, may they be like Jacob, who had to work seven long years to be able to marry Rachel and yet who loved her so much that those seven years seemed merely like seven days! With proper catechetic training, all this was possible. As a special treat to celebrate the young catechisees success, we ordered two bowls of strawberry hokey-pokey and a half bottle of Château Margaux, for the love of Mary Magdalene.

When I got back to work there was yet another celebration in the offing, this one with a decidedly techno-nuptial spin. Bottles of champagne popped open and all the spoons were fluted and accepting top-ups without restraint. Jean-Claudi and Horace danced chest to chest in technocide tuxedos (Gaultier) whilst Willie (*Wheelie*) manned the turntables. It was a party and no minor one at that. A three-tiered cake with two plastic grooms arm-in-arm at the top of it sat on a linen-covered table, along with a remarkable spread of bites from Fauchon.

'What's going on here,' I asked my nearest neighbour, who happened to be Yoga Spoon, calmly standing on her head (the Sīrṣāsana position).

'It's a party for Jean-Claudi and Horace. They just tied the knot at City Hall.'

'They got married?'

'Almost. They did the best they could. And now they'll have a better tax status.'

'I see.'

I thought a moment. Indeed there had recently been some modification in the Napoleonic code allowing for courthouse sanctification of same-sex relationships for tax and inheritance benefits. And indeed this *was* the best they could do. And while it wasn't quite enough – for they were true lovers and not profiteers – they were nevertheless throwing a kingly reception. Everyone in the office was there, including the accounting, finance and marketing people who are usually upstairs with the door shut. The only one of us who ever sees them is Top Spoon, and usually to discuss a bonus problem. But there they all were, new and unusual faces to me, loosening up their ledgers with bubbles, moving their market reports to the command of DJ Willie (*Wheelie*). The party was irresistible; even Yoga Spoon came down from her heady station and had a highball. Chin-chin!

A group of young men with platinum-dyed hair, each one wearing that tight sleeveless tee called 'a marcel', arrived all at once and in high spirits. I instantly recognized these marvellous ephebes as the swing performers. Small and compact in the manner of acrobats, they were perfectly made for that gentlemen's swing, which I have never seen yet have imagined so vividly that I might have sat upon it myself. Yes, so light on the feet, so handsome and sweet, why who else could they have been? The swing team made their way through the crowd to Jean-Claudi and Horace, who they hoisted up on to their (largely bare) shoulders, before proceeding to parade them around the reception like brides at a Berber wedding. A round of applause and the multiple firing of corks!

The boys bounced to the trance-like beat of Willie's (*Wheelie's*) techno wedding-march remix as they made their way twice around the room, stopping at last before the three-tiered cake. From this ambulatory loft, Jean-Claudi and Horace held the nuptial knife together and cut the first slice. Then a second. Lovingly they fed each other this sweetmeat as a symbol of their commitment to mutual nourishment in the days to come. More applause! The pouring of toppers! *Un discours! Un discours!* Yes, a speech was desired and due. Horace sat up as straight as he could upon his friends' shoulders and greeted his guests.

'We are honoured to have you here with us to celebrate our happiness which at this moment is very, very great. Our only regret, dear friends, is that we were not able to have a church wedding, which would have meant so much to us. Perhaps one day the Church will open the skirts of her sacraments to all of us, but for the moment we cannot get through that curtain. And so we have done the best we could which is really not so bad is it? Cheers, my friends. To the health of all.'

Thunderous applause. A magnum of champagne popped and shot like a fire hydrant, wetting the shrieking spoons. *Hooray!* Jean-Claudi and Horace descended from their perch and the swing pack dispersed. Willie (*Wheelie*) played a straight Strauss waltz. Jean-Claudi invited Horace's mumly to dance, whilst Jean-Claudi's mumly was twirled around the room in Horace's arms, Arthur Murray style. Did a bit of *pas chassé* myself, a step which inadvertently landed me in the arms of Monsieur Dufour, a dot-com accountant, and specialist in accountability technology. As we were spinning around, M. Dufour missed the floor and landed flat-footed upon my toes.

'I'm so very sorry. Please, Mademoiselle, let me make amends.'

And so I was willingly led to one of the back desks for an accountable foot massage, which was lovely indeed. So lovely, indeed, that I had rather a difficult time leaving M. Dufour, who was inclined to continue on up the limbs, as it were. Knowing that he spent his days in the upstairs office where the door was shut tight, and that I would most likely not cross paths with him again being as I am a stay-home spoon, I left him in that corner with a certain regret. Back at the party I bumped into Horace who was in grand form indeed.

'Congratulations, Horace!'

'Thank you, darling! I'm just thrilled myself.'

'Say, Horace, how interested are you *really* in the sacrament-o-marriage?'

'Remedy, dear, I regret terribly that Père Pouteaux wouldn't do it. He baptized me, first communioned and confirmed me, but now he won't marry me. It's very unfair, love, but what's a lad to do? Write to the Pope? He never answers, you know. His secretary, Dominic, does all the paperwork. I know Dominic – used to go to parties with him when I was in Rome. He would borrow the Pope's censer and use it as a purse. Usually it caught on fire.'

'I think I can help you, Horace.'

'How so?'

'I mean, I think I can marry you. Not in a church, but at home. A home wedding.'

'Could you, love, that would be fabulous! Do you know a priest who would do it?'

'Yes, I do,' said I, thinking of myself as rehearsal priest. 'Come by my place tomorrow night at nine p.m.'

Horace kissed me on the cheek.

'Miss Remedy, you're a peach.'

Well, I hope that I am. Manifestly Horace thought I had some bootlegging priest in mind. Perhaps it's me, Remedy! In these times of prohibition, a woman must keep to her mission. Despite the interdiction. If I excelled as a rehearsal priest, as a performance priest I would certainly exalt. But first I have to brush up a bit on the wedding sacrament, which I know so little about. A visit to www.catholictroth.com should provide me with all the necessary know-how. The rest will depend on my personal interpretation of the material, and choice of scripture. And, of course, there is also the sacerdotal collar to consider which I will have to confect myself, perhaps out of cosmetic cotton and starch.

Pondering the task ahead, I rejoined the party, to find that Djamila and Hadj Mohammed had just arrived.

'Djamila, Pilgrim, come and join us!'

'What? Join the infidels! Never. Not on the head of my mother! Ah! Look at this mess. Why were we not told? Our time's been taken by the drinking Infidels!'

'It's a surprise wedding party. Nobody knew about it. There's orange juice if you'd like some.'

Despite her distress, Djamila agreed to have a fruit drink.

'How's your son?' I asked, handing her the glass of juice.

In a way it was dishonest of me to ask this neighbourly question, for what I really wanted to know was not how her son was, but what her nephew, that moon of a Mouktar, had been up to. Yet I intuited that it was best to start out easy, to begin by degree of proximity to Djamila's heart.

'He is well, Daughter. He shunned the atheist, which was Allah's will. She was a cheat and had a second man – a perfumer and a Jew. She began wearing so much scent that she stank as infidels often do because they perfume but do not bathe. He swore upon my head that he would never touch her again and left her to spread her stink in the home of the Jew. And she will continue to stink until the last scream of judgement day. But so it was written by Allah.

'As for Mohammed, my heart, he is with an Algerian girl, a second cousin who veils and follows Muslim law to the best of her abilities. She's a bit slow in the head but dear of heart.'

'I'm glad to hear it, Djamila. You must be relieved.'

'I am indeed, Daughter. God-be-willing there will be a wedding soon. And God-be-willing my son will be blessed with sons.'

'Yes, may Allah will what he may. And, say Djamila, how is your nephew, the one who caught the fish and ate it with us?'

I tried to be as nonchalant as possible, to make it seem that Mouktar had just then and there flashed though my mind. As if he were some friendly afterthought rather than the preoccupying concern dominating both my head and my heart of late.

'Working hard, I tell you. He writes his doctorate in the day and delivers for Shlomi at night. Hardly does he have a moment's rest.'

My, my! I thought of that light in his eye, the kind that arises from the musing soul, that thoughtful, ever-ready illuminator. I grew quite interested in knowing more about Mouktar's scholastic efforts: after Vassar, I too, contemplated being a scholar, but then, because of the cost of shoes, decided otherwise.

'He is studying the poetry of our great Arabian poets and is so clever that he was given a full-paying scholarship. He only works to help his mother who must otherwise live off a widow's pension.'

Just like Mumly, I thought. If she doesn't start winning a few golf tournaments, I might have to moonlight too.

'He must be a very fine man.'

'A better one cannot be found, child. I only wish my Mohammed were more like him. How I wanted him to study medicine and become a doctor. But he never did like the studies. Now he sells refrigerators to the Muslims, which is not so bad a business. It is customary that a man have as many refrigerators as he has wives. Most Muslims prefer the Whirlpool models. Did you see my beautiful refrigerator, daughter? It's from America like you.'

'It's lovely, Djamila. It reminds me of home.'

Indeed, all refrigerators tended to remind me of home. How odd that I've never managed to keep mine full. Still, the very sight of it could warm my heart.

'Shall I introduce you to the hosts of the party, Djamila? They are believers.'

Perhaps the orange juice had loosened her up, for Djamila calmed the 'O Infidel!' cry and agreed to meet them. I guided her to Horace and made the introduction. To my great pleasure they took to each other straight away with curious Horace asking a number of questions and Djamila answering them squarely. Blew the swing boys a kiss and skipped out.

I took the metro home, wondering when oh when I would hear from Mouktar. How hard he worked and with no play? I had been awaiting his call, but perhaps he was carefully preparing it, imagining all possible telephonic conversations prior to the act. Perhaps he would require parental permission in which case I would have to send him to Djamila, my Muslim step-in mother. I have never dated a Muslim scholar before and so have no idea how such encounters transpire. Are we perhaps to meet clandestinely in the bustling marketplace? And do I ask him to carry my bag of figs? Best to sit tight. Best to get out the watercolours and paint a few scenes.

I painted a portrait of Mouktar in a cherry tree wearing a yellow turban. Another one of him in the National Library, taking calligraphic notes with an extravagant, foot-long, peacock plume. Then I hung them up to dry. Fed Jubilee a can of sardines in tomato sauce and had a pear myself. From nine to ten, I practised my finger cymbals and running choo-choo, a recurrent move in Samira's latest choreography, 'Eyes of Magic Fire', whilst imagining I was tankinied at the Red Sea with a boxer-shorted Mouktar. Observed my facial expression in the mirror. Having at last facially captured the essential emotions, I immediately applied a pore-cleansing mud mask so as to hold the expression in place and commit it to memory. Rinsed and retired. Counted Mouktars till slumber.

Oh Saint Pelagia, may you expedite my exit from celibatarianhood soon!

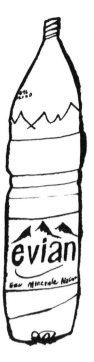

Feast of Saint Felicula

Alas! Felicula! And all because of that poor sport of a count who turned you over to the Roman magistrates. Why, you simply had to reject his crusty hand to better hold the Lord's! Oh, but you did end badly didn't you? Imagine suffocating in the pestilent sewers! I simply can't! Yours was a terrible martyrdom, yet it strengthened the Christian commitment to carry on, to forge ahead armed with the love of the Lord, noses clamped shut with clothes pins.

Indeed, while my little morning meditation on your martyrdom might have brought on the collywobbles, it instead increased my apostolic zest.

In excellent form, with a craving for a ham and egg breakfast even, I decided to go directly to the Café Beaubourg, where English breakfast is served until noon. Having found a comfortable armchair, I ordered scrambled eggs with goat's cheese and lardons. A sautéed tomato on the side. A café crème and freshly squeezed orange juice, too. Perhaps it's odd to brunch on a weekday, and yet the craving was so strong (here's to you Felicula!) I could not deny its appeal. Last night's activity had used up a good deal of my forces, much as would an evening of love. I pondered over my priestly performance and was pleased.

Jean-Claudi and Horace received the sensible and efficacious sign of God's love for humankind by way of the sacrament of marriage, which I myself single-handedly administered. Prior to the event I had spent an entire day as a sacerdotal scholar, learning all the words of the nuptial Mass by heart, minus the parts on multiplying the fruit-o-the-womb. By evening-time I was frocked, my entire being alive and humming, for I was invested with the supernatural action of the verb. Priestly grace had been granted to me. I had asked and received.

Whilst Jean-Claudi and Horace sat cross-legged upon velvet poufs, I read from the Corinthians and the Apocalypse too, not forgetting the Song of Songs. I pleaded with the Holy Ghost to unite what no man, excepting the Pope and the Palace of Justice, could bring asunder. I blessed the rings, initiated the pledging of troths and invited the groom to kiss the groom. I even made a wedding register which vapour-headed Neighbour Jeromino and Horace's mumly duly signed as witnesses.

As I dined on the ham and egg fare, I thought about those priests who suffer to repress their desire for the groom, when they join a couple in holy matrimony. Now I understood how this was. Lifted my glass of orange juice for a toast. To desire! Across the room a man perched on a pouf lifted his cup of coffee as if to toast me back. Desire indeed! It was Monsieur Lift! I was so preoccupied by my musings that I had not noticed him. But clearly he'd had his eye on me. And so I sent him another salute, this time with a different message. To solitude! I lifted my glass again, nodded my head Simone de Beauvoir style and shielded my own private party with the *International Herald Tribune.*

Solitude indeed! I said a quick prayer to Glorietta, supplicating for the speedy arrival of my moon man. Then the collywobbles set in from so many eggs so early in the morn (ah! They do it every time, Felicula. Eggs are nothing like martyrdom; they inspire not). But I managed to pay the bill and stand up to leave. I was even going to nod again to my toastee but found he was no longer there. Monsieur Lift? I asked my waiter. *Là-bas.* He pointed to a far corner of the café where another young woman sat alone with a cup-o-tea. Desire knows no bounds, I saw. Solitude has no favourites. Left quickly to get to work on time.

Top Spoon asked me to investigate the dust bowl look taken up by an emerging group of young New York-based designers paying tribute to their Oklahoma great-grandmothers. The look is very Martha Graham-like, pulled and distressed yet with loads of plissé and extra sleeves. Silk mixed with oatmeal tweed and plume. Perfect for dancing Medea in a chuck wagon which, I must say, was how it was presented at the collections. Wrote three articles and submitted two. Then I went to the ladies' room to powder my nose, and found, much to my relief, that the quarters were back to normal. No more unsettling decor to play havoc with the digestion. I practised my 'Eyes of Magic Fire' expression and found the exact attitude and allure right away. My mud mask was extra efficient. When I got back to my desk, the phone was ringing.

'Remedy! It's happened!'

'Oh, Joanna, I knew it would! What does it look like? Any chronometers?' (Chronometer breast plates, are, I should say, one of Motte de la Motte-Piquet's trademarks.)

'No, her latest collection is a bit different. The dress is a pink-lamé shell with a long silver skirt. Actually it's not lamé but topstitched tinsel with a few bolts of silvery attic insulation for the bustle. It has that off-kilter edge I find great for dancing. Remedy, it's just fabulous! By the way, have you done that article yet?'

'Top Spoon has it on the calendar for next month. I'll write it then.'

'Sooner would be better, but I suppose that'll do. Anyway, I pick up the dress in two weeks, right before the ball. Eléanore is a love, I tell you. An absolute love once you get to know her!'

I expressed my sincere delight and managed to get off the phone before she enquired about my choice of gowns. Lord knows, I simply do not have time to think about the Ball of Marvels right now. Of course Joanna would not understand, though in her coffee-table book days she would have been more sympathetic. But now that she has little to divert her attention from the ball, besides occasional Faubourg St-Honoré strolls with her shopping trolley, she is not equipped for hearing any hem-hawing. No matter how justified it may be.

Went downstairs to buy a bottle of Evian and blessed it in the privacy of the Gents (ladies' room locked). Now it was ready for St Joe's. There seems to be an aridity problem with the holy water basins in church and cathedral foyers in France these days: they've all run dry.

Only in Notre-Dame does the Bishop of Paris make an effort to refill because of the number of global pilgrims coming through. Otherwise it's like Jesus and his forty days of desert, all parched and dying for drink. I've decided to act as well-wench, bringing the holy water in and refilling as many sanctified basins as I possibly can. Today I would start close to home, at St Joe's.

Getting there at half eleven sharp, I surreptitiously poured the freshly blessed (and therefore electromagnetically charged) water into the shell-shaped stone basin. Then I sat down to pray, but instead wondered if, having grown accustomed to a dry fount, parishioners would at all be inclined to dip their fingers in and bless themselves. Why would they expect there to be anything other than a parched basin? I worried that my effforts had been for naught. But then, as Mass-goers began to arrive, I saw that their hands went from fount to forehead most naturally and entirely without surprise. What a relief! How quickly a dry spell is forgotten with a refill! The healing, electro-magnetic properties of holy water attract the believing hand. It was truly a wonder to witness!

Sister Dagobert and Yorik then arrived at the door, requiring my services to be escorted up the aisle. Sister Dagobert whispered that she had encountered some kind of trouble with her animist patient, Mr Macaba, in the Tropical Disease ward this morning. I inspected Sister Dagobert closely but did not find anything awry. Manifestly she had not been struck with a stick. I wondered what manner of spirits might have seized Mr Macaba, in the hothouse of that feverish ward? I prayed for him, that he may first and foremost recover from his tropical ill and be discharged from the Hôtel-Dieu asap.

Père Ricard made his slurred but much awaited greeting. And an

important Mass it was, celebrating Ascension, the miraculous eleva-
tion of Jesus Christ into the heavens. And I had completely forgotten!
How so? I thought back to Easter forty days ago. What had I done
then? Oh yes, I had gone on a private pilgrimage to Chartres for the
entire Holy Week. A lovely expedition, and one I would recommend
to anyone requiring yin therapy. The intensity of the Chartres blue
does wonders for the autonomic nervous system. Moreover, there is a
great deal to do at Chartres, particularly during Holy Week. I studied
the stem of the Tree of Jesse window with my opera glasses for quite
a while. So much prestigious growth from one groin! Overheard
the celebrated British Chartres scholar, Mr Piller, leading a group of
American women on his tour. How condescending he was towards
these well-bred matrons from Connecticut and yet so entirely dependent on their purses! Still the ladies didn't seem to mind a bit. They
dismissed his glib patronizing as a Britannic tic and invited him to
New Haven to speak at their Junior League assembly. A fully paid
round trip plus a pension. I bumped into Mr Piller near the holy water
fount after his noon nap and gave him my last dollar bill, for it is
important to support non-institutionalized historians.

Went to confession with a young priest who was born and reared
in Passy, where Roland's mumly resides. For penance he had me
purchase a finger rosary at the cathedral store, a very handy item so it
has proved. Perfect to use in movie theatres whilst the previews are
projected. I didn't go to Easter Mass, because of my never-on-a-
Sunday rule, but instead walked down by the brook and said grace
with the ducks before feeding them crumbs. Listened to the Cathedral
hum, the bellowing of its organ pipes rising up, beyond the Gothic
vaults, to the very heavens of France. My spirit soared with the

harmonic piping but was brought back down by the *bourdon,* that low pitched stop announcing the end of the musical advance towards the gods. I could not help but think of the Marquis de Bourdon, for it is said there is much in a name. In truth what *is* a *bourdon*? A similar stop in harmoniums? The lowest bell in a peel of bells? So it seems. It does not elevate but concludes, brings down to *finis.* It is the sinker at the end of the fisherman's line. As a fisher of men myself, one who prefers the blithe fly, I've never sunk my line. That is, until now. Ah Roland, Knight of White! That lowest of the baritone bells! That weighty stop which brings the music down! (Oh dear, I hope he's not treacherous like your count, Felicula!)

With the return of these Holy Week musings, I had quite a hard time concentrating on the miraculous Ascension of the Son of Man. I tried thinking instead of Richard II's fly-fishing trips on the El Dorado. With a quick flick of the wrist, he would expertly lift the squirming trout out of the water and into the airborne net Mumly held. Flying fish, much like the Son of God rising and landing in the heavenly mesh. My concentration improved immensely. Prayers became upwardly mobile. *Bourdon* phenomenon forgotten.

Leaving Sister Dagobert after Mass, I picked up lunch from the caterer on the Rue Montorgueil. My favourite dish of all, *tartiflette*! With the heated *barquette* gently swinging in a plastic bag around my wrist, I rushed back to the office to eat the potato-ham-n-cheese *régal* before the spoons returned from pump practice. Only Yoga Spoon was there, but not to worry. She would never touch lardons. I prepared tea for the returning spoons, who are always so thirsty after the gym, whilst sifting through collections photos for examples of VIP dresses. I found only two, both from the Coco house. Very ladylike and tweedy.

Then I pretended I was a VIP myself, drinking large pots of coffee like Balzac to keep up with other important people on the run. Imagined myself running through the corridors of airports in strappy sandals...

...*No hose. Cell phone ringing off the hook. Have to pee because of all the coffee. Ovaries running on gonad time. Make a mad rush for the loo but run into another VIP. A manly one, in VIP Wall Street Journal wear. Excuse me! Oh! But he sees that I am VIP too, rushed but ready for collision. Offers me a coffee, which I cannot refuse. My VIP bladder will stand it. Can make it through the talk without unleashing. I will* will *it to hold. Such are my VIP thoughts. Mind over matter, as Mary Baker Eddy, founder of Christian Science, always says. Her remarkable manifesto, Science and Health, will help me if I can only remember the right passages and the keys to scripture. My VIP gentleman is entirely attractive and entirely interested. He has no time but takes it nevertheless. Mind over Time. He pays me the highest VIP compliment. We chat, chat, chat and drink. We drink again and chat, chat, chat again. I am charmed by my VIP but my bladder is not. It screeches and screams and, seeing that I refuse to listen, finally lets loose. A warm wetness seeps through the VIP tweediness of the VIP dress. Oh dear! Not now! I will have to cover with my VIP Coco coat. Where is it? Where is it? I look around but realize I have left it in business class. Damn it! Not now! Why now? But there is little to do but tie the arms of my VIP dress jacket around my waist Jr High School style. Oh! Oh! Oh! No!!!*

I made a visit to the ladies' room all the same just as the spoons arrived.

'Tea's ready,' I called out.

'Oh, Remedy. You are wonderful!'

I do do my best.

Dutifully, I spent the afternoon writing the article on VIP dresses. Thought for a minute about the Ball of Marvels, then forgot about it. I left work early for dance class, where I learned a new move called the Vibrating Half Moon, a very rapid hip movement often used when dancing to Egyptian pop music. Got home and fixed an egg salad dinner which I ate not without wonder. I wondered when Mouktar's day off would transpire. Perhaps scholars never vacation? And yet how leisure can refresh the mind. I may have to call Mouktar myself if the lad doesn't avail soon. Could he be waiting for a new moon cycle? Does he augur with an astrolabe? I did wonder.

Retired with *A Turn of the Screw*. A chilling tale indeed (though less appetite inspiring than your martydom, Felicula). Jubilee thought he saw a ghost, which is not so uncommon for a cat. Slumber.

Feast of Saints Valerius
and Rufinus

The strains of Radio Notre-Dame woke me from a deep sleep this morning with a broadcast straight from Soissons! Wasn't this where you two suffered martyrdom at the hands of the then heathen Gauls? The Soissons choir was singing in your honour what sounded like a French version of 'On Eagle Wings', a funeral favourite if I'm not mistaken, often sung at Mass as a filler. Did the two of you soar towards the heavens, perched upon the wings of an eagle, your martyred heads tucked under your arm like Saint Denis? If so, I hope you held on tight! They say it's like the rodeo.

Unfortunately I couldn't listen to the choir's saintly tribute for long. As usual there was simply too much to do before work, such as showering with lots of foaming geranium shower product for good mental health, then powdering down and dressing. The uniform season is at last over now that summer has made an appearance. Only light, flowing dresses with strappy sandals will do. Like in Florida, only minus the polka dots.

Most of my morning was spent writing about the Swarovski accessory craze: Swarovski tiaras, patchwork purses, boa belts, and heart-shaped mules. Crystal accoutrements abound for glitter-giving purposes. Every girl wants to give and get glitter. So says Top Spoon, who paraded around the office this morning in a black Swarovski tankini with matching wonder shoes. How do you stay so thin, asked the admiring spoons? Five curious ambulance sessions a week for trouble spots, plus a diet of cornflakes and cabbage and black radish soup. Unlike the other spoons, who go to pump practice, Top Spoon has private lessons with her personal meditation trainer. She says you can meditate fat away. And there's nothing magic about it. It's work! Indeed, Top Spoon is a busy bee both as a spoon and a lotus!

At half eleven, a delivery boy arrived with a bouquet of flowers for me, a mixture of soft pink Charm of Paris roses, with white lilies and assorted greens. I set it on my desk and looked at the attached card with great curiosity.

'*In a week we shall meet, my fair rose. Ah! Love on the Elysian Fields!*'

My, my! Is love on the Champs Elysées his noble intention? If so will he have the back seat of his motor car properly arranged?

'*Oh là là…* Remedy! It's beautiful! Who's it from? You must tell us!'

The spoons of course wanted to know all about it.

'It's just a reminder that I have a date to the ball,' I explained.

Immediately the spoons pressed to know which ball and where?

'The Ball of Marvels, I believe. Somewhere near Versailles.'

'In the Château!'

'Yes,' I quietly admitted, 'in the very castle, I'm afraid.'

'*Oh là là*… How chic! *Quelle Chance*, Remedy!'

I breathed not a word about Roland, intentionally keeping his identity incognito. Being full-blooded Frenchwomen, the spoons might well take me for yet another ill-bred foreigner after the local patrimony. A marquis-thief as it were, ridding Europe of what has long been hers. I'd rather avoid such misunderstandings. Moreover I am tired of explaining to the French that I am a third generation American, which obviously means that three generations ago I was a European. True, I was perhaps not yet born, however, according to several Eastern philosophies, my soul was nascent and already voyaging between Cordoba and Killarney, the homes of my ancestors. Why it awaited until the marriage of Mumly and Daddy-gone to appear in the cousin land, I do not know. Indeed, to find out would clearly require a Ouija-phone. Yet the fact remains that the practice of hybridity, so habitual and necessary in the Americas, is often frowned upon by the Europeans. As I pondered upon this, I began to wonder what the Marquis could possibly see in the cross-bred Remedy. Yes, even my name suggests a medicinal mix, an amalgam of healing plants and minerals, a multi-vitamin elixir to cure the seven evils. Mumly named me so after the death of Daddy-gone, for my wee presence turned her sorrow to gold.

Was the Marquis, I wondered, an exception to his ilk? Doubtful.

Or did he see me as a brief, half-breed interlude in an overly ordered destiny? Was I merely a moment of good cheer, a diverting mix of Peasant Exotic and American Pie? For if he wanted full-bred exotics he would have chosen an active member of the pornocracy say, or a Swarovski-sequined Lido dancer. And yet if this were so, if I were but a passing whim, would he make a public appearance with me at the Ball of Marvels? The answer is certainly no. Clearly the Marquis was trying to extricate himself from the maternal yoke by publicly dating a crumb and thereby disgracing his mumly. How often this happens; it's really terribly banal, but I must say that in choosing me, Roland was going about it half-heartedly, for could such a one as me truly be a source of full-fledged dishonour? An Israeli Lido girl would have done the trick in a minute. Manifestly he was not entirely ready to cut the cord and bear that momentary loss of inheritance which is often a necessary step in the initial process of mumly-son separation. Of course the inheritance returns after the first boy-child is born at which point all amends are made for the family name continues on. Roland's resistance was somehow unnatural, and yet I suppose he should be given a degree of encouragement for trying, however sorrily and half-handedly, to reach beyond the Mumly Inclination.

I called to thank him for the flowers but spoke in the end to his maid, who explained that he was at the Auteuil hippodrome for the day. A good place for him I suppose. The mere sound of horses hooves does stimulate testosterone production. Moreover, by carefully watching the jockeys, one receives a free riding lesson.

Got back to Swarovski but was interrupted by the phone. Joanna calling with latest FYI.

'Remedy, guess what? There's been a big change in plans.'

'Tell, tell.'

'The ball is not going to be held at the Versailles Castle but right in Paris at the Hôtel Crillon. It's so much more convenient don't you think? To be honest, you know, I've never been a great Versailles fan. I suppose it has to do with Marie Antoinette. I've never cared for her.'

'Me neither, Joanna. I suppose we're lucky that we never had to play shepherdess with her. She would have had us on all fours dressed like lambs.'

'Well, anyway, the Crillon is absolutely gorgeous and so much more intime. And that soft golden decor looks great on blondes.'

Indeed this was an upgrade in my opinion too. The Hôtel Crillon has long been Mumly's favourite Parisian palace. She and Richard II stayed there every trip and always with a room looking out onto the Obelisk of Luxor. The obelisk was somehow a great comfort to Richard II. Later I believe he had one built on his ranch in Texas. The Knight of Amarillo he called it: bigger than a totem pole, better than a mining hole. It became a most prestigious landmark and once a year a corral was put up and a rodeo played around its stem (though without the eagles, Valerius and Rufinus).

Richard II was exceedingly generous with his private goods whenever he was able to be so. But I do remember Mumly telling me about the marvels of the Crillon and how in the early evening whilst Richard II took his nap, she would sit in the golden marble salon sipping a Kentucky highball. How agreeable it was to converse with some distinguished gentleman from Capetown say, or Jiddah. Always an international set with a stake or two in Texas. Mumly loved an aperitif at the Crillon but she also loved the breakfast, which came to her on a linen-covered ambulatory table set with fine silver and fresh Queen Elizabeth roses. She would be so excited when I gave her the news.

'And your dress, Remedy, what have you done about it?'

'Oh it's ready.' I lied. 'Very simple. *Crêpe de soie.* Vivienne Westwood, I believe. Found it in the closet.'

'Well does it fit? I mean you just can't pull things out of that communal closet and expect them to fit.'

'A few tucks here and there. My seamstress is working on it.'

Oh dear, I thought, I really must find a dress at lunch break.

'Well, if you have any problems, do let me know. I can always loan you something. I have a very nice Balmain that would do the job.'

I thanked Joanna for her thoughtfulness, her kind manner of looking after me. Felt a tad guilty for the lie, especially as Joanna is a Presbyterian, but knew it was for the best all the same. Cut out a few Swarovski paper dolls, glued them to emery boards and headed out to shop. Without Claudia, which I did regret a bit. I went to the Galeries Lafayette where all the gowns were beyond my stay-home spoon budget. No luck at all. Got terribly hungry and picked up a Lebanese tabbouleh salad. Then back to work for a Middle Eastern desktop luncheon.

Later I asked Top Spoon if she would perchance have any discount coupons? For the gown floor preferably. None at the moment it seems. I would have to wait till next month coupons arrived which would be much too late. Somewhat consternated, I looked through the left-hand side of cupboard and found a Florence Eisman dress, age 12–13: white mousseline with a single layer petticoat and navy blue embroidered fleur-de-lis motifs on the bodice. Just like my First Communion dress so long ago! I tried it on in the ladies' room. A bit tight in the bodice but otherwise an impeccable fit. Walked out to get a spoon review.

'*Oh là là!* Look at the little girl! Is it Shirley Temple? Where are your curls?'

Little Match Girl I might accept, but certainly not Shirley! I can't imagine wearing a sausage-curl wig! The spoons had it all wrong. Yet another cross-cultural misinterpretation.

'Where you going dressed like that, Miss Thing?' asked Willie (*Wheelie*) who had just stepped into the office.

'To the ball! To the ball!'

Being dressed as a young girl filled me with joy. I spun round feeling the air fill my skirts like a balloon. Indeed, with the addition of a starched mesh petticoat this could become cotillion-wear.

'And take a giant sucker as your date?' Yoga Spoon asked from the raven position.

'Very well,' I conceded, 'perhaps another time.'

There was no sense in fussing with spoon sense which is so different from my own. I changed and set the sweet dress back in the cupboard to await the next ball.

More work on the Gandini tweed explosion which seems to be affecting women of all sizes and ages. The herringbone fetish too, which is now accompanying the crust everywhere. Phone rang.

'Helloo?'

'Remedy?'

'Speaking indeed.'

'This is Mouktar. How are you?'

'Oh, Mouktar!' His soft Arabian accent melts something in me. His syntax stimulates my automatic pilot.

'I tried to call you earlier but I didn't have the right number.'

Oh dear, had I given him the wrong number? So it seems. How dreadful of me!

'Djamila gave me your work phone. I hope I'm not disturbing you.'

'Not at all. I'm delighted you've called.'

'It's my pleasure. In fact, Remedy, I'm calling to see if you are available next Saturday evening. I have the night off and it would be my great pleasure to take you out to dinner and hope that it would be your pleasure too.'

My, my! Spoken like a scholar! I adore it, I do!

'Oh I would love to! Except that I can't. I've been invited to a social function that I simply cannot get out of. Could we try for that pleasure next week?'

Mouktar agreed to call me back with pleasure and I hung up the phone all a-tremble. Yes, all a-tremble because of love, not weed. Would Neighbour Jeromino ever know this greater joy? Prayed that he would. Ah, beautiful Mouktar! With lucent eyes like dates and the manners of a modern scholiast. He would write his thesis with a pin on the corner of an eye for the circumspect. And be hailed by the Master Moors of the Sorbonne!

Pretended I was the great Christian Queen Ibrizah from *The Thousand and One Nights* capturing Musulman knights on the battlefield but leaving them untouched and unharmed. Filling my nunnery with POWs. Feeding them well but confounding them with my peaceful intentions.

'You are my guests,' I tell them. 'I will kill any man, be he Christian or Musulman, who tries to harm you. In my home you are safe.'

But unlike the Queen Ibrizah whose power was seated in her

virginity, and who, when the King Umar al-Numan slipped her a mickey and ravished her, became entirely pregnant and ruined, my power was protected by contraceptives. I chose the most beautiful and cultivated man among the Musulmans and invited him into my chambers. Being fair, the two of us, we fell in love with neither playing victor over the other. The POWs became my personal army, protecting my interests. They married lovely Christian girls but were allowed only one apiece. So it was in my kingdom...

'Remedy, do you mind putting the hot water on?'

Ah! I was being called to spoon service. Alas I have no servants! No nimble slave girl to run my nunnery. Remedy would have to rely on herself and her good Christian will. So be it. To help my colleagues maintain peak energy levels throughout the late afternoon, I attended to tea. Quite ceremoniously I might add, with paper tea towels and treacle cakes. And how delighted they were by such attentive stay-home spoon service! Did not have tea myself but finished off the day by reading the back page of the *International Herald Tribune*. An article on London's lady pipe-smokers. Spoke a bit to Djamila and Pilgrim Mohammed before leaving. Made a quick cabinet search and found a Hermès scarf for Djamila, lovely but for a slight oyster print defect that was hardly detectable. For him: a Hugo Boss bow tie with a bottle-o-champagne motif. Seeing that they have to clean up after heathens day in and day out, a perk was long overdue. I said nothing about Mouktar's unexpected phone call. Not yet. Would save it for a home visit. Goodbye, my friends. See you tomorrow if God is willing!

On my way home, I bought farm fresh eggs from the cheese shop, plus a very ripe Epoisses which Jubilee loves to sniff. A bottle of Chinon

314

and a freshly baked baguette. We would prop our eggs on a pedestal tonight and have them three minute style. Eat them with a *demitasse* spoon. A quick egg dinner accompanied with the right Chinon wine is a pleasure indeed. Julia Childs recommended it for an *après-theatre* treat. I was enjoying this light repast when the phone rang.

'Princess?'

'Speaking indeed.' Then recognizing my collocutor, 'How are you Mumly? How was Pebble Beach?'

'Wonderful!'

'Did you win? Did you keep warm?'

'Princess, I did!'

'I'm so glad to hear it, Mumly! That's wonderful news!'

'It is, Princess. I won lots of prizes! Even a trip to New York. I was thinking from there I'd fly to Paris to come and see you. What do you think? Could you get me a reservation at the Crillon? A room with a view please.'

Oh dear. I hope that Mumly was given cash prizes too. Richard II was no longer around to foot the bill, which I would have to remind her. Yet any talk of money makes her dropsy worse. Apparently this happens with Catholics quite a lot.

'I'll see what I can do, Mumly. When do you think you would come?'

'In the Fall, Princess. Just as the leaves change in the Tuileries.'

Very good, I thought. The off-season. When the Crillon lowers its rates a bit.

'Did I tell you I'm going to a ball at the Crillon this weekend?'

'Princess, you are? With whom?'

'With a friend of Joanna's.'

'I'm so happy to hear it. Joanna's always found you nice dates, Princess. Remember all those young Harvard gentlemen?'

'I do, Mumly.'

'Although maybe they weren't so much your type.'

'Mumly, what is my type?'

So Mumly understood and perhaps she would know!

'Well, Princess, it's hard to say exactly. But a man with a sense of poetry I suppose. A man who respects the failures of the human heart as much as its successes.'

'Oh, Mumly!'

'You'll find him, Princess.'

Yes, yes! But oh, would I?

I told Mumly to give me her travel dates as soon as she had them and wished her a good afternoon, for in Florida it was half past three. Finished dinner, practised dances and retired with *The Thousand and One Nights*. Around midnight I developed a baklava craving which I managed to satisfy by imagining myself lounging with Mouktar on poufs and pillows, a tray of oriental sweetmeats by our side. Love does appease the appetite.

Feast of Saint Elizabeth of Schönau

How do you do, Saint Elizabeth? The *Concise* says you used to converse with the Saint of the Day too! Only in your case, he or she would appear in the flesh and favour you with a vision, often before you had your morning Weetabix. I can't imagine anything so auspicious! You must have had momentous days at the convent what with all those holy helpers and levitating ecstasies (and let's not forget the mortifications!). Thank goodness you put all your visions down on wax tablets to save them for posterity. Weren't some of them used for that film with Linda Blair? What was that? *The Exorcist*?

Rather than have coffee at home this morning (I was a bit afraid you might appear in the boudoir, Lizzy), I made a thermos of it to take to work. With the *International Herald Tribune* under my arm, the thermos and a croissant in my purse, I arrived before the spoon crew and went into the conference room. There I set the table with paper tea towels, brought in my office coffee cup and began breakfast pleasantly. The conference room, occupied by Top Spoon reunions during office hours, is the finest in the house with a view over the rooftops of Paris: the coloured plumbing of the Centre Pompidou to the far left, the spire of St Joe's to the right. I read the paper quietly whilst sipping the sugared von Krysler coffee peppered with a cardamom pod. How peaceful the morning hour was with no neighbourly disruptions! How quiet was my breakfast room till the church bells rang nine thirty and the door was flung open. In walked a first batch of spoons, in strappy sandals, mid-length A-line skirts and flimsy handkerchief tops with a six-month shelf life. Then Willie (*Wheelie*) arrived on a unicycle, followed by several more spoon batches. The workday had begun. I picked up my picnic, blew a kiss to the rooftops, and went to my station.

Several communiqués on a new bus line offering exclusive overnight shopping trips to Milan plus duty-free shopping on board. The bus is equipped with two large screens featuring pre-tour videos of the designer outlets, three Ella Baché aestheticians performing traditional ozone facials and an aromatherapist-pedicurist on the return trip for tired noses and feet. The Moda Bus leaves from the Place de l'Opéra every Tuesday and Thursday at four thirty a.m. Thought this might interest Joanna, and was about to send her an FYI email with the full Moda Bus brochure, when she called. And with great urgency in her voice.

'Remedy!'

'What's up, Joanna?'

'I've got very bad news. Terrible news, Remedy!'

'Pray tell, what's wrong?'

'Roland's been in an accident.'

'What?!'

'An accident! It's terrible! Listen. He was motoring in the Bentley out by Fountainebleau where his family has their Château – I think you've heard about it. Well, anyway, he was driving through the forest when a deer ran out in front of his car. He swerved to miss it and ended up driving smack into a tree. The Bentley's dead!'

'Was he hurt?'

'He's in traction at the Hôtel-Dieu.'

'Oh no!'

'It doesn't look good, Remedy. I mean, he'll live and everything, but there's a lot broken.'

'*Mon Dieu!*'

'And he feels terrible about the ball. We went to see him last night. He insists you go anyway, Remedy. He'd never forgive himself if you didn't. We've been trying to arrange for his cousin Albert to take you. Albert de Castegnan. He's at the Gritti Palace in Venice apparently, but we haven't been able to get in touch. Plus his cell phone isn't working. We'll try to reach him tonight at Harry's Bar.'

'Don't bother, Joanna.'

'What do you mean Remedy? Don't tell me you don't want to go!'

'No, I'll be going, Joanna. Only not with cousin Albert.'

'Well with who then? I honestly don't know what you're thinking about!'

319

'With Mouktar. The Arabian scholar.'

'Get serious, Remedy! You can't go with someone named Mouktar. And what's his last name?'

'I'll be finding that out.'

'You mean you don't even know? Where does this guy come from? Is he presentable?'

'Oh very!'

'Roland won't appreciate that one bit you know.'

'But Roland insists that I go. He would never forgive himself if I didn't. And Mouktar is free. Mouktar is in Paris. Mouktar is a moon!'

'Damn you, Remedy! Don't blow this!'

'But it's been blown, Joanna. The lowest bell's been played. The Bourdon is flat down with limbs strung up. I'm free now to do as I please. And my pleasure is Mouktar.'

'God! What am I going to do with you?'

'Joanna dear, you've already done so much. Look, take a break and leave the rest to Our Lady of Victory. I will send Roland a recovery card and a box of chocolates. Please tell him I will pray to Saint Christopher for him. He'll understand.'

'I'm feeling so tired, Remedy.'

I could hear the lachrymal swell in her voice.

'Joanna, take a rest. I'm telling you, you've got to go easy on yourself. Listen, I'll make an appointment for you now at La Prairie.'

'Don't bother. I've got one already. At three o'clock. The full works.'

'Good for you.'

'Oh, Remedy, you're like a little sister to me. We've been through a lot together haven't we? I just want what's best for you.'

Joanna could no longer hold back her tears.

'Oh, Joanna, my dearest friend! I want what's best for you too!'

We both wept, then quieted our sobs enough to say goodbye. Joanna invited me to pass by the Ritz for a drink when she came out of La Prairie Beauty Institute. But I declined, knowing that the evening ahead would require all my time.

Skipped out to St Joe's where I lit a votive candle at the feet of St Christopher for Roland's sake. Then another at Our Lady's skirts for Joanna. May she get all the rest she needs. Preferably before the ball. Sat next to Sister Dagobert and listened the best I could to Père Ricard mumbling on about the new Catholic avant-garde, a group of Christian martyrs in China who are raising suffering to the level of high performance art. Apparently Père Ricard is friends with Père Girard who has taken his video camera along with a crew of four Dominican sisters to film them. Proper documentation is so important these days. The Holy See no longer declares martyrs on a whim, but requires solid cinematographic evidence. There's simply no getting around it. Using the Ouija technique, I wished Père Girard and his four sisters the best of luck on their journey to the Far Orient.

A quick lunch with Sister Dagobert and Yorik. Just the usual hamburger patty and fried egg fare with a *pichet* of Côtes du Rhône. I told Sister Dagobert what had happened to my date and asked her if she would visit him at the Hôtel-Dieu.

'Maybe tell him a bible story or two. Something from the Old Testament to cheer his mood.'

'I'll be glad to, child.'

'And Sister Dagobert?'

'Yes?'

'What do you think of the Moors?'

'Like my tribe, they're Semites. Therefore I must think of them as cousins.'

'And how does one become a Semite?'

'It is a matter of birth, Child. Depending largely upon the mother.'

'Like being an aristocrat?'

'Yes, I suppose it is not so unlike that.'

I must say that I was quite happy to hear this. For admittance to the Ball of Marvels depended entirely upon selective birthrights. Mouktar's claim would be that he was born a Moor, a descendant of the valiant though misled Othello. Daggerless now but armed with the might of poetics, Mouktar would not fall prey to any dupedom like his forefather. He was on a scholarship and could not afford to.

Returned to office and spent the afternoon in an agitated state of pre-prom mental preparation. No gown as of yet. I'd have to wait till Djamila came to get Mouktar's number. Would have to call him right away. Would have to arrange for a motorcar and chauffeur. Would have to make an appointment for coiffure. Would have to… Would have to…. To liberate my mind of the debilitating would-have-tos, I pretended I was a Surrealist with a large, Latin moustache and began an automatic writing exercise (a bit like you, Elizabeth, with your wax tablets). Writing furiously away whilst whistling 'Eyes of Magic Fire', I stumbled upon a solution in no time…

In shimmering green she enters the scene. Beads for the ball, belly for all.

Yes, there it was, the answer to that nagging gown question which had so fatigued Joanna. Clear as could be, made evident by an autonomic plume. Samira's costume, the text was telling me. Egyptian haute couture. How perfectly on the mark this was! It would be exotic, yes, but not overly so. Undoubtedly, it would bring to mind YSL's irresistible *turqueries*. Yes, I would arrive as an Arabian-dressed Desdemona with gold-embroidered babouches on my feet and a matching evening bag from the Marrakech medina. I drew several sketches of my ball attire and realized that I would have to do some veil draping to cover my midriff, at least incipiently. Best not to reveal too much early on. Only after champagne.

I worked for a while on my sketches, but was called away by Top Spoon who asked me to interview the Moda Bus people. Did so, quizzing them long and hard on Milanese shoe prices. The marketing director promised to send me a Ferragamo coupon. Worth ten Euros. Maybe I can get Mumly's Christmas present with it when I go to Rome.

At five thirty, and as if in answer to my prayers, Djamila and the Hadj arrived early. How reassured I was to see them; with so much on my mind, I couldn't wait to take care of business.

'Oh, Djamila! Can you give me Mouktar's number? It's an emergency!'

'What has happened, daughter? In Allah's name tell me if there's been some trouble?'

'None at all, Djamila. Rest assured. Only I have to reach Mouktar tonight. I'll tell you about it tomorrow. Can I come by around two? And can Leila help me with some sewing?'

'That will be fine. Go in peace, daughter. Tomorrow at two you shall be God's guest. *Inshallah.*'

I left work and metroed home, my mind much preoccupied. What if I couldn't get hold of Mouktar? What if he had been invited to a Poetics conference for the weekend? I had given him a rain check after all. When I reemerged from the metro and walked by Chez Shlomi's, I peeked in just in case. And good thing I did: there by the grace of God-be-willing was the very Mouktar himself, getting his delivery equipment ready. I knocked on the window to get his attention.

'Mouktar!' He smiled at me and his whole face illuminated like a summer moon. He set down his insulated pizza bag and came outside.

'Remedy, it is a pleasure to see you,' he said as we gave each other the suburban *bise*.

'Likewise, Mouktar.'

I felt a fluttering in my stomach. A yang rising, warming me up to my cheeks. His beauty was startling, his manners more than admirable.

'Say, would you still be available tomorrow night?'

Seeing how little time there was, I saw no sense in dilly-dallying. Best to put the question forth straight away.

'As a matter of fact I am. Why do you ask?'

'Well, I've had a change of plans. You see I had been invited to a ball some time ago. But my date just had a motoring accident and is now indisposed. I was wondering, you see, if you would come with me as my cavalier. Without meaning to disparage the fellow who is now lying unhappily in hospital, but in all truthfulness, I wanted to go with you anyway! Maybe some things happen for a reason.'

'Yes, things happen according to Allah's will.'

Indeed! If Allah wills me Mouktar, I'm certainly all for it.

'It would be my pleasure to take you to this ball.' Mouktar chuck-led. Indeed he seemed amused. 'But tell me more about it. What must I wear?'

'Your Arabian finery would be perfect. Something silky with a touch of gold. Maybe Djamila could help you.'

'I believe I have something. I was to be married once and although the wedding did not take place, I kept the traditional attire.'

'I'm sure that'll be lovely. By the way, you wouldn't know of any limo service, would you?'

Mouktar thought for a moment, then remembered his cousin Samir who buys wholesale Mercedes from the Turks.

'Samir can probably drive us. I will talk to him tonight. He has one very beautiful car that he rents to wedding parties. His wife decorates it very fancily with roses and nuptial laces.'

'Do you think she could decorate it Oriental style for us. So it would seem we were arriving from Baghdad? The old Baghdad I mean. Before all that US uranium hit it.'

'I believe she would like that.'

'Oh, Mouktar! I am very excited! I'm so happy you can come!'

'It is my very great pleasure, Remedy.'

We left each other in high spirits and despite our desirous longing to remain with one another. But Mouktar had a night of work ahead of him, and I had many preparatives. Our premature parting would only make our date all the sweeter. Skipped dinner for I was too revved to dine. Opened a can of Brittany sardines with four spices for Jubilee. Let the bath run till full to the brim. Blessed that entire expanse of water for a holy bath, the kind that calms, soothes and promotes miraculous graces. A home Lourdes grotto if you like, yet much more hygienic and without the wailing crowds. I've become remarkably good at water-blessing these days. Quite clever at it indeed. Bathed for an hour, imagining myself as a mermaid swimming with Mouktar in the Mediterranean. This pre-libation of seaside vacationing with M filled me with a well-being that must have been galvanized by the auspicious meeting of yin with yang, for I yawned so languor-ously.

I felt wonderfully calm once dried and robed, and able to pick-n-choose from the cheese platter. Yes, a bit of appetite returned. I had a ruby red apple too. Retired early, for the essential had been done. No sense in disrupting my quieted mind with prommy details. Completed a twenty-second Aquinal lesson straight from the teacher's manual (a good man, that Aquinas. Might you have met him, Elizabeth? I believe he's on the Board). Dropped off.

Feast of Saint Juliana Falconieri

Like many an ambitious bride of Christ, you mothered your sisters as the convent superior thus earning a good number of saintly brownie points. Though what set you apart, Juliana, was your unusual devotion to the Eucharist, which reached its apogee on the day of your death, when you were unable to eat. Did you know, Juliana, when you requested the host to be set upon your breast that it would penetrate into your body, miraculously and at speed, providing you with Christ's dearest sacrament, plus the daily recommended allowance of vitamins and iron, which you certainly needed as you were vigorously rushed off on eagle wings to Saint Peter's gates? Most likely you did, your loss of appetite heralding the moment of grace to come, as often happens with saints, who shun common food to better nibble upon the divine mysteries.

Meditating upon a miracle does set one up nicely for the day (so thank you indeed). I felt quite refreshed, though a bit of the amatory collywobbles, so different from the alimentary kind, did reduce my appetite (could this be a harbinger, Juliana? Is a miracle due?). Making coffee with the von Krysler contraption, I thought of Johannes briefly, and ever so sweetly. Yes, as I might have considered a bygone ambrosia – the food of a growing goddess.

Delightful bee-bread.

'May Johannes generously share his treasures with other appreciative ladies!,' said I, facing east.

'May others know the thrills that I have known!,' I added, turning myself westward.

Then I *déboulé* across the flat to the fountain where I blessed myself and Jubilee, for one can never receive enough sanctification, especially on prom night. Slipped on a sun dress and a pair of flimsy mules, more like boudoir slippers than summer togs, only without the powder puffs. Skipping out the door with my mannequin bag filled with bath products and green-sequined ball-wear, I headed straight for the vapours. To the Cleopatra Club! That haven of rest and beauty where I am sometimes admitted as a minor. But not today. Perhaps my face showed a new maturity because I had resolved all cotillion concerns swiftly, indeed expertly, and in an entirely adult way. Surely our accomplishments are visible upon us for all to read. We wear them as verily as we wear our failures. That we are charged more for them is simply the way of the world, a kind of reverse recompense. It seems one must buy one's own reward.

I paid a full price entrance and made my way to the hammam, taking in vapours for an hour before submitting myself to Samia's glove. Beneath it I was wrestled and sanded down, then left pink, more like Cuban shrimp than English rose. Back in the vapours for a second soak to eliminate all Parisian pollution: next to me the same Tunisian lady as last time, still complaining about Cleopatra's prices. This time I was inclined to agree.

'Say,' I asked. 'What is coiffure like in Tunis?'

'It is not to be believed! And for only a quarter of the price. They perfume your hair with orange flower water and treat you to tea and sweetmeats. Sometimes there is singing in the salon and always a great deal of flattery. Arab ladies are well versed in the art of coquetry, I tell you. All young Tunisian ladies know how to use blowers and brushes with perfection. Still we like the salon. For it is preferable to have your hair done than to do it yourself.'

Undoubtedly true. But all this talk of coiffure reminded me that I hadn't made a hair appointment. I'd completely forgotten about it! Oh dear! What now! But I managed to calm this sudden sensation of imminent calamity with the reassuring thought of Claudia. Yes, I could always put her on and look the part perfectly. Joanna may not recognize me at first, but perhaps this is not such a bad thing. And I did not anticipate any shock or distress from Mouktar. He was certainly so accustomed to henna reds, that Claudia's auburn tresses would merely remind him of home. And it is a good thing to remind a man of home, isn't it? Except for those who dislike whence they came. And I avoid that kind.

329

I bid my Neighbour goodbye and left the steam room to shower and get dressed. Went to Chez Bichi for tea and chickpea salad. Then off to Djamila's.

'Why didn't the Nazarene tell us? She keeps secrets from us. Naughty Nazarene!'

So they knew without my telling them. Women have their ways it is true. Leila is pouring mint tea. Her hands are rust coloured from henna paste. No-one notices this but me. I'll keep no secrets from you. I'll tell you all.

Sarrah throws a velvet cushion at me, a pillow with an olive complexion.

'He's our favourite, you know. We can't marry him, but you can. Leila is jealous of you!'

I set the pillow on the floor and sit next to Leila on the couch.

'Are you, Leila?' I am slapped on the arm and pinched on the thigh.

'Oh I am, Nazarene! He was once my kissing cousin. Now he thinks nothing of me. But never mind! Allah wants it so. You may have him, Nazarene. He is a pearl among men!'

I do not disagree.

Another cushion is flung, landing against my heart.

'Is this the way we treat God's guest?'

Behind us we hear waterworks. Djamila exits the ladies' room and enters the salon.

'Is this the way we treat the Nazarene? What will she do now when we go to her home? Knock our noses with the crucifix? Serve her some tea. Where are the cakes?'

Leila saunters into the kitchen and comes back out with a platter of almond and date cakes. Tunisian cakes, it seems, brought back from Tunis by a local friend.

'Not so good.' Leila frowns. 'Our Constantine cakes cannot be beat.'

The Tunis cakes are decorated like Christmas ornaments, cut into diamonds, frosted white and pink. Tiny, silver confectioners' balls are pressed into them for a tinsel effect. I think of Joanna's Motte de la Motte-Piquet gown. Its silver leaves, soon to glitter at the Crillon palace. Plucked a frosted date cake from the tray and popped it in my mouth.

'How is it?'

I nodded my head. Deliciously sweet, though perhaps slightly overaged. Djamila pours me a cup-o-tea.

'They are only two weeks old, but because they do not know how to make them properly in Tunis, they go stale before the month is through. Yet they are perfumed with orange flower water which is pleasant.'

Djamila hands me the tea. I take it by the golden minarets, the top of the glass, so as not to burn my fingertips. I begin to wonder what is jest and what is not. I begin to quiz my welcomehood.

'Is it wrong of me to take Mouktar…?'

But Djamila understood my question even before it was finished.

'On the contrary! We are delighted, Daughter! True, a Muslim girl might have been better, but a Nazarene who believes is also quite welcome. You are a fine young lady with a job. Where will you be going tonight? My sister said, but I do not remember.'

I wave my hand southward.

'Near the Obelisk of Luxor.'

Then I reach down to my mannequin bag and undo the zipper.

'Could you help me with my party dress? It just needs a few alterations. Nothing too drastic. Perhaps just some draping?'

The women look down at my bag expectantly.

'Leila can do that in no time. Yesterday she turned two nightgowns into a lovely maternity smock for the Constantine cousin. Thanks be to Allah, our cousin Fatima is already pregnant. God-be-willing it will be a boy!'

Leila takes the bag now on my lap and pulls out the siren suit. Then gets up and digs through the fabrics in her sewing basket. Pulls out mousselines and silks, brocade and sequined bands.

'Put on your costume, Nazarene, so that I can pin.'

Obediently I undress and dress. Stand upright and at attention. Leila wraps a piece of green Lycra voile around my midriff. Cuts and pins.

'In Egypt, a dancer who shows the true skin of her belly is arrested. It is better this way, Nazarene.'

I see that my belly will be veiled in green.

'Will there be any way to undo it? As the party takes off?' Djamila shakes her head. Best not to. Then a wide piece of a sari, golden with an emerald green fleur-de-lis motif, is strewn around my shoulders. This too is measured and pinned.

'Off with it, Nazarene. Let Leila work.'

Carefully I step out of the two-piece suit, soon to be a one-piece gown, apparently more appropriate for the ballroom. Leila takes it and begins her stitching. With a certain gusto for she is good at it. Sewing is Leila's gift. Yet I wonder if her jealousy has passed. If this is her reconciliation, *timeo Danaos et dona ferentes*? Yes, fear the Greeks even when they bring gifts. But Leila is not a Greek and has no ties to Constantinople. She is from Berber land where gifts are given with a peaceful heart.

Djamila puts on a live recording of the legendary Egyptian diva, Oum Koulsoum. Like the Egyptian army during the War of Six Days, we are brought down by our diva. With our souls lifted from their niches, we cannot be victors either. And yet because there is no reason to be revving to win, we are fine. Leila stitches along. She is able to do two things at once: sew and soar. I see why there are so many cushions, for now I want to nap. Like the Moors I am inclined to recline after tea. I lie down amongst the pillows where dreams are the sweetest, lighter than they are upon a bed. Cushion dreams do not have seams, one floats in and out of the conscious stuff…

…I go to Damascus and sit beside a gurgling tiled fountain, then come back when I've drunk my fill. Off to Marrakech next for a bowl of sweet oranges. There I wait till Mouktar comes and leads me to his library…

My journeys alight and subside. I am like a bird that must have the sea.

'Tell the Nazarene I am done. Wake her up.' Leila's voice is soft but firm, like a clock. 'Tell her I would like a gift.'

But I have nothing to give her now. She will have to be patient. Patience pays.

I rise from my cushioned comfort, refreshed despite all the travels.

What about shoes?

Djamila leaves the room and comes back wagging a pair of green babouches with golden appliqués depicting doves upon branches.

And a purse?

Djamila leaves again, returns with a matching evening bag.

'These are from Constantine. Made by my uncle, a very well-known cobbler. Size thirty-eight which is the Nazarene's size.'

How right Djamila is!

The slippers and purse fit perfectly.

'Nazarene, let me paint your nails.'

It is Sarrah's offer. A beauty offer which I have to turn down for the clock strikes five. The ball begins at eight thirty. The chauffeur is to arrive at eight. There is no time for a Muslim manicure. Bid my farewells and press all God-be-willing bouquets to breast. Promise Leila a cupboard gift, something she can sew if she cares to or roomily wear.

'*Ma' as-salaam!* Goodbye! Farewell!'

I then rushed to the twenty-four-hour Louvre post office where I dictated my telegraphic missive in record time.

DEAR ROLAND. STOP. SENDING BEST WISHES FOR SPEEDY RECOVERY. STOP. WILL THINK OF YOU AT THE BALL. STOP. SHALL SPEAK LATER. STOP. REMEDY. STOP.

Best to express compassion in a no-nonsense way. Much like Jesus did with Mary Magdalene. Best to keep in mind that Roland had many Balls of Marvels ahead of him if he so wished. For me, it was a one shot deal, or perhaps a shot in the dark, which Roland himself acknowledged by insisting I attend without him. A form of crust compassion I suppose. Joanna had been wrong: the Marquis had never been crazy about me. I was simply his fall-girl, his way of bringing his mumly down a bit. Yet now that he and I no longer harboured illusions, we could cut our losses and call upon compassion.

The moon is palest when she sets; only pretended love forgets.

Yes, soon enough we would forget our short-lived love story, sweep aside both crust and crumb…

In the meantime may his traction stay be quick! Must stop by the hospital soon to bless his crutches.

Back to the flat, lifting a prayer of thanksgiving to Glorietta. Oh kindly ancestor, at last you have availed me. Thank you for the moonshine! Thank you for the Moor! May our evening be one of love as sweet as the pairing of doves! May he dance like Arthur Murray and not be in a hurry! Glorietta had understood far beyond what Joanna could fathom, for she had Ouija-ways which outshone in efficacy the most nimble planning of the here-and-now matchmakers. Oh, Joanna had done her best I will concede. Perhaps with a different girl, one more naturally daring by profession and birth, her ploys would have worked. Surely there is some Lido dancer out there dying for Joanna's intercession. A lovely, long and scissor-legged vixen from Leeds say, perfectly willing to help Roland cut his mumly ties. Made a mention of this to Glorietta.

Ah! So much to do to get ready and so little time! I took a quick shower and applied a mud beauty mask; waited for twenty minutes whilst reading an article in the *International Herald Tribune* about France's two major exports: armaments and cheese. Washed off the mask and applied various 'rapidly absorbed' beauty creams (a bit like your last hostie, Juliana, only enriched by chemicals, not the Holy Ghost), give-aways all of them and so helpful when the time comes. Waited thirty seconds while my skin worked hard absorbing the creams' seven leading chemicals. Then I turned on the radio.

Radio Notre-Dame. Live from the Vatican City: the Pope was leading the World Rosary! My God, was it today? Indeed it was! I had completely forgotten despite the many Mass-time warnings in the early week. Quickly I pulled my finger rosary from the Chartres gift

store out of my pocket and began to pray along but was soon speed-
ing so far ahead of the Pope and his Marian masses, that it behoved
me to stop and let them catch up. Still, I managed to finish before they
did which gave me time to go back into the bathroom and apply a
gratuity foundation (not quite the right tint, but with Claudia on my
head, the discrepancy shouldn't show), decorate my eyes Egyptian
style with kohl using a toothpick, apply mascara, rouge and a cupboard lipstick simply called For Redheads Only (Lancôme). At last it
was time for coiffure: I combed and carefully pinned my hair back,
flattening it against my head to make room for Claudia, my crowning
glory. My carbuncled queen!

The overall effect of this cosmetic transformation was rather
Arabian indeed, though with a slight European twist. I looked, I must
say, not unlike an Alexandrian aristocrat, a Copt, as it were, with roots
in Constantinople and a terraced home abroad in Cannes. Paris' *beau
monde* adores having such guests. Well-bred exotics are always a plus
at a party. Disguised as an Arabian, I could play upon all the European
notions of Oriental noblehood and pass beautifully: no-one would ask
me questions I couldn't answer.

In the boudoir, I slipped into a pair of green Brazilian-cut panties,
then pulled the one-piece siren suit out of my mannequin bag and
stepped into it. Fastened the waist belt, then twisted my arms behind
my back to fasten the top strap – a painful, shoulder-wrenching
manoeuvre which could have been avoided had a lady-a-waiting been
employed. Alas I had none, yet did in the end manage the fasten-
ing myself and eventually emerged from the boudoir in this most
arabesque of ball gowns. The belly veil Leila had sewn in added a
peek-a-boo effect bound to catch a roving eye or two. I would cover

discreetly at first with the sari wrapper and only reveal the transparency of my gown after midnight. I then accessorized with green sequined pull-on sleeves (courtesy of Samira) and my heirloom necklace, the cross with seven rubies the size of pomegranate seeds and pearls from the Black Sea. Usually I wear it hidden under the uni along with my cleavage, but tonight was a night to display jewels, and although this one was long ago stolen from the inquisitor Foulques de Saint-Georges, there was no cause for shame. Most heirloom jewellery owners are descendants of a thief or two and if it weren't for the holy and forgiving waters of baptism, we would be burdened by their guilt. And yet if one believes in the virtues of Robin Hood's thievery, which indeed I do, then one would understand that in stealing this sacred ornament from a devil-conspiring inquisitor, my tortured ancestor had spared the dignity of the cross. And so I wore it proudly, fearing not the crusty gazes I was bound to endure, but anchoring my faith in the noble act of my ancestor, the cat burglar. Sprayed myself from head to foot with *Ce Soir ou Jamais*.

Now I was ready. I spun thrice round in front of the mirror, and approved. The skirt twirled high, the sequins sparkled, Claudia held on tight. It was eight o'clock and Mouktar would be arriving any minute. I decided to do what Mumly would do if she were in my shoes, which is to say, fix a highball. A ladylike one, as she had taught me to make, with a teaspoon of sugar. Sat myself dreamily on the *canapé* and sipped my drink. It calmed the collywobbles a bit and warmed my chest quite nicely. Yes, I was feeling deliciously fine indeed and got up to put some music on – Samira's CD featuring 'Fill the Cup O Beautiful!' I swayed gently eight-wise, careful not to perspire before the ball began. A bit of O Infinity! to start the evening on the right hip. How soothing this was, and mentally stimulating too, for I remembered just then that I had forgotten to prepare my evening bag. I turned off the music, nursed my drink a tad and went to fetch the necessary: small comb, lipstick, cotton ball, spare change, finger rosary and keys. Just as I was dropping these prom sundries into Djamila's evening bag, the doorbell rang. I turned to answer it but found myself stricken by a major collywobble pang.

'Coming!'

Nearly doubled over, I found my way to the boudoir and stepped into the babouches.

'Be right there!'

Did some quick prana breathing just as Yoga Spoon had taught me to do in the ladies' room. Glorietta! Now he's here. Avail me! Managed to stand up straight and walk to the door.

'Mouktar!'

At my humble door stood a prince of astounding beauty. A prince versed in poetry, the books of science and the words of Musulman sages. A prince dressed in a saffron yellow silk robe sewn with golden needles, babouches of the softest leather with silver embroidery spelling the name of God, and on his head a deep azure turban like those worn by the Blue Men of the desert. The sight of his splendour forced me to take a step back: to approach him I desired a word of welcome, an invitation as it were.

'Remedy, are you ready?'

I answered him with my hand which he brought to his lips. He then carefully escorted me down that stairwell so treacherous for babouche wearers. Quietly, regally, we descended.

On our way we passed M. Phet's lodger. He was ascending with a bag of leafy greens ready for stir-fry. I nodded my head. Top of the day! M. Phet's lodger stepped aside and bowed his head deferentially. Perhaps he had seen such sights in Singapore. But then perhaps he had not. We were ambassadors of the Middle East not the farther stretches of the Orient. And although not vizier and princess, so we seemed.

When we reached the ground floor, Mouktar gallantly guided me out of the building and onto the sidewalk where a most astonishing motorcar, strangely elephantine in appearance, sat awaiting us. It was entirely covered from hood to wheel with tapestries of the richest, earth-drawn hues of red, orange, purple and gold; thick brocade ropes with pearled pom-poms draped down the sides of it like some rustic bridal coiffure and over the windows and windshields, the tapestries were cut to form horseshoe-shaped apertures each with an arabesque point at the tip. Candlelit wrought iron lanterns with green and blue glass inlay hung from ornate poles attached to the front sides of this motoring beast.

'Mouktar!'

'Does it please you?'

'It'll be like riding in the belly of an elephant! I love it! I do!'

Mouktar then, like a knowing knight, lifted one of the draperies and opened the car door. I climbed in, gently sliding my way down the velveteen-covered seats, pulling my skirt along as Mouktar followed me in. The perfume of musk and benzoin enveloped us deliciously. A bit like at High Latin Mass only so much more romantic! In the driver's seat was cousin Samir, wearing a fez, dark glasses and a forest fragrance with notes of bergamot called Paris by Night. Sold exclusively at the local grocery store.

'*Salaam.*' I greeted him with a word of peace, which is the recommended greeting for drivers. Cousin Samir replied with a splendid Arabic responsory that was a bit beyond me, I must say.

'How lovely you are, Remedy. As lovely as the moon. What a pleasure it is to spend the evening with you!'

Mouktar spoke formally but true I could tell, for he was a seeker of truth, a lover of poesy. He held my hand and again kissed it.

'It is like a dream, isn't it?'

The perfume was certainly inebriating, making us both more lax than the hour usually permitted.

'Oh my heart! Mouktar, my heart!'

Cousin Samir hit the gas as if upon cue, and Paris sped by us, quaintly window framed by our arcade of carpet. If we had bothered to watch, we would have seen the city through the eyes of caravaners. Yet Mouktar and I were busy in our back seat. Samir had put on the music of an Algerian diva, and we clapped to her mesmerizing bendir, bounced upon the seat (me) and sang along (he). Together we then slid beneath the music and into a lover's silence. Mouktar whispered Arabian love poetry, the verses of Antar ibn Shaddad, into the softest part of my ear. So sweet and tickly. Irresistible. And all in Arabic. Yet I understood, for love has its recognizable sounds.

'*Ya habaybin ya ghaybin!*'

My dear, my dearest heart!

Our amorous recital gained in momentum and might have gone beyond pre-ball preliminaries had Samir not honked expressively and with excitement at the Obelisk of Luxor. Cars arriving from the four corners of Paris sped around the Place de la Concorde's totem like impatient dancers at the maypole, beaming ribbons of light. We held

340

out our lanterns too, shining our beacon before us till we reached the Crillon palace and joined the line of limousines parked before it.

Crillon men in comely bellboy suits were opening the car doors and carefully helping coutured lady guests out. Photographers from the crustier magazines were snapping away. Samir turned the music down. Mouktar and I watched the spectacle whilst quietly holding hands. Suddenly I was not so sure I wanted to leave the car, this belly of an elephant in which we declared our love just moments before. What would we find in the Crillon that we didn't have here? Couldn't we just nuzzle in the car and play Vizier-see, Vizier-do? But Mouktar was more disciplined than me, more outward looking. It was not a matter of finding anything but simply of going to the ball as planned. Yes, we had made deliberate plans and carefully dressed for them. We would play our games in the Palace.

'*Mademoiselle?*'

The car door was opened and I was given an arm for getting out. '*Merci, monsieur.*'

I handed him a sequin that had fallen off my sleeve. Mouktar came around from the other side and took my arm. Already we were being watched and commented upon. Noses turned, heads nodded and there were a few knowing winks.

'It's a lovely night, isn't it?' I said, making small talk with the guests we passed.

I nodded, Princess Lala-style, and held my posture straight and slim. Mouktar, I noticed, did the same only with more ease and an enigmatic smile to boot. Crust carriage came so naturally to him! We passed through the Crillon's revolving door, together in the same pie slice, not separately as the other guests. We were in love, and lovers always share their cut of cake, at least early on. A tuxedoed gentleman greeted us at the door.

'*Bonsoir Madame, Bonsoir Monsieur.* Your names, *SVP.*'

I gave him mine, Remedy O'Riley de Valdez, which appeared to be on his exclusive checklist list.

'Adoptive daughter of Richard II, Texas Tycoon.'

This I added just in case and for Joanna's sake.

From there we were ushered across the lobby's gold and black-checkered floor past its caramel coloured marbled walls and crystal lustres.

'This way please, to the Salon Marie-Antoinette.'

Oh not her again! Joanna will not be pleased. Perhaps we will have to have a go at Mary-had-a-Little-Lamb after all! The Salon Marie-Antoinette, he explained, could hold four hundred and fifty guests. Tonight there would be two hundred.

'*SVP,*' I enquired, 'did Marie-Antoinette ever stay here? Perhaps for a slumber party?'

'This,' said our tour guide, 'was her boudoir.'

Oh dear! Now we were in for it.

'Do you believe in revenants?' I asked Mouktar.

'I believe in djinn as do all Muslims. Ghosts are of a different sort. But I have seen one so I believe in them.'

'Did you see it in a palace?'

'No, I did not. I'm afraid I saw it in the latrines at the university. It seemed to be the ghost of that Descartes fellow.'

'How did you recognize him?'

'By his breeches, at first. But then he took a black marker and wrote *Cogito ergo sum* on the wall.'

342

I picked up Mouktar's right hand, the hand with which he holds his scholarly plume, and kissed it.

'So he is still thinking away!'

'A very determined man.'

'Shall we go in?'

The Marie-Antoinette room was already filled with luxurious members of high society, sipping champagne and conversing in hushed tones. Mouktar took my arm in his and escorted me into the sumptuous salon, luminous and prism-like with chandeliers enhancing the brilliance of all family jewels. The sensual, wide sweep of the midnight blue velvet draperies filled me with a childlike desire. I was tempted to play behind them, and perhaps as the evening drew on I would. Mouktar and I must have looked like Bollywood stars, straight off the plane from Bombay and superbly versed in sentimental family films, for we were asked by a Pakistani champagne waiter to sign his sleeve.

'For my children please.'

'But I'm nobody!' said I.

'And who are you?' Mouktar asked, turning to the waiter. 'Are you nobody too?'

The waiter nodded his head. Did not insist on the signature but humbly offered us a drink. Nobody indeed!

But I was learning about my nobody man every minute. Mouktar, it seemed, knew the Dickinson. Could recite her at whim and perhaps the Whitman lad too. I felt so at home just then. Set at my ease with Emily. Now we would not be public like a frog, but enjoy our private anonymity and laugh at the bog. We both took a champagne flute and lifted our glasses for a toast. I looked at Mouktar questioningly. He lifted the glass to his lips and drank the bubbly as soundly as any infidel.

'I am a part-time Muslim,' he said laughing. Splendid thought I. Me too! Just as I was about to propose a toast to the prophet's wealthy wife Khadija, Joanna and her husband dropped by.

'Remedy!'

'Joanna! Jean-Marc! You look stunning, Joanna!'

Indeed, the Motte de la Motte-Piquet showed off her slim waist and high riding breasts (best not to set a hostie on these!), brought out the lightest shade of blue in her eyes, and even revealed a long stretch of shapely right leg. Her blonde hair had been washed in imported waters and exquisitely set in a Hepburn-style chignon to show off her tassel-shaped Chaumet earrings in white gold with pavé diamonds. Like a rich French cream, gloriously whipped and spread across a display cake, her skin tempted the desires of the senses with its flawless, velvet smoothness. Well done indeed!

Joanna possessed that particular grace which endows a woman with an irresistible degree of edibility. This time, she had gone beyond the call of beauty. For beauty is really a humble affair and requires only cosmetic rudiments and a happy disposition. Joanna had taken that extra step and benefited from the beauty care ever available to obliging ladies at La Prairie and the European Institute of Hair and Aesthetics.

I politely introduced my friends to Mouktar and after a bit of small talk, Joanna pulled me away from our foursome for a briefing.

'He's gorgeous, Remedy! Where did you find him?'

'At the pizza parlour.'

'You didn't!'

'I did, Joanna. He works part time at Chez Shlomi. The rest of the time he's a doctoral student.'

'What's he studying? Not philosophy I hope. Nothing in the humanities!'

'He's a scholar of medieval Arabian poetry. But he knows Emily Dickinson too.'

'Bad news, Remedy. There's no future in it. He'll just end up being a professor, you know, the kind in tweed with the patches on the elbows. Always needing a haircut. Listen, Remedy, you can do better. Much, much better! You just need more confidence in yourself. I know you can do it! Roland'll be out of the hospital next month. It's not over you know.'

'Oh it is, Joanna. It is!'

'Well, I know for a fact that it's not, but you have to be willing to try.'

'But, Joanna, Mouktar and I are in love. Terribly in love. He's brilliant and romantic. He's funny and he loves me!'

Not wanting to upset Joanna, I brought our attention back to the ball.

'Isn't it wonderful that we're finally here, Joanna! At the Ball of Marvels! Didn't you always dream about this when we were at Vassar? And now look at you! You're gorgeous and you're swishing around in the hush-hush luxury of this palace!'

Joanna beamed with pleasure. Her eyes sparkled as they must have when she was a little girl eyeing the presents beneath the New England Christmas tree.

'Yes, Remedy. We're really here aren't we!'

'We are!' I pinched her arm.

'Remedy, let me see your dress.'

Joanna has always been quick to change the subject whenever the slightest dash of worry taints her mental palate. Obediently I opened my wrapper-covered arms like a butterfly.

'My God! That's your belly-dancing outfit! Jesus, Remedy!'

'Joanna, it is. Although I've had some additions made. Now it's a gown, you see.'

I plucked at the greenish gossamer Lycra midriff covering.

'It looks like you're wearing green pantyhose around your waist. It's awful, Remedy!'

'I disagree. It's a matter of what you're used to. In Egypt, if a dancer isn't covered with this stuff she's arrested.'

'But we're not in Egypt, Remedy. This is Paris, the capital of Couture! Listen, just keep that wrapper on. Already people are wondering about you. Best not to mention Florida. Now that you've dressed the part, you'd better pretend you're from Kuwait or something.'

'Will do, Joanna.'

'By the way, where is Mouktar from?'

'He's a Moor.'

'A Moor? Remedy, maybe it's never occurred to you but nobody's used that word since the Brontës!'

I thanked Joanna for her FYI.

'Jesus! Sometimes you really worry me. You're just not living in the here and now.'

'But I try so hard!'

'You really should take a yoga class.'

Indeed, if only there were time to take one. Joanna was right of course, but she truly had no understanding of my hectic daily schedule of activities, which afforded me so little spare time!

Having finished our private interview, we returned then to where we had left our gentlemen. Mouktar and Jean-Marc were discussing the mature work of Victor Hugo, a subject which interested me greatly. I was about to add a word or two on the dear patriarch and poet who would have gotten me to Afghanistan if only there were Ouija-phones, when Jean-Marc began praising recent musical adaptations of Victor's work by Disney and Broadway. Mouktar put his hand to his heart. I curled one of his locks, a turban escapee, around my index finger to comfort him. Joanna joined in then and talked at length about the campy sing-a-long *Sound of Music* which is all the rage in London. She went to see it two weeks ago when she was really needing to wind down a bit. It seems that everyone dresses up as characters in the film. Joanna sat beside someone who came as crisp apple strudel. She herself had gone as Julie Andrews' Swiss Mother Superior, a role which I'm sure she played wonderfully although a Presbyterian.

The Pakistani waiter came by again with his tray-o-champagne. No toppers but always a new glass at the Crillon palace. A delightful way to start anew. Like calling upon an ancestor. More conversation on various topics such as Marie-Antoinette and leg-o-lamb, a recent website on mushroom hunting in Fontainebleau, and the brand of cutlery used at the Cordon Bleu. Another round of champagne. Chin-chin! Jean-Marc and Joanna, I saw, were not insensitive to Mouktar's charms. Witty and well-versed in occidental matters, he had swiftly won them over. His extraordinary smile, which beams as luminously as the crescent moon, disarmed Joanna, for I saw her blush several times at the sight of it. But this is Mouktar's gift, I wanted to say. Take

347

it happily; it is the smile he offers out. Know that there is a special one reserved for me, quieter yet more radiant than the seven stars that sit above the Koran.

We were about to head to the buffet when the barking voice of a Master of Ceremonies called our attention to a velvet-covered platform. The debutante roll-call, it seemed, had begun.

'The Countess Alexia Wamarowski!'

A young lady, American but of Russian ancestry, and with the ambition of passing her MBA, walked pleasurably down the platform staircase and along the gold metered line. A Crillon usher walked behind her holding a placard that bore the name of her dress designer. In this case, YSL.

'The Countess Juliana von Swarzmark!'

A second unmarried miss whose ambition is to work with people as opposed to vegetation walked painfully down the very same path. Uncomfortable but lovely in a Christian Lacroix strapless dress which pushed her cleavage into what the French call a 'perfect balcony.'

'Mademoiselle Melina de Milly!'

Although only fifteen, and very busy in a Wiltshire boarding-school, this mademoiselle has the ambition to play badminton. She would like to visit Africa and is wearing Dior.

And so on and so forth. The presentation ran on, the girls both nervous and poised, trying to please mumly and daddy whilst displaying their nubility in the best light possible.

Whilst these young ladies came out, Mouktar and I migrated to the buffet table and happily fed each other lobster tails as do birds of a feather. How delightful it is to love and feed! To love and be fed! Mouktar was just about to lay a caviar canapé on my tongue when I heard what sounded like my name. Pronounced French style, which is to say with a very democratic use of the tonic accent, and over the loudspeaker.

'Mademoiselle Remedy O'Riley de Valdez!'

How now? I cocked my ear and heard again what I thought I heard the first time, which is to say my name with the added de Valdez as a Cordoba reminder. Could it possibly be my name-day? I had no idea there was a Saint Remedy. But no, it was the barker harker with his microphone, the roll-call attendant inviting me to the podium to introduce me as marquis marriage material. This can't be so, I thought. Not possible. I'm thirty-two and by *beau monde* standards an autumn chicken. How could I have possibly made the deb list?

A terrible mistake had been made! Indeed!

'Can't do it,' I said to Mouktar.

But Mouktar chuckled knowingly, gave me that smile brighter than the seven stars shedding light on the Koranic verses and said, 'We are here to play, are we not? It would be my great pleasure to see you on the podium. You are being called, my heart.'

Indeed, my name was barked over the microphone once again, impatiently this time as if to highlight my bad manners. Mouktar gave me a playful wink and with courage that was more Marie-Antoinette's than mine, for I was certain that she had returned to her boudoir to help me as part of her purgatory penance, I stepped up upon the blue velvet podium whilst my name was called yet once again.

'Remedy O'Riley de Valdez. Young lady journalist. Part-time catechist. Ambition to make the world a better place through the democratization of fine shoes. Dress of unknown origin.'

Had Joanna, I wondered, given them the FYI on me? No matter. There I was on the podium in my Arabian attire facing the impatient crust crowd. All eyes were on me, eyes of wonder, eyes awaiting magic fire. With Marie on my side, confidence as trustworthy as a little lamb came and availed me. I looked out boldly at my public and smiled in a subtle but welcoming way. Then with a stunning flourish which Simone de Beauvoir herself might have mastered had she studied tap-dancing say, I spread open my butterfly arms and *pas chassé* down the podium whilst coyly rolling my shoulders Samira style and revealing my green sequined skin.

Oh là là!!

Reaching the gold line marker, I switched to an alternating maytag/pistol hip shimmy which, I must say, truly stole the show.

Oh là là…! How extraordinary! Who is that girl?!

Three arabesques, two grammar rolls and a tricky Hindu head move. Now the crowd stood back in astonishment. Some turned up their noses indignantly whilst others gaped helplessly, but in the end, the applause was nearly unanimous. The menfolk especially cried out for an encore, forgot their crustiness and behaved like hot-blooded crumblies. Not so unusual for the Latin aristocracy. Their Britannic homologues would have politely excused themselves to visit the Gents. I caught a glimpse of Joanna: her jaw had dropped, yet she applauded all the same. Not vigorously but gently for a friend.

Yes, my hippy interlude had astonished the felt-lined sensibilities, yet I had learned, from dealing with Roland, that a desire for rollicking, perhaps even uncouth fun, lay in abeyance in the aristocratic heart. It merely required the appropriate coaxing to revive and breathe fully. With my arms now wings, I flew back to Mouktar who embraced me sweetly and fed me another morsel or two. A prawn and a stuffed mushroom.

The rest of the evening passed in a swirl of waltzes, rumbas, and cha-cha-chas. Mouktar danced, not like an Arthur Murray man, but more continentally, which is to say in the manner of the African continent. Rather than twirl, we shimmied; rather than swirl, we swung; and never once did we leave each others' arms. Love may be blind but not necessarily unto itself. Mouktar and I had eyes only for each other: it was the peripheries we did not see, the guests floating by us, the sartorial and societal concerns which pruned the soirée.

And yet there were interruptions to our intimacy. Several tuxedoed gentlemen tapped Mouktar's shoulder for a Remedy-spin, but we both refused the offer firmly yet politely. No exchanging tonight. Love kept us free from all barter. We swung and sunk down into the rhythm of our hips and hid behind the long blue draperies. Yes we did make a curtain call or two for the thrill of hide-n-go-peek. No-one knew we were behind them, I believe, and we took remarkable liberties. Curtains, I should say, do enhance passion which the Muslims know very well. Head curtains or bed curtains. Velvet draperies too.

At last, when Marie-Antoinette's *horloge* struck midnight and a half, perhaps at that hour when she once closed her *bergerie* and called it a day, we decided to leave the palace and its noblehood which had just begun dancing a rather sloppy limbo beneath the cane of the Count O'Connor of Ireland. The Ball of Marvels had passed before our eyes like a splendid backdrop, the idyllic setting of our nascent love.

Arm in arm, Mouktar and I strolled out of the salon, stopping every few steps to kiss and love. We walked slowly down the sumptuous hallway, alone now, with the ball behind us. The palace offered us its own private party. We saw a couple embracing in the mirror and tried to divine who they were. The Prince Toussoun of Egypt and the Princess Lili'uokalani of Hawaii? Mouktar thought not. Believed them to be peasants on their way to a mutton feast. But dressed so richly? Peasants fancy dress too I am told when the occasion so requires. Let us eat mutton then! Mouktar lifted me in his arms like a catch and spun me around. Not so unlike Johannes von Krysler only closer to the ground. Mouktar is not a flight man, a trapeze would mean little to him. He might even see the need to cut its ropes. No, it was not his limbs that required the heady risk, but rather his imagination and spirit. In a word, Mouktar was romantic in a way that an acrobat could not be. A word to von Krysler meant a somersault. To Mouktar, a word became a wing.

Walking more casually now, with our arms around each other, my head leaning against his shoulder, we strolled through the lobby, bathed in its golden aura. The heady perfume of its voluptuous bouquets arranged as meticulously as coiffures, enveloped us delicately as does sleep after an evening elixir. This palace was for people with soft hued lives, for those who slumber in feather-bedded comfort, not for the crumbs of whom greater fortitude and moonlighting are required.

Farewell fair palace! *Adieu*!

We left through the revolving door without looking back. No, we were forward looking, now searching for our peregrinating elephant, which, having made what the French call a *tour*, we found parked on the Rue du Faubourg St-Honoré. From the street outside our tapestried beast we heard the haunting strains of the Orient's favourite diva,

Oum Koulsoum, calling us in to Egyptland. Samir had the window rolled down and was smoking a Marlboro. His sunglasses were still in place perhaps to protect him against moon glare.

'Hark!' Mouktar said in Arabic. And 'Allah's peace be with you.'

Samir tossed the cigarette.

'And with you his peace.'

With this greeting we climbed in and were driven to a place that served midnight mutton, a dimly-lit Algerian restaurant with a tattooed proprietor by the name of Lady Fatima. It was an all-night eatery, kept open for hard-hatted Magrebin workers on the underground night shift. But there were no other diners there at our hour. We sat at a table for two, holding hands, recounting our histories. The moment might have been melancholic had our hearts not been fortified. Some sadness unfolded from our stories, it is true, and yet this only served to expand the circumference of love and unite us more intimately within it. Mouktar's arms appeared to me now as boughs filled with the intelligence of sap, knowing from having withstood what each season brought down, both the kind and the cruel things. These were boughs that could bend, boughs with a heartbeat and like a mysterious Celt, I would wrap them around me in the quiet of the forest and listen.

Lady Fatima came out of her kitchen with steaming couscous and a plate of mutton stewed in saffron and cumin. She tapped at Mouktar's turban, and pointing at me, smiled and laughed.

'Who is she? And why are you dressed like this? What is this game, my son? Vizier-see, Vizier-do?'

Mouktar laughed with her and introduced me. I was taken instantly as a daughter and told to begin.

'Eat, child, while the mutton is hot! Love requires stew for strength.'

Mouktar served me, then himself. We ate and drank a bottle of Sidi Brahim. I felt myself swell with a kind of joy which begins as a taste then deepens in the heart place. Love has a will of its own, I knew, and now it wanted to nest in me. A heated bliss flooded me as the dove settled in, bringing his bedding in his beak. I felt his sudden architecture taking shape, becoming a humble abode in which my heart could perch.

On our way back in the caravan, Mouktar and I held hands silently whilst spreading the heat in our palms. We peered out the arcaded windshield as Paris passed by us more silent than we had ever seen it. Vain Paris, still yet illuminated; even at night this prince does not let his beauty sleep in the dark. The *lampadaires* on my own street stood rooted like trees. Trees with moons caught in the branches. Mouktar lifted me from our limousine and carried me through the threshold, then up the four flights of stairs. In his arms I was the nest and the boughs would not break.

It is best to be brief when speaking of the love which transpires between a Moor and a Christian maiden. Desdemona has told us little. I will tell you less. Suffice it to say that we passed a night together such as is worthy to be enshrined among the historical love nights of the world. Indeed! Every word that lovers say was said. In the four languages between us. Some were shouted whilst others were whispered. Still more were spoken with the eye, for in its corner are inscribed words so tender to the heart, so fragrant to the senses, that only lovers can read them.

Before falling to sleep, I sent a word of thanks to Glorietta. Dear Ancestor you have sent me the beautiful Mouktar! You have spoiled me no doubt but I love him so! Please leave him with me so that our happiness may grow! As ancestors have a reputation for taking back what they have given upon an Ouija whim, it is best to insist and to praise them expressly for their generosity. How generous of you Glorietta! How hospitable and on the mark! I fell asleep just as the *lampadaire* by my window was blown out. Day had risen, but Remedy and Mouktar now slumbered in each other's arms.

Epilogue

Feast of Saint Aloysius (Luigi) Gonzaga (Patron Saint of All Young Men)

Fancy finding you here on the calendar, Luigi! Today of all days, just as I've decided at last to make the pilgrim plunge and begin anew. You are, after all, a saint of fresh starts; from a family of aristocratic pornographers (the *Concise* says your daddy's porno plays were prohibited in France. Imagine that! Even the naughty French wouldn't have them!), you did emerge to join the company of Jesus, renouncing your princehood and the erotic pageantries for a life of service and poverty. The *Concise* claims that you described yourself as a 'piece of twisted iron needing to be twisted straight.' I know what you mean, Luigi, for we all need to be fixed a bit, we're all looking for a remedy, aren't we? A way to put things aright, a way to the pilgrim path? Bless you! If only the plague hadn't brought your saintly doings to a precocious end, you would have gone on to Jerusalem like Sister Dagobert, perhaps straightening some of the crooked iron works there. Lord knows the Holy Land needed a handyman back then too.

As the Patron of All Young Men are you also a lifetime member of the YMCA? In any case, Luigi, I thank you for taking special care of Mouktar, who, you know as well as I, is a prince among the many peacocks. Let me tell you, it was sweet indeed waking up to Mouktar's hand smoothing my brow whilst I laid there draped by a mere sheet. He himself had risen according to bird time, had opened and shut his books already, had studied his versification before going down to the bakery for a crescent run whilst Remedy slept on, dreaming she was Coco Chanel attending a barbecue on Coney Island, wearing a monochrome pantsuit but surrounded by polka-dotted bikinis, trying to set a fine example whilst nobody could give a damn. I was most relieved to exit that one and be invited to breakfast.

Mouktar makes excellent coffee in the von Krysler, better than myself, I must say, and with the addition of cardamom. We had a superb breakfast all around whilst listening to the BBC shipping forecast. I would have liked to linger, and perhaps return to the boudoir for a time, but Mouktar who must balance studies with work at all times did not have the leisure to do so. With utmost respect for his unending labour, I washed my face, threw on a dress and was out the door with my arm pretzeled through his in no time. At the Gare de l'Est, that station known for sending young men eastward on military romps, (you do look after them, don't you, Luigi?), we parted with a kiss which I purposely made linger regardless of the labour imperative. Mouktar happily complied and continued on to the National Library, that most prestigious thinkery, looking rather *amoureux*, I must say.

At the office I bumped into a bronzed Jean-Claudi, recently returned from his bungalow honeymoon with Horace in Bora-Bora. He was chatting with the spoons over coffee. Actually he was drinking a multi-vitamin drink (A, C and B-minus) with lots of carrot juice which is supposed to help him keep his excellent tan for an extra two weeks.

'Pray tell, Jean-Claudi, how was the honeymoon?'

'Seventh heaven, Remedy. The cat's miaow.'

'Did you swim with tropical fish? And did they follow you like you were their daddy?'

'They did!'

'That's wonderful news! I'm so happy for you!'

Indeed I was. For it seemed that a taste of fatherhood might be just what he needed. Horace had confessed to me that they were contemplating welcoming some fruit-o-the-womb into their newlywedded lives. Maybe a babe from Warsaw, say, straight from the Verbum Dei Convent, which is now an adoption centre for unwed lasses, co-managed by Weronika. I would certainly tip them off if they asked for my advice. Blew all the spoons a double kiss and settled in at my desk.

How painless work can be when one is in love. Personally speaking, love gives me *plumephoria*, a well-being of the pen promoting smooth and easy inkage. I wrote an article on a new fashion phenomenon launched by imaginative amateurs called 'wearable art'. No ink stoppage or spilling to report. Named the piece 'The Way Fashion is Going'. Tried imagining myself going to one of these gatherings, in a licorice-lined sausage membrane dress, under a salmon skin coat with fishhook buttons. On my head a cloche hat made of spare parts. Mittens confected with business cards and Pomeranian hair. Tried smiling. Pretended I felt great, but was terrified that I smelled bad. Had the new couturiers discussed the odour problem? Would they be coming out with a lemon-scented petticoat? I wrote a letter to the Wearable Art Commission to this effect. I do hope my concerns will be duly considered. Went to visit the ladies' room but was called back precociously by the phone ringing.

'Remedy?'

'Speaking.'

'It's Joanna, Remedy. I thought you would have called me by now to excuse yourself.'

'Oh! I'm so sorry, Joanna. Please excuse me!'

'Running off and not even saying goodbye! Honestly! It was a social event, Remedy. We were looking around for you everywhere.'

'Oh Joanna! I'm so sorry. Really. We just got carried away. It was our first date, you know. Though we've been in love for a while. Please excuse us. We certainly meant well.'

'Well anyway, we'll try to have you both to dinner sometime. But probably not until the fall though because I'm leaving for summer vacation next week.'

'You are? Already? Where are you going?'

'To the family home in Saint-Tropez. I can't tell you how much I need the rest! God knows I deserve it! Then Jean Marc and I are going to spend August at his great aunt's villa on Lake Como. She'll be gone so the place will be ours alone. Keep it quiet, Remedy, but we're going to do all we can to get pregnant while we're there.'

'I've heard that's a wonderful place to conceive, Joanna! I'm so happy for you both!'

'We'll see how it goes. You can say a prayer if you like.'

'Oh I will, Joanna!'

I wished my friend fruitful vacationing and made mental note of the prayer obligation. Dear Joanna! At last she would be getting the rest she required. I was sure that a month in Saint-Tropez would do her ovaries a world of good. There's nothing more important for a potential mother, of course. Joanna insisted that I come and spend a week with her in Saint-Tropez but I declined, as I am not at all fond of helicopters.

Headed back to the powder room to attend to my nose. Locking the main door, I practised 'Fill the Cup' and 'Eyes of Magic Fire' in front of the mirror until there were several knocks. And so I turned off the Red Sea, shut the camel in the garage. And at last decided to let the lass in, seeing that, from the sound of it, the Gents was busy. You can hear everything between that divider, I'm afraid. French architects design the lavatories this way to lessen the communication gap between ladies and gentlemen.

Back at my desk, I sifted through more recent communiqués. Wrote a special report on the customization craze, an Anglo-Saxon trend that is challenging the most precious fashion rules. To this résumé I added an autobiographical mention, describing my unis, with a detailed account of how I carefully customized them with hems and accessories. Indeed, I may have to ask Jean-Claudi to photograph me in my winter and spring editions so that our visitors may have a visual testimony.

Off to Mass. Ten minutes late, I'm afraid, though on time by divine standards. Sat through a rather uninspired homily comparing Jules Verne's *Around the World in Eighty Days* (quite fun but apparently fruitless in the end) to the spiritual voyages proposed directly by the Lord, that greatest of tour operators. These holy travels have been declared far more interesting than their literary counterparts by His Majesty the Pope and the Board of Saints (of which, if I'm not mistaken, you are vice-president, Luigi).

I made a special prayer to Our Lady for the success of Joanna's ovaries, and another one to Jesus himself on Jean-Marc's behalf, for it does take two to tango. Whispered to Sister Dagobert to ask that she do the same. Which she did, after communion I believe, by putting both hands on her belly and mumbling unto the Son-o-Man.

Afterwards, Sister and I had a quick lunch on the corner café terrace: chef's salads with lemon Perrier and a half bottle of Tavel rosé. The utter deliciousness of a fair-weathered Paris coaxes the sensuality of any girl from out of its well-bred box. Sister Dagobert pulled up her skirts a bit for a taste of the sun on her legs. And how right she was; her legs truly needed a toast! And I, already in a short-cropped sundress, crossed my legs, letting my mules drop off my feet. Thought of Mouktar. Thought of myself and Mouktar loving in the sun! Gentlemen walked by and gave us both a wink. With her Peggy Guggenheim dragonfly sunglasses, Sister Dagobert has a mod kind of charm. She deserves an admiring eye.

I blessed a piece of bread and fed it to the girdled Yorik at our feet. Did Sister Dagobert see under the table? I wonder. Apparently she has made all her travel arrangements and will be leaving for the Holy Land in two weeks. She's very excited about it, but also concerned about getting her packing done on time. There are so many errands to run, including buying an extra set of AA batteries for the Perrier fan. I promised Sister Dagobert that I would help her however I could: would she need another suitcase, I wondered? (I have a personalized one that used to belong to Richard II. On it is inscribed the Roman numeral II, which is what people called him in Texas. Never Richard but always 'Two'. Sometimes 'The Two', for courtesy and respect.) Sister Dagobert declined the offer, thanking me very much all the same. She has a special Holy Land suitcase provided by her tour operator. From her description it sounds like a bowling ball bag, which, she insists, is big enough – although I'm not so sure. All these vacation plans! How little thought I've given to vacationing myself. Why? I'm not sure, but perhaps this has to do with Richard II, who always took Mumly on vacation, but never me. In truth the only vacations I've ever taken were those Joanna so graciously invited me on. My very first vacation was taken with her family in the Hamptons while on summer break from Vassar. A wonderful sojourn although the ticks and the Presbyterianism did disconcert me a bit. It was the first time I had been to a church service where no-one in the pews had even a trace of an accent, and everyone spoke the exact same language. Mass is simply not like that, especially in Florida. But how kind of Joanna's family all the same. They did take me in like a daughter and introduced me to whisky sours.

Yes, vacationing and the art of travel. Miss Koltun who wrote *The Complete Book for the Intelligent Woman Traveller*, exhorts young women to go unafraid of the foreign and foreigners, to go with zest, curiosity and common sense, to go because knowing more of life, a young lady will enjoy and cherish it all the more. Indeed! It's time I took the matter into my own hands. Not wait for an invitation, but like Miss Koltun did during the first post-war spurt of tourism, fly to Rome.

It's to Rome that I'm being called, after all. Not to vacation, if the truth be told, but to make a pilgrim's journey – the difference being that the latter provides the feet with a deeper purpose. Better shoes are undoubtedly required, as well as a thick wool cape in the winter months. A pilgrimage, if you like, may be amusing; but its purpose is not to amuse. It is a way of forging ahead, of taking one's testimonies to their destination, which is always an Orphic place, serving as both oracle and ear, and dressed in extraordinary raiment. St Peter's for example, with its Duomo, which Michelangelo designed especially for the flight of angels, is a wondrous jewel beneath which pilgrims may freely fall to their knees and untether their talking hearts. The scarlet and gold plume-helmeted Swiss Guards herald their arrival to encourage the tired feet. And the pilgrims march on, making confessional acquaintances along the way, exhausted but determined to reach the pilgrimage point. The Muslim will cast his stones at the three devilish pillars, the Christian will kneel and jubilate before the altar and the Jew will rock in his temple. They are the fortunate ones who yet maintain the pilgrim's prerogative.

With Rome in mind, I asked Sister Dagobert if she knew of any retreat houses near the Holy See for incoming and stay-around pilgrims. As I strongly suspected, she did. The Catholic orders have retreats throughout the world in prime places, both on and off the beaten track, including conceptionary hot spots like Lake Como. Whilst many of these retreats are for celibatarians only, some accommodate couples. Married couples. Sister Dagobert stressed this point clearly. No problem, thought I. I could marry us in a minute after all.

366

Mouktar and me. I have the entire sacramental ceremony on flash cards. A quick quiz review and we were ready. Sister Dagobert gave me the number to call, insisting I use her name as a shoo-in.

I'm to call her sorority's Vatican branch asking to speak to Sister Maria Antoinetta. A Roman nun friend of Sister Dag's, named I dare say, after you-know-who. Certainly it would be most convenient to have the convent's wedding suite with a kitchen on the side. This way I could do my pilgrim duties while Mouktar pursued his thesis at the Bibliotecca Nazionale. Our evenings would be spent dining on calamari and confited tomatoes, romancing on the Spanish Steps beneath the Roman moon! On our days off from St Pete's and the library, we would swim and love at the lido! We would be citizens of Rome for a summer. I thanked Sister Dagobert profusely and insisted she call me if she required Richard II's valise *tout de même.*

Back to the office, where I spent most of the afternoon drinking iced tea. Four of the spoons did not return from pump practice, but left directly for vacation after towel drying at the gym. The remaining ones were planning theirs on office time. So it happens in France, where holiday leisure is considered a national obligation, as it is believed to enhance the love connection. With the democratization of romantic love, which was once the privilege of the courtly class, comes the benefit of *five weeks paid vacation.* I do appreciate the French after all. And whilst I am here, I will try to do as they do. At least some of the time. Yes, from time to time. Perhaps when it behoves me.

Translated several articles, then sent an email to the queen bee, Top Spoon herself, announcing my imminent vacation departure. No dates yet. But a warning that it would be soon. Certainly within the month, for summer passes quickly. Top Spoon will inevitably pick up the message in Thailand where she is vacationing at the moment with her husband and her Blackberry.

Left work after visiting a moment with Djamila. She and the Hadj are leaving town, too. They're going to Constantine for the month of July and from there, Djamila will prepare her holy pilgrimage to the Mecca, God-be-willing. Apparently she was unable to accompany her husband two years ago when he alighted for the *Kaaba* with his bed-sheet. It seems she had an egg problem at that time which needed rest rather than those hectic, counterclockwise circuits.

'Are your eggs better?' I asked, concerned.

'They were taken out, Child. It was Allah's will. But I am doing quite fine without them. It must be said that they were never so well and only gave me one child. Thanks be to Allah it was a son. My Mohammed! My heart!'

'It was the same for my Mumly,' I added. 'Only she had a daughter, not a son. And I am her Princess! I am her heart!'

'But that is not the same.'

'Perhaps not.'

'There is nothing like having a son. It is a mother's highest honour.'

'But you don't have a daughter, do you? How can you compare? What do you know about daughters?'

'I was one once!'

True enough, she had been. Djamila raised her brow like a storm cloud from the north, and shook her head at me: she knew all about it. She had been a daughter from her day of birth till the day she married. There had been little glory to it. How could it be called an honour to sweep her brothers' rooms and wash their clothes whilst they were away at school, profiting from Koranic education and

Islamic spelling-bees? At night she stole her brothers' books and learned her letters under the light of a finger lantern. As a daughter she had been allotted the leftovers. The remains of her brothers' day.

'It was good you had a son,' I conceded, for seeing in her face the bellicose emotion my mention of the girl-child provoked, I feared she would have unleashed this bile upon a daughter had she had one.

Perhaps Allah had known what was best for her and arranged the egg situation accordingly. Though this is not so certain for Allah is first and foremost preoccupied with the menfolk and their matters. Ladies and other mammals come in second and therefore often have to rely upon the recourse of djinn.

I wished Djamila an excellent pilgrimage and headed home, walking not to the metro but to a yonder bus stop. A warm evening encourages the pilgrim spirit. Encourages the legs to blithe locomotion. I imagine the Parisian sidewalk underfoot to be a carpeting of ground-growing roses that can withstand only the firmest of footholds. The foot steps knowingly, which is to say, assuredly, firmly, and yet does not trample the flowers. A paradox perhaps, but there is fluidity, even a kind of lightness, to the steady step. A kind of respect for what lies below and a cousinly connection to it. This is how a pilgrim walks.

I bused my way down to the Rue Saint-Dominique and walked some more. Passing by a lingerie boutique, I thought of Roland. Poor, dear Roland in crust contraction. I must stop by the hospital to visit him and give him the number of Djamila's healer. Looking more closely at the lacy negligées, my mind then switched to Mouktar. Dearest Mouktar! On a whim I went in and bought what seemed to be a baby doll nightgown. A transparent number in violet and black with

369

a matching see-through panty! Even more risqué than Esperanza! Do I dare wear it? Indeed, but only if I bless it first.

I continued down to the Rue Cler to buy the evening comestibles. A serving of *lapin à la sauce moutarde* with accompanying potatoes and a bottle of Anjou Villages. For Jubilee, the usual brioche plus two anchovy fillets.

Back at the flat, I showed Jubilee my lingerie purchase for a sniff test before blessing it. Jubilee's approval was unanimous. I blessed then hid the purchase in a drawer to preclude further olfactory enquiries. Dined quietly by candlelight, though the evening sun had not yet set. Would not set until ten o'clock, lengthening the pleasures of the day for those who cared to enjoy them.

A delicious repast with a fine wine accompanying. What felt like a delicate breeze floated in through the open window sending a ripple through the water in the fount. But in truth it was not the wind at all, but an angel passing by for a bath. A quick one with no need for towels, as angels air-dry beautifully. Poured myself another glass of Anjou and contemplated the mysteries of the angels. Thought of Bernini's piazza, that Roman masterpiece thoughtfully designed as a landing strip for these divine messengers. Soon I would be there, hand in hand with Mouktar, a pilgrim in love, a freshly landed angel on my shoulder. I indulged myself luxuriously in the prelibation of bliss. A foretaste of all the happiness that would be ours for the taking. Then the phone rang, interrupting the sweetness a bit.

'Princess?'

'Mumly!'

'Just thought I'd call to see what's new. Tell me how you've been.'

'Wonderful, Mumly. I'm in love.'

'You are, Princess? That's wonderful news! Is this Joanna's gentleman? The one who took you to the ball?'

'I'm afraid not, Mumly. It's Mouktar that I love. He's a scholar and a poet. He's financing his doctoral degree with four scholarships and a part-time job.'

Mumly prefers the facts straight away.

'Well, Princess, you always did like your teachers in school didn't you?'

'Oh I did, Mumly.'

How true. My years at Vassar were foggy ones, dewed by the mists of collegian love. The objects of my classroom passion were always professorial-erudites in the various sciences of the humanities. With Mouktar of course it was different. He was not my professor but my classmate, perhaps one who continued farther along the scholarly road than I, but nevertheless my peer in love and life. He would write me sonnets. I would buy him shoes.

'And guess what, Mumly.'

'Yes, Princess?'

'We're going to Rome. Any day now. I just have to make the reservations.'

'That's wonderful news, darling! You're going at last! I knew you could do it. And will you have a private audience with His Holiness?'

'I will certainly try, Mumly. I believe I have the right connections.'

Indeed. I kept Harold's friend in mind. The one who runs off with the papal censor at night and answers Holy See junk mail by day.

'When you see him, Princess, remember to cover your head and wear long sleeves. No jewellery and almost no make-up. And when you go to kiss his ring, be sure to keep your tongue in your mouth.'

'Oh I will!'

'Princess, this is wonderful news! Remember to send me a letter from the Vatican Post Office. I waited in line there once and realized that the Padre Pio was standing behind me, queuing too! My postcard to the Epsteins arrived in Florida two days later. It was a miracle, Princess! And the Padre Pio was in on it.'

'I'm sure he was, Mumly. Isn't he a member of the Community of Saints now?'

'Yes, Princess. Died and gone to heaven. Now a saint without a complaint.'

'Mumly, it's amazing to be in love, isn't it?'

'It is, Princess.'

'And to go to Rome too!'

'Princess it is. Just remember to thank the angels whose wings have prepared the way.'

'Will do, Mumly.'

Promised to send Mumly a postcard a day, sent with a papal stamp from the Holy See. Wished her all my love transatlantically, and went to thank the angels. Did so spinning about the room which, as the whirling dervishes have known for centuries, is the best way to communicate with the agents of grace. I then retired to my boudoir with the first complete English version of *The Romance of Tristan and Iseult*. Read weepily about the hapless lovers for a while, then switched to a day-old *Wall Street Journal* wherein I learned that the European power-tie (Hermès) as well as its American homologue, the Harvard cravat, are making a tremendous comeback. Wished the tie bearers well. More power to them of course. I then folded the *WSJ* and returned to Tristan's tristesse. And fell asleep just as things were looking up a bit.

At midnight, I was woken by the doorbell. Mouktar! Having just finished work at Shlomi's, he had come as quickly as he could. Mouktar, my heart! Though groggy from naptime, I kept my wits about me and before answering the door, slipped into the baby doll affair which was meant after all for love. And Mouktar, though exhausted from his day of double duties, was driven to an even higher duty. Yes, pleased at once, he recharged on the spot. And a tremendous night we spent. Moor and Maiden. Loving in all manners! Ignited by that lacy thing!

> *Wild Nights – Wild Nights!*
> *Were I with thee*
> *Wild Nights should be*
> *Our Luxury!*

Why Emily knew all about it! The dear Dickinson. Perhaps she merely dreamed it, but dreams do portend.

> *Rowing in Eden –*
> *Ah, the Sea!*
> *Might I but moor – Tonight –*
> *In Thee!*

Indeed, to moor in the Moor. To sink my anchor down in the bed of love. Now I can toss the compass! Now I am done with the chart! Yes, in the end the Dickinson knows better than the Dolittle. Away the doctor! For what does she know? A loving man does not go. Adult Sex after all wears thin, wears out like a fashionable sin. When a man loves you he stays around and if you must leave on your journey, he will accompany. In the past this was not so but rather just the reverse with ladies following their gentlemen around and requesting naught. Now when a woman asks, she receives. And if she asks a young man to follow her, he will (you'll make sure of that, right Luigi?). Though the love must be sure.

SHE   Shall we go to Rome, my love? As pilgrim and scholar shall we?

HE   God-be-willing, oh delicious slice of the moon. With you it will be a pleasure to go. My heart!

So our voyage was settled, in that most contented moment following love when women are advised to do the asking. Good night my heart! Dream sweet dreams. Dreams of the Appian Way. With our feet we will walk it! With our souls we shall sing it!

I fell asleep with my ear to his heart. Listening to the sounds of my seabed. Listening to the beating heart of my Moor.

The End

Acknowledgments

With deepest gratitude to my enlightened readers, whose insights and loyal support – as good as any the saints could supply – have sustained me all these years: Susan Marson and Ray Watkins.

And to the angels who have made this happen: Violaine Huisman and Laura Barber.